Escapade

Also by Walter Satterthwait

Cocaine Blues
The Aegean Affair
Wall of Glass
Miss Lizzie
At Ease with the Dead
Wilde West
A Flower in the Desert
The Hanged Man

Escapade

Walter Satterthwait

St. Martin's Press
New York

Production Editor: David Stanford Burr

Library of Congress Cataloging-in-Publication Data

Satterthwait, Walter.
Escapade / Walter Satterthwait.
p. cm.
ISBN 0-312-13068-6
1. Doyle, Arthur Conan, Sir, 1859–1930—Fiction.
2. Houdini, Harry, 1874–1926—Fiction. I. Title.
PS3569.A784E83 1995
813'.54—dc20 95-15462
CIP

First Edition: July 1995

10 9 8 7 6 5 4 3 2 1

This book is for Dr. Olga Taxidou,
me pollá filákia

Acknowledgments

THANKS to Dominick Abel, my agent; Reagan Arthur, my editor; and Jeanne W. Satterthwait, my mother. And thanks and hello to Derek and Alma Harding in Exeter; John and Jane Pack at the Aegean Center for the Fine Arts; Lelli Rallis in Athens; Heidi Reich in St. Moritz; Mike Ripley at heathside; Susan Rose at the Snoop Sisters Bookstore in Bellaire Bluffs; Eva Schegulla in New York City; Yianni and Marsha Spiridoyiannakis at Delphini; Maggie Steed in "Harvey Moon"; John Tilke at the Centre for Police and Criminal Justice Studies, University of Exeter; and George and Gigi Wolff, nice folks, in Knightsbridge.

Thanks for earlier help to Ted and Barbara Flicker, of Santa Fe and points west.

And especial thanks to the extraordinary Sarah Caudwell, of London and points north, who slogged through this book in manuscript and who stole huge chunks of time from the writing of her own eagerly awaited opus to offer invaluable suggestions and advice. Hi, Sarah.

The magician is an actor playing the part of a magician.

—Jean-Eugène Robert-Houdin

Sex is worth dying for.

—Michel Foucault

Part One

The Morning Post

12 Yeoman's Row, Knightsbridge

August 15, 1921

Dear Evangeline,

No catty complaints from me today. Today I have some good news, really quite splendid news, in fact. Tomorrow morning, the Allardyce and her paid spinster companion are romping off to Devon for a séance.

Yes, you poor envious wretch, a séance. In Devon. In a haunted manor house, no less. Clanking chains and spectral voices and dripping ectoplasm and one of those overweight mediums with cryptic messages from dear departed Aunt Delilah. *And* a train ride through the West Country! The wild moor, the open countryside: an escape from the grime of grim grey London! I'm really quite witless with excitement!

The Allardyce has spent the last two days crowing about her aristocratic connections. She's a cousin—no doubt distant (meow)—of Alice, Viscountess Purleigh, whose husband, Robert, the Viscount, is the son of the Earl of Axminster. The séance will be held at Maplewhite, the Earl's estate. So, Evy, as of tomorrow, I'll be mingling with the peerage. But you needn't worry—I'll never forget the simple honest folk, like yourself, who were so terribly kind to me before I rose to greatness.

I'm packing the luggage (hers and mine), so I haven't time, just now, to scrawl more than a few lines. But I did want to tell you that I've begun to read the book you sent to me, Mrs Stopes's 'Married Love'. It's curious and rather delicious to see all those body parts swaggering so boldly across the printed page, cool Latin names draped like togas over their smooth warm shoulders. I'll be ferrying the book to Devon, but discreetly of course. Should the Allardyce ever suspect what it is I'm reading with such zeal she would become quite puce with shock. I've very cleverly stripped away its original cover and replaced it with the cover to 'Mansfield Park'. I suspect that this would delight Miss Austen nearly as much as it would dismay Mrs Stopes.

How is that charming brother of yours? How is Mary?

I must go. I shall write to you when I arrive at the haunted mansion and I shall let you know *everything.*

All my love,
Jane

Chapter One

THE GREAT MAN was skating the big Lancia around blind turns on the slick road as though he had received a personal telegram from God that guaranteed his immortality.

"You're driving too fast, Harry," I said. I had said it before and it hadn't accomplished anything. I didn't really expect it to accomplish anything now. But occasionally you want to put these things on the record.

The Great Man smiled at me. He had a wide, wild, charming smile. It made you believe that he felt extremely lucky to be in your company, and usually it made you believe that you were extremely lucky to have your company to offer. It hadn't been working so well since he got behind the wheel.

"Phil, Phil," he said. "You worry too much altogether. I have spent countless years honing my reflexes. As you know. With a lesser man, yes, for certain, you would be in jeopardy. But with me, you are as safe as a little tiny baby in its cradle."

That was the way he talked.

"Don't look at me," I said. "Look at the road."

"Peripheral vision," he said, and he smiled again without taking his eyes off me as he coasted around another turn. His teeth were white. His eyes were grayish blue and shiny and the smile deepened the lines that angled from their corners. "That, too," he said. "With practice, with work, it can be brought to a level of achievement most men would never believe possible."

"Harry," I said. "Look. At. The. Road."

He laughed. But he turned to face the road, showing me his profile. Curly black hair, a bit unruly and a bit gray at the temples. A strong nose, a wide mouth, a strong chin. Not a handsome face, in fact almost an ugly face. But a dynamic face, as forceful as the blade of an axe.

I squinted through the smeared windshield. The wipers squeaked back and forth, slapping water around the glass without ever getting rid of it.

We had left Dartmoor behind us, the cold gray mist and the endless rollers of bald gray hill. It had been grim and empty, but at least you could see the cars that were coming your way. It had been better than this.

This was gray rain ahead and tall black hedgerows looming up on either side, and endless possibilities of collision. Sometimes there were trees just behind the hedgerows, left and right, and their black branches and black leaves arched over the road and formed a long dark tunnel. The headlights were on but they weren't working any better than the wipers.

I sat back and sighed.

Usually I was the driver. It was part of the job I had been hired to do. Usually, the Great Man and his wife sat in the back seat. But the Great Man's wife had been too ill to leave Paris and we had gone to Amsterdam and then to London without her. The Great Man hadn't cared for that.

He had sulked until Lord Endover offered him the Lancia—"Keep her as long as you like, old boy." The Great Man had glanced out the window of Lord Endover's Belgravia town house at the Lancia parked at the curb, its long white body as sleek and as promising and as dangerous as a banker's second wife. A gleam had come into his eye and at that moment I knew I would probably never get behind the wheel of the beast.

The rain sizzled along the hood of the car, splattered along the glass. The wipers chirped.

In England, you're supposed to drive on the left. But on this road there wasn't much difference between left and right. If I stuck my arm out the passenger window, I could have touched the hedgerows. Except they weren't really hedgerows. Hedgerows were plants and they gave way when you hit them. These were stone walls thinly screened with ferns and bushes and they would have snapped my arm in two.

Once again now, he went racing through a left-hand turn. But this time the Lancia's rear wheels slid away beneath us and the car lurched toward that towering wall on the right. I stopped breathing and I braced myself.

As though being braced would make a difference when a ton of speeding metal met a hundred tons of rooted rock.

The Great Man eased up on the gas pedal, steered ever so slightly into the skid as the Lancia swept within inches of the wall. Black branches snatched at the bodywork, scrabbled at my window. Then, in the last possible fraction of a second, just when I knew it was all over, the tires bit into the road again. The Great Man downshifted, punched the pedal, and the car surged forward into the gray rain. He turned to me and laughed. "Reflexes," he announced gaily.

He was a wonderful driver. He was better than I was, and I was good. But enough was enough.

I exhaled. Then I inhaled. Then I said, "Okay, Harry. Stop the car."

He turned to me and he frowned. "What?"

"The car. Stop it. Now."

The frown reached his eyes. "You want me to stop?"

"Now."

"But . . ."

"Now."

He stopped the car and looked over at me, still frowning. I grabbed my fedora from the back seat. I opened the door, stepped out into the rain, and slammed the door shut behind me. I screwed on the hat. I tugged up my coat collar, buttoned the buttons, tied the belt, and I started marching back the way we'd come.

The rain wasn't all that heavy when you weren't racing through it at sixty miles an hour. But it was as wet as rain usually is, and it was cold. The air temperature was probably in the forties. This was August. Oh to be in England now that summer's here.

I heard the car come up behind me.

"Phil?"

The car was in reverse. He had the window down and he was leaning across the seat so he could talk to me through it. Rain was pattering onto the leather seats, but I doubt that he noticed, or cared. If the seats were damaged, he would buy Lord Endover a new Lancia. He could afford it.

I saw all this without looking at him directly. Peripheral vision. I kept walking and he kept driving. The car remained at exactly the same distance from me all the while, about two feet away. He was a wonderful driver, even in reverse.

"Phil? Where are you going?"

I didn't look at him. "Back to New York."

"But what about your job?"

"I can't do my job if we're both dead."

"But what about Bess? What will I tell her?"

Bess was his wife. It had been her idea to hire me.

I said, "Tell her whatever you want."

"Phil," he said. "You're upset."

He said it as though he had just now figured it out. Probably he had. He was one of those men who honestly believed that everyone was as thrilled by him as he was.

"Yeah," I admitted. I still hadn't looked at him.

"Why don't *you* drive the car, Phil?"

I stopped walking and he stopped driving. I turned and looked down at him. Some water toppled from my hat and splattered onto my shoes. He was peering up at me through the window, blinking against the rain. His face was earnest.

He hadn't apologized. Why should he? He hadn't done anything wrong. He couldn't do anything wrong. Ever. But I was upset, for whatever reason, and he liked me, and so he would mollify me. He was a generous man.

Despite myself, I smiled. His self-involvement was so total it was almost a kind of innocence.

"Harry," I said, "you are really a piece of work."

He smiled up at me, that wide charming smile, and he nodded. He already knew that.

WE REACHED THE narrow gravel driveway to Maplewhite at a little after nine-thirty that night.

The rain had stopped, darkness had come. The full moon was a dull gray blur behind dark scudding clouds edged with silver. Leaning toward us on both sides was a dense forest of tall black trees, oaks and elms and pines. We drove up through these into the smell of damp earth and moldering leaves, the drive turning back and forth upon itself like a grifter's alibi. At the top of the hill the trees fell away and all at once we were among the clouds and not below them. In the moonlight they were slowly rolling across acres and acres of parkland.

Directly ahead of us, with more clouds streaming like pennants from its towers, was the house.

It was black and it was huge, as big as a cliff. The towers, one at each side of the main building, were taller than the giant twin oak trees that flanked the entrance. The lighted windows were tiny narrow vertical slits in the craggy mass of rock.

It looked like the kind of place you couldn't get into without an invitation, and maybe not even then. That was fine with me.

"It's big, eh?" said the Great Man.

"Yeah," I said.

"In the thirteenth century, it was built. The Normans. Observe the towers."

"Hard not to."

To the right of the building was a carriage house—slate roof, stone walls, two broad wooden doors. In front of this was a graveled area for cars, roofed over to protect them. Six cars were parked there. I wheeled the Lancia in and parked it beside an elegant Rolls-Royce tourer.

I turned off the ignition reluctantly. The big automobile had driven beautifully. A couple of times, rain or no rain, I had been tempted to hit the gas and see what the car could do. I hadn't mentioned this to the Great Man.

We got out of the car and I put on my hat. I went around to the trunk and opened it. The Great Man joined me, rubbing his hands together. Even in the dimness I could see his smile. He was excited. He was about to make an entrance.

Impatiently, he waved a hand at the trunk. "Leave the bags, Phil," he said. "The servants will take care of them."

"Why should we bother the servants?"

I pulled my bag out of the trunk.

He was shorter than I was, by almost a foot. But his shoulders were as broad as mine and he could pick me up and hold me in the air for pretty much as long as he liked.

It wasn't merely strength, although he had plenty of that. It was a refusal to recognize that, for him, anything at all was impossible.

If he decided he didn't want to carry his bag, there wasn't much I could do about it. Except carry the bag myself, to prove a point.

He grinned up at me and he clapped me on the shoulder. "You are a pure democrat, Phil. A true American. That is what I like about you. I am exactly the same myself." He reached in and swung his bag out of the trunk. Black alligator leather, with gold fittings. The kind that all true Americans carried. I had stashed the bag in the trunk, so I knew that it weighed about seventy-five pounds. He handled it as if it were filled with popped corn.

I slammed the trunk shut and together we walked to the enormous wooden door at the entrance to the house.

An electric light glowed above the door. Poking through the door's center was the head of a big brass lion who was chewing on a big brass knocker. The Great Man lifted the knocker and rapped it once, hard, against its brass plate. The lion didn't seem to mind.

For a moment we stood listening to drip-water plop against the puddles. Then the door swung open and a butler stood there in the light. A tall man, heavyset, white haired, in his sixties. His round English face was red, the face of a man who knew where they hid the cooking sherry. He was dressed in black, elaborately. If kings wore black, they would dress the way he did.

"Gentlemen?" he said. His features were blank and expressionless.

"Harry Houdini," said the Great Man, like Santa Claus announcing Christmas. "And Phil Beaumont," he added. Remembering the reindeer.

The butler nodded without changing the look on his face, or adding one to it. "I am Higgens," he said. "Please come in."

He stood back. I moved to one side, to permit the Great Man his entrance. He stepped in grandly, sweeping off his hat with a flourish, and I followed him. We set down our bags. To the right of the butler was another servant. This one was also dressed in black, but not as magnificently. He glided smoothly forward, as though he were wearing roller skates, and he began to help the Great Man with his coat. The Great Man smiled pleasantly. He liked having people help him with his coat.

The butler said, "Lord and Lady Purleigh are in the drawing room, with their other guests. Would you like to join them now, or would you prefer to go to your rooms first?"

"Go to the rooms, I think," said the Great Man. "Don't you agree, Phil?"

I shrugged.

The servant glided toward me, but I had already taken off my hat and coat. If this was a disappointment, he didn't show it. He just nodded and took them, his features as blank and expressionless as the butler's. But he was shorter, and younger and much thinner, with black hair and a pale, pinched face.

"Very good," said the butler. "You'll be staying in the east wing. Briggs will take you there."

Briggs had hung up the coats and hats. Now he lifted both our bags and said, "Please follow me, gentlemen."

We had been standing before a hall big enough to land an airplane. An electric chandelier hung from the center of the beamed ceiling, but the ceiling was so high and the walls so far apart that the room's upper corners were cobwebbed with darkness. Below the chandelier a long wooden table ran for twenty-five or thirty feet. The walls of the room were made of pale brown stone and they were draped with murky oil paintings of dead people wearing old costumes. Embroidered curtains hung at the sides of the narrow mullioned windows. The pale gray marble floor was covered with broad dark Oriental carpets, seven or eight of them.

Ahead of us, Briggs glided across the marble floor toward another wide, open doorway. I noticed that the far wall of the hall, off to my left, held no paintings. It held weapons: lances, pikes, broadswords, cutlasses, rapiers, wheel-lock muskets, flintlock rifles, an enormous blunderbuss, some shotguns, a Sharps buffalo gun, a scoped Winchester Model 1873, a selection of handguns. Most of the handguns, like most of the long arms, were black powder antiques. But there was a Peacemaker Colt, a long-barreled artillery officer's Luger Parabellum, a Colt Army 1911 automatic, and what looked like a Smith & Wesson .38 caliber revolver. If the Apaches attacked tonight, we would be ready.

I don't know what the Great Man noticed. Maybe everything. He was glancing around, calmly appraising, like someone who was mulling over the idea of adding all this to his private collection.

We followed Briggs up some stone stairs and through a wide doorway, then down a wide hallway with parquet wooden floors. More dead people hung from the walls. We climbed up a wide, worn, wooden stairway and we went down some more hallways. The place was a maze.

Carpets flowed along the wooden floors. Cabinets and chests and tables clung to the stone walls. Perched on these were vases and bowls and lacquer boxes, statuettes of porcelain and ivory and alabaster. I've been in museums that owned less bric-a-brac. Maybe most museums did.

We came to another corridor. On our way down it, we passed ornate wooden doors, left and right. Each door had a small card thumbtacked to it. On the cards, names had been written in a flowing cursive script. *Mrs Vanessa Corneille,* said one. *Sir David Merridale,* said another. *Mrs Marjorie Allardyce and Miss Jane Turner,* said the card on the door opposite. *Sir Arthur Conan Doyle,* said the card on the last door to the left. On the door opposite, the card said, *Mr Harry Houdini and Mr Phil Beaumont.*

The corridor ended up ahead, about thirty feet. In the stone wall was another door, unmarked. Probably it led to a stairway.

Briggs set down the Great Man's bag, opened the door, and gestured for us to enter. As usual, I followed the Great Man. Briggs picked up the Great Man's bag and followed me.

Chapter Two

IT WAS A BIG ROOM, tall stone walls and a beamed ceiling. The wooden floors were spread with carpets. To the left was another door, opened, and beside this, a small writing desk and a chair. Directly ahead, against the wall, was an antique cupboard and an antique dresser that held a ceramic basin and a ceramic pitcher. To the right was a huge four-poster bed covered with white satin. White satin curtains were drawn back to each of the posts. Large night tables stood on either side of the bed.

Briggs set the Great Man's bag down on the nearest of these. "The bathroom is through here, gentlemen." Carrying my battered bag, he moved through the open door. Inside, he opened a door on the left, to show us the bathroom. A sink, a towel rack hung with heavy white towels, a huge tub squatting on big brass lion's paws. Paws from the same lion, probably, whose head was trapped in the front door.

Briggs opened a door on the right to show us the toilet. It was a fine toilet.

The second room was beyond, and smaller than the first. But it was as comfortable as the other, with a second writing desk and chair, a second cupboard and a second four-poster bed. The bedspread here was also white satin.

"Your room, Mr. Beaumont," said Briggs. He placed my bag on the nightstand. "Will there be anything else, gentlemen?"

"No," said the Great Man. "Thank you, Briggs."

Briggs nodded, his face still expressionless. "When you're ready, please ring the bellpull beside the bed. Someone will come for you."

The Great Man nodded. "Yes, certainly, thank you."

Briggs glided off.

The Great Man looked around, smiling. "Not bad, eh, Phil? This is a very pleasant room, don't you think?"

"Well, Harry," I said, "I'm glad you like it. Because this is the room you'll be taking."

He frowned.

"I'll take the outer room," I said.

He looked at me for a moment and then he said, "But Phil! Surely you don't believe that anything will happen here? With people present, with all those servants?"

"Something happened at the Ardmore. With all those house dicks and all those cops."

"But that was a *hotel!* And the newspapers had *announced* that I was there. No one knows that I am staying at Maplewhite."

"Maybe that's true," I said. "Maybe it's not."

"But Phil—"

"Harry. You remember when you made me take that oath? About not giving away your secrets? You promised me something too, remember? And you promised Bess."

He stared at me. Finally he nodded. He drew himself fully upright. This usually meant that an announcement was coming. "Houdini always keeps his promises," he announced.

"I know that," I said. "So we'll switch rooms."

He nodded and he compressed his lips. He had made a promise and he would keep it, but no one had said he couldn't sulk.

He looked around the room with a sour expression on his face.

I took my suitcase into the main room, exchanged it for the Great Man's bag, carried his bag back into the other room. The Great Man was sitting on the bed with his shoulders slumped, staring at the floor. He didn't say anything when I put the suitcase down.

"Harry," I said.

He looked up.

"It's for your own good," I told him.

He nodded glumly.

"Let me know when you're finished washing up," I said. "We shouldn't waste too much time. They're all waiting for you."

He frowned for a moment, considering this. Then he smiled. "Yes. Yes, of course. You are right, Phil."

IT WAS BRIGGS who came to get us. The Great Man was feeling better by then. The idea of hobnobbing with lords and ladies always cheered him up.

Briggs led us down the corridor again, and up and down some more stairways until we came to another doorway. We followed him through it.

This room was smaller than the hall. Not enough space to land an airplane, but enough to park it. More Oriental carpets were spread along the floor and the walls were swathed with tapestries. Running across the tapestries were some plump naked people chasing other plump naked people through a forest. The plump people were naked in a refined way—their vital parts were all hidden by rushing arms or pumping legs or by a leafy bush that happened to spring up in exactly the right place. The forest looked damp to me, but everybody up there seemed to be having a pretty good time.

Against the far wall stood a long trestle table. Atop the table were liquor bottles and champagne buckets and stacks and pyramids of glasses, silver teapots and china cups and saucers, silver platters and china plates. There was also a gramophone. It was playing Dixieland jazz, the horns and the piano sounding thin and tinny this far from home. Behind the table was another servant who wore a black uniform and a blank expressionless face.

Throughout the room, in cozy glowing pockets created by the electric lamps, there were small clusters of people sitting.

Briggs led us off to the right, to a cluster of two women and one man. The man sat in a stout padded leather chair, the women in a small upholstered sofa behind a coffee table of dark polished wood. The three of them looked up.

Briggs said to the man, "Excuse me, milord. Mr. Harry Houdini and Mr. Phil Beaumont."

"Ah, thank you, Briggs," said the man, and stood up.

Briggs disappeared. His employer offered a hand to the Great Man. He was short and burly in his gray tweeds, and his hair and his mustache were thick and white. So were his eyebrows, which were big and bristly and looked like a pair of albino beetles. He had blue eyes, a large beaked nose, pink cheeks, and a wide fleshy mouth. "Houdini," he said, grinning. "Great treat for us, your coming. Glad you could make it."

Smiling happily, the Great Man shook hands. "It is a great pleasure to be here, Lord Purleigh."

"Now, now. None of that nonsense here. It's Bob. Always has been, always will be. And this is Beaumont, is it?"

"Phil Beaumont," said Houdini. "My secretary."

Bob—Lord Bob?—glanced at the Great Man as his beetle eyebrows rose. "Secretary, eh? Getting up in the world, are we? Exploiting the poor workers now, eh? Well, pleasure to meet you, Beaumont." He shook my hand. "First time in England?"

"Yes," I told him.

"Dreadful place, isn't it? Rain and fog and mist. Attractive women, though, eh? A couple of 'em right here. Mrs. Allardyce. Cousin of my wife's. And Miss Turner, her companion. Marjorie, Miss Turner, let me introduce Mr. Harry Houdini. And his secretary, Mr. Phil Beaumont."

Calling them attractive had been gallant, or optimistic, or maybe nearsighted. In her sixties, Mrs. Allardyce was built like a blacksmith, but without the daintiness. Her shoulders and her arms were thick and meaty. Her round breasts and round stomach were taut against the pink floral pattern of her black dress. Her gray hair had been carefully chiseled from granite. Someone had stenciled circular patches of rouge on her round cheeks. Her gray eyes were small and shiny and avid, glistening birdshot trapped in a pale puffy muffin.

Miss Turner was an improvement. She was young, maybe twenty-three, and she was tall for an Englishwoman. Although she wasn't beautiful, she had that horsy English handsomeness that sometimes seems elegant and sometimes seems stiff. Right now, with her back rigid and her knees locked together beneath her plain gray dress, it seemed stiff. Her hair was pale brown and it was tightly clenched back along her skull. Behind wire-rim glasses, her large eyes were a deep, clear, and startling blue. They were her best feature, and they would look good on anyone. They looked good on her, but extravagant, like sapphires on a nun. She wore no make-up along her cheeks or anywhere else that I could see. Her wide pink mouth was turned down slightly at the corners, as though she disapproved of something but couldn't remember exactly what it was.

Smiling, Houdini made a small, quick formal bow to each woman. *"Madame,"* he said. "And *mademoiselle."*

I nodded and I smiled, politely. I had been working on my politeness.

Mrs. Allardyce and Miss Turner both sat with cups and saucers on their laps. Mrs. Allardyce lumbered her bosom out over her cup and said to the Great Man, "What a *thrill* this is, Mr. Houdini! Jane and I have read *all* about your exploits. Will you be doing some of your *wonderful* magic for us?" She batted her eyelids at him.

"Now, Marjorie," said Lord Bob. "Houdini's a guest. No one here need sing for his supper."

"Oh no, of course not, Robert," she said and now she batted her eyelids at him. She turned back to the Great Man. "But surely Mr. Houdini could perform just one teensy weensy little trick for us?"

Houdini shrugged theatrically. "Alas, madam," he said. "Unless I am much mistaken, I fear I am too late. For observe . . ."

He bent forward at the waist, used his left hand to pluck the lid from the silver teapot on the coffee table. He poked the first two fingers of his right hand inside the pot. When they emerged, nipped between them was a crisp five-pound banknote, folded into quarters. With a graceful twirl of the wrist he held it out toward Mrs. Allardyce.

Lord Bob laughed. "Marvelous," he exclaimed.

Mrs. Allardyce produced a delighted little chortle, clapped her hands, and then leaned forward and grasped for the banknote. The Great Man surrendered it. If he hadn't, probably she would have ripped his arm off.

She unfolded the thing and examined it. A five-pound note was almost as big as a road map. "It's authentic, too," she said, looking up at him. "Absolutely *genuine*. And to whom does it belong?"

"Well, madame," he said, "since it was in your teapot, then clearly it must belong to you."

Five pounds was enough money for a long week in Paris.

"Yes, of course," she said, and chortled again as she folded up the note. "It must, yes, of course." She picked up a small black leather purse that lay beside her on the sofa. She opened it and carefully slid the note inside, then closed the purse and clutched it to her bosom. "All *mine,*" she said, and she shivered with a kind of pretended avarice. Hidden behind the pretense, it seemed to me, was the real thing.

I looked at Miss Turner. She was watching Mrs. Allardyce and her mouth was still turned down in disapproval. She must have felt my glance, because suddenly she turned and her blue eyes dazzled up at me from behind the glasses. Then, blinking, she looked toward the floor. The corners of her mouth veered down another notch.

"Marvelous," said Lord Bob again. He slapped his hand against the Great Man's shoulder. The Great Man beamed. Applause always made his face open up like a flower in the sunshine.

Mrs. Allardyce most likely believed that she had established her position by commanding a performance, and getting it. What she didn't understand was that in the Great Man's eyes, she was merely a member of the audience. Like all the rest of us.

She smiled up at the Great Man. "Are you interested in ghosts, Mr. Houdini? Robert was just telling us, before you arrived, the most *fascinating* story about Lord Reginald, the ghost of Maplewhite."

The Great Man smiled. "Ghosts are not one of my main fields of interest," he said. "I feel—"

"You don't believe in them?" She had her eyebrows raised.

"Whether they exist or not is irrelevant to my own—"

"But *surely* one wants to keep an open mind?"

"My own feeling is that—"

"I must confess that I *do* love a good ghost story," she said.

"Wicked spirits and bloodcurdling screams in the night. Stories of that sort—so long as they're done *well*—in the *best* of taste, I mean—they give one of the most *delicious* chill, don't they?"

"Yes," said the Great Man. "of course. But you see—"

"And Lord Reginald—Robert's ghost—is really *quite* chilling. He wanders into one's bedroom in the very *dark* of night, it seems. In a long white nightgown, isn't that right, Robert?"

Lord Bob nodded patiently. "So the stories have it."

"Absolutely *spectral,"* she said, and she put her hand to her chest and produced another small shiver. "I'm sure I should *die* with fright." She turned to Lord Bob. "But what exactly does he *do* after he arrives?"

"Nothing, Marjorie. How could he, eh? Dead, isn't he?"

"Oh, Robert," she chided him. *"Must* you be such a cynic?"

Lord Bob smiled. "A realist, Marjorie," he said. "Dialectical materialist." He turned to the Great Man and me. "But come along, you two. We'll find you a drink and introduce you to the others."

We said our goodbyes to the two women. Mrs. Allardyce was smiling happily, Miss Turner was still faintly frowning.

The Evening Post

Maplewhite, Devon

August 16

Dear Evangeline,

A few words hastily scribbled on the Exeter train.

As usual, at breakfast the Allardyce gorged herself on muffins and buns and on crumpets dripping with butter; a moment or two after the train left the station she slipped into a providential (if occasionally stertorous) coma. She sits opposite me, mouth agape, holds folded in her lap, her broad body sprawled back against the seat like a drugged Buddha. The compartment is crowded with the smell of the mint bonbons she consumes, on the hour, whenever she is away from home. But in effect I am alone.

It's been drizzling since we left Paddington, but a soft, thoughtful, introspective drizzle: seen through trailing wisps of mist, the landscape looks impossibly romantic, like a painting by my famous namesake. I sit and watch the panorama unfold outside the window—towns, villages, fields, meadows, everything dim and hushed and tranquil beneath that grey silky sky.

Sometimes I dream a bit. Have you ever, while on a train, picked out some piece of scenery, a solitary tree standing sentinel on a swell of ridge, a small faraway thatched cottage tucked amidst a huddle of elm and oak, and (so to speak) mentally thrown your consciousness there? So that, in your imagination, you are standing beneath that tree or beside that cottage, watching the tiny distant train roll toward its mysterious destination?

No, of course you haven't. You're *much* too sensible a person.

I've read a bit more of your Mrs Stopes. I confess that, despite what are no doubt the best intentions in the world, she has made me feel thoroughly depraved and dissolute. According to her, 'the average healthy type of woman' experiences sexual desire only once every fortnight, when it promptly arrives and just as promptly departs—like the electric meter reader, apparently, but with a slightly more demanding schedule. What would Mrs Stopes make of me, I wonder. My own meter reader rides upon my shoulders, pickaback, from the time I arise in the morning until the time I totter back to my empty bed at night.

I had believed that the absurdity of sexual longing would disappear with adolescence, like lisle stockings. But as I grow older, it has only grown stronger and more preposterous. Sometimes, suddenly, without warning, my face flushes, my flesh wilts. My knees become plum jam. I wander utterly lost into a warm humid haze, sluggish and stupid; I collide with walls. All too often, in order to function, I am forced to resort to that beastly trick you taught me so many years ago, when you were such a wicked little girl. Because of you, no doubt, I shall roast in hell, like a suckling pig, forever.

The railway guard has gravely announced that in a few minutes we shall be arriving at St. David's Station in Exeter. Time to change trains. More later.

We're at Maplewhite now. Evy, it's marvellous! The countryside hereabouts is so incredibly beautiful that its sweetness pierces the heart, like a honeyed thorn. Isn't it remarkable that every sweetness you meet, once you leave Youth behind, inevitably carries within it some pain? These days I find the music of Mozart so filled with heartache that I can scarcely listen to it.

But really how lovely all this is—the lushly forested hills and the trim green fields billowing off into the misty grey, the tiny sheep grazing pensively in the pastures, the toy villages with their slender church spires needling above the dark nestle of yew. Is there anywhere in the entire world more beautiful than England?

Maplewhite itself is wonderful. Even in the rain, the place is extraordinary. The enormous lawn stretches out in every direction, like a vast Russian steppe; there are grand old oak trees and grey clusters of pine shouldering through the fog. There is an extravagant formal garden, immense, dreamy, looking in the grey smoke somehow immensely significant, like serene ruins left by some once powerful but long-vanished race. And the manor house itself—enormous, ancient, with tall brooding walls of rough grey granite and a pair of monumental, massive, moody towers.

And inside—you cannot imagine the abundance of treasure scattered so casually about! When I entered the Great Hall, my breath was snatched away. One wall is covered with dreary old guns and knives and things, but the rest are bedecked with the most handsome and accomplished family portraits, generations of Fitzwilliams going back to the Middle Ages. Two or three of these, I'm convinced, are Gainsboroughs. And sprawled across the marble floor, as though they were tatty old hearth rugs, are eight of the largest and most exquisite silk Tabriz carpets I have ever seen. Eight of them!

Everywhere the eye turns there is some new delight. Here in my room, where I sit (on a delicate Louis XV walnut chair) writing this (on a delicate Louis XV walnut desk perched on graceful fluted legs), I need only glance around me to spy another marvel. On the Sheraton secretaire sits a Meissen tobacco box, as red and shiny as an polished apple. On the wall beside it hangs a mirror framed in the most gorgeously detailed walnut marquetry. Behind me is the bed in which I shall sleep tonight: a Chippendale four-poster as big as a yacht, its smooth satinwood posts inlaid with ivory, its dainty linen bed hangings embroidered in red silk.

And the people. The Right Honourable Robert Fitzwilliam, Viscount Purleigh, is adorable. I realize that viscounts are not universally esteemed for their adorability; but Lord Purleigh is adorable. He reminds me of Trelawny, Mrs Applewhite's gardener, all comfortable tweed and hearty pink flesh, except that Lord Purleigh's white Guardsman's moustache is considerably grander and more flamboyant. So are his eyebrows, which put me rather in mind of birds' nests.

He insisted that I address him as Bob. *Bob.* I think I should more easily address him as 'Lord Snookums'. We have compromised on 'Lord Robert', a solecism which would no doubt horrify the scribes at Debrett. He is, it transpires, a Bolshevist. (!) He plans, upon the death of his father, the Earl, to open Maplewhite to what he calls 'the toiling masses,' although where he will find toiling masses in the Devon countryside I cannot imagine. Perhaps he'll have them freighted in by train from Birmingham.

Lady Purleigh is charming, a lovely woman with a natural, effortless kindness and grace. I like her enormously.

If Lady Purleigh is lovely, her daughter, the Honourable Cecily Fitzwilliam, is dazzling. She is poised and perfect. Her "bobbed" blond hair is immaculate. Her clothes are Parisian. (An opalescent silk frock this afternoon, low waisted, with a hem that fell to her knees and not an inch farther.) Her figure is slim and suave and flawless and uncluttered by the disagreeable hillocks and mounds that decorate the clumsy form of, say, a typical paid companion. Someone less compassionate than your correspondent might be tempted to suggest that her elocution is perhaps a shade or two more arch than is absolutely necessary. Or that her thought processes are not perhaps sufficiently evolved for any behaviour more complicated than breathing. But breathing, I expect, is all that the Honourable Cecily will ever be required to do.

The Allardyce has at last emerged from her bath. Aphrodite arising from the foaming sea. I've only just managed to unpack the luggage (hers and mine). There is a box for the guests' post in the hallway. I have time enough to dress for dinner. I'll drop this into it and I'll write again as soon as I can.

Much love,
Jane

Chapter Three

AS WE CROSSED the Oriental carpet, walking toward the trestle table, the Great Man asked Lord Bob, "And the medium? She has arrived?"

"Tomorrow sometime," said Lord Bob. "With Conan Doyle. You know Doyle?"

"Yes, certainly. We are close friends. We correspond frequently."

Lord Bob nodded. "Beyond me how he invents those stories of his. Ah, there you are, my darlings."

Two women were standing before the table. They turned, saw Lord Bob, and they smiled. The older woman's smile was friendly and open. The younger woman's was thin and bored, and then it was gone.

"Look what I've bagged," announced Lord Bob. "The famous Mr. Harry Houdini himself. And this is his assistant, Mr. Phil Beaumont, also from America. His first time in England. Gentleman, my wife, Alice, and my daughter, Cecily."

They were obviously mother and daughter. They were the same height, about five feet six inches, and they had the same fine coloring and the same fine bones. In her fifties somewhere, the mother had aged nicely. Her hair was pale blond, shoulder length, its soft waves threaded with silver. She wore a pearl necklace and a black dress that would have been simple if it hadn't been made of silk.

Unlike most of the aristocrats I'd met since we arrived in England, she actually looked like one. Regal without being cold, composed without being stiff. But according to the Great Man, she hadn't been born one. She came from a family that had made its money, a lot of money, in publishing, here in England and on the Continent.

Her daughter looked aristocratic, too, but there was no silver in her blond hair. The hair was straight and neatly bobbed just below her ears, cut longer in front to emphasize her slender neck. The gauzy scarlet scarf loosely wrapped around her throat helped with this. So did the scooped neckline of her pale gray dress, also silk.

She was maybe a bit too aristocratic. She held a champagne glass in her left hand. Her right hand hovered just to the side of her face. Between her extended first and second fingers, she held a lighted cigarette. When she decided that she wanted a puff, all she had to do was swivel her head a few inches. You got the impression that even this would be a terrible chore.

"Hello," she drawled at a space somewhere between the Great Man and me. She was maybe a year or two younger than Miss Turner.

"How do you do," said Lady Alice. There was more life in her eyes than in her daughter's entire body. "I'm so *very* pleased that the two of you could join us. I do hope you'll enjoy yourselves while you're here. If you need anything, you've only to ask." Then she turned to her husband and put her hand along his tweeded arm. "I was just coming after you, darling. I'm afraid we have a small problem."

"Eh?"

She glanced at us very briefly, looked back at her husband. "Upstairs," she said, and her shoulders moved in a small quick elegant shrug.

Lord Bob's bristling eyebrows dipped downward, two pale beetles struggling to embrace each other. "Carrying on again, is he?" Scowling, he stroked his white mustache. "The swine. Comes the revolution, we'll string him up with the rest. He'll be the *first* to go." He punched his right fist into the palm of his left hand.

"I know, darling," said Lady Alice, "but let's deal with today first, shall we? I'll go up there with you."

He nodded. Her hand still held his arm, and now he put his own hand atop hers. "Thank you, my love." He turned to his daughter. "Cecily, be the good little Girl Guide, would you, and introduce Mr. Houdini and Mr. Beaumont to the other guests?" He turned to us. "Sorry. Domestic problem. Back as soon as I can. Come along, my darling."

Lady Alice said to us, "I'm so sorry. Please, do have something." She smiled apologetically, and then she and Lord Bob went off, arm in arm.

The Great Man said to Cecily, "There is some trouble?" He was only making polite conversation. Other people and their troubles didn't interest him much and didn't trouble him at all.

"It's such a bore," she drawled, and swiveled her head to inhale on her cigarette. "My grandfather," she said, exhaling smoke. "He has these fits."

"Ah." He nodded sympathetically. He had learned to do that somewhere. "Brain seizures. A great pity."

"Temper tantrums, actually," she said in her flat drawl. She tapped her cigarette against an ashtray on the trestle table, then raised her hand and put the cigarette back within reach. "You know, of course, that Daddy's a Bolshevist." With her cigarette hand she plucked a flake of tobacco from her lower lip.

We hadn't known, or I hadn't. If the Great Man had known, he had probably forgotten. It had nothing to do with him, so it was irrelevant.

"Daddy's only waiting," she said, "for Grandpère to die so he can give Maplewhite to the peasants and workers. And that makes Grandpère furious, of course. He's bedridden, he's been that way since the accident, years ago. So he can't flog Daddy, which of course is what he'd like to do." She swiveled her head, inhaled on the cigarette. "Once a week or so he starts screaming and throwing things about his room. It drives the poor servants mad." She showed us her thin smile again. "What would you like to drink? Champagne? We've whiskey, as well, I should think."

Houdini shook his head. "Thank you, no. I neither drink alcohol nor smoke tobacco products. I never have. They sap the strength and deplete the will. And without strength and will, I would never have become what I am."

Her left eyebrow edged upward. She took a puff from her tobacco product. "Yes," she said, and blew out some smoke. "Some sort of magician, I gather."

A lesser man might have been derailed by this, which is maybe what she intended. The Great Man steamed ahead at full throttle.

"Not merely a magician," he said, and smiled indulgently. "Anyone can become a magician. A few gimmicked props, some sleight of hand. Child's play. Nothing. I, on the other hand, am an escape artist. A self-liberator. I was the very first self-liberator, anywhere. I have many imitators, in many countries, but it was I who invented the art. And, if I may say so, with no false modesty, Houdini is still the greatest of them all." He turned to me. "Would you agree, Phil?"

"Sure," I said. It was true, after all.

"Really," she said, pronouncing every letter in the word. A faint light had begun to flicker behind her eyes, and a faint note of irony had slipped into her voice. "And just what is it you escape from, exactly?"

Irony, faint or otherwise, was wasted on the Great Man. He waved a hand. "Everything. Anything. In the beginning it was handcuffs and shackles. But anyone can escape from handcuffs and shackles. Always, you see, I try to go beyond what others can do, what even *I* can do, and that is the greatest challenge of all, naturally. Nowadays Houdini escapes from everything. Locked trunks. Coffins. From coffins under water, or buried in the earth. And naturally this requires enormous physical strength and stamina. Tremendous stamina. Would you like to hit me in the stomach?"

"I beg your pardon?" she said.

He opened up his suit coat. "Go ahead. Hit me. As hard as you like. Years of conditioning have turned Houdini's muscles into steel." He nodded toward his stomach. "Please. Feel free."

"Ah," she said. I saw that she was blushing. Quickly, she glanced around the room. She wasn't as jaded as she pretended to be. She looked back at him and cleared her throat. "Thanks awfully, of course," she said. "But perhaps some other time."

Houdini flexed his arm and held his biceps out to her, like a proud butcher presenting a prime slab of porterhouse. "Here. Go ahead. Feel."

She looked over to me, as though expecting a rescue. I didn't have one. She hesitated. The Great Man still held out his arm.

She said, "Oh, well," and she shrugged lightly, as though it didn't really matter in the long run. And she reached out and touched it, tentatively, experimentally.

"Amazing, isn't it?" he said. "Exactly like steel. Feel it."

"Yes," she said. She touched it some more. She blinked again as her fingers moved along the tight black fabric. "Yes, it's really quite . . . firm, isn't it?"

"Yes, naturally," he nodded. He let his arm drop. "Conditioning, exercise," he said, "years and years of it, every day without exception. Alcohol would ruin that in an instant. It destroys muscle tissue, you know. Eats it away, like sulfuric acid. A glass of plain water is what I would like, if I may."

She was staring at him with her lips slightly parted. She blinked again, like someone waking from a daydream, and she closed her mouth. Blushing once more, she glanced around the room. "Yes," she said. "Yes, of course." There was a faint sheen of perspiration on her forehead.

I had seen it happen before. People were never prepared for the Great Man's bald, boundless ego. Some people were repelled by it. But a lot of them were attracted.

And some people are also attracted to firm muscles.

The Great Man hadn't noticed the girl's reaction. He had turned away from her and he stood now with his hands behind his back, his head held high. He glanced thoughtfully around the room, like a theater director gauging the house and its profits.

She turned to me. She cleared her throat. She had wrapped her world weariness back over herself, but I think she realized that it didn't fit nearly as well as it had before. "And you, Mr. Beaumont?"

"A whiskey, thanks. With a little water."

She turned and she stabbed her cigarette into the ashtray. Her movement was so quick and violent that I felt sorry for the cigarette.

She ordered the drinks from the servant. She didn't look into the Great Man's eyes when she gave him the glass of water, but her hand was rock-steady. She handed me the whiskey and water. No ice. The English don't trust it. "You *must* meet the other guests," she told me.

Chapter Four

THE GRAMOPHONE WAS tinkling out a Scott Joplin rag as she led us from the trestle table. We walked across some Oriental carpets and past a fireplace big enough to roast a woolly mammoth. There was no mammoth inside. There was no fire either, even though the air was chilly. The English don't believe in heating their homes before January. If then.

Beyond the fireplace, we came to another cluster of people, three men and a woman sitting in a circle around another coffee table. One of the men was saying, "And it is this, you see, this completely wish-fulfilling nature of the dream, that Herr Doktor Freud discovered."

He was a small, slight man with a thick German accent and a thick beard, neatly cut and shot through with curling wires of gray. His scalp was completely bare and it gleamed as though it had been waxed and buffed. He wore sparkling black pince-nez glasses, a neatly pressed black suit, glistening black patent leather boots, a crisp white shirt with a stiff wing collar, and a tiny, tidy black bow tie. He was immaculate. He was spotless. Dust and disarray would never touch him. They wouldn't dare.

"Excuse me, Dr. Auerbach," said Cecily. The flat, weary drawl had returned to her voice. "Daddy's appointed me hostess. This is Mr. Phil Beaumont, from America, and Mr. Harry Houdini." I thought she gave the word *Houdini* a soft, sour spin.

The other men and the woman remained seated, but Dr. Auerbach bounded to his small shiny feet. "Mr. Houdini!" he said. He displayed his small shiny teeth as he groped for the Great Man's hand. The Great Man granted it.

"Dr. Erich Auerbach," said the doctor. "What a truly gigantic pleasure this is! I witnessed myself your magnificent performance in Vienna several years ago! Astonishing!"

The Great Man looked down at the doctor and smiled his charming smile. "Thank you so much." Flattery always brought out the best in him.

Dr. Auerbach whirled toward Cecily. His brown eyes were opened wide behind the glasses. "You will please permit me, Miss Fitzwilliam, the introductions?"

She smiled her thin listless smile, and she shrugged indifferently. "Yes. Certainly."

"Wonderful!" he said. "Thank you so very much. Well, then, gentlemen. Gracious lady." He bowed toward the seated woman to our right. "Allow me to introduce the extraordinary Mr. Harry Houdini. As you heard, I had myself the honor to witness in Vienna his performance there. *Overwhelming,* absolutely! Mr. Houdini, allow me to introduce to you first the extremely charming Mrs. Corneille."

The extremely charming Mrs. Corneille was the seated woman. She was probably over thirty years old and she was probably under fifty. That was all that I could tell about her age and it was probably more than she would ever tell. She wore black high-heeled shoes, sheer silk stockings, and a pleated black silk dress that exposed her long pale arms and her smooth pale shoulders. Her hair was cut like a pageboy's and it was straight and black and glossy. Her cheekbones were feline, her nose was small, her mouth was red and wide. Beneath long black lashes, her eyes were large and almond shaped. They were the same color as her hair and they looked like there wasn't anything in the world that they hadn't seen at least twice.

In her hand, lightly, she held a long brown cigarette. She inclined her head toward the Great Man and she smiled.

"And this gentleman," said Dr. Auerbach, "is Sir David Merridale."

Sir David was in his forties. His shoulders were broad beneath his tailored black coat, his stomach was flat beneath his tailored black vest. His hair was black, too, except for the elegant waves of gray that lapped elegantly back over his temples. He had a high forehead, a strong nose, a black mustache, and a dark broad mouth. He sat comfortably, sprawled back in a padded leather chair, his hands along its arms, his legs crossed at the knees. He held a glass of champagne in his left hand, comfortably. He seemed permanently bemused.

Sir David nodded hello. The Great Man said, "And this is my secretary and close personal friend, Mr. Phil Beaumont."

I nodded and I smiled. Politely. It was easy once you got used to it.

Sir David said, "Do join us. Dr. Auerbach was just explaining psychoanalysis."

"Oh no, no," said Dr. Auerbach quickly, and semaphored his small manicured hands. He had obviously taken charge. "We finish this now, with the great Houdini here. Please, Miss Fitzwilliam, you will sit beside me?"

She did, on the embroidered love seat. The Great Man chose the empty leather chair at the head of the table, which wasn't much of a surprise. The only seat remaining was the one beside Mrs. Corneille, on the sofa, and I took that. She inhaled a puff from the cigarette and exhaled pale blue smoke through her delicate nostrils, and she looked at me from beneath slightly lowered eyelids. She was wearing a perfume that had been distilled from flowers grown in the Garden of Eden.

Sir David was studying the new arrivals. He was still bemused.

"So," said Dr. Auerbach, leaning toward the Great Man, rubbing his hands together. "You are here for a test of the medium, isn't it? To verify her genuineness, yes?"

Houdini nodded judiciously. "I see you know of my work. Yes, I have had much success uncovering the fraudulent techniques used by these people. But in my youth I was a noted stage medium myself—although only for a brief time, and only for the purpose of healthy family entertainment. Since then, I have made a lifelong study of the occult. I have put together the finest and most extensive library on this subject in the world. And so naturally, Houdini is better equipped than most men to determine trickery and fraud." He smiled. "Only as we grow older do we acquire wisdom."

Sir David said, "Do you really think so? In my experience, people seldom actually acquire wisdom. They merely accumulate evidence."

Houdini put a polite expression on his face. "Oh?" he said.

"Evidence of what, Sir David?" asked Dr. Auerbach.

"Their own fundamental correctness," said Sir David.

The Great Man kept the polite expression on his face while he waited for the others to stop talking.

Mrs. Corneille glanced at Sir David. "You include yourself, do you, David?" Her voice was dark and thick, like sealskin.

"Certainly." He smiled. "But of course, my own correctness is more fundamental."

"Of course." She turned to the Great Man. "So you're not a believer then."

"I am neither a believer nor a disbeliever, madam," the Great Man announced. "I approach these things objectively, in the manner of a careful scientist. But a scientist who has had much experience in this field."

"Dr. Auerbach," said Sir David. "Does your colleague Dr. Freud have an opinion about Spiritualism? He seems to have one about everything else."

Once again Houdini put a polite expression on his face and waited.

Dr. Auerbach said, "Herr Doktor Freud has yet to write about Spiritualism specifically. But he is rationalist, yes? I think it is not presumptuous of me to say that he would consider it a form of superstition. And as such, he would of course see it as a regression."

"A regression?" said Mrs. Corneille.

He nodded. "A retreat, so to say, to an earlier level of development. Even the most well-adjusted individual, as a relief from anxiety, does this from time to time. He may bite his nails, for example, or indulge in unusual sexual activities, or read mystery stories."

"I'm all for unusual sexual activities, of course," said Sir David, smiling. "But if I were you, I shouldn't mention mystery stories in the same context to Conan Doyle when he arrives."

"As a psychic evaluator," said the Great Man, "I often discover that medical doctors and academic professors, when they approach this field, are the most easily misled of investigators. They work with matter, you see, and with physics. And neither of these, no matter how complicated they might be, possesses an *intent* to deceive. But all the so-called psychics I have unmasked in my career, they *have* possessed this."

"How fascinating," said Mrs. Corneille. She turned to me and said, "And what of you, Mr. Beaumont? Are you a skeptic?"

"I never gave it much thought," I told her.

She smiled. Her black, almond-shaped eyes looked into mine. "You mean to say you've never wondered what happens to us when we die?"

"Seems to me there's only one way to find out. I'm not in any hurry."

She smiled again, more widely. Her teeth were very white.

"Personally," said Sir David, "the Spiritualist notion of the Great Beyond sounds terribly tedious to me. Not a single *caneton à l'orange* in sight. Nor a single *grisette.* I much prefer Paris."

Mrs. Corneille smiled at him. "But David, they wouldn't let you in. You've spent so much time there already. You'll probably be sent somewhere quiet and unpretentious. Like Brighton."

"I *will* go to Paris," he said. "I shall travel incognito."

"Yes," said the Great Man. "It is a wonderful city, Paris. The good people of Paris have always been very kind to me, very appreciative. It was in Paris, several years ago, that I introduced my famous Milk Can escape."

Cecily raised her champagne glass and drawled, "Mr. Houdini escapes from things." She sipped at the champagne.

Sir David was bemused again. "Whatever were you doing in a milk can?"

"Escaping from it," said the Great Man. "No one had ever attempted this before."

"I can well imagine," said Sir David.

Sir David, Dr. Auerbach, and the Great Man. It was like watching a three-way taffy pull. If you scooped up all the ego gathered around that table and dumped it on an ocean liner, the ship would keel over and sink like a stone.

"It is a most extraordinary illusion," said the doctor. He was back in charge. "Into a milk can somewhat larger than normal, and filled with water, Mr. Houdini is locked. With four padlocks."

"Six," corrected the Great Man.

"Six, yes, better still. You must imagine—he has no air to breathe, no key, no means of escape. Before the milk can a screen is drawn, to conceal it from the audience. The audience awaits. Time passes. One minute, two minutes, three. The people grow concerned, yes? They grow apprehensive. Surely no one can, under the water, survive for so long? But then at last, suddenly, Mr. Houdini steps out from behind the screen and he waves. Great, *great* applause. The screen is withdrawn, and *there* is the milk can, still locked. When unlocked, it is shown to be filled, still, with water."

The Great Man spoke. "A very accurate description. Except, if you will excuse me, for the word *illusion*. The milk can is real. The water is real. Houdini is real."

Dr. Auerbach nodded quickly. "Yes, yes, of course, it is a word only."

The Great Man smiled and waved a hand, grandly forgiving.

Dr. Auerbach didn't notice that he had been forgiven. His eyes narrowed and he said, "It is almost mythic, yes? In a way, it is a re-creation of the trauma of birth, the escape from the womb. The darkness of the womb you have there, inside the milk can. And the amniotic fluid, which is the water, yes? You yourself are quite curled up, like the fetus. And then, like the fetus, you burst all at once into the light of day." He shook his head in admiration. "Extraordinary."

Houdini had shifted uncomfortably in his seat. "Dr. Auerbach, if you will excuse me, perhaps such language is not entirely appropriate at the moment." He made a courtly nod toward Mrs. Corneille, and then toward Cecily.

Dr. Auerbach frowned.

Sir David blandly said, "Pity you weren't here when the good doctor was explaining Dr. Freud's Oedipus complex. Really a wonderful notion. Seems we're all of us men a bit fonder of our mothers than we ever imagined. Secretly we'd like to topple the old dear onto the breadboard and have a go at her. Did I get that right, Doctor?"

"You oversimplify, Sir David, I am afraid." Dr. Auerbach

turned to the Great Man. "What Herr Doktor Freud has established, you see, is that the young male child craves exclusive sexual possession of the mother. After the witnessing of the Primal Scene—that is, of sexual intercourse between the parents—the child develops a hostility toward the figure of the father."

"Dr. Freud has obviously never met *my* mother," said Sir David. "One look at Evelyn and he'd chuck that theory straight away. Along with dinner, I expect. Any child in his right mind"—he smiled at Mrs. Corneille—"and I include my younger self, of course—any child would be perfectly happy to let an entire rugby team take their chances with the old cow."

"David," said Mrs. Corneille, "you really are a dreadful man."

"If you think *me* dreadful, Vanessa, then you really must meet Evelyn."

Dr. Auerbach was shaking his head. "It is not at all important what the mother looks like, Sir David. It is only important that—"

"Excuse me." This came from the Great Man, who was rising from his chair. His face was white. His voice was weak and his body seemed unsteady. "I feel not well. Excuse me."

Holding his hand against his stomach, he nodded once, to no one in particular, and then he turned and stiffly walked away.

Mrs. Corneille looked at me. "Is it something he's eaten?"

Sir David raised his eyebrows blandly. "His mum, perchance?"

Mrs. Corneille turned to him, frowned, turned back to me. "He looked quite ill. Will he be all right, do you think?"

"Probably," I said. "But it's been a long trip."

"You motored down from London?" asked Sir David.

I nodded. "And took the boat from Amsterdam, day before yesterday."

"That explains it then," he said. "English food on top of Dutch. A marvel he can still walk."

I said to Mrs. Corneille, "I'd better go check on him."

She raised an eyebrow, as though mildly surprised. "Yes," she said. "Perhaps you'd better."

The Morning Post

Maplewhite, Devon

August 17 (Early Morning)

Dear Evangeline,

Night time, cuddled up against the bolster in my four-poster, toasty warm beneath the sheets and blankets, scribbling away, so ridiculously happy that from time to time (no one else being present) I hug myself. And from time to time I quite forget that the Allardyce is snoring away in the next room.

Maplewhite actually *is* haunted, Evy; there is at least one ghost in residence. Isn't that wonderful?

It was at dinner that I first learned of the ghost. We were all of us sitting round the table, Lady Purleigh at one end and Lord Robert at the other. It was the Allardyce who brought up the subject, between the turbot and the brandied chicken. 'Now, *Alice,'* she said, and even a blind man could have perceived how very much she relished this familiarity with the lady of the manor: the pleasure in her voice was so thick it had clotted, like Devon cream. 'You really *must* tell us *all* about this ghost of yours. Rebecca de Winter mentioned a *few* things, but she was *very* vague about the details.'

Lady Purleigh smiled. She has a lovely smile. She is, as I said, a lovely woman. (She was wearing a dress of black silk crepe de chine, cut on the bias; there are desperate women, I expect, who would kill to obtain this dress.) 'But I've never really seen it,' she said. 'I've heard it, of course.'

'What does he *say?'* asked the Allardyce.

'He doesn't say anything, actually. He only moans and groans. And only sometimes, late at night.' She seemed very nearly apologetic. That she is in any way related to the Allardyce will forever remain one of life's great mysteries. 'He's not an awfully interesting ghost, I'm afraid.'

'But that's only one of them, Mother.'

This came from the Honourable Cecily, the daughter. The

paragon. (Who was wearing a lovely sleeveless little thing in grey silk, scooped at the neck to flaunt her aristocratic throat.)

'There are *more?*' said the Allardyce, turning to her.

'There are three of them,' said the Honourable Cecily in that plummy voice of hers. 'There's Lord Reggie and there are the other two. One's a woman and the other is a young boy.'

'Cecily's been listening to MacGregor again.' This was from Lord Robert, who was smiling at his daughter with a kind of impatient fondness. She sat to his right.

'And *who* is MacGregor?' asked the Allardyce.

'The gamekeeper,' said Lord Robert. 'Soundest chap you could ever find at minding deer. But a trifle over-imaginative. A Scot,' he added, as though this explained everything.

'But he's seen them, Daddy,' said the Honourable Cecily. 'At the pond, down by the old mill. Beneath the willow tree. A woman in a long white dress, holding the hand of a young boy. MacGregor says the boy is ten or twelve years old. The two of them stand there, MacGregor says, staring out over the water. Whenever you approach them, they simply vanish.'

'Rubbish,' said Lord Robert. He turned to the Allardyce. 'Before MacGregor, no one ever said a word about ghosts down by the pond. Only ghost story here at Maplewhite was the story of the ghost in the East Wing. Been there for centuries, so the story goes. Supposed to be an ancestor. Reginald Fitzwilliam, the third Earl. Exploitive old swine. Worst relic of the feudal system. Got half the girls in the district in the family way. One of the tenants killed him in the end. Enraged father. Jumped out of a tree while Reggie was out riding, landed on Reggie's neck and snapped it. Snapped his own ankle, as well. He was hanged, of course, poor devil.'

'When was this?' asked Mrs Corneille.

'It must have been in the autumn,' said Sir David Merridale, 'if the tenants were falling from the trees.'

Sir David fancies himself a wit. He *is* clever, in a jaded way, and also handsome, in a jaded way; but neither so witty nor so handsome as he believes. I confess that I dislike him. Whenever he says something mildly clever, he glances at me significantly, as though he expected me to hurl myself, simpering, at his aristocratic feet.

But even more irritating are his un-significant glances. Have you noticed the way that certain men, when they believe themselves unobserved, observe women? They examine them as though the women were offerings, and as though they, the men, were coolly trying to decide whether to accept or reject them. Sir David is one of those.

Lord Robert answered her, 'In 1670. Under the Stuarts. Charles the Second.'

Cecily said to her father, 'But I thought you didn't believe in ghosts, Daddy.' Listening closely, one might possibly have imagined that one detected a faint feline purr in Cecily's aristocratic voice.

'I don't,' he said gruffly. 'A lot of bourgeois rubbish, ghosts. But it's the ghost in the East Wing I don't believe in. *That's* the ghost people have been talking about for ages.'

'Has anyone ever seen him?' said Mrs Corneille. She's a widow, stunning and slender and almost unbearably *chic.*

Lady Alice smiled at her. 'He's quite harmless, Vanessa.'

'He wasn't always, though,' said Sir David. 'According to the stories, no virgin was safe anywhere in the East Wing.' He glanced at me and faintly smiled.

'Rubbish,' said Lord Purleigh. 'Bourgeois fairy tales.'

Talk of ghosts dwindled along with the chicken, but it was picked up later, and once again by the Allardyce. We were all sitting in the drawing room, where every wall is hung with the most beautiful and probably priceless Belgian tapestries, each depicting scenes from the Rape of the Sabine Women. (You do remember the Sabine Women? That afternoon in the garden of Mrs. Applewhite's Academy for Young Ladies? I seem to recall a rather forceful performance, by yourself, as a Roman.)

Another guest had arrived after dinner: a Dr Erich Auerbach, an Austrian psychologist. (Not a very interesting man, I think; and short; several inches shorter than I.) He was sitting at the other end of the vast room with the Merridales and Mrs Corneille. When Lord Robert—out of sheer kindness, I suspect—sat down with the Allardyce and me, she said to him, 'Do *tell* us, Robert. This dreadful ghost of yours. What does he *look* like?'

'Never saw him, Marjorie. Told you, I don't credit all that nonsense.'

'Rebecca said that he's in his seventies. And that he has this *terrible* long white hair and a long white beard. He holds his head at a *peculiar* sort of angle.'

'Rubbish.' Here he turned to me and smiled. 'Not to worry, Miss Turner. Hundreds of women have stayed in the East Wing, thousands of 'em. And a fair share of virgins among 'em, I dare say. And not a one of 'em's been bothered by a ghost.'

We were interrupted then by one of the footmen, who was escorting the two newest arrivals, one of whom was the famous American magician, Harry Houdini. He's much shorter than I should have imagined, but very exotic looking and very energetic. And talented, as well: he 'found' a five-pound note in the Allardyce's teapot (a lovely piece of rococo silver, flower-chased, that one of the footmen provided for her when she explained that she simply *couldn't* drink coffee). Mr Houdini made her a present of the banknote, which thrilled her, needless to say. She would have been thrilled by a ha'penny, but of course he wasn't to know that.

The other arrival was Mr Houdini's secretary, a tall, swarthy American named Beaumont who seems to spend most of his time smirking. Obviously, and for no reason that I can determine, he is extremely taken with himself. Like Sir David, but without even his feeble wit.

Enough. I really ought to try to sleep, Evy. There is, in any event, scarcely anything else of note to recount.

So I shall tiptoe past the snorting form of the Allardyce and post this in the hallway, and then tiptoe back to my comfy nest. And perhaps during the dark hours I shall be visited by a ghost!

All my love,
Jane

Chapter Five

I KNOCKED.

"Who is it?" The Great Man's voice, sounding flimsy through the thick oak door.

"Beaumont."

"Come in."

The Great Man was sprawled, face up, on the bedspread as though he had toppled there from the edge of a cliff. He was wearing all his clothes and his right arm was flung over his eyes.

"What's up, Harry?" I asked him.

"Filth," he said. Even though I was in the same room with him, his voice still sounded flimsy. "Filth. I have never in my life heard such filth."

"Which filth is that, Harry?"

He swung his arm from his eyes. He sat up and swept his feet off the bed. "You heard him, Phil? That vile little German dwarf?"

"I thought he was Austrian."

He shrugged. "Austrian, German, what difference? Did you *hear* him? The child craves *sexual* possession of his mother! His *mother!*" He closed his eyes for a moment, then opened them again. "Phil, if my own dear mother were alive to hear this, the shock of it would kill her in an instant. Did you ever *hear* such an obscenity? I was afraid I would vomit."

"Well, Harry," I said. "I've read about these psychoanalysts. I don't think you have to take them all that seriously. They've got a lot of theories."

He shook his head and looked off into the distance. "And this Sir David—how could he possibly talk like that?"

"Sir David likes to shake people up, I think."

"But to say that about his mother." He looked at me and said earnestly, "Phil, I truly believe that if ever an angel walked the earth, it was my mother."

He had said that before, and often.

It was the death of his mother, I think, that had sent him chasing after mediums. Looking for one he could trust, but knowing too much to trust any of them.

I said, "Sounds like Sir David doesn't feel the same way about his."

Abruptly, he stood up. "We are leaving, Phil. I cannot remain here, among such people."

I leaned back against the stone wall and put my hands in my pockets. "What about the séance?"

He waved a hand. "They can hold their ridiculous séance without Houdini."

"Won't look good," I said.

He frowned. "What do you mean?"

"You leave now, you're admitting defeat."

He drew himself fully upright. "Houdini never admits defeat."

"That psychic, Madame Sosostris, she'll claim you lammed out because you couldn't prove fraud."

He snorted. "The famous Madame Sosostris. Where is she? She hasn't arrived yet, even."

"Looks worse, then. You wouldn't even hang around till she showed up."

He screwed up his face and chewed pensively at his lower lip. He turned and walked over to the window. He put his arms behind his back and grasped his left fist in his right hand and he stared out through the glass.

Maybe he wasn't staring through it. All he could see through it was darkness. Maybe he was staring at his own reflection.

"Why not just ignore them?" I said. "You've got the rest of the world in your pocket, Harry. After this weekend, you'll never see those two again."

"Filthy vermin," he said. He stared at the window.

"What about Conan Doyle?" I said. "Isn't he a friend of yours? Won't he be disappointed if you're not here?"

What I wasn't saying was that my job would be a lot easier out here in the country than it could ever be in London.

I also wasn't saying that if we left now, the drive back to London would take us all night. I was too tired to do it myself and too fond of living to let him do it.

"And Lord Bob and Lady Alice," I said. "You'll hurt their feelings. That might get around. Maybe you wouldn't get invited to any more of these soirees."

He thought for another moment and then he turned from the window. "Yes. Yes, of course. You are entirely right, Phil. They are extremely fine people, Lord and Lady Purleigh, are they not? Extremely gracious. I cannot abuse their wonderful hospitality."

"Right."

He nodded. "Very well. We will stay. I can rise above this, above the other two. The vermin. I can ignore them, as you say. What are they to me? Nothing. Less than nothing."

"Right."

"Yes. Good." Once more, he nodded. "But now I think I shall retire for the night. I find myself curiously fatigued."

"I think I'll pack it in myself. Mind if I use the bathroom?"

"No, no. Of course not."

I left his room, walked past the bathroom into mine. I circled around the four-poster bed to the night table. I opened my bag. I hadn't locked it. People don't usually bother with an unlocked bag.

But when I dug around a bit, I realized that someone had bothered with this one. Someone had gone through it. Carefully, but not carefully enough.

I lifted out the clothes and set them on the bed. I took out the case that held my razor and my toothbrush and I put it beside the clothes. I lifted out the pint bottle of bourbon and put that beside the case.

"Phil?" The Great Man stood at the doorway between our two rooms.

I straightened up and looked at him across the satin bedspread. "Yeah?"

He was frowning, puzzled. "Someone has attempted to unlock my bag."

I nodded. "Anything missing?"

He shook his head impatiently. "No, no. The locks are made to my own design and, naturally, they are impregnable. But someone has clearly tried to pick them. To an expert like myself, the signs are unmistakable." He frowned again. "You seem very calm about this, Phil."

"Someone got into mine. Didn't take anything, looks like."

"But who would do such a thing?"

"Couldn't be any of the others. They were all downstairs. One of the servants, maybe."

He was standing fully upright. "Phil," he said, "we must report this at once."

"Let's hold off on that for a while, Harry."

Another frown. "But this is a personal violation. A defilement. And if one of his servants is a thief, Lord Purleigh must learn of it."

"Whoever he was, he didn't take anything. And if we tell the boss, all the servants will know we know. Including the one who did it. Maybe things will work out better if he doesn't know."

The Great Man considered this. Then he nodded. "We shall possess knowledge that he does not."

"Like a magician and his audience."

He nodded again. "It provides us an advantage. And possibly it will enable us to catch him in the act."

"Right."

He grinned. "Excellent. I approve. Mum is the word, eh?"

"Mum," I said.

"Excellent."

After the Great Man went back inside his room, I reached down into the empty bag and pressed the two concealed snaps with my thumbs. I raised the bag's false bottom. The little Colt .32 was still in there. So were the spare magazines.

I replaced the bottom. I hung some clothes in the wardrobe, took my watch from my pocket, placed it on the night table. I undressed, climbed into my pajamas and robe, grabbed the toilet case, went into the bathroom and washed up.

When I opened the bathroom door, the Great Man was standing outside it in his own pajamas. They were impressive. They were black silk and the lapels were piped with gold, and a large ornate golden *H* was stitched over the chest pocket. He was carrying his toothbrush in one hand and his tooth powder in the other and he was wearing his black silk blindfold across his forehead.

"Good night, Harry," I said.

He stuck the toothbrush into his left hand, with the tooth powder, and then reached up to his ear and twisted out the lump of beeswax. "What was that?"

"Good night."

He smiled and nodded. "Good night, Phil. Many pleasant dreams." He corked up his ear again.

At night he put the blindfold across his eyes and the lumps of wax into his ears because he believed he was an insomniac. He wasn't. All night long, maybe, he dreamed he was awake. But I had slept in the same compartment with him on the train from Paris to Amsterdam, and for hours I had listened to snores that sounded like coupling hogs. In the morning he told me he hadn't slept a wink.

I returned to my room, shutting the dividing door behind me. I took off my robe and hung it on a hanger in the wardrobe, then slipped into bed and turned off the light.

I lay there for a while wondering who had broken into my bag. I decided there was nothing I could do about it now. A few minutes later I was asleep.

SOMETHING HAD AWAKENED me.

The door to the suite opening? A footstep?

My eyes were wide open. I narrowed them slightly. I was lying flat on my back. My head was facing the door, my hands were outside the covers.

I kept my breathing slow and regular.

The clouds must have cleared away outside. A slab of moonlight slanted across the room and painted a rectangle of colorless design on the dark Oriental carpet.

I listened.

I heard the faint ticking of my watch on the night table. Nothing else.

With my eyes still narrowed, I peered through the gloom toward the door.

Was there something there, *someone* there, a lighter shade of gray lurking over there in the darkness?

There was. Something tall and thin. Something the color of ash. It had moved toward me.

It moved again. Very slowly. Silently.

I found myself wishing that I had taken the Colt from the suitcase and tucked it beneath my pillow. I hadn't thought I would need it tonight.

The thing came closer. It was only a pale smudge against the sooty background and it made no sound at all. And then it floated into the spill of frosty moonlight and I saw that it was a figure shrouded from head to toe in white. It wore a hood that made an empty hole where the face should have been. It held something in its right hand, something that gleamed for an instant in the light of the moon.

It came still closer. It glided out of the moonlight and it became a silhouette, black against silver.

Four feet away.

Three feet.

Two feet from the bed.

It leaned toward me.

I whirled over, swinging my arm. Aiming my fist into the hood, at the spot where its chin should be.

My knuckles clipped the corner of something.

The figure toppled to the carpet, boneless and slack.

I sat up, turned on the light, jumped from the bed, bent down and turned the figure over. The hood fell away

Cecily Fitzwilliam lay there, out cold.

I said an impolite word.

★ ★ ★

CECILY'S EYES OPENED. "What?" she said. She blinked.

I took the damp washcloth away from her face and dropped it into the ceramic basin I'd set on the floor. "Everything's okay," I said.

She blinked again. Her eyes were still unfocused.

I moved the lamp on the nightstand a bit farther away. "Everything's okay," I said.

She looked at me. "What happened?"

She was lying on my bed. It wasn't a shroud she was wearing, it was a white silk robe with an attached hood. She was naked beneath it. I had learned this when I scooped her up and stretched her out along the bed.

"You tripped," I said.

"I . . ." She winced. She reached up and put her fingers to her chin. "I *hurt,*" she said. She looked vulnerable and lost and about twelve years old.

"Must've banged yourself when you fell. Probably what knocked you out."

Suddenly her eyes opened wide. She looked quickly around the room, then back at me. I was sitting on the edge of the bed in my bathrobe. Her own robe was belted shut but she clutched at it with both hands and tried to draw the front of it closer together. She moved to sit up and then winced again and fell back to the pillow. "What are *you* doing here?" She was whispering now.

I smiled. "I was just going to ask you the same question."

"But this is Mr. Houdini's room!"

"We switched."

She frowned. "Switched?"

"Exchanged rooms. What did you want with Mr. Houdini?"

She lowered her eyebrows. Her hands still gripped the front of her robe. "I don't see that it's any of *your* business."

Her flat, bored drawl was gone. Maybe it was something she hung up at the end of the day, with her clothes. Before she started wandering into other people's rooms.

"I handle his appointments," I said. "Usually he doesn't have any at two o'clock in the morning."

"I . . . If you really *must* know," she said in a ferocious whisper, "I wanted to ask him something." She winced again and she brought her left hand up to her jaw. *"Ow."*

"Ask him about these?" I held up the object she had brought into the room. I had found it on the floor after I picked her up. A pair of handcuffs.

Her hand dropped to her chest and she blushed. It was a spectacular blush, a deep crimson that tinted her face from the hollow of her throat to the top of her forehead. It told me everything I wanted to know about her coming here, and then some.

I tossed the handcuffs onto the bed.

She looked down at them and then looked back at me. She raised her head. "They're my grandfather's," she whispered defiantly. "Part of his collection. I thought it might be amusing if Mr. Houdini taught me how to unlock them."

I nodded.

"It's the *truth,"* she hissed.

"You don't have to whisper," I said. "No one can hear you."

She glanced toward Houdini's door. Looked back at me. Carefully, as if trying to decide whether I was telling the truth. She caught her lower lip between her teeth. She blushed again. Not as spectacularly, but still fairly well. She opened her eyes wide and she said, "Are you saying that, about no one being able to hear me, because you have designs on my virtue?"

"Your virtue is safe," I said.

She looked down at her hands again, and when she looked up into my eyes she was smiling. She was trying for boldness and she got there. "Are you quite certain of that?" she said.

I smiled. I think it was a paternal smile, but I could be wrong. "Time for you to get back to your room," I said.

She watched me. She lifted her left hand from her chest and ran her index finger down my own hand, from the back of my wrist to the first knuckle of my thumb. She canted her head slightly to the right. "Are all Americans so noble?"

I nodded. "We take an oath."

Her fingertip was soft and warm. So was the second fingertip, when it joined the first. So was the third. She was still watching me, saying nothing.

I should have stood up. I should have moved away from her. I told myself I was only sitting there because I was curious. Someday I'll sell myself the Brooklyn Bridge.

"Bedtime," I said.

"You probably think," she said, "that I'm a nymphomaniac."

"A nymphomaniac?"

"A woman who desperately—"

"I know what the word means."

"I had a friend, Gwendolyn, who was declared a nymphomaniac. They put her into an lunatic asylum. She was smitten with one of the footmen at her father's estate. I've always felt that one couldn't blame her for it, really. Peters was absolutely dishy, and we all had a crush on him, all of us girls. But her parents took her to the family doctor and he signed some papers saying she was a nymphomaniac, and that was that. Now she's locked away with all the lunatics."

"Why didn't her parents just dump the footman?"

"Dump? You mean dismiss him? Oh, they did that, first thing, of course. But Gwendolyn ran off, to be with him. She was totally smitten, you see. But they caught her. And then they had her put away with the lunatics."

"I'm not sure that one footman makes a nymphomaniac."

She nodded seriously. "I think that nymphomania, the idea of it, it's something men invented, don't you?"

"Probably," I said. "Come on, Cecily. It's time for bed."

"I'm already *in* bed," she said. She smiled, and then winced again. "Ow." Her fingers squeezed lightly at my hand. "We have a rule. Here in England. If someone has a pain, a sore chin, let's say, someone else has to kiss it. To make it better, you see."

"We have a rule in America. We don't fool around with the host's daughter."

She made a face. "Or his horse, or his automobile. I'm not just a *daughter,* you know. I'm not a piece of property. I'm a person in my own right. I'm a human being."

"I can see that."

"So. Do I get my kiss?"

She had gotten comfortable with the part she was playing. So had I. That was the problem.

"C'mon," I said. "Let's go."

Her fingers left me. She plucked the handcuffs from the bed and held them out with both hands. She looked at me playfully over the connecting chain. "Who should wear them first, do you think? You? Or me?"

"Let's go, Cecily."

She moved pretty quickly for someone who had been unconscious just a few minutes ago. She swung a cuff at my arm and it clicked shut around my wrist. "You, I think."

I stood up, away from the bed. The handcuffs dangled from my left wrist. "The key, Cecily."

She laughed. A light musical laugh. She crossed her arms over her chest and she shook her head. She smiled, as smug as a burglar in a bank vault on a rainy Sunday afternoon.

I took a step toward her.

It was then that I heard the scream.

A woman's scream.

Hard to tell where it came from. But the walls were stone. It had to be somewhere nearby.

Cecily had heard it too. Her head was cocked. The smug look was gone. She was listening, puzzled.

It came again, louder this time. A long frightened shriek. A wail.

I said, "Give me the key, Cecily."

Cecily's forehead was furrowed, her mouth was open. She closed her mouth and reached into the pocket of her robe. She frowned. She looked at me. "It's gone." She dug around in her pocket. "It's *gone!*" Her voice had become shrill. "I had it, I know I had it, but it's *gone!*" She looked quickly around the room, looked back at me, her face awry.

Fallen out of the robe when she hit the floor? I glanced around the carpet, didn't see it.

There had been no more screams. I didn't know if that was a good thing or a bad one.

I said the impolite word again.

I snatched the handcuffs up into my left hand and stuck both of them, hand and cuffs, into the pocket of my dressing gown. I took a last look at Cecily. She was on her hands and knees now atop the bed, slapping at the bedspread, her short hair flapping frantically as she looked back and forth. I ran to the door and yanked it open and I rushed out into the hall.

Chapter Six

THE ILLUMINATION IN the corridor came from dim electric lights set in brass sconces along the stone walls. Sir David Merridale stood in front of the next doorway to my left—the door to the suite occupied by Mrs. Allardyce and Miss Turner. Just as I saw him, Sir David opened the door and plunged into the room. I sprinted toward the door—with one hand jammed in my pocket, it was an awkward sprint.

I went inside. I stuck my other hand, my right, into the right pocket of the robe. With both hands in my pockets, I might be able to pass for a normal person. Out for a casual stroll.

By the dim light of the electric lamp on the nightstand I could see three figures in the far corner of the room. Two of the figures had their backs to me. One was Sir David. The other had to be Mrs. Allardyce. Unless there were two or three people under that bulky robe, traveling as one.

The third figure stood with her back against the stone wall. She was tall. She wore a long pink flannel nightgown and her head was lowered and her hands were covering her face. Her long brown hair was loose and it spilled down over her shoulders. Miss Turner.

The door to the next chamber was open. A light was on in there.

"She's had a nightmare," said Mrs. Allardyce to Sir David.

Miss Turner's head jerked up. "It was no nightmare!" she said. "I *saw* him."

"Saw whom?" said Sir David. He was patting Miss Turner on the shoulder. Paternally. He was also admiring her body, I noticed. I didn't blame him. The thin pink material clung to the curves and it draped nicely over the hollows. All the curves and all the hollows seemed to be in exactly the right places. Miss Turner, at nighttime, was a surprise.

"The ghost," she said. "Lord Reginald." She looked from Sir David to Mrs. Allardyce to me. "I know it sounds absurd, but he was *in* there!" she said, and pointed to the open door of her room.

"Nonsense," said Mrs. Allardyce. Her make-up was gone and I could understand now why she wore so much of it. She had no eyebrows and no lips. "You've had a long day. All this talk of ghosts has overstimulated you."

"I *saw* him!" With her glasses gone, her thick toffee-brown hair streaming free, she looked five years younger.

"Now Jane, for *goodness'* sake," said Mrs. Allardyce. She spoke with that elaborate patience that always conveys its opposite, and always intends to. *"Do* stop making a *nuisance* of yourself. It's time we all went back to bed."

Sir David curled his paternal arm around Miss Turner's shoulder. "I suspect that the young lady could do with a stiff tot of brandy. I happen to—"

Miss Turner turned and pushed his arm away with her forearm. She backed up. "Please don't patronize me," she said stiffly. "I'm telling you, I *saw* him."

Sir David smiled his bland smile. "I'm sure you saw *something,"* he said. "Something that appeared to you to be—"

"I saw a bloody ghost, you fool!"

"Jane!" said Mrs. Allardyce. "You forget yourself!"

Miss Turner turned to her. Her hands were down at her sides, balled into fists. "He was *there!"* she said.

"Even if he *had* been," said Mrs. Allardyce deliberately, "which I do not for one *moment* believe, there would *certainly* be no need to use such language."

For a moment Miss Turner's blue eyes flashed and her wide lips parted. It seemed to me that Mrs. Allardyce was about to learn something interesting about language. Maybe I could have picked up a thing or two myself. But then Miss Turner shut her mouth and bit her lip and looked away.

I said, "What did he look like?"

She turned to me and frowned and she narrowed those dazzling eyes as though trying to figure out what I was up to. Finally, hesitantly, she spoke. "He was an old man," she said. She turned to

Mrs. Allardyce. "Just as you said." She turned back to me and took a deep breath. I don't think she really cared whom she talked to, so long as it was someone who listened. "He was very old. Ancient. And thin. Skeletal. His beard was white, white and yellowish and long, like his hair."

"You had the light on when you saw him?"

"Yes. I switched it on as soon as I heard a noise. I wasn't sleeping."

"What noise?"

She frowned, remembering, trying to get it right. "A sort of clicking sound," she said. "Like claws on stone." She put her hands to her shoulders, holding herself, and she closed her eyes.

"What was he wearing?"

The blue eyes opened. She took another breath. "A long white gown. A sort of nightgown."

"He was tall? Short?"

"Tall," she said. "Not so tall as you, but tall. And his head was bent over to the side. Tilted. Twisted." She shivered again. "It was horrid. It made him seem demonic."

"Did he say anything?"

"He said—" She caught herself. She shook her head. "No. He said nothing."

For the first time I got the feeling she was lying. She had imagined the ghost, maybe. But if she had, she had also imagined him saying something. "Did he do anything?" I asked her.

Once again she shook her head. Once again I thought she was lying. "No," she said. "But he was *there!*"

"Gentlemen," said a female voice. I turned. It was Mrs. Corneille in a belted red silk robe. Her heavy black hair was still sleek, still perfectly groomed.

"I suggest," said Mrs. Corneille in that dark furry voice, "that you all return to bed and permit me to care for Miss Turner."

"For some reason, Vanessa," said Sir David, "I have a difficult time imagining you as Florence Nightingale." I thought I could hear irritation in his voice, running through it like a tight thin wire.

"For some reason, David," she said, "I have a difficult time imagining you as Dr. Livingstone. Miss Turner? Would you like to come with me? I should imagine that you'd rather not attempt to sleep just yet. And, if you feel you need it, I've some brandy, as well." She smiled sweetly at Sir David. He smiled blandly back. To Miss Turner she said, "And there's another room in my suite. You're quite welcome to it."

Miss Turner glanced toward the open door of her room, looked around at the rest of us, finally turned back to Mrs. Corneille. She raised her head. "Thank you. Yes. It's very kind of you. I *would* like a brandy. But I must fetch my robe."

Mrs. Corneille said, "I'll be happy to fetch it for—"

"No, no," said Miss Turner. "Thank you." She dropped her arms to her sides, turned, and walked into the door that led to her room. She kept her head held high, as proud as an Egyptian queen. And Egyptian queens almost never wore pink flannel nightgowns.

Mrs. Allardyce said in a stage whisper, "You really *shouldn't* encourage her."

Mrs. Corneille smiled pleasantly. "I'm sure you're right, of course. But what harm can it do if she gets away for a bit? No doubt she could do with a few moments to pull herself together. She seems basically a sound young woman."

Mrs. Allardyce frowned. She was dubious but she would go along. Maybe because Mrs. Corneille was being sensible, but more likely because Mrs. Corneille somehow outranked her. "Very well," she said. "But I'm not entirely sure that I *approve* of brandy at this hour."

Mrs. Corneille smiled again. She was better at that than I would have been, if I'd been the one smiling at Mrs. Allardyce. "You needn't worry," she said. "Only a thimbleful."

Sir David started to say something to Mrs. Corneille but just then Miss Turner returned to the room. She was wearing her glasses now and she was buttoning up the front of a shapeless gray bathrobe. None of Miss Turner's clothes lived up to her blue eyes. Not many clothes could.

"Come along, then," said Mrs. Corneille. She took Miss Turner's left arm and patted it. She turned to the rest of us. "Pleasant dreams."

Miss Turner glanced at all of us again but she said nothing.

They walked off. They made an interesting pair—Mrs. Corneille sleek and glossy in her red silk, Miss Turner taller and stiffer and almost drab now in her gray wool. You wouldn't think it was possible for someone to look drab and proud at the same time, but Miss Turner somehow managed to pull it off.

Without looking back, the two of them walked out the door into the hallway.

I said to Mrs. Allardyce, "What was it, exactly, that woke you up?"

She blinked. She was surprised, I think, by my asking. "Why, that awful screaming, of course. The silly girl gave me a *horrible* start. I thought my poor heart would stop." She put her hand on her heavy chest. Probably she had a heart and probably it was in there somewhere.

"Miss Turner screamed twice," I said. "Which scream woke you up?"

"The *first* one. It would've awakened the *dead.*"

"When you heard the scream, what did you do?"

"I sat up and I switched on the electric light." She frowned. "Why on earth do you ask?"

"An excellent question," said Sir David. "What are you playing at, Beaumont? Amateur sleuth?" He was annoyed at Miss Turner, I think, for calling him a fool. And probably at Mrs. Corneille, for plucking Miss Turner away. He was taking his annoyance out on me, probably because I was a witness, and a male. I could live with that for a while, if I had to.

"Mr. Houdini will want to know," I said. "This is the kind of thing he came here to investigate." It sounded reasonable to me, but it seemed to bother Sir David.

I looked at Mrs. Allardyce. "You turned on the light as soon as you heard the scream?"

"Yes, of course."

"What happened then?"

"Well, the—the poor girl screamed again, a *dreadful* scream, absolutely *pitiful.*" She was on her best behavior now. She was assisting the Great Houdini with his research. "I had no *idea* what to think. But I got out of bed and I put on my robe—I was concerned about Jane, you see, and I thought I should go and have a peek at her. And then she came *running* through the door. She was *completely* hysterical."

"You didn't see anybody else coming from her room."

"No, of course not. Only Jane. There was never anybody else *in* her room. Jane's a charming person, good-hearted, but *clever,* of course, and *terribly* imaginative. It's all those books she reads. And last night, you see, Lord Purleigh told us all some truly *horrifying* stories about the ghost who's supposed to haunt this part of the manor. An ancestor of his, the third Earl, Lord Reginald Fitzwilliam. Far be it from me to *criticize,* Robert's a *dear* sweet man, but really, he ought to have known better—anyone can see that Jane's an *excitable* person. What must've happened is that after hearing all that, Jane *dreamed* she saw Lord Reginald, and then, of course, because she was sleeping in a strange bed, she was *disorientated.* And so she thought the dream was *real,* you see."

I nodded. "You heard two screams," I said.

"Yes, didn't I just *say* so?"

"Uh-huh. You mind if I take a look in Miss Turner's room?"

If she'd had eyebrows, she would've raised them. Instead she raised the ridge of her forehead. "Is that *absolutely* necessary, do you think?"

"Absolutely. I've got to make sure everything's okay. Mr. Houdini will ask about it."

She frowned. "Well, if you think . . ."

"Thanks." I walked through the doorway.

It was the same set-up as the Great Man's room—first a bathroom and a toilet and then the sleeping area. There was no one in it, anywhere. The bed was a tangled mess and one of the pillows was on the floor, near the door. There was no one under the bed and nothing in the wardrobe except Miss Turner's clothing and the clean smell of talcum powder. The floor was wooden and the walls were made of stone. The window was too narrow to let anyone in or out.

Sir David had followed me in. Like mine, his hands were in the pockets of his dressing gown. Maybe he was hiding a pair of handcuffs of his own. His smile had gone from bland to ironic. He said, "Searching for clues, are we?"

I glanced once more around the room. "Right," I said.

"Aren't we going to produce our magnifying lens?"

I looked at him. "You think it was a really small ghost?"

His smile became bland again. "As an American," he said, "you probably wouldn't know this. But a gentleman never enters a lady's room without her permission."

I nodded. "Then I guess we'd both better leave." He stood in my way, so I walked around him and back out into Mrs. Allardyce's room.

"Thanks for your trouble," I told her.

"Not at all," she said. She put her hand to her chest again. "Will Mr. Houdini wish to speak with me?"

"Sure he will," I said. "Count on it. Thanks again. Good night." I nodded to Sir David. He didn't return the nod.

But I could feel someone behind me as I walked out into the hall. I took a few steps down the corridor and he called out, "Oh, Beaumont?"

I stopped and turned. "Yeah?"

He approached me. His handsome face was thoughtful. "You know," he said, "I don't think I care for your manners."

"No? You in the market for a new set?"

He nodded as if that was pretty much the answer he had expected. He stroked the left side of his mustache with the tip of his index finger. "Perhaps we'll have an opportunity to discuss this at some other time."

"Look forward to it," I said. "See you later."

"ORGHH."

"Harry?"

"Orgh."

"Harry?"

"Whumph?" In the light from the open doorway I could see him tug up the silk blindfold and stick it to his forehead. He unscrewed the wax from his ears. "Humph? What?"

"Sorry to wake you up," I said.

"No no no. I was merely resting my eyes." Probably the wax had kept him from hearing the snores.

"Okay if I turn on the light?" I asked him.

"Yes, yes, certainly. What is it, Phil? What is wrong?"

I turned on the light and held out my left hand. "I was wondering if you could get these off."

Cecily must have slipped away from my room while everyone was talking next door. If she had found the key to the handcuffs, she hadn't left it for me.

The Great Man looked at the handcuffs dangling from my wrist. He raised his eyebrows, surprised. "A Mueller and Kohl spring-loaded. An antique. Where did you find it, Phil?"

"A long story, Harry. Tell you in the morning. Can you get it off?"

He smiled. "Phil, a child could remove those. Here. Observe."

In less than a second, the cuffs were off.

The Morning Post

Maplewhite, Devon

August 18

Dear Evangeline,

You'll be appalled, I know. You'll be disgusted with me. I can scarcely blame you: I'm thoroughly disgusted with myself. I've been an absolute and utter fool. If the earth suddenly groaned open before me, I would leap immediately into the smoking chasm and I would feel, I promise you, nothing but intense gratitude and relief as I whistled down toward the Abyss.

Oh, Evy, I've been such an idiot! If you had seen me standing there, half naked, with all those people gaping at me! If you had heard me babbling like a lunatic about the ghost—

Yes, the ghost. A *real* ghost, or so he seemed at the time, slathering and foaming and hissing obscenities. Those wild eyes, that leering mouth, and that monstrous *thing* of his rampant and red!

But now, as the light of dawn begins to sift through the window, pale and cold and relentless, I begin to suspect that I must have suffered some attack of mania.

I've returned to my own room. The ghost is gone, if indeed he was ever present. In the room beyond, which reeks of her mint bonbons, the Allardyce sleeps, as always, the sleep of the just. One of the other guests, Mrs Corneille, was kind enough to offer me a brandy and, had I wanted it, the extra room of her suite. She's a wonderful woman, but I knew that wherever I might be I shouldn't sleep at all tonight, and so I returned here, determined to write to you and describe this fantasy that terrified me so. For a fantasy it *must* have been.

And yet, Evy, he seemed so very *real!* I can still hear his beastly cackle and the dreadful, *filthy* things he said. I can still taste the fear in my mouth, stale and slippery and bitter, like old pennies.

I'm babbling again. I shall do this properly.

Ah well. I'm afraid the ghost must wait. I hear something

stirring next door. Either the Allardyce is awakening or a hippopotamus has wandered into her room in search of a place to wallow. If he spies the Allardyce, he will no doubt attempt to breed; the clamour will unnerve the entire household. In any event, I must go. I shall get this in the morning post, and I shall send its continuation to you this afternoon.

All my love,
Jane

Chapter Seven

WHEN I AWOKE the next morning, a bright bolt of sunlight lay across the room. Tiny motes of dust floated slowly through it like microscopic creatures drifting in a golden shaft of sea.

It was the first sunshine I had seen since we left Paris. I had started to think that I would never see it again.

I picked up my watch from the night table. A quarter to nine. Late.

I eased out of bed, climbed into my robe, padded to the Great Man's door and knocked.

"Come in," he called out.

He was wearing his gray socks and his gray pants, a shirt and a tie, an opened gray vest. He was sitting on top of the bedspread, his back against the tall dark wood headboard. There was a pen in his hand and a notebook on his lap.

"Good morning, Phil," he said cheerfully.

"Morning, Harry. Why aren't you downstairs?"

He smiled. It was an innocent smile, and his innocent smiles always made me nervous. "But, Phil," he said. "I am under orders not to leave without you, am I not?"

"Being under orders isn't the same as taking them."

"But for me it is, Phil. I gave my word." He changed the subject. "Did you sleep well?"

"When I slept," I said.

His face became thoughtful. "Do you know, I must have actually slept myself last night—for a time, at any rate—because I had a dream. It was a most curious dream. You were in it and you were wearing a pair of handcuffs. You asked me to remove them for you."

"That was no dream, Harry. That was my life."

"I beg your pardon?"

"You weren't dreaming. I was wearing a pair of handcuffs last night, and I asked you to take them off."

"They were made by Mueller and Kohl?"

"According to you. Spring-loaded, you said."

"Amazing. Where did you get them?"

"They were a gift. From Cecily Fitzwilliam."

"A gift? Why would Miss Fitzwilliam give you a gift? And why a pair of handcuffs?"

"They weren't really for me. They were for you. Mind if I sit down?"

"No, no," he said, and waved a hand toward the seat by the writing desk. "For me? What do you mean?"

I sat down. "Well, Harry, it looks to me like Miss Fitzwilliam is smitten."

He frowned, puzzled. "Smitten? What are you saying, Phil?"

"She wanted to get to know you better. So she came to the room. She got me instead."

"Better?" Suddenly he blushed. "You mean . . . ? Miss *Fitzwilliam?*" His voice had risen slightly. "Phil—*no*. Her father is an English *lord.*"

"Harry. Calm down."

"But doesn't she know that I'm a married *man?*"

"She's just a kid, Harry. She only wanted to talk."

He looked off, toward the window, and stared at it for a moment. Then he took a deep breath and slowly let it out in a kind of moaning sigh, long and low. He shook his head. "So it begins again," he said.

"Again?" I said.

He looked at me sadly. "This has happened before, Phil. Many, many times. It is a terrible curse. Women of a certain . . . ah . . . animal nature, they inevitably find me irresistible. Perhaps my great physical strength attracts them. Or my virile demeanor. Perhaps it is merely the fact that Houdini is the most famous man alive."

He shrugged sadly. "Who knows, Phil? Who can plumb the hearts of these women? Certainly I never encourage them, never give them reason to believe, even for a moment, that I would respond to their advances. You know that my darling wife is the light of my existence. She is my beacon in life's storm-tossed sea, the only woman who has ever meant anything to me. Except, of course, for my dear departed mother. I would never betray Bess, Phil."

He looked off again. "I suppose I must try to find it within me to forgive them, these women. They cannot help themselves, naturally." He shook his head. "But I would never have believed that the daughter of an English lord . . ."

He looked back at me. "What shall we do about this, Phil? Shall we go to Lord Purleigh and ask him to keep a closer watch over this daughter of his?"

I smiled. "I don't think so, Harry. Cecily won't bother you again."

He raised his dark eyebrows hopefully. "Really? What did you say to her?"

"All the stuff you just said. About Bess and all. The beacon in the storm-tossed sea. I explained everything. She understands."

"Ah. Wonderful, Phil. A good thing that you are a man of the world, like myself." He frowned suddenly. "But why on earth did she bring the handcuffs?"

"She wanted you to see them. They're her grandfather's. She thought you might be interested."

"In an ancient pair of Mueller and Kohls?" Mildly indignant.

"She didn't know, Harry. She was only trying to be friendly. After she left, I was playing around with them and I accidentally locked myself up. Sorry I had to wake you up."

He shook his head. "You did not actually awaken me. As you know, I have difficulty sleeping. I was merely resting."

I nodded. "There's one other thing you should know, though."

He frowned. Worried, probably, about some other woman with an animal nature. "And what is that?"

"Looks like we had a ghost here last night."

"A ghost?"

I told him about Miss Turner.

When I was finished, he asked me, "How did she seem to you, Phil? Miss Turner?"

"Like someone who'd just seen a ghost."

"She was hysterical?"

"Not hysterical. Upset. Whatever she saw, she thought it was a ghost, and it scared her. But she seemed to be handling it fairly well."

"Yes. From my brief meeting with her, I would say that she has a good head on her shoulders."

And a good pair of shoulders under her head.

"As I may have told you, Phil, hauntings do not much interest me. If the accounts are true, ghosts seem to be completely unaware that they are actually dead. Which makes them, in my view, remarkably stupid creatures. What would be the point of communicating with them, even assuming that one could? But, you know, perhaps our Miss Turner is a sensitive. A natural medium. Unwittingly, without her own knowledge. I have heard of this, although never encountered it." He nodded thoughtfully. "I shall speak with her."

"Right."

"Shall we go have breakfast?" he asked me.

I looked down at my bathrobe, looked back up at the Great Man. "I thought I'd get into some clothes first."

"Excellent. I shall finish up this letter to Bess."

DOWNSTAIRS, ANOTHER SERVANT—one we hadn't seen before—told us that breakfast was still available in the conservatory. We followed him along some more hallways.

The conservatory was a large sunny room. All around, lush ferns and squat palms spread lacy fans and plump shiny fronds. Bright saffron light streaming through the walls of glass warmed the smooth gray marble floor. Beyond the glass was a view as still and as perfectly composed as a landscape painting. Blue sky overhead, a few white puffs of cumulus hanging there. An expanse of green lawn sloping down to a broad formal garden neatly blocked with squares of red and yellow and purple.

Sitting in the middle of the room was a long table covered with white linen. On a sideboard to the right were five or six silver warming pans, all of them the size of washtubs. There were stacks of porcelain plates, teapots and coffeepots, cups and saucers.

Lord Bob was sitting at the end of the empty table, in another gray suit.

"Ah, Houdini, Beaumont," said Lord Bob cheerfully. "Up at the crack of dawn, eh?" He chuckled. "You've missed the others, sorry to say. Gone into the village, all of 'em. Shopping, seeing the sights. Both sights, presumably. The church and the pub." He chuckled again. "Grab some grub, why don't you. Isn't that how you Americans say it? Marvelous language, American. Help yourself, we're informal at breakfast. And coffee, tea, whatever. Probably need your coffee this morning, eh, Beaumont? Comforting damsels in distress all night long, eh?"

He was in too good a mood to be talking about his daughter. I smiled at him as I lifted the lid of a warming pan. "You heard about last night?" Inside the pan were glistening layers of chunky pork sausages. I picked up a fork and stabbed a few, levered them off the fork onto a plate.

"Everyone has," said Lord Bob. "Talk of the town, eh?"

I said, "How is Miss Turner this morning?" I looked inside the next warming pan. A small beached school of stiffened fish stared up at me with scorched cloudy eyes. I returned the lid.

"Fine, fine," said Lord Bob. "None the worse. Funny, though, wouldn't you say? Never would've pegged her for the flighty type."

The next dish held rashers of bacon. I took some. "Me neither."

Like me, the Great Man was piling food on his plate. He asked Lord Bob, "This ghost was your ancestor, Lord Purleigh?"

"Supposed to be." His bristly white eyebrows dipped. Impatiently, he waved his teaspoon. "But too nice a day for that sort of thing, eh?"

Both the Great Man and I had filled our plates. We sat down next to each other and the Great Man turned to Lord Bob. "You have a lovely home, Lord Purleigh."

"Bob," he said. "Nice of you to say so. Can't take all the credit, of course. Been here a lot longer than I have. Make a lovely golfing club, though, won't it?"

"A golfing club?" said the Great Man.

"For the toiling masses. Idea of mine. Poor chaps don't get enough fresh air, do they."

"Ah," said the Great Man. "Yes. Miss Cecily mentioned something about this, I believe."

"Cecily did, did she?" He stroked his mustache. He nodded, faintly, sadly. "Doesn't approve, Cecily. Neither does her mother. Upbringing, you know. But they'll see the light. Know they will."

He leaned forward. "Think of it. A golfing club for the proletariat. Plenty of good fresh air, plenty of sound, healthy exercise. And we'll have more, of course. Nursery school for the young 'uns. Free medical care for everyone. And research facilities with first-rate people, eh? Finding ways to improve the quality of life. Everyone's life. And educational classes, as well, readings from *Das Kapital.* Not all those statistics, mind, but the gist of the thing. The meat. Read it, have you, Houdini?"

The Great Man blinked. "Not as yet, Lord Robert."

"I'll give you a copy. Got hundreds of 'em. It'll change your life. Changed mine, for a fact. Would've started this thing years ago, the golfing club, if it hadn't been for the Earl. My father. Dead set against it. Well, what can you expect? Complete reactionary. But he can't hold on forever, thank goodness. Soon as he pops off, we get to work. Should be any day now, too. Got a bad ticker, the swine." He grinned happily.

"Well," he said. "I'm off." He stood up. "There's coffee, tea, whatever. Help yourself."

"You are going into the village?" asked the Great Man.

"No, going for a ride on my new motorbike. Arrived just yesterday, straight from the factory. A Brough Superior, one-liter engine, four gears, hundred miles an hour top speed. Real beauty."

He smiled at the Great Man. "Almost forgot, Houdini. You're in the *Times* this morning. Maplewhite, too. The society page. Well, you two want anything, food, whatnot, just ask one of the servants. The others should be back soon. Tea at four o'clock. Till then, enjoy yourselves, eh?"

Lord Bob left the room, as the Great Man looked over at me.

"The *Times?"* I said.

His eyelashes fluttered. "I know nothing about it," he said. He leaned forward and plucked up the folded newspaper that lay in the center of the table. He opened it, turned the pages. I waited.

He read silently. After a moment he began to smile with pleasure. Then he looked in my direction and he frowned. He said, "I had nothing to do with this, Phil."

"Let me see it."

He handed me the newspaper. I glanced over the society page until I found it. It was only one small paragraph in a long column, but it was enough.

> Viscount Purleigh will this weekend be entertaining Sir Arthur Conan Doyle, creator of one of England's, and the world's, most popular fictional characters, Sherlock Holmes, Consulting Detective. Also present at Maplewhite, the Devon estate of Lord Purleigh's father, the Earl of Axminster, will be the famous American Escape Artist, Mr. Harry Houdini.

I closed the newspaper, folded it, tossed it to the table. This, I thought, was why he had been so cooperative. "Damn it, Harry," I said.

He showed me the palms of his hands. "I did nothing, Phil."

"That wasn't supposed to happen."

"It must have been Carlyle." His manager.

"Uh-huh. And how did Carlyle know?"

"I cannot imagine. I shall telephone him. I shall tell him I am furious."

He snatched up the newspaper, started to read it again.

"It's a little late for that," I said.

Still peering at the page, he said, "Why do you suppose they mentioned Sir Arthur first?"

"Harry, we've got more important things to worry about right now."

He lowered the paper, looked at me. "But perhaps Chin Soo is not in England yet. And even if he is, perhaps he did not read the *Times* this morning."

"Is that something you want to bet your life on?"

He frowned.

I reached into my pocket, took out my watch.

Ten-thirty.

"What are you thinking, Phil?" he asked me.

"Let's say that Chin Soo *is* in England. Let's say he's in London. Let's say he read the paper this morning. The earliest he could read it would be eight o'clock, maybe. Let's say seven, to be on the safe side. I don't know how many trains are running from London to Devon on a Saturday, but there can't be that many. And the trip takes six or seven hours. So we've got a few hours of leeway."

"Yes? And what do we do with them?"

"We don't do anything. *You* stay in your room."

"Phil—"

"Just for a few hours, Harry. Read a book. Write a letter. Meanwhile, I'll take a look around the grounds."

"And why will you do that, Phil?"

"To see if I can figure out how he's going to come at you."

Chapter Eight

THE GREAT MAN and I went up the stairs and down the halls. He didn't say anything, but his mouth was set in a thin petulant line and I knew that trouble was coming. When I closed the door to our suite, he turned to me. And on me.

"Phil," he said. "This is entirely unfair. You are treating me as though I were a child."

"It's for your own good, Harry."

"But you said yourself that we have a few hours of leeway."

"Sounds like you've got something on your mind."

He drew himself to his full height. "I refuse to stay here, cooped up in that tiny room."

"Cooped up? Harry, you're the guy who spends his time in coffins."

"From which I can escape whenever I wish." Somehow he managed to draw himself still taller. He shook his head. "No," he said. "I refuse."

"Harry, you told me—"

He shoved his hands into his pockets. He raised his strong chin. "I know what I told you. That I would do whatever you said, whenever it involved matters of security. But this does not. You're insisting on this because you wish to punish me for that silly article in the *Times.*"

There was maybe some truth in what he said.

"That was Carlyle," he announced. "I had nothing to do with it. If I *had* been responsible, the article would have been more than an insignificant little filler."

I didn't really believe that he was innocent, but I believed that, right now, he believed it. "So you're suggesting what?"

"That I come along while you inspect the grounds."

I shook my head. "It's too open out there."

"But Chin Soo is not there. He cannot be. You said so. And what if he is? Tell me, Phil, am I in any less danger inside the building? What about the Hotel Ardmore? Was it not you who pointed out that he nearly reached me there? What happens if he comes for me here, in my room, while you are outside?"

He had a point.

I walked over to the bed and sat down. I looked over at him. "Harry. Listen. Maybe it's time to bring the cops in on this."

"No. I told you. That is out of the question."

"Or at least let me wire New York," I said. "Have them send some people from London."

"And how would I explain *those?* Shall we tell Lord Robert and Lady Alice that they are *all* my secretaries?"

"Why not just tell them the truth, tell them—"

He shook his head. "Absolutely not."

"Harry, why is seeing the grounds so damned important?"

"The grounds of Maplewhite are *celebrated,* Phil. The forest, the extensive lawn, the fabulous gardens." He pulled his hands from his pockets and held them out to me. "Would you deny me a chance to see all these, to drink in their legendary beauty? And what will I say when people ask me about them? Shall I say that Houdini never saw them, because he was busy cowering in his room?"

I slipped my watch from my pocket. Ten minutes to eleven.

It was probably safe out there. Better to give way now, I told myself. If I did, maybe he would listen to me later, when it wasn't safe.

"An hour or two," he said. "Only an hour or two. And then we can return to the rooms."

I sighed again. "Okay," I said.

"Ah, Phil, wonderful!" He stepped over to the bed, clapped me on the shoulder. *"Wonderful!"* When I was sitting down, his eyes were level with my own. They were shimmering with pleasure.

He was easy to please. All you had to do was give him whatever he wanted.

"Okay, Harry," I said. "Okay. Go on downstairs. I'll be right there."

"Certainly, Phil," he beamed.

When he left, I opened my traveling bag and lifted the false bottom. I removed the small automatic Colt and one of the spare magazines. I replaced the bottom, closed the bag, dropped the magazine into the left pocket of my coat.

I hefted the Colt. It wasn't much of a gun and it didn't really have much heft. But that was why I'd brought it along—if anyone found it, it would seem like the sort of gun that might be carried by the sort of person I was supposed to be.

I pulled back the Colt's slide and released it. The slide jumped forward, chambering a cartridge. I flicked on the safety and slipped the pistol into the coat's right pocket.

THE MANOR HOUSE sat broad and monumental in the center of six or seven acres of mowed lawn, a solitary square mountain in the center of a rolling green prairie. There were some trees scattered around, alone or in clusters, and a garden or two, and some fountains. But most of it was open space. If I could stick a couple of men in each of the two towers, no one would be able to approach the building during the day without being seen. I didn't have a couple of men to stick in the towers.

The Great Man and I walked along a gravel path that ran around the perimeter. We kept the trees to our left. Even in the sunshine, the woods were dark. Tall shaggy pines crowded the ragged maples and oaks. Black plumes of fern drooped in the dense gray shadows. An entire army could hide itself in there, and some dancing girls, and all their relatives.

Walking beside me, the Great Man was drinking in the legendary beauty. He strolled with his head held high and his eyes wide open beneath the brim of his fedora. His arms were behind his back, left hand clutching right hand.

He took a deep breath and he hummed for a moment with pleasure. "Smell that air, Phil," he said.

"Yeah."

"It is a magnificent place, isn't it?"

"Yeah."

"And a magnificent day."

It was. The air was warm and clear and it smelled of new beginnings, fresh starts. Birds chattered and chittered in the trees. The blue of the sky and the green of the grass were as bright and slick as fresh paint. I resented it. I had things on my mind and all that brightness and beauty were distractions.

I said, "Yeah."

"You know," he said, "being here, amidst this loveliness, this serenity, makes me think that perhaps I should begin to consider my retirement from the stage."

"Yeah?"

"Have I not produced enough astonishments for mankind to marvel at? Have I not sufficiently baffled the most sophisticated audiences in the most cosmopolitan cities of the world?"

"Probably."

He sighed. He shook his head. "You cannot imagine how fatigued I sometimes become, Phil. How weary. Always creating some new way to enthrall and astound them. Always devising some new and even more impossible escape. Sometimes I actually wish that I could . . ." His voice trailed off. He sighed again, shook his head again.

I smiled. "Escape from it all?"

He turned to me and nodded. "Exactly, yes. Exactly. Perhaps the time has come for me to live as other men do. Perhaps, finally, the time has come for me to think only of myself. And of Bess, too, naturally. Perhaps it's time for the two of us to find a haven of our own, a place where we can—" He stopped walking. "Look there, Phil!"

I stopped and I looked. A squirrel bounded across the lawn, a ripple of red fur atop the grass.

I said, "It's a squirrel, Harry."

He grinned, excited. "But it is an *English* squirrel, Phil. My *first* English squirrel."

"You've been in England before."

"Yes, but I was trapped in London then. I've never seen the countryside, never seen the wildlife."

"It's a squirrel, Harry."

"Think of it, Phil. Ancestors of that squirrel may have witnessed the signing of the Magna Carta."

"Maybe even signed it themselves."

He looked at me and frowned. "You have no romance in you, Phil."

"Probably not," I said.

WE KEPT FOLLOWING the gravel walkway around that immense sunswept lawn. To our right, a hundred yards away, beyond some clumps of trees, the rear of Maplewhite rose up like a castle.

I kept telling myself that it was safe out here. That there was no one around who represented a threat. Not yet.

We were about halfway around the walkway when I saw someone coming toward us. On horseback, about a quarter of a mile away, at the far curve of the gravel path.

The Great Man had stopped drinking in the legendary beauty. He was telling me about the time he had jumped from the Belle Isle Bridge into the Detroit River. It had been in December, he said, and the river had been frozen, and he had jumped into a hole in the ice wearing handcuffs. The current had been stronger than he expected and it had carried him away beneath the ice, seven inches thick, and he had survived by breathing the thin layer of air just beneath the ice's surface. Not much of this was true but I didn't bother to point that out.

Then he said, "Someone is coming, Phil."

"Yeah," I said. "A woman."

She was dressed in black. The big black horse beneath her moved in a lazy walk as they came toward us along the gravel path.

"Not Miss Fitzwilliam?" the Great Man said.

"Looks like Miss Turner."

Chapter Nine

IN A FEW minutes, when she was closer, I could see that it was Miss Turner. She wore a small black bowler hat, a white blouse, a black bow tie, a black jacket, a pair of black riding breeches, and black leather riding boots. It seemed to me like a lot of clothes for such a warm day. But English people don't pay much attention to the weather. If they did, they wouldn't live in England.

Miss Turner's blue eyes were squinting a bit as she approached us. I realized she wasn't wearing her glasses.

She sat stiffly upright but she looked like someone who knew what she was doing. She knew how to put on the brakes, and the horse stopped a few yards from us and moved its head up and down. Her long legs straight against her stirrups, she leaned forward and stroked its strong sleek neck. The horse moved his head up and down some more. He liked that. I didn't blame him.

"Mr. Houdini," she said. "Mr. Beaumont. How are you this morning?" A few strands of her brown hair had freed themselves and draped down against her slender neck. Her face was bright and shining and once again she looked younger than she was.

"Quite well, Miss Turner," said the Great Man, taking off his hat. "And you?"

"I'm fine, thank you," she said, and suddenly she smiled. It was a big, fine, delighted smile. It went very well with her eyes. "It's really a marvelous day, isn't it?"

"Magnificent," agreed the Great Man.

I removed my hat and I said, "You're feeling better?"

She blushed, looked down, looked back up. "I'm glad of a chance to apologize for last night. I made a complete idiot of myself."

"You don't owe anyone an apology," I said.

"Oh, but I do. I was a silly hysterical child."

"Miss Turner," said the Great Man. "If possible, when you have a free moment, I should like to discuss with you this apparition you witnessed last night."

She shook her head. "But that's just it, you see. There *was* no apparition. There *couldn't* have been. It was all just a terrible dream, and like a fool I persuaded myself that it was real."

I said, "Sounds like you're trying to persuade yourself today that it wasn't."

She frowned and her face flushed again, with anger this time. She sat back, stiffer than before. "It wasn't," she said curtly. "I was a fool. I apologize for disturbing you last night. Good day. Good day, Mr. Houdini."

She tapped her heels lightly against the horse's flanks and the animal edged forward, around us. We put our hats back on and watched the horse move from a walk to a trot to a canter.

"A temperamental woman," said the Great Man.

"Uh-huh."

WE WALKED AND WALKED. As we came into the home stretch along the walkway, I was coming to the conclusion that no one could be kept safe here at Maplewhite. Not outside it, at least. Not unless he had an army of his own. There were too many approaches to the house, too many places to hide.

Just ahead, to the right of the path, a huge tree with dark bronze-red leaves towered over it. Two white-enameled wrought-iron benches were planted in the shade of the tree and I saw that one of these was occupied. Mrs. Allardyce and Mrs. Corneille.

"Yoo hoo! Mr. Houdini?" Mrs. Allardyce. She was wearing a brown dress and white gloves and she was holding a pale blue parasol over her head, maybe to protect it from all that shade. "Won't you join us?"

The Great Man and I joined them. We took off our hats and said hello and sat down on the other bench. I pulled the watch from my pocket, glanced at it. Twelve-fifteen.

Still safe, I thought.

I was wrong, but I wouldn't know that for a few more minutes.

"Are we keeping you from something, Mr. Beaumont?" said Mrs. Corneille, smiling. On her lap was a white straw hat with a broad brim. On the rest of her was a white linen dress that made her shiny black hair seem even blacker. The hem of this dress was lower than the hem of last night's dress, but it was high enough to show off a fair amount of her legs. They were still very good legs.

The broad blue sky, the broad green lawn, Miss Turner's eyes, Mrs. Corneille's legs. There were a lot more distractions around here than I liked.

I slid the watch back into my pocket. "Mr. Houdini and I had a bet. How long it would take to circle the grounds on foot."

"And who won?"

"We haven't finished yet."

She turned to the Great Man. "Are you feeling better today, Mr. Houdini?"

"Very much so," he said. "Thank you."

"I shouldn't *attempt* to circle the grounds," said Mrs. Allardyce. "Not even on a horse." She frowned. "Did you see Jane? She's off riding somewhere." She glanced around vaguely.

"Yes," said the Great Man. "We spoke with her a while ago. She seems a very accomplished rider."

"Yes, I suppose she is. And that's *surprising,* really, when you consider that basically she's such a *bookish* sort of person. When she's not writing one of those *interminable* letters of hers, she has her poor head buried in a book. Personally, I've never found Jane Austen all *that* fascinating."

She heaved her heavy bosom forward and looked eagerly at the Great Man. "Mr. Beaumont *did* tell you about our excitement last night? Jane's ghost? Well, today, of course, the poor girl realizes that it was all merely a nightmare, a figment of her imagination, but last night she was absolutely *hysterical,* wasn't she, Mr. Beaumont? It was all I could do to calm her. She can be so *emotional* sometimes."

The Great Man nodded. "Mr. Beaumont has told me of this. I—"

He was interrupted by the cheerful *toot toot* of a horn. We all turned toward the south.

A big motorcycle raced toward us along the walkway, gravel and earth spitting from its wheels. Lord Bob and his Brough Superior.

Lord Bob hit the brakes. The motorcycle skidded for ten or twelve yards on the gravel, wavering left and right, and finally it stopped in front of us.

Lord Bob was wearing the tweed suit he had been wearing earlier, but now he also wore a leather cap and a pair of goggles. He ripped up the goggles and let them slap back against his forehead. He grinned. Except for the white circles at his eyes, like a raccoon's mask, his face was coated gray with dust. His mustache had been swept back along his cheeks. "Capital machine! *Capital!* What an adventure! Reached a hundred on the main road!" Beaming beneath his goggles, he looked around at all of us. "Anyone care to give it a go? I'd be—" Suddenly he looked off, down the walkway. "Good Lord. Is that Miss Turner?"

Once again, we all turned.

About fifty yards away, the big black horse had just burst from the forest. It reared up, forelegs clawing at the air, but somehow Miss Turner held on. Then the powerful legs came back to earth and the horse wheeled toward us and began racing along the walkway. The reins were flapping loose against its neck. Miss Turner was bent forward, her arm groping for them. Her bowler hat was gone and her long brown hair was streaming like a banner in the wind.

"Oh dear," said Mrs. Allardyce. Mrs. Corneille stood up from the bench, maybe thinking she could do something. I realized that the Great Man and I were already standing.

But Miss Turner had found the reins and brought the horse under control. About twenty yards away she started slowing it, and by the time she reached us the animal was moving in a walk. The horse was panting. So was Miss Turner. Its eyes wide, the horse stopped and pawed the ground, once, twice, then raised its head and shook it and whinnied.

A few feet away, Lord Bob was standing now, too, his legs braced on either side of the big motorcycle. "Miss Turner! You gave us a terrible fright! Are you all right?"

"*Jane.* What on *earth* did you think you were doing?" Mrs. Allardyce. She was still sitting down.

Miss Turner's face was white and it was shining with sweat. She took a breath. She put her hand against her forehead. She licked her lips and she looked around at all of us. "I . . . I'm so sorry. I . . ."

Just then a number of things happened very quickly.

From somewhere in the forest behind us, to the south, came the flat hard crack of a rifle.

And something made a thunking noise somewhere as I spun to look at the Great Man. He had turned toward the sound of the shot and I knew without being able to see it that his chin was raised and he was daring the rifleman to try again.

All the others had turned, too, and frozen in position.

I shoved my hand into my pocket, going for the Colt.

And then, behind me, Miss Turner said "Oh," very quietly, and I turned back to her and her eyelids fluttered and her blue eyes rolled upward and became white and she slumped sideways off the horse.

Chapter Ten

I RIPPED MY hand from my pocket and I sprinted toward Miss Turner. Just as her leg slipped over the saddle, I caught her shoulders with my left arm and I scooped my right arm up beneath her knees. She sagged into the crooks of my elbows, her head lolling, her arms loosely swinging. I carried her over to the bench and laid her out on it and I squatted down beside her. I was looking for the bullet wound. I couldn't find it.

I sensed the people crowding around me. Mrs. Corneille, Mrs. Allardyce, Lord Bob. I searched for the Great Man, found him standing just behind me. He looked puzzled, maybe even worried, but he was alive and unwounded. There hadn't been a second shot.

Miss Turner was breathing but her face was white. I put my hand against her forehead. Cold and damp. I put my fingertips against her wrist and felt for her pulse. It was there, fluttering like the wings of a wounded bird.

Mrs. Corneille said "Is she . . . ?"

I said, "I think she's just fainted."

"A bloody poacher!" growled Lord Bob. "Filthy *sod!"* His beetle brows were lowered and a bright furious red was glowing beneath the gray dust that coated his face. He snapped his goggles down over his eyes, leaving two rings of indented flesh on his forehead. "I'll show the swine!"

He scurried off to the motorcycle, a flurry of tweed. I turned back to Miss Turner. I heard the howl of the motorcycle behind me as I unknotted the tie at her throat. Lord Bob, revving up the machine.

"Mr. *Beaumont!"* said Mrs. Allardyce.

The motorcycle exploded away with a roar of engine and a clatter of gravel.

"She needs air," I said. I unbuttoned the first two buttons of her blouse. Lightly, I tapped Miss Turner's cheek. Nothing from her. I noticed that her skin was as soft as a child's. I ignored that.

"May I?" Mrs. Corneille. She was beside me now, on my right. Her shiny black hair swung forward like a silk curtain as she leaned toward Miss Turner. I could smell her perfume. I ignored that too.

She took Miss Turner's right hand between hers and rubbed it gently.

I tapped the cheek again. "Miss Turner?"

She took a deep staggered breath and her lids snapped back and those dazzling blue eyes looked at me.

Twice now in less than twelve hours I had been the first thing a young woman saw when she came back to earth. Miss Turner didn't seem any more thrilled than Cecily Fitzwilliam had seemed last night.

She frowned. "What happened?"

"You've fainted," said Mrs. Corneille.

Miss Turner looked at her. She raised her head from the bench, as though trying to sit up. Mrs. Corneille touched her shoulder gently. "Not just yet, Jane. Rest a moment."

I stood up.

Mrs. Allardyce said to Miss Turner, "You gave us a *terrible* fright. What on *earth*—"

Mrs. Corneille turned and glanced back at her. She didn't say anything, but her eyes were narrowed and her lips were grim. Mrs. Allardyce shut her mouth.

Off to my right, two small black figures were running toward us, down the slope from the manor house. Servants.

I stepped over to the Great Man. Under my breath, I said, "Go back to the house with the rest of them. Wait for me in your room."

"Phil—"

"Just do it, Harry. I'll be back." I set off in a run after Lord Bob.

I LOPED ALONG the walkway and then down the lawn toward the formal garden, following the trail of the motorcycle across the lush green grass. The machine was parked beside a row of hedges at the garden's far end, along the edge of the woods.

That was about right, I thought. The rifle shot had seemed to come from the forest somewhere near here.

Ahead of me there was a narrow path into the forest. I marched up to it, stopped, looked back toward the tall tree with the bronze-red leaves. One of the servants was leading the horse down the walkway, along the course I had just taken. Everyone else was walking in a loose group up the gentle green rise to the house. In the sunshine, under that clear blue sky, they looked like they were returning from some sultry summer picnic.

Right here, I thought. Right here is probably where he stood when he fired.

About a hundred and fifty yards from here to the tree. Not an easy shot, especially firing slightly uphill.

I glanced around. No repentant snipers down on their knees, begging me to run them in. No signed confession nailed to a tree. No empty cartridge anywhere. The mossy ground was still spongy from last night's rain and there were footprints in it, but too many of them. Lord Bob had gone tramping through here.

The trail twisted down the hill for twenty or thirty yards until it ended at another path. This one was wider, almost a road, with a surface of crushed black stone. To the right it led up the hill, in the direction of the house, which was out of sight now. To the left it led down the hill and disappeared about forty yards away, behind the trees.

Lord Bob came around the bend in the road and stopped. I walked down the pathway, toward him.

"Beaumont," he said. "Seen anyone?"

"No."

"Look here," he said. "You're an American. How's your wood-craft, eh? Following a trail, Fenimore Cooper, all that?"

"You mean broken branches, bent twigs?"

He brightened. "That's it, yes."

"No good at all."

"Ah."

"Where does this go?" I nodded down the path.

"Eh? Oh. Down to the river. No luck there. Went down that way myself just now. Nothing." He looked around him, at the forest that seemed to go on for miles. "Bloody bastard could be anywhere."

"What's up here?" I nodded up the path.

He seemed puzzled by the question. "The manor, of course."

"Could we take a look?"

He frowned. "You can't be thinking a poacher would go *that* way?"

"Worth a look."

He stared at me for a moment and frowned again. Probably wondering why a personal secretary was so interested in poachers. But he was a gentleman, and finally he shrugged. "Very well. Come along."

The two of us trod up the gravel road. The earthen banks on either side of it grew higher until they rose above our heads. The road became a kind of narrow valley running between the steeply sloping ground and the tall trees climbing off the ridges up there. We ended at a tall, broad, double wooden door set into a wall of stone about fifteen feet high. I could see a green line of hedge beyond the top of the wall. We were beneath the level of the formal garden, and at its far side.

"What's this?" I asked him, and nodded to the door.

"Freight tunnel," he said. "Goes under the garden, into the house. Comes out near the kitchen. They used to bring goods this way. Barges on the river, horsecarts up the road here, and then down the tunnel to the house. Faster back then. Don't use it nowadays."

On the door to the right, at waist level and just where it joined the other door, there was a rusted lockplate with a large keyhole in its center. I bent forward and examined the keyhole. It looked like no one had used it in years. But I was no expert at locks. I glanced down. No tracks in the crushed stone, that I could see. But, as I had told Lord Bob, I was no expert at tracks.

I stood straight. "You have the key?"

In those white circles that surrounded them, his gray eyes

blinked. "Not with me, no. Wouldn't make any difference, though. Barred from the inside."

I pressed against the door. It didn't budge.

Lord Bob was frowning again. His aristocratic patience was beginning to unravel. Or maybe it was his Bolshevist patience. "What is it, exactly, you think you're looking for?"

I pulled out my watch. Five minutes to one. "Could I meet you somewhere inside, in about an hour?"

"Whatever for?"

I shook my head. "I've got to talk to Mr. Houdini first. But it's important."

Yet another frown. Obviously I had overstepped some boundary that a secretary wasn't supposed to step over. "Perhaps you could tell me," he said, "what this is all about."

"I sorry, but I can't right now. An hour?"

A small sigh. He reached into his vest pocket, plucked out his watch, glanced at its face, looked up at me. "Very well. In one hour. In my study."

"Where's that?"

"Someone will show you."

"Right. Thanks."

"HARRY," I SAID, "we've got to tell him."

"But Phil—"

"I went back there," I said. "Before I came here, I went back to that big tree. The one we were all standing under. There's a hole in the trunk, Harry." I reached into my pocket. "This was inside the hole. Good-sized slug, from something like a thirty-thirty. I worked out where all of us were standing. If he fired the rifle from where I think he did, this thing missed your head by about two inches."

We were back in his room. He was sitting on the bed, his back against the headboard, his arms folded stubbornly across his chest. I was sitting in the chair by the writing desk.

"But Phil," he said. "Lord Purleigh believes it was a poacher."

"Lord Purleigh doesn't know about Chin Soo." I tossed the slug onto the bed.

He pretended not to notice it. "But it *could* have been a poacher."

I shook my head. "The sound of the shot. It was sharp and clear. Not muffled. Whoever fired it, he fired right at the edge of the forest. Not inside it. He wasn't aiming at a deer or a wild pig or some damn rogue elephant. He was aiming at you."

He pressed his lips together and looked off.

I said, "I'm sorry, Harry, but it's over. If you won't tell him, I will."

He looked back at me, surprised. "But you gave me your word."

"I said I'd stay under cover as long as I worked for you. But if you don't tell Lord Robert, I don't work for you. I quit. I tell him myself, and the two of you do whatever you want, and meanwhile I'm on the train back to London."

"But Phil—" His voice was cajoling.

"There's something else, Harry. If he'd missed you by two inches in the other direction, he would've hit Mrs. Corneille. Maybe he'll hit her next time. You can risk your own life as much as you want. That's your privilege. That's what you do for a living. But you're not going to risk the life of anybody else."

He inhaled slowly, deeply, and then he sighed. He nodded. "Yes. Yes, of course. You are quite right, Phil. We must tell him."

The Evening Post

Maplewhite, Devon

August 18

Dear Evangeline,

I'm losing my mind, I've become certain of it. I've also become certain, however, given this particular organ's many obvious defects, that its loss will occasion hardship to no one. Least of all, perhaps, to myself.

I know that I promised you a ghost. I'm going to renege on that promise, or at any rate on that ghost. I don't really want to talk or write or even think about him any longer. I'm sick of him, frankly. What he said and what he did, if in fact he actually said and did them, are things best forgotten. If not forever, then at least until I sort out the rest of it.

The rest of it?

You may well ask. Since breakfast, in addition to stumbling upon two *additional* ghosts, I've been fondled and propositioned; I've been badly bruised; I've been trapped, flopping and flailing, on a runaway horse; I've once again made an absolute fool of myself; and I've been peered at and prodded at by an Austrian psychoanalyst. And somehow I've misplaced an antique tortoise shell comb that I liked very much.

And, oh yes, mustn't forget, I've been shot at.

The bullet wasn't actually intended for me, or so at any rate I am assured. But certainly it deposited itself near enough to my person for me to have taken, at the time, a certain proprietary attitude regarding it. I felt rather cheated later, when I learned that this was mistaken.

Such are the ways of Devon. Of course, we seasoned travellers take all this in our stride. For, really, when you've seen one ghost, then in a sense you've seen them all, *n'est-ce pas?* One is enough, surely, to prove the point; the presence of two (or three, or four, or four hundred) is simply redundant.

And what, come to that, do propositions and fondlings

ultimately signify? When you've experienced as much of the world as I have, Evy, when you've encountered, as I have, everything from the giddy heights of Knightsbridge to . . . well, the giddy heights of Kensington, you realize that in the supreme scheme of things, the grand expanse of Time and Space, our passions and indeed our lives are, at bottom, puny little things.

And as for bullets—ah well, what are bullets, finally? How petty they are, how *common,* these little bits of lead whizzing through the air and crudely plunking themselves into nearby trees.

As for the comb, I probably did something silly with it while my attention was wandering. Misplaced it, perhaps. Or ate it.

I *am* rather upset about the comb.

I'm losing my mind, as I say. And *I don't care.* I refuse to keep playing the wide-eyed (if ageing) ingenue, even if that is the role for which, by general agreement, I am best equipped.

Enough. We shall begin this narrative where I ended the last.

I told you that I hadn't slept at all last night, after seeing the first ghost. And I think I told you that I stopped writing to you because I'd heard the sound of something stirring in the Allardyce's room. After folding up the letter and sealing it into an envelope, I eased myself off the bed, threw on my robe, and tiptoed over to the door that connects her room to mine. I was less than eager to confront her, still smarting with shame at my performance last night.

Sitting at the dressing table in her robe, her heavy body slumped, her arms slack along the arms of the chair, her hands limply dangling, she was staring at the mirror.

She wore no make-up. I've seen her like this before, of course, countless times: all the paints and polishes stripped away, all the oils and cosmetics. I had indeed seen her like this only a few hours before, while I was demonstrating my flair for hysteria. But this morning, for some reason, her face appeared curiously naked and vulnerable.

Vulnerable is perhaps the last label that I should normally attach to the broad back of the Allardyce. Perhaps it was the sunlight this morning. Outside, for the first time in weeks, the clouds were gone. A cold yellow shaft stretched across the room and struck her white round face like the beam from an electric torch.

I think I told you that she has no eyelashes and no eyebrows. This morning, in that stony sunlight, their absence made her face look shocked, astonished, as though only a moment before she had glanced into the mirror and realized, all at once, that she had grown old, and stout, and alone.

For, at some time, however many years ago, before however many bonbons and muffins and buns, even the Allardyce must have been a small child. Once she must have chased butterflies across a meadow. Once she must have felt *surprise:* at a sunset, a rainbow, a sneeze. Once she must have giggled and squealed.

I don't mean to say that I thought all this out, rationally or even consciously. What came over me, and it came over me within the course of merely a second or two, was a feeling of profound and infinite sadness for the losses she had sustained, whether by accident or by her own design (which of course would have been worse); and a sense that I had, up till now, in a way *betrayed* what was best in her by not recognizing the possibility of its existence; and betrayed, too, by doing so, what was best in me.

As I say, all this happened within only a second or two. And then she realized, abruptly, that I was there in the room, and she turned to me and frowned. Beneath her pale peeled forehead, her tiny black eyes puckered. 'You nasty, *vulgar* little thing,' she said.

Whatever it was I attempted to say, it came out as a hopeless stammer.

She drew her robe more tightly about herself. 'Waking up *everyone.* Screaming and howling like some Irish *washerwoman.*'

Shame burbled hot and thick to the surface of my face. 'Yes, I'm terribly sorry, I—'

'It was a *dreadful* embarrassment. What must my friends *think* of me? When I awoke this morning, my *first* thought was that I should dismiss you.'

My own first thought was to spit in her beady little eye.

My next thought, less appealing but more rational (alas), was that this just would not do. The spitting, I mean. I reminded myself that I had been suffering this insufferable woman for a purpose. After only one more year in her employ—assuming that both of us did in fact survive one more year—I should have saved exactly one hundred pounds, which will provide a cushion for me to sit upon while I make an attempt to decide what I shall do with this life of mine.

I suppose I could have spat in her eye anyway. And perhaps struck her in the mouth with a Meissen snuffbox. Both notions were enormously tempting. I could have left her outstretched on the floor like a beached whale, packed my luggage, begged a ride down to the railway station, caught the first train back to London.

But I remembered the months I had spent without employment, the cramped cold meals in my tiny room, the hunger and the humiliations and the murderous London solitude that scorches the soul.

Thus calculation doth make cowards of us all.

I said nothing to the Allardyce. She, for several long seconds, said nothing to me. For my part, I was too proud to beg for my position; and yet, despite my pride, too craven to throw it in her face. She, I think, was deliberately prolonging the moment, to impress upon us both the dimensions of her power.

'I am, however,' she said at last, 'and with *quite* a few misgivings, going to give you one more chance. I am going to make allowances for your youth and your obvious ignorance. But I *warn* you. If you do not do as I say, from this moment on, you will be dismissed immediately. And I shall see to it that *no one* of decent family has *anything* further to do with you. You *do* understand me?'

'Yes,' I said.

She narrowed her spitless eyes and pursed her unbruised mouth. 'It is customary,' she said, 'when someone has been *good* enough to show us a kindness, that we *thank* them for it.'

This too? I thought.

'Thank you, Mrs Allardyce,' I said, and privately I wondered how much spittle I could accumulate over the course of a year.

But the Allardyce was not finished with me, not yet. 'There will be no more *nonsense* about ghosts,' she said. 'Your behaviour last night was *inexcusable.* And your treatment of Sir David was particularly offensive. You will apologize to him as *soon* as possible.'

Earlier this morning, in the midst of my performance, Sir David Merridale had pretended to comfort me by stroking me in a manner that was designed less to calm my nerves—Evy, I *know* this—than to arouse his own. I had been rude to him, yes; but the man had taken deliberate advantage of my distress. If the Allardyce had sat up all night contriving one single act which would disgust and enrage me, it would have been exactly this, *my* apologizing to *him.*

But I swallowed my pride, the few wretched shreds of it that remained, and I nodded. Mrs Applewhite, that staunch believer in principle, would have retched.

'Very well,' the Allardyce said. 'You may go and dress.'

Breakfast was not quite the torment I had anticipated. I had been dreading it: confronting in daylight the people who had witnessed my lamp-lit hysteria. If not for the Allardyce, however, I believe that no one would have said a word. Even Mrs Corneille acted as though it never happened, despite my having spent a shaky half-hour in her room. She merely smiled at me pleasantly, and nodded in my direction.

Sir David smiled his ironic, knowing smile at me, but Sir David is forever smiling his ironic, knowing smile at me.

Mr Houdini and his secretary, Mr Beaumont, incidentally, never arrived. Despite their legendary get-up-and-go, Americans evidently prefer to lie-down-and-stay.

We ate in the conservatory, an airy room with a view of the lawns and, below us, the formal garden. The meal was an informal affair; we helped ourselves to eggs, bacon, kidneys, etc., from silver chafing-dishes on the sideboard.

I wasn't hungry—those shreds of pride had caught in my throat and I could swallow very little else. I said nothing. Afterward, the Allardyce, her face and her good humour restored, talked at length about a mindless musical comedy to which she had towed me the month before. Lord Robert waxed ecstatic about some new motor bicycle he had purchased.

The Honourable Cecily surprised me by turning in my direction and asking me if I rode. Caught off guard, flustered, I could only reply, like a perfect idiot, 'A motor bicycle, you mean?'

She smiled sweetly and said, 'No, no. Do you *ride?*'

I said that I once had, with great pleasure, but not for many years. She surprised me once again by offering me her own horse.

'But I've no proper riding clothes,' I said.

She shrugged lightly, and lightly glanced over my drab cotton frock. 'My cousin left hers here. They'd fit you, I expect.'

Surprised by this unexpected generosity, and wondering what had prompted it, I nearly stammered again. 'That's extremely kind of you,' I managed to say. 'Yes, then. Thank you. I'd love to. If you're quite sure you don't mind?'

'Not at all,' she said in her plummy tones.

The Allardyce spoke.

'Jane, dear,' she said sweetly, 'I don't *really* feel that riding is a good idea. After *all* that excitement last night, I shouldn't want you to *tire* yourself.'

Beneath this feigned concern, of course, was a determination to demonstrate her authority anew by refusing me something which I clearly desired. I felt anger wash through me, and then caution, and then shame, and I looked down at my plate without seeing it.

'Eh?' said Lord Robert. 'Which excitement is that?'

'Oh, you didn't know?' brightly said the Allardyce. 'Poor Jane had a *frightful* nightmare last night. She *persuaded* herself that she'd seen your famous ghost, and she felt *compelled,* poor dear, to wake up everyone within earshot.'

I looked at Lord Robert and saw that he was staring at me. He had gone as pale as a—well, he had gone quite a deadly shade of pale, Evy. He opened his mouth, closed it, then opened it again and said to me, nearly in a whisper, "You saw Lord Reginald?" He cleared his throat.

I was a bit surprised at his reaction and I could only stutter, 'I, no, Lord Robert, I—'

'Robert, dear,' said Lady Purleigh, smiling up at him from the opposite end of the table. 'It was a nightmare. Only that.'

'Yes,' I said. 'A nightmare. I'm very sorry, Lord Purleigh, that I disturbed your guests.' My voice was raspy and not at all my own.

Mrs Corneille sat across from me, and she was staring at the Allardyce, her lips compressed. To her left sat Dr Auerbach, the psychoanalyst, who was watching me with his eyes wide in psychiatric interest behind his pince-nez spectacles.

The skin of my face was hot again, and as taut as a sausage casing.

Lord Robert's face had gone from white back to its usual brickred, and suddenly he ginned at me. 'A nightmare. Well, 'course, it was a nightmare. 'Course it was. Hah hah. Nothing to be ashamed of. Happens to the best of us, eh? Don't give it another thought.' He narrowed his eyes. 'Riding, that's the ticket. Best thing in the world for you. Good fresh air. Healthy exercise. You take Cecily's horse, like she says. Damn good idea, Cecily.' He turned to the Allardyce. 'Best thing in the world for her, Marjorie, trust me.'

Coming from her host, this was for the Allardyce less a suggestion than a command. Blinking her eyelids, she smiled sweetly. 'Well, of *course*, Robert. If you really *think* so.'

Is it possible, do you think, that she is secretly a creature from some other world, Mars or Venus, obliged to disguise her true feelings in order to masquerade as a creature of this one?

Said Cecily, 'She could take Storm for a run while we all go into the village.'

And Mrs Corneille, bless her, said, 'But perhaps Jane would enjoy a trip into the village. Wouldn't you like to come with us, Jane?'

'I would, yes,' I said. 'But some other time? If I could? If you don't mind, I'd really love to go riding.'

She smiled beneath those finely arched eyebrows of hers. 'As you like.'

'Best thing for you,' said Lord Robert. 'Cecily, take Miss Turner upstairs, why don't you, and fit her out, eh?'

I glanced around the table. Sir David was still smiling

knowingly. Dr Auerbach was still eyeing me with professional curiosity.

As I left with Cecily, enormously relieved to be going, another thought occurred to me: it is quite rude not to remove one's back from the room when people are about to discuss one behind it.

Cecily has her own suite in the West Wing of the manor, a small sitting room and a boudoir with an attached dressing room. Everything everywhere was perfect, of course, and French—the mahogany armoire, the elegant Empire bed, the Louis XIV chairs in crimson velvet. And the clothes crowding her cupboards, the silk and satin and velvet and lace and . . . etc. Envy is *so* tiresome, don't you think?

Cecily lay on an upholstered camelback sofa in the sitting room, leafing through a *Vogue* magazine, while her maid, Constance, helped me locate the cousin's clothes. They smelled faintly of Chanel (of course) and they fitted me really rather well, I must say. When I looked into the tall looking glass in the dressing room, I was surprised and absurdly pleased. The cut of the jacket with its trimly tucked sides was immensely flattering, minimizing that awful chest of mine and emphasizing my waist, which is, no matter how currently unfashionable, one of the few decent features I possess. (And *please* don't tell me otherwise.) I spent, I confess, a moment or two swirling like a dervish before the glass, admiring my fatuous smiling self over my shoulder.

When I returned to the sitting room, carrying the riding crop in one hand and the bowler in my other, Cecily closed the magazine and languidly laid it on the coffee table. She looked me over and frowned, as though for some reason displeased.

I stopped walking. 'Is something wrong?' I asked her.

'Oh, no,' she said. 'Nothing.' Lightly, athletically, she swung her long legs off the sofa and stood. She was wearing a dress of cream-coloured linen, simple but elegant, with short sleeves and a low waist and a hem that fell to just beneath her pert perfect knees. Opalescent silk stockings, also, and beige leather pumps. She looked smashing, as always.

She removed a cigarette from a black lacquered Chinese box on the coffee table and put it between her lips. She looked over at me again. 'It suits you,' she said. 'The jacket.' With a small gold lighter she lighted her cigarette.

'Do you really think so?'

'Yes,' she said, exhaling smoke. 'You're quite the dark horse, aren't you.'

'Excuse me?' I said.

She merely smiled her superior smile and shrugged her slender shoulders. 'It's only that you seem so much . . . I don't know, really . . . *healthier* in that outfit.'

Fatter, I assumed she meant; and perhaps I frowned.

But she smiled again, less rigidly. 'I mean to say,' she said, 'that you do look really quite lovely.'

I thought that was very sweet of her, and I thanked her: flushing, of course, like a schoolgirl.

Together we marched from her room through several corridors and down several stairways and through several more corridors until we arrived, rather breathless, at the Great Hall, where the going-to-town contingent had assembled: Lady Purleigh, Mrs Corneille, Dr Auerbach, and Sir David. Lady Purleigh said something gracious about me and my plundered finery, and again I blushed and gushed; very becomingly, I'm sure. And then, as the others began to trickle out into the sunshine, the Allardyce towed me aside and growled, under her minty breath, 'Time for your apologies, young lady.'

She wheeled her bulk around and whinnied, 'Oh, Sir *David?* May we speak with you for just a *moment,* please?'

Sir David turned and then strolled over to us, smiling that odious ironic smile.

'Sir David,' mooed the Allardyce, 'Jane has something *most* important she wishes to say to you.' She smiled at me sweetly: once again attempting, and with the same crashing lack of success, to impersonate a human being. 'Now don't *overtire* yourself today, dear,' she said. And then she waddled off, leaving me alone with my bowler and my riding crop and Sir David. I felt rather as a sacrificial goat must feel when it has been staked out amidst the brambles, beneath the roaring sun.

'I must say, Jane,' said Sir David, 'you look ravishing in that outfit.' He smiled, as though ravishing, word and deed, had been much on his mind of late.

'Thank you,' I said.

'A fine riding crop,' he said, stroking his moustache. 'May I see it?'

I gave it to him. He thwacked it very lightly against the palm of his left hand, then looked up at me knowingly. 'Nice spring to it. Stiff and yet supple.'

I felt the skin of my face begin to stiffen and singe. 'I am sure it will prove adequate,' I said.

He smiled at my blush; my blush deepened; his smile widened. 'Oh, I'm quite sure it will,' he said, tapping the crop rhythmically against his palm. 'You had something to say to me?'

'Yes. I wanted to apologize for my behaviour of last night. I was rude.'

There. It was done. In a year's time, the Allardyce would be richer by half a pint of spittle.

Still smiling, still tapping the crop, he said, 'You've ridden before, you say?'

'Yes.'

'I'd have thought so. You've a splendid seat, I fancy.'

And then, his glance holding mine, his eyebrow raised speculatively, he lowered the crop to my side and moved it, in a lickerish, leathery caress, up along my hip.

I was so startled that I merely stood there.

He took that as acceptance: he stepped forward, his lips still smiling, but parting now. I slapped him full across the face, as hard as I could.

I suspect that I was as surprised by this as he was. And he was stunned. His head snapped up and his face went white. And it went *wicked,* Evy: his eyes narrowed to dark shining slits and his thick lips snapped back from his teeth. And then, backhanded, so swiftly I could hear it hiss, he raised the riding crop.

(to be continued)

Chapter Eleven

LET ME SEE," said Lord Bob, "if I understand you."

We were in his study, a large room on the ground floor. It smelled of new flowers and old money. It had probably always smelled of old money, but the smell of flowers came from a tall vase of red roses on Lord Bob's desk. The desk was big enough to make the vase look like a tiny skiff floating on a lake of cherry-wood.

The Great Man and I were sitting in red padded leather chairs studded with brass tacks. On the dark paneled walls hung framed etchings of elegant hunting dogs. Beyond the casement window hung a postcard view of green grass and distant trees.

Lord Bob was staring at me as though I had just offered him a bite of tarantula sandwich. "You're not a personal secretary," he said.

"No," I said.

"You work for the Pinkerton Detective Agency, in America."

"Right."

He stroked his mustache. "It was a Pinkerton spy, wasn't it, broke the Molly Maguires in Pennsylvania?"

I nodded. "James McParlan."

"And it was Pinkertons got sent in to protect those blacklegs in Homestead. Big workers' strike against that Scottish swine, Carnegie."

"Right."

"Armed thugs. Capitalist mercenaries."

I nodded. "We don't do that anymore."

His furry eyebrows climbed up his forehead. "Oh? Work for the labor unions now, do you?"

"Right now I work for Harry." I shrugged. "You don't like the Pinkertons, Lord Purleigh." He didn't ask me to call him Bob.

"That's your privilege. But I'm not here to clobber steelworkers. I'm here to protect Harry."

Lord Bob scowled. He turned to the Great Man. "You've retained Beaumont here—" He looked back to me. "It *is* Beaumont? You're not traveling under some sort of . . ." He paused, searching for the word, or maybe for a nasty equivalent.

"Alias?" I said. "No."

Back to the Great Man. "You've retained Beaumont because someone is attempting to *kill* you?"

The Great Man frowned. "It was not actually an idea of my own. I believed, personally, that I could deal with the matter myself. But my dear wife, Bess, was concerned. She worries about me, you see. And after what happened in Philadelphia, she insisted I hire someone who might be able to guarantee my safety."

Lord Bob was looking puzzled. "What was it," he said, "that happened in Philadelphia?"

"I was staying in a hotel. The Ardmore. Chin Soo entered my suite in disguise, dressed as the room service waiter. He attempted to kill me. Or the person he believed to be me. In fact, he nearly killed a member of the Philadelphia Police Department. A Sergeant Monahan."

"Lanahan," I said.

Lord Bob frowned at me. So did the Great Man—he didn't like being corrected any more than he liked being interrupted. "Whoever he was," he said, "he was masquerading as me. It was a trap, you see. The police were there to apprehend and arrest Chin Soo."

"Which they failed to do," said Lord Bob.

"Yes. He escaped down a fire escape."

Lord Bob stroked his mustache. "And so you employed the Pinkertons. In the form of Beaumont."

"Yes. As I said, it was my wife's idea."

That was true. But it was obvious that Lord Bob didn't like the Pinkertons, and probably the Great Man didn't mind putting some distance between himself and me.

Still stroking his mustache, Lord Bob nodded. "This Chin Soo person. He's a disgruntled magician, you say?"

"A rival, yes."

"Takes his rivalries damn seriously, I must say."

"The man is deranged. Completely demented. He claims that I stole my coffin escape from him. This is total nonsense, of course. I was performing the coffin escape years ago, while Chin Soo was still catching bullets in second-rate vaudeville houses."

"Catching bullets?" said Lord Bob. His bushy eyebrows floated up his forehead.

The Great Man shrugged dismissively. "With his teeth."

The eyebrows dipped. "Good Lord."

The Great Man shrugged again. "It is dangerous, yes, to some extent, but it is merely a trick."

"And you honestly believe that this chap would follow you all the way from America?"

I said, "I got a wire from my agency while we were in Paris. A man who was probably Chin Soo bought a ticket on the La Paloma. It arrived in Rotterdam last Monday."

Lord Bob looked at me. "Why didn't your chaps notify the Dutch police?"

"They did. The guy never got off the boat. He disappeared."

"Disappeared?"

"No one knows what Chin Soo looks like. He wears make-up on stage. No one knows what his real name is. Chin Soo's a stage name. We're pretty sure he's not Chinese. And we know he's good at disguises. When he came for Harry at the Ardmore, he made himself up to look like an Italian."

Lord Bob frowned.

"He's smart and he's determined," I said, "and right now there's no way at all to locate him."

"How d'you expect to capture him, then?"

"That's not my job. My job is to keep Harry alive. Which is why getting him out of London, coming to Devon, seemed like a pretty good idea. There wasn't supposed to be any publicity." I glanced at the Great Man, who blinked and glanced away. "I thought it'd be safe. I was wrong. Chin Soo must've seen that article in the London *Times.*"

Lord Bob stroked his mustache again. "But you can't *know* that it was your Chin Soo who fired the shot this afternoon."

"Whoever he was, he missed Harry by about two inches. That's good enough for me."

"But you can't be certain, can you. Not absolutely."

"I'll only be certain about anything when Chin Soo's in jail. Or when Harry's dead. But in the meantime, seems to me, all your other guests are in danger."

He frowned at me again. He was doing a lot of frowning today, most of it at me. He sat back in his chair and put his elbows on its arms and he steepled his hands together beneath his chin. "And what is it you propose we do?"

"Harry and I can leave. Go back to London. That's one possibility. That way, at least your other guests aren't in danger. And that's what gets my vote."

"But Houdini's the only one this chap wants to kill. Eh?"

"If he's trying to kill Harry, he could miss him and hit someone else. He could've hit Mrs. Corneille this afternoon."

He nodded. Reluctantly. "Fair enough. But you're putting people in danger wherever you go, eh? Isn't that right?"

"Yeah. It's something I'm not too happy about. I'd like to have another twenty men working with me. But Harry wants to keep this thing simple. Only one man. Me."

Lord Bob turned to the Great Man. "And why is that?"

"The more people who become involved," he said, "the greater the likelihood that the press will learn of it. My entire career is based upon the remarkable dangers into which I place myself. If it should be thought that I was frightened by a mere individual, another magician, and an inferior magician at that—"

"Got you," said Lord Bob. "Got you. Well, look here, old man, naturally if you'd like to leave, no one at Maplewhite would hold it against you. Entirely up to you."

The Great Man bobbed his head lightly toward Lord Bob. "I am sorry, Lord Robert, but I disagree. It is up to you, entirely. But so long, of course, as you and Lady Purleigh wish my presence, I should prefer to remain."

"Goes without saying," Lord Bob said. "Welcome as long as you like." He grinned. "No jumping ship, eh? Stout fellow."

He turned back to me, without the grin. "You're welcome as well, of course. In the circumstances."

"Thank you," I said.

"So you remain here," he said to the Great Man. "That's settled. What now?"

I said, "We tell all the other guests what's going on."

Lord Bob glared at me.

I said, "They've got a right to know the score—to know what the situation is. If they want to stay, fine."

He glanced down at his desktop and thought for a moment. At last, he said, "We could tell 'em all at tea time, I suppose."

"Next," I said, "we tell the local police. Have them mount a guard on this place."

He looked across the desk at me and he snorted so hard that his mustache flapped. "Got an inflated idea, I see, of the local constabulary's resources. Their competence, too."

"Anything's better than nothing."

"Not in this case. Met the Superintendent a time or two, over in Amberly. Honniwell. A nincompoop. And Constable Dubbins, down in the village, he's a buffoon, plain and simple. Besides, even if they were geniuses, both of 'em, they haven't got enough people to watch over us here. Simple as that."

"What about the police in London?" I asked him. "Couldn't they send someone down here?"

He shook his head. "Too busy up there. *Your* sort of work—breaking strikes, bullying workers. Even if they could spare some of their thugs, they wouldn't be able to get 'em here till tomorrow, at the earliest. And all the guests are leaving tomorrow, eh? Not much point in that, is there."

He paused. "Tell you what. I'll have MacGregor get some of the tenants together. The local farmers. Have them search the grounds. They're good lads, all of 'em. Know the country like the back of their hands. If Chin Soo's anywhere about, they'll flush him out."

I said, "They're not cops, Lord Purleigh."

"My point exactly."

Someone knocked at the door.

"Yes?" Lord Bob called out.

The door opened and the butler stood there, looking as magnificent and as blank and expressionless as he had looked last night. "Forgive me for disturbing you, milord."

"Yes, Higgens?"

"Sir Arthur Conan Doyle has arrived. With Madame Sosostris and her husband."

"Ah," said Lord Bob. "And what have you done with them?"

"The lady and her husband are being shown to their room. Sir Arthur is waiting in the library."

Lord Bob nodded. "Very good, Higgens. Please tell Sir Arthur that we'll be joining him shortly."

Higgens inclined his head. "Very good, milord." He pulled the door shut.

Lord Bob turned back to the Great Man. "Doyle's something of an expert on all this, eh? Guns, disguises, mystification. Let's put this before him, shall we, and see what *he* has to say?"

SIR ARTHUR CONAN DOYLE stood tall and massive at the library window, blocking the light like the trunk of an oak tree. As we entered the room, he was gazing out at the grounds with his lips thoughtfully pursed and his hands thoughtfully clasped behind his back. He turned toward us and raised his eyebrows and opened wide his brown eyes and he smiled at us from beneath a plump prosperous white mustache. The smile was more boyish and open than you would expect to see on the face of someone so famous, or someone so large.

"Houdini!" he called out in a rumbling bass voice. "And Lord Purleigh!" He strode briskly across the room and held out a ruddy hand that looked as big as a flounder.

In his sixties, he was at least six feet four inches tall. His shoulders seemed almost as wide. He must have weighed two hundred and fifty pounds but he carried it with a relentless vigor, like a retired athlete who still took his strength for granted, or still wanted to. He was so charged with physical energy that he appeared even larger and more imposing than he was. He made the Maplewhite library feel frail and flimsy and cramped.

The Great Man smiled his own charming smile but he remembered his manners long enough to let his host take Doyle's hand first.

"Looking splendid, Doyle," said Lord Bob. Doyle pumped at his arm as though he were trying to raise water from thirty feet below ground.

"Feeling splendid, Lord Purleigh!" said Doyle. His large white irregular teeth were sparkling. His thinning hair was ginger and gray where it ran back along his wide pink crown, but at his temples it was white as his mustache. He was wearing a double-breasted suit of dark gray wool, a white shirt, a blue and red silk tie, and a pair of the biggest brogues I'd ever seen, black and bulbous and shiny. You could have carried mail in those shoes. Across the Mississippi River. "Absolutely tiptop!" he said to Lord Bob. "How goes it with you? And Lady Purleigh?"

"Fine, thank you, fine, both of us. But it's 'Bob,' old man. Told you a hundred times. You know Houdini, of course."

"My *good* friend," said Doyle. He grabbed the Great Man's hand and buried it within the lumpy mass of his own and he pumped the Great Man's arm. He reached out and his left hand slammed down, affectionately, onto the Great Man's shoulder. "Grand to see you again," said Doyle. "How *are* you?"

"Excellent, Sir Arthur," said the Great Man, nodding and grinning up at him. The top of his head was below the level of Doyle's square red jaw. "Please let me introduce my . . . ah . . . friend, Mr. Phil Beaumont."

"Delighted!" said Doyle, and he smiled down at me, crinkling up the corners of his eyes. He captured my hand and he imprinted some creases in my palm that felt like they would be there until the day I died. "American, are you?" he asked as he pumped at my arm.

"Yes," I said.

"Topping! Welcome to England!" He released my hand.

My fingers were still attached to my body but it was a good

thing that nobody would be asking me to play the piano any time soon.

Lord Bob was glowering at me as if I had slithered out of a hole in the wainscoting. He turned away. "Listen, Doyle," he said. "Something's come up, I'm afraid."

Chapter Twelve

WHAT AN EXTRAORDINARY tale!" said Doyle. He sat on one of the padded leather library chairs, his great red head thrust forward, his heavy forearms planted on knees the size of pineapples. He shook the head a few times in amazement and then turned it toward the Great Man. "And you're quite all right, are you?"

"Oh yes," said the Great Man, tapping his palm lightly against his thigh. He sat opposite Doyle in another leather chair, beside my own. "I am in perfect health, as always."

Seated, Doyle was more subdued. It was as though his age somehow caught up with him when he stopped moving, and then settled over his heavy shoulders like a shawl. "And the young woman? Miss Turner?"

"She's fine, considering," said Lord Bob, who sat to my right. "Resting in her room. Poor girl's had rather a thin time of it. Disturbances last night, and then her horse ran away with her. And now this. Some filthy sod firing a bloody rifle. Can't blame her for feeling a bit under the weather, eh?"

Beneath his white mustache, Doyle's lips tightened. "Disturbances, you say? Last night? What sort of disturbances?"

Lord Bob waved his hand lightly. "A nightmare."

"She believed," said the Great Man, "that she had seen the ghost of Lord Purleigh's ancestor."

Doyle nodded his big head at the Great Man and said to Lord Bob, "That would be Lord Reginald?"

"Yes. My fault, I expect. Shouldn't have told her the story. Cousin of my wife's pried it out of me. Persistent woman."

"But perhaps Miss Turner *did* see Lord Reginald."

Lord Bob frowned, as though he didn't want to discuss this possibility. "Irrelevant, isn't it?" He held up a placating hand. "Sorry, Doyle, know you're fond of all that—ghosts, spirits, et cetera. Fair enough. One man's meat, eh? Agree to disagree, eh? But just now, seems to me, we've got to deal with this Chin Soo fellow."

"I concur," said Doyle. He sat back in his chair and I noticed a small brief wince of annoyance flicker across his mouth. Rheumatism, or arthritis, or maybe just ligament and bone that had grown wary of sudden movements. Whatever it was, he wasn't as limber as he would've liked to be. Probably no one was, except the Great Man.

Doyle reached into the right-hand pocket of his coat, looked over at Lord Bob. "May I smoke?"

Lord Bob waved his hand. "Course you may." He smiled. "A two-pipe problem, eh?"

Doyle smiled back, but wanly, as though he had heard this before, often. He pulled from the pocket a meerschaum pipe and a leather tobacco pouch. He opened the pouch and dipped the pipe into it and he glanced over at the Great Man. "When did all this begin?"

The Great Man put his arms on the arms of the chair. "One month ago," he said. "In the city of Buffalo, in New York State. Both Chin Soo and I were performing there. I was at the Orpheum, he was at the Palace. You know, perhaps, that the vaudeville houses in America are extremely competitive these days, due to the increasing popularity of the cinemas."

Doyle had pulled out a small box of Swan Vespa matches. He struck one alight. Nodding at the Great Man, he held the flame to the bowl of his pipe.

"Naturally," said the Great Man, "I myself have no trouble filling a house, even in these difficult days. But for a performer of lesser magnitude, such as Chin Soo, the situation can be truly formidable. And when Houdini is playing the same town, at the same time, well, of course, the situation becomes in fact hopeless."

With a lot of puffing at the stem of his pipe, Doyle had finally gotten the thing lit. He slipped the matches back into his coat pocket and blew out a streamer of smoke. The smoke drifted across the room, smelling like smoldering burlap.

"Not surprisingly," said the Great Man, "Chin Soo's ticket sales were very poor. He grew desperate. He ordered his minions, common hoodlums of the street, to begin pasting his boards—his advertising posters—over my own. Naturally, to protect myself, I retaliated by having my assistants do the same to his. But interfering with my advertisements was not enough for the man. He began denouncing me on stage, before his performance, calling me a fraud, a charlatan. He went so far as to claim, in a press interview, that I had stolen my legendary coffin escape from him. *Him,* a mediocre trickster who had never in his life given a coffin a second thought."

"Only fair to point out, though," said Lord Bob to Doyle, "that the chap *does* catch bullets in his teeth."

"A trick, merely," said the Great Man. "But no matter. What then happened, I called a press conference and I revealed the truth to the assembled reporters. That it was Chin Soo who was the fraud. That the man was a liar and an incompetent. I challenged him to appear on stage with me, bringing any restraint of his own choosing—chains, handcuffs, shackles, whatever he liked—and attempt to render me captive. I would, in turn, provide a restraint of my *own* choosing, for him. Whoever succeeded in escaping in the least amount of time would be considered the winner. This seemed to me utterly fair-minded."

Doyle nodded, puffing at his pipe.

The Great Man shrugged. "But naturally, Chin Soo declined the challenge. And, naturally, as a result, he was ridiculed in the newspapers. His last performance played to an empty house. Or it nearly played, I should say. When he discovered that most of the seats were unoccupied, he stormed from the stage. Typical behavior, from such an egomaniac. He left the theater and removed all his things from his rooming house. He simply disappeared."

The Great Man paused for a moment, letting that sink in. Then he said, "That night, as I left the Orpheum by the stage door, someone attempted to shoot me."

"Good heavens," said Doyle, and raised his eyebrows.

"He missed me, but by a matter of inches only. My quick reflexes enabled me to dash back to the safety of the theater. The police were notified, and when they arrived I explained the situation. They immediately suspected Chin Soo, of course. But when they attempted to locate him, they learned he had gone."

"One moment," said Doyle, taking his pipe from his mouth. "You said earlier that no one knew what Chin Soo actually looked like, without his stage make-up. And yet he had taken lodgings. Wouldn't the people there—the landlord, for example—wouldn't someone have seen him as he truly appeared?"

"No," announced the Great Man. "Before Chin Soo arrived in a city, he retained someone to engage a room for him, and pay for it in advance. Chin Soo would arrive on the date specified, but he would be wearing his make-up. No one would ever see him without it, at least wittingly." He sniffed dismissively. "It was something he did to make himself appear fascinating. Part of his so-called mystique."

"And you're quite sure," said Doyle, "that it *was* make-up?"

"Oh yes. No one has ever seen Chin Soo arrive in any city in which he was performing. Not by automobile, by train, or by boat. He travels undisguised. Or perhaps disguised as someone else."

"But how—and just when, exactly—does he transform himself into his Chin Soo identity?"

The Great Man shrugged. "If he travels by means of an automobile, perhaps he changes inside it. Perhaps he uses public lavatories. Perhaps he engages some other lodgings, from which he can come and go unseen."

"Extraordinary," said Doyle, and shook his head. "And you're certain that it was Chin Soo who attempted to shoot you?"

"He himself admitted as much to me. On the day after the incident, I returned to my home in New York City, and that evening he telephoned me—on my *private* number—and spoke with me. He used his stage voice, and he asked me whether I would like him to give me lessons in catching bullets. I told him, of course, that I needed no lessons of any kind from *him*. And I suggested to him that perhaps he required some lessons himself, in marksmanship."

Doyle smiled around the pipe stem. "Good man. Giving him his own back." He frowned slightly. "But you say he used his stage voice?"

"On stage he speaks in a singsong Oriental manner. It was in such a voice that he spoke with me."

"And this Oriental voice is assumed, I take it?"

"Yes. He possesses, I admit, some accomplishments as a mimic. He has telephoned me several times since then, and each time he used a different voice, a different accent. A feeble attempt at wit, I suppose. But always he has made his identity clear."

"How did he obtain your private telephone number?"

"From someone in the telephone company, no doubt. No doubt he paid bribes. I have had the number altered several times, and each time he has somehow acquired the new one."

"And he threatened you, you say, before you went to Philadelphia?"

"Yes. That was my first appearance after the engagement in Buffalo, and it was to be my last in the United States, before I sailed for Europe. He telephoned me two days before I left, and said that he was looking forward to seeing me in Philadelphia. At my wife's suggestion, I discussed the matter with the Philadelphia Police Department. As I told you, they attempted to capture him, and they failed."

Doyle nodded. "And between the time you appeared in Buffalo and the time you appeared in Philadelphia, no one has seen Chin Soo?"

"No one. He had several bookings, small theaters in insignificant cities, but he canceled them all."

"And he made no attempt to harm you while you were in New York City?"

"No. Perhaps he is aware of the esteem in which I am held there. Or perhaps he wishes to harm me only while I am on tour. Perhaps he feels that this would be more dramatic."

"And it was at the start of the tour that you retained Mr. Beaumont's services?"

"Correct, yes."

Doyle turned to me and took the pipe from his mouth. "Do you have anything to add, Mr. Beaumont?"

Across the carpet, Lord Bob scowled.

"A couple of things," I said. "First off, although Harry doesn't agree with me, I think that maybe Chin Soo isn't really trying to kill him."

"We have discussed that, Phil," said the Great Man. Suggesting that there was no point discussing it again.

"What do you mean?" Doyle asked me.

"Maybe Chin Soo is just trying to rattle Harry. Shake him up. Make him nervous, so he'll lose his concentration on stage, botch up the performance. Bungle it."

"Phil," said the Great Man, *"nothing* could make me lose my concentration. I have never bungled anything in my life."

I smiled. "Like I told you, Harry, maybe Chin Soo figures there's a first time for everything."

Doyle said to me, "You're basing this notion upon what? Your understanding of Chin Soo's character?"

"Partly," I said. "I think Chin Soo would love the idea of Harry screwing up—making a mistake. But also, Harry's told me about this bullet-catching trick. In order to pull it off, you've got to know a fair amount about guns and bullets. You've got to be a pretty good shot yourself."

"Just how *is* the trick performed?" Doyle asked me.

"Sorry," I said. "It's Harry's cat." I turned to the Great Man. "He'll have to let it out of the bag himself."

The Great Man smiled sadly. "I regret to say, Sir Arthur, that—"

Doyle held up the palm of his hand. "I understand completely. I should never have asked." He turned back to me, took hold of the bowl of his pipe, puffed. "You were making a point about Chin Soo's marksmanship."

"Yeah. He's a good shot. But one of our ops—operatives, agents—examined that alley in Buffalo. The one where the shooting took place. Harry was standing only about fifteen feet from the spot where the gun was fired."

Doyle nodded. "And yet Chin Soo's bullet missed him."

The Great Man shifted in his seat. "The alley was dark, Phil."

"The gas lamps were lit," I said. "Harry, you were a sitting duck, and he missed you."

Doyle said to me, "But I understood that he did shoot a police officer in Philadelphia."

"When the guy was trying to nab him."

The Great Man said, "But you have no way of proving that Chin Soo wouldn't have shot *me,* if I had been in the room." He was dead set on getting shot at.

Doyle said to him, "The shot that was fired today." He puffed at the pipe. "That missed you, as well."

"Yes," he said, "but it was fired from—what was it, Phil?—something like two hundred yards."

"A hundred and fifty."

"Still, his missing me is entirely understandable."

"Why didn't he fire again?" I asked him. "You were standing there and he just walked away."

"A single-fire rifle, perhaps?" suggested Doyle.

Lord Bob said, "Filthy sod spotted me chasing after him."

"A single-shot rifle, maybe," I said to Doyle, and I turned to Lord Bob. "But if it wasn't, he had plenty of time to let off another shot before you got to him. And plenty of time to shoot you, if he wanted to." I looked at the Great Man. "And, Harry, it was a handgun he used in Buffalo. A Colt forty-five, a semi-automatic. Cops found the slug and the spent cartridge. Why didn't he empty the whole clip into your back?"

"Phil," he said, "as I have explained to you countless times, I moved too quickly for him to attempt a second shot."

"Seems to me," I said, "if he was serious, he would've given it another try."

Doyle took his pipe from his mouth and narrowed his eyes and he said, "You do realize, Mr. Beaumont, that even if these speculations of yours are correct, your own position remains essentially the same."

"Sure," I said. "Even if he's just trying to spook Harry, I've still got to stop him. He could make a slip, and kill him by mistake. But the idea that he's trying to shake him up, not kill him, that's the only thing that gives me a sliver of hope. Because if I buy the idea that he really wants to kill Harry, I might as well pack up and go home. There's no way that one man can stop him."

"And," Doyle said, "despite your doubts, you must proceed *as though* the man were in fact determined to effect Houdini's death."

"Yeah," I said. "That's why I want to bring in the cops. Lord Purleigh and Harry disagree with me."

Lord Bob leaned forward in his chair. "What do *you* think, Doyle?"

The Evening Post
(continued)

Again, as I had before, I simply stood there. Sir David held the crop; I held still; so did Time.

Evy, I wish I could tell you that I drew upon some secret reservoir of courage; but in fact I was still functioning on another plane, in a dimension slightly out of step with this one, slightly behind it. I had not yet reached even the stage of disbelief. If he *had* hit me, I think that I should not have realized it until sometime the next day.

He didn't hit me. He lowered the crop and grasped its ends in his hands. Slowly, the wickedness and the fury left his face. He drove them away, Evy, by an effort of will, an effort I could sense and could, from within my curious remoteness, very nearly admire. When he spoke, his voice was completely under control and laced with that familiar mocking irony. 'A saint,' he said lightly, 'would turn the other cheek.'

I said, 'A saint would have no need to.'

He reached up and touched the cheek. The marks of my fingers were stencilled bright red against the pale skin. 'You are,' he said, 'a plucky young woman, Jane.'

'And you, Sir David, are a boor.' I said it without thinking; had I stopped to consider, had I remembered the wickedness I'd glimpsed, I should have said nothing, perhaps.

But he merely smiled again, then faintly shrugged. 'We've done the introductions and exchanged the mutual appraisals. What do you say to our getting to know each other better?'

'The others are waiting for you. May I have my crop?'

With a small bow, he presented it. He smiled. 'We're not finished, Jane. You know that, don't you?'

'They'll be wondering why you're late, Sir David.'

He smiled once more, looked deep into my eyes, or, rather, pretended to, and then, with another bow, turned and walked away.

And that, Evy, is the story of the fondling and the proposition.

But I do think I did that rather well, don't you? 'A saint would have no need to.' Mrs Applewhite would have been proud of me, don't you feel?

He alarmed me, though, I admit it. I saw, for a moment, the cruelty and the evil that lie beneath his surface. There is a great deal more of it, I think, than there is of surface. I wonder how many others have seen it.

But we move now from the swine to the horse. And the ghosts.

Cecily had given me directions to the stable, where a young groom saddled my mount, a gorgeous black gelding named Storm, and equipped me with a handful of sugar lumps to offer as bribes. The horse was lovely. Despite his name, and his size—above fifteen hands—he was a lamb, gentle and responsive; I scarcely used, scarcely needed, the reins. Initially, at any rate.

He and I sauntered out onto the grounds. For a while we drifted lazily along, following the footpath that ambles around the edge of the vast park of Maplewhite. Evy, how I wish I could convey to you the beauty of it all. No; not convey it; somehow *present* it, actually hand it over to you, physically, so that you might share it with me.

The sun was shining, gloriously. I sometimes believe that we poor English are allowed only a specific (and very small) number of bright, madly beautiful sunny days; and often it seems to me that I spent my entire allowance in childhood. Sunlight sweeps through all my early memories: streams through the lace curtains in the family parlour, dapples the rosebushes in Mrs Applewhite's garden, rolls in from the flat blue sea at Sidmouth to wheel down that broad green ribbon of meadow along the cliff tops. But since the War, since my parents died, the days seem to have clouded over. The world has gone grey.

I speak here of meteorology, not sentiment. The weather *was* better then.

Today, however, was spectacular. The sky was a dome of blue, with only a few fluffy white clouds slowly sailing beneath it. Larks trilled. Thrushes and blackbirds flitted between the elms and the maples and the oaks. Squirrels scampered along the tree trunks and played hide and seek with me as I passed. To my left,

Maplewhite rose grey and stately from the lake of emerald grass, like a castle in a dream.

But dreams, in the end, must surrender to reality, and mine finally buckled under to the prickle and itch of the riding habit. Perfectly appropriate to any other day of the year, the black woollen habit hung on me this afternoon like a penitential suit of sacking. I began, as Mrs Applewhite would have put it, to glow. I began, in fact, to melt.

At the very moment that I was thanking Fortune for not flinging witnesses helter-skelter about the landscape, I saw, at some distance, two people strolling toward me on the path. I had put my spectacles in my pocket, for fear of losing them, and I couldn't identify the two until I was nearly on top of them. They were Mr Houdini and Mr Beaumont.

In the larger scheme of things, I suppose it hardly matters that Mr Houdini and Mr Beaumont should observe my disarray. But, Evy, you know that I tend to live within the (much) smaller scheme of things; and of course it did matter. I resolved to confront the catastrophe with typical British fortitude: by denying it. *This is not perspiration; this is dew.*

We chatted a while, inconsequentially. Anxious to be away, I was somewhat abrupt, I suspect; but I doubt that Americans would notice this.

As soon as I was free, I made a run for the shade of the forest. Some twenty or thirty yards ahead, a small trail led off from the main path, into the trees, and I urged Storm onto it.

The smaller path hadn't been used in some time. Our progress was slow and unpleasant. Brambles crowded in on us from either side. Spider webs as thick as shrouds stretched like great bats across the track. Gnarled muscular roots with flaking bark twisted from the earth and snaked along it.

At last we came to another, broader path in the looming forest; an ancient road, it seemed, roughly perpendicular to the track. I gave Storm—my brave unflinching mount—some sugar and then urged him to the left.

The forest was dark and silent. In light of what happened, you will claim that, now, retrospectively, I invent the silence. Forests, you will claim, are never silent, no matter what the poets say. Always, birds whistle and chirp, insects buzz and whine and whiz annoyingly about. But, truly, all I could hear was the dry whisper of Storm's hooves as they moved through brown decaying leaves, and an occasional sharp crackle as they snapped a dead twig. Beside the path ran a narrow brook, its water clear but tinted the colour of rust, as though some large creature had bled away its life upstream; and even the brook was soundless.

I've whimpered often enough about the noise and bustle of London, but I found this stillness unsettling. The trees, with their black, deformed trunks, seemed to grow taller, wider, blacker and more deformed, and to edge more closely together, and closer to the path. Overhead, the dense netting of limb and leaf seemed to grow denser. My brave unflinching mount, perhaps sensing its rider's unease, twitched his ears and flicked his head from side to side. He whickered—nervously, I judged. I was about to turn him back, return to the comfort and safety of the manor, when I saw that, up ahead, the path opened onto a sunlit clearing. I kicked Storm lightly, and he trotted reluctantly forward.

We stopped when we reached the light. In the clearing was a pond, perhaps fifty feet across, smooth and glossy in the sunshine, but as black as a pool of tar. Grey rushes sagged along its banks. To the right, some twenty feet away, crouched an old mill house. It was a ruin: the grey thatched roof was torn and tufted, the grey stone walls were crumbling, the big grey wooden wheel, collapsed from its shaft, lay atilt in the murky stream, buckled and smashed.

Beneath that gaudy sun, under that taut blue canopy of sky, the ruin should have seemed quaint, rustic, picturesque. It did not. It seemed to me (and again you will claim that I invent) ominous, even sinister. The exposed ribs of the roofing, gaunt and rotting, seemed somehow grotesque. The grey stones of the disintegrating walls seemed to radiate a kind of bitter, empty cold. One got the feeling, *I* got the feeling, that the mill had been abandoned because of some long-ago, horrific death which took place here: some slaughter or pestilence.

I suddenly realized that this was the old mill Cecily had mentioned at dinner. The old mill where came, so she said, the two mysterious ghosts, the mother and the small boy.

I glanced to my left, and there, across the pond, was the willow tree, its pale branches draped over the black water like a woman's hair over a basin. And there, in the shade beneath it, as real and as substantial as everything else, as real as anything I have ever seen, the two of them stood. A tall slender woman and a slender young boy.

Do you know the opening to Bach's Toccata and Fugue in D minor? Those three abrupt notes from the organ, so swift and harsh and chill? When I saw the two figures silently standing there, exactly where they ought to be, but could *not* be, I felt those notes hammer through me, blood and bone, as if my spine were an organ, and some demented organist were flailing at it.

They were there, Evy. I saw them. They were there, under the willow tree, the woman and the young boy.

At first they were gazing at each other, the woman's hand along the boy's cheek. She was wearing white, he was wearing black. Then, as I watched, she dropped her arm and the two of them turned toward me. They gazed at me from across the glistening, pitch-black pond.

I feel that, whatever my faults, I am a woman of basically sound mind. Or so I once felt, before I arrived at Maplewhite. At any rate, my reaction, when they turned to me, was less stalwart than I should have hoped. And certainly less so than Mrs Applewhite would have demanded of me.

I panicked completely. I tugged at the reins, snapping poor Storm's head around. As he spun about, lunging back down the path, I raked his flanks with my spurs. I whacked at him with the crop, again and again, like a maniac.

But how we raced! Storm was a marvel, swift and strong and powerful, and we thundered over the earth like some mythological beast. Trees whisked by us, the path spun away beneath. It's been years since I've had a horse under me: if I hadn't already been reeling with fear, I should have been reeling with excitement. I think that perhaps I was, even so.

I rose higher in the stirrups and turned around, to look back. This was an error. A low-hanging branch smashed into my shoulder and I toppled, buttock over bonnet, from the saddle.

I cannot remember alighting. I was unconscious for a time—I couldn't say for how long—and then I was lying on my back and something was thumping me in the side.

Storm.

I attributed his concern, at first, to a laudable equine loyalty; but realized, when his nose nudged at me again, that he was after his sugar. I clambered to my feet and determined that I was more or less intact. No bones appeared to be broken.

The horse, big boorish brute, was still prodding me. I gave him a few lumps of his damnable sugar and then climbed stiffly back into the saddle.

Speed seemed less crucial now. No ghosts pursued me. My body throbbed all over. I let Storm walk at his own pace for a bit, and then, when we came to a path that looked as though it led back toward the manor, I eased him onto it. I didn't see the snake until Storm reared up and nearly tossed me from the saddle again.

I haven't the faintest idea what sort of snake it was. It was no adder, I believe, and it was perfectly harmless, and far more terrified than I.

But not more terrified than Storm. His forelegs came pounding down and he thrust his head forward and bolted up the path, muscles pumping, hooves thudding. The reins slipped from my grasp. I was only barely holding on, one arm around his wide slick neck, the other groping frantically for the reins, when we burst from dimness into sunshine and green. I realized that we were on the pathway that circled Maplewhite; and, just then, finally, I managed to snag the reins.

When I had the horse under control again, I discovered that my return to civilization had not been effected in altogether the privacy I should have preferred. Ahead of me, in an excited group by the side of the pathway, beneath a big copper beech, were Lord Purleigh, Mrs Corneille, Mr Houdini, and Mr Beaumont. And, of course, the Allardyce.

As soon as I was near enough, they all began to hurl questions at me. I couldn't find my voice, Evy. I could only stare at them, hopelessly, and mumble.

And then, off to my left, there was a bright quick flicker of light, and a sharp explosive *crack.* I believed—in a kind of delirium, I suppose—that my two ghosts had stalked me all this way, followed me back to the manor, and that now they were *shooting* at me. And so, with the quickness of mind common to all gothic heroines, I fainted dead away.

Enough for now. My hand is cramping. I'll post this and I'll write again, later.

All my love,
Jane

Chapter Thirteen

DOYLE CROSSED HIS right leg over his left knee, and again a small wince flickered quickly across his lips. He puffed once more at his pipe and then took it from his mouth. "To begin with," he said, "I think that in these matters we should defer to Mr. Beaumont's expertise. He is, after all, the professional here. I am merely an amateur, a simple scribbler."

"Come, come," said Lord Bob, sitting back. "Don't be modest, old man. Whole country knows how you saved that Hindu fellow's life. Nuralji, Moralji, whatever." He turned to the Great Man. "Poor devil was arrested for maiming some animals. Cattle, dreadful thing, all the locals in an uproar. Shropshire, this was. Bloody police needed a scapegoat, ran this fellow in, no real evidence. Bloody court convicted him. Typical capitalist cockup. Then Doyle got onto it. Sniffing about. Just like that Sherlock Holmes chappie of his, eh? Deductions right and left. Digging up clues and whatnot. Proved the fellow innocent. Got him released, eh, Doyle?"

Doyle looked over at me and smiled sadly. "I'm afraid that Lord Purleigh overstates both my efforts and their results. By the time I took an interest in his case, George Edjali had already been pardoned and released. He was completely innocent, of that I had no doubt. But I was far from being the only one who felt so. I merely attempted to persuade our Home Office that his conviction should be quashed, and that he should be paid some compensation for having been unjustly imprisoned for three years."

He put the pipe back in his mouth. "Unfortunately," he said, puffing smoke, "I was unsuccessful."

"No surprise there," said Lord Bob. "Typical capitalist bureaucracy, eh? Protecting themselves and their lackeys. Gutless swine, the lot of 'em. Still, you're the one found the evidence. Saw the proper direction to take, eh? That's what we need here, Doyle. Bit of direction. Be grateful for it, don't mind telling you. Crazed magicians, assassins, not my thing at all."

Doyle smiled and puffed again at his pipe. "But neither, really, are they mine. As I say, this is Mr. Beaumont's parish. And I must admit, Lord Purleigh, that I believe he's entirely justified in insisting upon informing the police."

"Bob," said Lord Bob. "But look here, Doyle. Local police simply haven't enough men to do us any good. Told Beaumont the same thing. And what men they do have are dolts. Won't have those louts tramping across the lawn, tracking muck about, pestering the guests. *My* guests, Doyle. *My* responsibility. Being spied on by the police, not what they came here for, is it? Wanted a bit of company, relaxation, spot or two of fun with that medium of yours."

Doyle took the pipe from his mouth, rested his hand on his thigh. He frowned thoughtfully and he said, "Lord Purleigh, I know your feelings regarding Spiritualism. However much I may disagree with them, I do, of course, respect your right to express them. But I really must point out that Madame Sosostris is a gifted and remarkable woman, possibly the most remarkable woman I have ever met. She has come here at your invitation, and at no small sacrifice to herself. She believes, as I do, that Spiritualism—"

"Quite right, Doyle," said Lord Bob, holding up his hand again. "Rotten bad form. Put my foot in it, I admit. All apologies. But the police? Here at Maplewhite? Prowling around all weekend? You see my point, of course. Simply wouldn't do, would it?"

It seemed to me that the Great Man had been silent for a long time. Probably it seemed the same way to him, because now he leaned slightly forward and he said, "Sir Arthur, I am inclined to agree with Lord Purleigh. As I explained to him before, I know that I, personally, would prefer that the police not become involved in this. And I suspect that Lord Purleigh's other guests will feel much the same way."

"Harry," I said. Three faces turned toward me, and two of them were unhappy. "You're not thinking this out. These other people don't have any reason to avoid the cops. Once they find out about

Chin Soo, they're going to want to leave, or they're going to want protection."

I turned to Lord Bob. "And if they want it, *real* protection, are you going to tell them they can't have it? A regiment of farmers and kitchen staff doesn't really make the grade."

Lord Bob glanced at Doyle. Doyle said, "I'm afraid I must agree."

Pursing his lips, Lord Bob stared down at the pattern in the carpet.

The Great Man was staring, too, but at me. In pretty much the same way that Jesus had stared at Judas.

Doyle puffed at his pipe. "Lord Purleigh?" he said.

"Bob," he said without looking up. He took in a deep breath and he slowly sighed it out. He looked up, at Doyle. "Very well. We'll discuss it with them at tea time. Four o'clock. Suit you?"

"Entirely," said Doyle. "I do believe that this is the right decision."

"Expect we'll find out," said Lord Bob. He stood up. "Now, if you'll excuse me, I've some things to attend to."

Everyone stood. Lord Bob crossed the carpet, held out his hand to Doyle. "Good to see you again, Doyle. Glad you could come. Apologize for all this excitement, eh?"

Doyle pumped his arm. His vigor had returned and once again he seemed larger even than he was. "Not at all," he said. "It's a delight to be here, in any circumstances."

Lord Bob turned to the Great Man and smiled. "Houdini," he nodded. He turned to me and frowned. "Beaumont." He didn't nod. To the others he said, "See you at four. The drawing room." And then he left.

It was a bit abrupt, I thought. But maybe that was the way the aristocracy did things. Even when they were Bolshevists.

I was about to sit down again when the Great Man aimed his charming smile in my direction. Either he had recovered from his betrayal or he had decided he wanted something. "Phil. Would you excuse us, please? I should like to speak with Sir Arthur for a short while."

Fair enough. The two of them were old friends, they had lives and wives to catch up on. "Sure, Harry," I said. "Just do me a favor and don't go wandering around outside."

He nodded impatiently. "Yes, yes. I understand. But please, Phil, do not mention any of this to anyone until tea time."

"Okay, Harry. Tea time. Nice to meet you, Sir Arthur."

I held out my hand to Doyle, so he could pump my arm some more. He did.

"I very much look forward," he said, "to talking with you at length."

I AMBLED THROUGH the big house and out of it. The place seemed empty, no other guests around, no servants. I followed a flagstone path that stopped at the gravel walkway and started again on the other side of it. It meandered toward the formal garden, and so did I. In the garden a few wrought-iron benches were scattered among the neat rows of flowers, benches painted with white enamel like the two under the bronze-red tree. I sat down on one.

The air was still warm, the sun was still shining, the sky was still blue.

The Great Man was still alive, and so were all the other guests. Fairly soon, the other guests would find out what the situation was and they would all have a chance to decide whether they wanted the police here. I was getting my own way, which didn't happen very often around the Great Man. Except to him.

I should have been happy.

But I was bothered.

It was too big a job for one man. If the cops didn't show up soon, somehow I had to convince the Great Man to bring in some more people.

I looked off at the forest, dark green and dense and draped with shadow. Chin Soo could have been anywhere in there. Maybe he was watching me right now.

I heard the crunch of gravel to my right and I wheeled around on the bench.

"I'm sorry," said Mrs. Corneille. "I didn't mean to startle you." She held out her slender hand and she gently waved me down.

"No, no, please don't get up. Do you mind if I join you?"

"No," I said, "of course not." It was the truth. She was as much of a distraction as she had been before, but I was in the mood for a distraction now.

Hanging from her trim shoulder was a white leather purse. Beneath her white straw hat, the wings of thick black hair were sleek and glossy. Her white linen dress was as bright as a spill of snow. She sat down and crossed her long legs and the sunlight shimmered on her pale silk stockings. From the purse on her lap she removed a silver cigarette case and a silver lighter. She opened the case and held it out to me. I could smell her perfume again, and again it put me in mind of Gardens and temptations.

"No thanks," I said. "I don't smoke."

She lightly arched one eyebrow and it disappeared behind her shiny black bangs. "You have no bad habits, Mr. Beaumont?" she asked me.

"Not that one," I said, and reached for the lighter. She handed it to me and I clicked it alight and held it out. She leaned forward and touched the tip of the brown cigarette to the flame. Below the broad brim of the hat, below the sleek bangs, her large eyes gazed calmly into mine. The eyes were so dark that the pupils melted into the irises. She took a deep drag and plucked away the cigarette and sat back to exhale a slow billow of blue smoke. I handed over the lighter and she put it into the purse, along with the cigarette case.

"Thank you," she said.

I asked her, "How is Miss Turner?"

"Much better."

"What happened?" I asked. "How did she lose control of the horse?"

"The horse saw a snake," she said, exhaling smoke, "and it bolted."

"But why did she faint?"

"I'm not sure. She *has* had a rather trying time of it lately. But it's fortunate for her that you were there. When she fell." Even in the glare of sun, there were very few lines in the pale soft skin beneath those almond-shaped eyes. Thirty-six years old? Thirty-four? "If you hadn't managed to catch her, she might have been seriously injured." She inhaled on the cigarette. "You're extremely resourceful, for a personal secretary."

I was a personal secretary until tea time. "You should see my shorthand," I said.

She smiled, but her eyes narrowed a bit. "What were you reaching for?"

"Reaching for? When?"

"When the man, the poacher, whoever he was, when he fired that rifle. We all turned toward the shot, and when I turned back and looked at you, you were reaching into your pocket."

"Yeah?" The little Colt automatic was still there. I shrugged. "I don't remember. Looking for some chewing gum, maybe."

She smiled again, but briefly this time, and patiently. In a polite way, she was letting me know that she didn't believe me. "You let it go, whatever it was, when you ran to help Jane."

"You can't worry about chewing gum when it's time to be resourceful."

She laughed. She took another drag from the cigarette, exhaled another streamer of smoke. "It's just that you've never really impressed me as looking very much like a personal secretary."

"No? What does a personal secretary look like?"

"Well," she said, "I confess that I've met only a few of them. But most of them were little men, rather prissy and self-important. And physically cautious, I should've thought." She smiled. "I can't imagine any of them running off into the forest after someone, as you did. Particularly someone in possession of a rifle."

"No big deal. Just trying to help out. Would you mind if I asked *you* a question?"

"Are you any better at asking them than you are at answering them?"

"Maybe we'll find out."

She nodded. "Go ahead, then."

"Is this something you usually do? Attend séances?"

"Heavens, no." She inhaled some smoke, exhaled. "It's my first time, and probably my last. Sitting around a table in the dark, holding the damp hand of some stranger, isn't exactly my idea of fun."

"But not all these people are strangers. Sir David, for example. I got the feeling you knew him pretty well."

"David? For ages. He was a friend of my husband's." She paused. "By the way. Have you said anything to David to upset him? Or done anything?"

"Not that I know of. Why?"

"I could be wrong, of course, but he seems to be harboring some sort of resentment toward you."

"It's news to me," I told her. "You said he was a friend of your husband's. Past tense. They're not friends these days?"

"My husband died in the War."

"I'm sorry," I said. The phrase sounded thin and frail, the way it always sounds when it comes up against endings.

"There's no need to be," she said.

"No?"

She looked at me. "Were you in the War, Mr. Beaumont?"

"For a while."

She smiled briefly. "Then perhaps you know that not everyone who died in the course of it was a hero."

I nodded. I said nothing. There was a bitterness simmering beneath her words, and I was curious about it. But to learn more, I would have to open her up—and to do that, I would have to open up myself.

She took a final drag of the cigarette, long and deep. Exhaling, she said, "My husband and I separated from each other a very long time ago." She dropped the cigarette to the ground. Elegantly, she uncrossed her legs and bent forward, her hands against the bench. She watched as the sole of her white pump carefully crushed the cigarette into the grass and buried it there. She sat back, knees together, hands atop the purse on her lap, and she looked over at me. "At the time he died, we hadn't seen each other for nearly ten years."

I nodded. "Getting back to the séance. Why'd you come?"

She smiled. "You *are* rather better at asking questions."

I smiled back.

"Well," she said, "in the end it's difficult to say no to Alice. Impossible, really. She's been a friend for years, and a good one. She's quite enraptured with this woman, this Madame Sosostris, and she wanted me to meet her. And when she mentioned that Sir Arthur Conan Doyle would be coming, she knew she had me."

"When did she ask you?"

"On Tuesday. We lunched together."

"Did Lady Purleigh say anything about Houdini being here?"

"No. I didn't know about that until I arrived yesterday." She looked at me, her eyes narrowing slightly once again. "Why do you ask?"

I shrugged. "Curious."

She nodded, but I think she had scratched another mental chalk mark against my honesty. "Have you been working with Mr. Houdini for a long time?"

"Not long, no."

"He's quite a legend in his own right, isn't he?"

"Yeah. Quite."

"Ah, there you are, Mr. Beaumont!" It was Doyle, striding tall and hardy down the walkway between the flowers.

Chapter Fourteen

HE PLUCKED OFF his hat as he approached us. He was smiling that big boyish smile of his, the boxy teeth gleaming like old polished ivory beneath his bristling white mustache.

"Excuse me for interrupting," he said, bobbing his big pink head at Mrs. Corneille.

I stood up. "Mrs. Corneille, this is Sir Arthur Conan Doyle." As though she hadn't figured that out already. "Sir Arthur, Mrs. Corneille."

Still sitting, she smiled as she held out her hand. Doyle took it gently between his bulky fingers and he bobbed his head again.

"Delighted," he said.

"What a great pleasure to meet you," she said. "I've enjoyed your writings for many, many years."

Doyle beamed and released her. "Not that many, surely?" His hands clasped behind him, he hovered over her like a schoolteacher over a prize pupil. "I know that I'm been writing them for many, many years. But surely it's impossible that you've been reading them for so very long."

"You are most *gallant,"* she said, smiling up at him from the shade he cast.

"Ah, well," he said, standing upright and shaking his head sadly. "I'm afraid you may have cause to revise your kind opinion. As it happens, I've come to disconvenience you, and most ungallantly. Would you mind terribly if I absconded with Mr. Beaumont for a few moments? It's a rather pressing matter or I shouldn't think to disturb you. I promise you that I shall return him to you in perfect health."

"You disturb me not at all," she said. "Actually, I was just about to return to the house. The sunshine is wonderful, but I believe I'm beginning to burn." She stood up. "Mr. Beaumont, thank you so much for entertaining me." I couldn't tell whether she was playing around with the word *entertaining*. "Perhaps we can continue our discussion at some other time."

"I'd like that," I told her.

His face concerned, Doyle asked her, "Are you certain that I'm not intruding?"

"Entirely," she told him. "It's been lovely to meet you. I hope I'll be seeing you again."

"That you shall," said Doyle, giving her another bob of his head, "if I have anything to say about it."

With a final glance at me, she lightly turned and lightly walked away, her dress as white as a wisp of cloud against the brightly colored rows of flowers.

Gallantly, Doyle edged his big body to the side, so he couldn't watch her leave. He put on his hat and he lowered his head toward me and lowered his voice and he said, "What a handsome woman."

"And then some," I said.

"And clever into the bargain, I'll wager."

"That's not a wager I'd take."

He chuckled, and then we both glanced over at the retreating Mrs. Corneille. She was floating up the flagstone walkway now, toward the house. A gust of breeze flapped at the hem of her skirt. The broad brim of her straw hat fluttered. She inclined her head forward as she put her hand atop the hat.

"Well," said Doyle, turning to me again, eyebrows raised. "Shall we walk for a while? Need that at my age, you know. Don't get out as much as I'd like."

We walked through the garden and turned right at the gravel walkway, heading back toward the tall tree with bronze-red leaves. His long legs churning up the gravel, Doyle set a pace that would probably get us to Labrador by nightfall.

We scurried along for a while. I didn't say anything—the footrace had been his idea. At last he said, "You know, I've met William Pinkerton."

"Yes?"

"Several times. A fascinating man, I thought. And a wonderful raconteur. We traveled on the same ship once, a transatlantic crossing, and he was kind enough to provide me with some splendid material. Really gripping stuff. I used bits of it in one of my novels."

"No kidding." *The Valley of Fear*. Everyone in the Agency knew that Doyle had used the story of McParlan and the Molly Maguires in the book, and everyone knew that William A. Pinkerton had been steamed at Doyle for doing it without his permission. But the smart money was on the notion that the Old Man had really been angry because Doyle hadn't given him credit for the story.

Doyle said, "He also told me quite a lot about his agency. I was most impressed. He made the point that all of his agents—operatives, isn't that right?—that all of them were responsible, intelligent, reasonable men."

I smiled. "Harry's been talking to you," I said. "He's been trying to persuade you to persuade *me* to forget about the police."

Doyle chuckled. "His agents were insightful as well, Mr. Pinkerton told me. Is that the tree, up ahead?"

"Yes." The bronze-red tree.

"May I examine it?"

"Be my guest."

When we reached the shade of the tree, Doyle reached into his inside coat pocket, found an oblong leather case, opened it, took out a pair of spectacles. He slipped the case back into his pocket and then slipped the spectacles over his nose. I showed him where we had all been standing when the shot was fired. I showed him the hole in the tree trunk, where I'd dug out the slug.

"And the shot," he said, "was fired from where?"

I pointed down the long green rolling slope. "There. At the back of the garden. That small opening in the tree line."

"A fair distance."

"Yeah."

He frowned. "You were both on the walkway, and the walkway passes within thirty yards of that opening. Why is it, do you think, that he didn't wait until you'd approached more closely?"

"We weren't walking on it at the time. We were standing around, talking. Maybe he'd just gotten there himself, maybe he didn't know we'd be coming closer." I shrugged. "Or maybe he got tired of waiting."

Doyle nodded. With his big hand he indicated one of the white wrought-iron benches. "Shall we sit?"

We sat. Doyle exhaled deeply. Once again, now that he was sitting, some of his vitality seemed to escape with his breath. Almost wearily he reached into his coat pocket and took out the leather case. He removed his spectacles, folded them, put them in the case, slipped the case back into his pocket. He leaned forward, parked his heavy forearms on his knees, clasped his hands together. He turned to me. "Mr. Beaumont," he said. "Houdini does, of course, realize that you're in the right, so far as informing the authorities is concerned. He knows full well that so long as Chin Soo's whereabouts are unknown, the guests here are quite possibly in jeopardy. It goes without saying that he's deeply concerned about them."

Went without saying by the Great Man, anyway. At least to me.

"But he's also concerned," said Doyle, "as you know, about the effect that the arrival of the police will have on his career. And in this, I believe, he is correct. Purleigh is a small town and doubtless has its share of gossips. Houdini's career, as you know, depends almost entirely upon his reputation."

"I'm not worried about his reputation. I'm worried about his life. And the lives of all the other people here."

"Of course. And your concern does you credit." Slowly, wincing very slightly, he sat back. He crossed his arms over his chest. "But hear me out. What Houdini proposes is that we inform New Scotland Yard, in London."

I shook my head. "According to Lord Purleigh, they can't get here in time."

He smiled. "Ah, but you see they *can* send a telegram to P.C. Dubbins, and to the police station at Amberly, the nearest large town. They can insist, in the telegrams, that Dubbins and the Amberly constabulary preserve the absolute confidentiality of this matter. I know a man at the Yard, quite highly placed, who could help arrange this. I could get in touch with him by telephone, after tea, after we've discussed this with the other guests."

I thought about that for a moment. I looked at him. *"Houdini proposes,* Sir Arthur?"

He smiled. "Well . . ."

"This was your idea, wasn't it?"

"Well. Yes." His smile widened and he bobbed his head. "I confess. Forgive me for saying so, but it seemed rather a good solution to the problem."

"It is," I told him.

He grinned now, pleased. "Do you really think so?"

"It's good. Have you talked about it with Lord Purleigh?"

"Not as yet. But he's already agreed that the police are necessary. Why should he object to keeping confidentiality?"

"Okay."

"Then you're agreed?" Doyle asked me.

"Sure."

"Excellent!" he said. "Topping!" He held out his big hand and I took it. He put some more creases in my palm.

WE WALKED BACK to the house more slowly. Maybe Doyle was growing tired now. Or maybe, now that he had confronted me with his compromise, he was no longer in a hurry.

I asked him, "Have you known Harry for a long time?"

He looked up, blinking at me. "I beg your pardon? Oh. Not terribly long. We met just last year. And you, I take it, you've known him for only a month or so."

"A little over a month."

He nodded. "A truly exceptional man, don't you think?"

"One of a kind."

"Brave and gifted. I've never seen any man display such absolutely reckless daring. The man is constantly risking life and limb."

The Great Man was brave, I knew that. But I had seen him prepare for his performances and I knew that he was anything but reckless. He was risking life and limb more by staying here, out in the English countryside, than he ever risked them on stage.

"He's an extraordinary showman," said Doyle. "A marvelous performer."

"Yeah. Marvelous."

"And a medium, of course."

I looked at him. "A medium what?"

He smiled. "Come now, Mr. Beaumont. A medium. A clairvoyant. And most assuredly more. This is a man who clearly possesses stupendous powers. How else could he achieve the miracles he achieves? Oh, he denies it, I realize, for reasons of his own." The smile became indulgent and he shook his head. "Modesty, perhaps."

"Modesty," I repeated. I was still looking at Doyle. He seemed completely sincere. Just to make sure, I said it again. "Modesty?"

He nodded. "I realize, of course, that on the face of it he does sometimes seem rather taken with himself. I've heard people refer to him as conceited, and I suppose I can understand their confusion. But as I see it, his assurance is but the supreme self-confidence of a unique individual who has, through a God-given gift, overcome the boundaries of time and space."

He looked over at me, smiling. "But you know all this, of course. You know the man. You've traveled with him. No doubt you've actually seen him dematerialize."

"Dematerialize."

"I envy you, I must say. I've read through the literature, it goes without saying. Comprehensively. The accounts in the Bible. The stories of Daniel Dunglas Home. And of Mrs. Guppy—you know that she actually teleported herself from Highbury to Bloomsbury? How I should've loved to see that!" He unclasped his hands, slipped them into his pants pockets, shook his big head a few times, then looked over at me. "But to live, as you've been doing, at close quarters with such a marvel. I truly envy you, Mr. Beaumont."

He looked down, at the gravel walkway, and he sighed.

"Sir Arthur," I said.

"Hmm?"

"Harry doesn't dematerialize."

He looked over at me and he furrowed his wide brow. And then, after a moment, he smiled at me, the way a father smiles when his son tells him that the missing cookies were stolen by a band of gypsies. "Come now," he said.

"He's a magician, Sir Arthur. Those are tricks up there, on stage. Good tricks. But tricks."

For another few moments he stared at me. Then, once again, he smiled. He nodded sagely. "I understand completely. Not another word."

I didn't have any other words. Neither of us spoke any until we reached the entrance to the manor house.

"And here we are," he said. "Back again." He looked at me thoughtfully. "I do hope this Chin Soo business won't affect the séance tonight. Madame Sosostris is acutely sensitive, you know. Her abilities may be impaired by all the ill will drifting about."

He looked around him and then up at the sky, as if the ill will might have gathered into storm clouds up there.

He turned to me. "You'll find her remarkable, I'm sure. She'll be joining the rest of us for tea. Well, I believe I'll rest for a bit. Long drive from London. It's been delightful talking with you."

He held out his hand. I gave him mine and let him crush it for a while.

Chapter Fifteen

THE GREAT MAN wasn't in his room when I returned to our suite. I looked at my watch. Three-thirty, and tea was at four. I undressed and took a quick shower. I put on clean underwear and a clean shirt.

My suit had been harvesting fruits of the forest all day—twigs and leaves, a thorn or two. I brushed them off and then I climbed back into it. The .32 Colt was still in my jacket pocket and it was going to stay there until I left Maplewhite.

I left the room. I was opposite the door to the suite that held Mrs. Allardyce and Miss Turner when Cecily Fitzwilliam sailed around the corner up ahead. She was walking toward me and she was wearing some clothes this afternoon, a long-sleeved red dress. I stopped.

"Mr. Beaumont!" she smiled. "What a wonderful coincidence. I was just coming to see you." She stopped and curled up her shoulders in a soft quick shrug, then put her hands together below her stomach, left hand cupping right. "How are you?" She looked sweetly up at me as if she expected a kiss on her pert little mouth. I tried to remember the jaded young thing who had drawled at me in the drawing room last night.

"Bringing back the key to your handcuffs?" I asked her.

She frowned, puzzled. "But what . . . You *have* the key. I put it"—she glanced quickly around, lowered her voice—"I put it on your bed."

I shook my head.

She nearly stamped her foot. "But I *did,"* she said. "I found it under the bed, after you left, and I put it exactly in the center of the mattress. Where you'd be certain to find it."

"I didn't."

"But that's impossible. You *did* look?"

"I looked. How'd you manage to get back to your room without anyone seeing you?"

"The front stairs." With a nod of her head she indicated the end of the corridor, behind me. "Mr. Beaumont, I swear to you, I put the key on the bed. I'd never have left you . . ." She shrugged, smiled. "Well . . . *you* know . . . *stranded* like that."

"Okay," I said. "You put the key on the bed."

Her smile vanished, buried beneath a pout. "I *did.*"

"Okay," I said. She hadn't asked me how I'd gotten out of the cuffs. Probably she was too busy thinking about whatever it was that had brought her here.

She glanced around again, leaned slightly toward me. She fluttered her eyelashes a few more times and she smiled again. A coy smile. "You didn't tell anyone about last night, did you?" This was why she'd come—to learn if I'd been spilling any beans lately.

"I told Mr. Houdini," I said.

She leaned back and her face went suddenly stiff and red. "How *could* you?" she said.

"I needed to get the cuffs off."

Her brow puckered up, her lower lip dropped. "But I left you the *key.*" A wail was quavering just behind her voice.

"I never found it," I said. "Look. Don't worry. I told him you wanted to talk. I told him you brought the handcuffs because you thought he might want to see them."

"But you told him I was *there!*"

"He won't repeat it."

Some kind of understanding flashed across her face. "Is that why he was avoiding me? Just now? Every time I came near him, he was blinking like a madman. And then he went racing away." Her eyes opened wide in horror. "He thinks I'm a nymphomaniac!"

I smiled. "He doesn't think—"

"I'm *not* a nymphomaniac!"

At that moment, the door opened to my left. Miss Turner stood there, looking out at us with her mouth turned down in disapproval. Her hair was wrung back behind her head again and she was wearing another shapeless dress. Brown, this time.

For a second or two she stood there and those wide blue eyes silently stared. And then she flinched and her long body jerked abruptly forward, as though she had been whacked in the back. The voice of Mrs. Allardyce shrilled out—"Get along with you, Jane, don't *dawdle* so." And then both of them were out in the hallway and Mrs. Allardyce was coming around Miss Turner like a hungry crab scuttling around a pearl. She clutched her purse against her stomach as though it were a shield. A broad eager smile was pasted to her round shiny face. "Why, Cecily. How very *lovely* you look." The smile slipped only a bit when she nodded to me. "And good day to you again, Mr. Beaumont."

I nodded. Politely.

"Aren't you taking tea, dear?" Mrs. Allardyce asked Cecily, and put her hand on Cecily's forearm. Cecily seemed to shrink away, but Mrs. Allardyce didn't notice, or didn't care. She said, "I can't *tell* you how much I'm looking *forward* to meeting Sir Arthur. I *adore* his work, just *adore* it. I saw Mr. Gillette in that *wonderful* Sherlock Holmes play at the Lyceum and he was simply *brilliant!* He's so terribly *handsome,* isn't he? So terribly *distinguished."* She edged her bulk closer to Cecily. "And tell me, dear. Has Sir Arthur brought along that *medium* of his?"

"Yes," said Cecily. "Everyone is in the drawing room." Her aristocratic drawl had returned, but it lay over the strain in her voice like a first coat of paint, thin and transparent. "Mr. Beaumont asked me to show him around Maplewhite." She was too young, maybe, to know that you never volunteer a lie. Or maybe too upset to remember.

Once again, Mrs. Allardyce didn't seem to notice. "How *fortunate* for him," she said, "to have you as a guide." She patted Cecily's forearm. "Well, dear, we'll leave you to your tour. I'm sure we'll see you later. *Au revoir!* And you too, Mr. Beaumont. Come along, Jane."

"Mr. Beaumont?" Miss Turner had stepped closer to me.

I turned. Behind her, Mrs. Allardyce wobbled to a surprised halt.

Miss Turner's uncanny blue eyes looked into mine and they

were unwavering. She held herself straight, her back rigid. "I don't recall much of what happened," she said. She pressed her lips briefly together. "My fainting spell, this afternoon. But Mrs. Corneille told me that if you hadn't been so quick to help, I should have injured myself. I wanted to thank you."

"No need to," I said.

"There is," she said, "and I do. And I apologize, once again, for causing you trouble."

"No trouble. I'm glad you're all right. Mrs. Corneille said your horse saw a snake?"

"Yes. It startled him. In any event, I thank you for your efforts." She nodded once, as if pleased with herself for pulling something off, and then she nodded to Cecily. "Miss Fitzwilliam."

"Come along, dear, come along," said Mrs. Allardyce, and she swung her thick arm like a gaff into the crook of Miss Turner's elbow. She smiled again at Cecily, quickly, almost fiercely, and then she led Miss Turner off, toward the stairs.

As they disappeared around the corner, Cecily said, "What a perfectly horrid little woman."

I smiled. "Miss Turner?"

"No, silly. That awful Allardyce person. She's a cousin of my mother's. And what a positively sick-making idea *that* is." Suddenly she turned to me. "She couldn't have heard what I said, could she?"

"Mrs. Allardyce?"

"Miss Turner. What I said about . . ." She raised her eyebrows, took a deep breath, let it out in a weary sigh, *"You* know . . ."

"About being a nymphomaniac?"

"I am not—" She heard herself squeal, glanced around, leaned toward me. "I am not a nymphomaniac," she said between clenched teeth, and then she thumped me on the chest.

"I know," I said. "And no, I don't think she heard. And no, Mr. Houdini doesn't think you're a nymphomaniac either. No one thinks you're a nymphomaniac. Except maybe you."

She eyed me suspiciously. "What is *that* supposed to mean?"

"Nothing. Look, Cecily. I've got to go. Don't worry about Mr. Houdini. He won't say anything."

She canted her head thoughtfully to the side. "Do you think she's prettier than I am?"

"Mrs. Allardyce?"

She made that almost-foot-stomping motion again. "*No.* Miss Turner."

"She behaves better," I said.

She tried to thump me again and I caught her wrist and held it. "See what I mean?" I said.

Her eyes were narrowed and she was staring at my hand. "Let me *go,*" she said, her voice low and threatening. The rules of the game had been changed, and she didn't like it.

"No more hitting," I said.

She tossed her head back and she aimed her glance down along her cheekbones. "Or *what?*"

"Or we'll talk to Daddy."

"He won't believe a word you say."

"I guess we'll find out."

She glared at me for a moment, and then her shoulders slumped and she scowled. I let go of her wrist. Wincing furiously, her mouth twisted open, she rubbed at the wrist as though she had been shackled for a lifetime to an overhead beam.

"I don't know why I care what you think," she said darkly, glowering up at me. She raised her head. "I'm sure I *don't* care. After all, you're only a *servant,* really, aren't you?"

I nodded. "That's right."

"And why on earth should I care what a *servant* thinks?"

"No reason at all."

"Well, I *don't,*" she said, and she wheeled about and stalked away. She whirled around the corner and I could hear her feet go stomping down the stairs.

I waited there in the hallway for a while, to give her time to find her drawl again.

ON THE WALLS, across the faded tapestries, plump naked people were still chasing each other in a refined way through the forest. Around the room, well-dressed people were gathered in clusters once again. No one seemed bothered by the idea that a sniper had shot at someone today. But maybe they were all rising above it. The English like to do that.

"Mr. Beaumont," said Doyle, lumbering up from his seat at the coffee table to my right. "There you are. Please join us. Come and meet my friends."

The table held platters of food, porcelain cups and saucers, a porcelain teapot, a silver coffeepot, a small silver cream pitcher, a small silver sugar bowl. There were six people sitting around all that. I knew four of them—Lady Purleigh, Cecily Fitzwilliam, Mrs. Allardyce, and Miss Turner. I didn't know the woman in the wheelchair or the man sitting beside her.

"Mr. Phil Beaumont," said Doyle, and held out his hand toward the woman, "this is my very good friend, the remarkable Madame Sosostris."

Remarkable was right. The woman made Mrs. Allardyce look like a wood nymph. Probably she weighed as much as Doyle did, but she was half his height. Her body was draped in a gown of red and gold silk, like a medicine ball bundled in gift wrap. Her huge mane of white hair was swept back from her wide white forehead into a pompadour the size of an ornamental shrub. The hair fell in thick waves to her shoulders and cradled her white puffy face. Her bushy eyebrows and her long eyelashes were jet black, and so were the small sly eyes that glittered beneath them. And so was the star-shaped beauty mark on her cheek, stuck there like a fly on a rice pudding.

She nodded to me the way a queen bee would nod to a drone. "So very charming to meet you," she said. She spoke with an accent but I couldn't tell what it was.

"And this," said Doyle, "is Madame's husband, a very kind and generous man. Mr. Dempsey."

Mr. Dempsey was bony and angular and he probably weighed less, clothes and all, than one of his wife's thighs. He was in his fifties, with sunken cheeks and sunken eyes and a thin bitter mouth. He wore a loose gray suit, a white shirt, a black bow tie, and a narrow black toupee that looked liked it had been oiled and then run over with a truck.

He unfolded himself out of the chair like a carpenter's ruler and gave me a handful of knobby knuckles. "How do you do?" he said, and smiled painfully. His accent was American.

"Won't you join us?" Lady Purleigh said, looking up at me from her chair. Beside her, Cecily Fitzwilliam raised her head and elaborately looked away.

"Thanks," I said, "but I've got to talk to Mr. Houdini."

Lady Purleigh smiled pleasantly. She looked good again today, slim and elegant in a long white silk dress that made her gray blond hair seem even lighter in color. "You're entirely too conscientious, Mr. Beaumont. I admire your energy but this is the weekend, after all. I do hope you'll set aside some time to enjoy it."

I smiled back at her. "I will. Thanks." I nodded to Madame Sosostris and to Mr. Dempsey, and then to Doyle.

He nodded and lumbered back to rejoin his table. I strolled across the room to the table where the Great Man was sitting alone. He was writing something in a notebook, probably another letter to his wife.

"All by yourself, Harry?"

"I refuse to sit with that woman. You saw her hair?"

"Kind of hard to miss it."

"She could hide every manner of prop and gadget inside that monstrosity. Trumpets, bells, several *pounds* of ectoplasm." Suddenly he grinned at me. "She's a physical medium, you know. She produces apports."

"Apports?"

"Physical manifestations," he said. "From the spirit world. Although, strangely enough, upon examination they seem invariably quite mundane." He rubbed his hands together. "Ah, Phil, I do look forward to this. Her control is a Red Indian, did you know that?"

"Her control?"

"Her Spirit Guide." He grinned up at me and he rubbed his hands some more.

"Have you seen Lord Purleigh?" I asked him.

He shook his head impatiently. "Not since we spoke in the library."

"I talked to Sir Arthur about the London idea. The police. I think that'll work."

"Excuse me." A woman's voice to my left, and a light touch upon my arm. The scent of ancient flowers.

"I apologize for interrupting," said Mrs. Corneille, smiling first at me and then down at the Great Man. "I was returning to my table and I thought I might ask all of you to join us there."

The Great Man glanced toward her table, which held Sir David and Dr. Auerbach. He still ranked them as vermin, probably, because when he turned back to Mrs. Corneille his smile was small and polite. "Thank you," he said, and nodded. "Perhaps in a short while."

She looked at me. "Mr. Beaumont?"

"Sure," I said. "Thanks." I nodded goodbye to the Great Man and then I walked to the table beside Mrs. Corneille and her perfume. Dr. Auerbach shot to his feet, his tiny teeth and his pince-nez gleaming. He gave me a small crisp nod. "Mr. Beaumont. A great pleasure to see you again."

From his seat, Sir David nodded curtly and looked away.

Sir David, Lord Bob, Cecily. I was making a big impression on the uptown swells.

"Would you care for some food?" asked Mrs. Corneille as I sat down beside her. Opposite me, Dr. Auerbach neatly tugged up the knees of his trousers and he sat down and crossed his legs.

Like Doyle's table, this one was piled with food. I realized that I hadn't eaten since breakfast. "Yes," I admitted. "Thanks."

Mrs. Corneille leaned forward for the teapot. "Tea?"

"Please"

She ignored him and poured the tea. She looked over at me. "Sugar? Lemon? Milk?"

"Nothing, thanks," I told her.

She set the teacup before me. "The sandwiches are quite good," she said.

I took a plate, took a sandwich from the silver platter. Bit into it. Smoked salmon and creamed cheese. Quite good.

Sir David said to Mrs. Corneille, "Dr. Auerbach was explaining that he has a literary as well as a psychological side." He turned to Dr. Auerbach comfortably, almost proudly, like an inventor waiting for his favorite windup toy to start performing.

"Oh no," Dr. Auerbach said to Mrs. Corneille. "Literary, no. I have myself produced a very few original monographs only. Studies of some interesting cases I have encountered. But I have, as I told Sir David, translated Herr Doktor Freud's 'Wit and Its Relationship to the Unconscious.' This I did for your University of Leeds."

Smiling, Sir David idly stroked his mustache with his index finger. "Leeds, was it?"

Dr. Auerbach showed his little teeth to Mrs. Corneille. "But this was quite some work, I can tell you. Because of the nature of humor, it was necessary that I substitute English jokes of my own for Herr Doctor Freud's German jokes."

"Perhaps," said Sir David, "you would favor us with some of these?"

"Whatever is wrong with Lord Purleigh?" said Mrs. Corneille, looking off toward the entrance to the drawing room.

I turned. Lord Bob had arrived. Standing a few feet from Doyle's table, he was waving his bushy eyebrows up and down and running his hands back through his hair, his face twisted. Doyle stood frowning before him, his big fingers on Lord Bob's elbow as though supporting the man. Across the table, Lady Purleigh had risen from her seat. She looked worried.

"Excuse me," I said. Reluctantly, I set my food back on the table and I stood up.

Doyle and Lord Bob were walking now toward the Great Man's table. Both their faces were grim. I reached the table at the same time they did. The Great Man had seen them coming and he was already standing.

"Beaumont, good," said Doyle. "We can use you, I expect."

"What happened?" I asked him.

Doyle turned to Lord Bob, who scowled at me and then looked at the Great Man. "Some sort of accident," he said. "The Earl. My father. His valet heard a noise in his room. Pistol shot, he thinks—

but that's impossible. Bloody impossible. Thing is, we can't get in and the Earl won't answer. Bloody door is locked. Some problem with the key."

The Great Man raised himself to his full height. "Houdini will open it, Lord Purleigh. This I promise you."

Chapter Sixteen

IT WAS A broad massive wooden door studded with black wrought-iron nails and belted with black wrought-iron bands. The little man named Carson who was the Earl's valet showed us with trembling hands that his big metal key wouldn't fit into the keyhole. He was in his white-haired seventies and right now he didn't look as if he would make it very much further. "It won't *fit,* sir," he kept saying, stabbing the key again and again into the hole, looking back frantically at the Great Man.

"Of course not," said the Great Man. "The interior key is blocking the channel."

We stood behind them—Lord Bob, Doyle, Higgens, the butler, and me. Most of us were panting. Lord Bob was gasping, leaning forward with his hands on his knees like a marathon runner at the end of the race and the end of his tether. His face was as red and shiny as a glazed beet.

We were at the northwest corner of the manor house, on the third floor, and it had taken us a while to dash over here. Along the way, puffing, Lord Bob had explained to the Great Man and Doyle that Carson had been in the anteroom—where we stood now—when he heard the shot. He had tried to open the door, discovered he couldn't, and gone next door to his own room, to call Higgens on the emergency telephone. Higgens had found Lord Bob, Lord Bob had come up here, tried the door, and then come for the rest of us.

The anteroom was a kind of antique parlor with bare stone walls and heavy, roughly finished oak furniture scattered around, and another Oriental carpet on the floor. It was a strange room, looking like something out of the Middle Ages. But all of us were more interested in what was on the other side of the massive wooden door.

"Permit me," said the Great Man and stepped forward. Carson glanced anxiously at Lord Bob, who was upright now but still puffing. Lord Bob nodded and weakly waved his hand. Carson tottered back and wrapped his arms around himself as though he were afraid he was going to explode.

The Great Man reached into his back pocket, pulled out his wallet, opened it, slipped out a thin steel pick. He bent over, peered for an instant into the keyhole, eased the pick into the hole and gave a sudden flick of his wrist. Then, gently, once, he tapped the pick into the lock. Its length vanished in the hole and I heard a distant slapping sound that might have been a big copper key landing on a wooden floor.

"Child's play," said the Great Man. He flicked the pick again and I heard a metallic click that might have been a bolt snapping back into a lock housing. The Great Man smiled and straightened up and pushed on the door. Nothing happened.

He turned to Lord Bob and frowned. "It is barred, unfortunately." He looked around the room, searching for something. "I need—"

"Blast!" said Lord Bob. His white mustache was limp. He staggered around the Great Man and raised his fist and pounded it down on the door. The door didn't move but the Great Man stepped nimbly aside, his eyebrows raised in alarm. Lord Bob pounded at the door again. "Open up!" he roared. He sucked in a deep ragged breath. "Open up, you blithering old fool! You reprobate! You filthy, sniveling, whining, reactionary *swine!* Open the bloody *door!"*

"Calm yourself, Lord Purleigh," said Doyle. He put his big hand on Lord Bob's shoulder. "This doesn't advance us. Is there no other way in?"

Lord Bob wheeled away from the comforting hand and he shouted, "Not unless we fly in, like bloody ducks!"

The Great Man said, "Gentlemen . . ."

"The bench," I said. I pointed to a long oak bench that ran beneath the windows. It had been a section of single peeled log once, years ago, before someone sawed away one side of it and stuck eight tapering wooden legs into its curved bottom surface.

"Perfect!" said Doyle. "Lord Purleigh! Higgens! Quickly now!"

"Sir Arthur," said the Great Man, but Sir Arthur was busy.

The four of us scrambled over to the bench and each of us grabbed a leg and we lugged the thing off the floor. It didn't weigh much more than a ton. We gripped it beneath our curled right arms and swung it awkwardly up into the air. Doyle was at the front, Lord Bob and Higgens followed, I was last. I noticed that Higgens's face was as blank and expressionless as usual. Maybe this was something he did every day. Carson still hovered off to the side, hugging himself, shaking his gray head, biting his lower lip. The Great Man stood with his hands on his hips, frowning. "Phil," he said to me.

"Careful now," said Doyle, who had taken charge. "Step back a bit, would you, Houdini, there's a good chap."

The Great Man threw up his hands in frustration and then backed off to stand beside Carson.

"On the count of three, men," bellowed Doyle, like a scoutmaster. "One. Two. *Three!*"

We ran forward and the end of the bench slammed into the door with a huge booming crash. The bench jumped and shivered under my hands. The door shuddered but didn't give way.

"Once more, men!" cried Doyle. "Back!"

We took some clumsy shuffling steps backward. Doyle called out, "Ready? One. Two. *Three!*" We ran forward again and the end of the bench whammed into the door and this time metal screeched suddenly against stone and the door burst suddenly inward and slammed itself against the wall.

"Down!" said Doyle, and we lowered the bench to the floor.

Doyle was the first one into the room, then Lord Bob, then Higgens, then me. The Great Man and Carson trailed in behind us.

The smell of gunsmoke hung in the stifling, musty air. A fire was burning in the huge stone fireplace and all the windows in the room were shut. It was a big room but a simple one, like the living room—a rough oaken dresser to the right, a rough oaken wardrobe to the left, a rough oaken bookcase beside it. In the center of the room, set against the far stone wall, was a huge bed with a towering, carved oak headboard. Beside the bed, on the left, sat a wheelchair of chrome and leather, smaller and more spindly than the wheelchair used by Madame Sosostris. Lying on the bed, the covers drawn up to his chest, was a very old man. He was clean-shaven and nearly bald. His thin right arm, sleeved in white flannel, lay above the covers and it was stretched out sideways. The withered right hand hung over the floor, palm up, long yellow fingers curled toward the ceiling. Beneath the hand, on the floor, was a dark revolver.

There was a small black hole in the old man's temple.

"Dear God," said Lord Bob.

"Steady," said Doyle, and clapped him on the shoulder.

I moved toward the body. I put my fingertips against the wrist of the frail old arm. The thin translucent skin was still warm but there was no pulse beating beneath it. I looked over at Doyle, looked at Lord Bob, shook my head.

Lord Bob said, "The swine's gone and killed himself." He took a step toward the pistol and he bent to pick it up.

"Don't!" I said.

He glared up at me once, a quick annoyed glare, then picked up the weapon.

"Not a good idea," I said. "The police won't want anything moved. And now your fingerprints are on the gun."

Lord Bob was inspecting the pistol. He moved it from his right hand to his left, frowned at his right hand, idly wiped it against the breast of his suit coat. "Dust," he said vaguely.

Doyle was glancing around the floor. "Ash," he said. "From the fireplace. It's everywhere. Blew out when we forced open the door."

On this side of the bed, the ash lay everywhere, a thin gray coating atop the wooden floor. I could see the footprints we'd made. There weren't any others.

Lord Bob was still looking at the gun, and still frowning.

I said, "He didn't keep a gun in here, did he?"

Not looking up, Lord Bob shook his head.

"Lord Purleigh," I said. "Put the gun back on the floor."

Lord Bob glared at me again. He was dazed, I think, but even through the daze his indignation was automatic. "I *beg* your pardon."

"That's an American thirty-eight Smith and Wesson," I said. "Not a very common weapon over here, I'm guessing. It looks a lot like a Smith and Wesson I saw downstairs, part of that collection in the big hall."

Lord Bob looked down at the gun. "Yes." Puzzled, he looked over at the old man lying in the bed. "But why . . . how did *he* get it?"

"That's what the police will want to know. Please, Lord Purleigh. Put the gun back."

Doyle said, "Best do as he says, Lord Purleigh."

Lord Bob glanced at him. "The police," he said. "But I won't have the police . . ." His voice trailed off. He stood there staring off into the distance.

"You've no choice, I'm afraid," said Doyle. "Not in a situation like this." He put his hand on the man's shoulder again. "Please, Lord Purleigh. Replace the gun."

Lord Bob looked at me, his face empty. He bent forward and put the gun on the floor, then stood up.

Lord Bob turned to Doyle. He still seemed dazed. "And now . . . what now?"

"We touch nothing else," said Doyle. "We keep the room sealed and guarded." He turned to the valet, who stood at the foot of the bed. "Carson? It's Carson, isn't it?"

Carson looked up at him, his face pale. "Yes, sir." His voice was quavering and his eyes were blinking. He raised his head. "I'm sorry, sir," he said to Doyle. "I apologize. It's just the shock of it, sir. The Earl . . . he seemed indestructible, sir." He blinked again. He pulled himself up, looked at Lord Bob. "I'm very sorry, milord." To Doyle, he said, "Sorry, sir." He moved his shoulders in a small sad shrug, a gesture without hope. "It's the shock, I expect."

Behind the valet, the Great Man had moved to the massive wooden door, and he was bending forward to peer with what looked like professional curiosity at the wooden crossbar that had blocked our entrance to the room.

Carson's shock had jarred Lord Bob out of his. He crossed the room and came around the bed to the old valet. "Carson," he said. His voice was soft. "Are you quite all right?"

"Yes, milord." He was staring straight ahead, over the body of the dead man.

Behind them, the Great Man looked up from his examination of the wooden bar, and he examined Lord Bob and the valet.

Lord Bob gently said to Carson, "Course you are. Course you are. But still, you know, all this excitement, better to catch our breath, eh? Snatch a bit of rest while we can. You go have a lie down. I'll ask Mrs. Blandings to look in on you. And I'll be 'round myself, once we've sorted all this out."

His lips compressed, still staring ahead, Carson nodded. "Yes, milord." He blinked again, turned to Lord Bob. "Thank you, milord."

Lord Bob reached out and briefly put his fingers against the man's arm. "Good man. Good man." Carson blinked. Lord Bob turned to Doyle. "Eh, Doyle?" he said heartily. "That's for the best, don't you think?"

Doyle nodded his big head. "I agree completely, Lord Purleigh."

"Right," said Lord Bob to Carson in the same bluff tones. "Off you go, then."

"Very good, milord." His glance flickered down at the old man in the bed. He blinked and then turned and walked away. His body was still rigid, his movements stiff.

Lord Bob turned to Doyle. "You were saying, Doyle?"

"We keep the room sealed. And guarded."

"Higgens can perform guard duty," Lord Bob said. "Temporarily. We'll be needing him downstairs. Eh, Higgens? I'll send someone up to relieve you."

Higgens nodded. "Very good, milord."

Doyle said to Higgens, "No one to enter the room until the police arrive."

"Very good, sir."

"The police?" said Lord Bob.

"We *must* inform the police."

Lord Bob frowned.

"If I may use the telephone," said Doyle, "I can speak with a friend of mine at Scotland Yard. I feel certain that he'll be helpful. And discreet."

After a moment resisting the idea, Lord Bob finally surrendered. "Very well."

Doyle turned to me. "Do you have anything to add, Mr. Beaumont?"

I said, "I'd like to take a look at that gun collection."

Doyle nodded. He turned to Lord Bob. "Lord Purleigh, no doubt you wish to inform Lady Purleigh of this tragedy."

Lord Bob lowered his bushy eyebrows, as though just now remembering that Lady Purleigh existed. "Yes. Yes, of course." He shook his head slightly, looked away. "She'll take it badly. Fond of the swine." He glanced at the body on the bed. "Mustn't tell the guests, though."

"Not tell them?" said Doyle.

Lord Bob turned to him. "Put a bit of damper on the weekend, wouldn't it? They'd leave, wouldn't they?"

"No doubt they would. But in the circumstances . . ."

Lord Bob shook his head. "Won't have it. Came for a pleasant weekend, that's what they'll get. Not their fault the old swine died. Alice will agree with me. Sure of it."

"And how will you explain the presence of the police?"

"Don't see that I need to. Trot 'em in, trot 'em out. Stop 'em tracking muck about, of course. And no one the wiser, eh?"

Doyle looked doubtful, but he said, "As you wish."

I said, "You *are* going to tell them about Chin Soo."

He looked at me, blinked. Irritation flickered briefly across his face. "Yes, yes."

"Houdini?" said Doyle.

The Great Man was bent at the waist, peering at the big copper key that lay on the floor, just inside the door. He looked over at Doyle.

"Have you anything to add?"

The Great Man looked at him for a moment. He pursed his lips. Finally he said, "No. Houdini has nothing to add."

"Very well, then," said Doyle. "I propose that we all meet again in the Great Hall." He slipped a watch from his vest pocket, glanced down at it, looked up. "In, shall we say, half an hour. Is that acceptable?"

It was.

WE LEFT HIGGENS in the anteroom, guarding the door to the bedroom. The rest of us trooped downstairs. When we got there, Lord Bob and Doyle went off together. Houdini tagged along with me. Probably because I was the only person he could complain to.

"You know, of course," he said, "that I could have removed that ridiculous bar." We were pacing through the corridors, toward the Great Hall. "In an instant. Less than an instant."

"I know that, Harry."

The Great Man couldn't take yes for an answer. "There you were," he said, "all of you, running around like schoolchildren. Throwing furniture. Breaking doors. It was absurd. All I required was a simple wire clothes hanger."

I nodded.

He shook his head and sighed. "I am very surprised at Lord Purleigh, I confess. I would never have expected such behavior from an English lord."

"It was his father trapped in there."

"Yes, of course, but I could have opened the door more swiftly. And with less damage, too, of course."

"He needed to do something besides stand around and wait. You saw him, Harry. He was going nuts."

The Great Man frowned. He turned to me. "This is why you suggested using the bench?"

"Yeah."

He pursed his lips again. He nodded. "Yes," he said at last. "Yes, you did well, Phil. I was so concerned with defeating the door and aiding the unfortunate Earl that for a brief moment I forgot myself." He nodded again. "You did well, Phil."

"Thanks, Harry."

We had come to the Great Hall. Even at the entrance, fifty feet from the gun collection, I could see that the Smith & Wesson was missing.

Chapter Seventeen

"YOU FORGOT TO mention, Harry," I said, "that Sir Arthur is crazy."

The Great Man frowned. "Sir Arthur? Not at all. He has, I think, been reacting to all this with great intelligence."

The two of us were in the Great Hall, at the end of the long table, near the gun collection. We were sitting on uncomfortable wooden chairs with tall straight backs, waiting for Doyle and Lord Bob.

"I don't mean that," I told the Great Man. "I had a talk with him this afternoon. He thinks you pull off your tricks by dematerializing."

"Ah. Yes." He nodded sadly. "I have tried to persuade him otherwise, of course, but he refuses to believe me. Spiritualism has become with him an *idée fixe.* A fixed idea, that is, in French."

"Thanks."

He remembered something. "Incidentally, Phil, you must never mention fairies."

"Fairies," I said.

"Yes. You must never mention them to Sir Arthur. He believes that fairies exist, you see. He has some photographs, two young girls playing with a tribe of fairies in an English garden. They are an obvious hoax—the girls are clearly holding cardboard cutouts—but Sir Arthur believes them to be genuine. He has actually written a book about them. If you mention fairies, he will begin to explain the photographs, as he did in the library this afternoon, after you left. Much as I like and respect Sir Arthur, I have already heard as much about fairies as I care to."

I shrugged. "Like I said, Harry. He's crazy."

"Phil, he is perhaps the best-known and the most respected author in the world. He was *knighted.* By Queen *Victoria.* Aside from his credulousness in these matters, he is an extremely rational and intelligent man."

"Pretty big *aside.*"

"Phil, he lost his son in the War, and his dear mother only this past year. He *wishes* to believe, and so he believes." He shrugged his muscular shoulders. "Who knows? Perhaps if I lacked my extraordinary expertise, perhaps I too should become a credulous believer." He looked off, frowning, as he considered that.

I read his mind for him. "No," I said. "Not you, Harry. You're too sharp."

He nodded. "Yes. That is true, of course."

THE SMELL OF smoldering burlap filled the room. Sitting back in his chair, Doyle took his pipe from his mouth. "They're sending their best man," he said, talking about Scotland Yard. "Fellow named Marsh. An inspector. I've heard of him, and he's reported to be extremely good. Unconventional, so I understand, but intelligent and very thorough." He turned to Lord Bob. "And discreet."

Lord Bob snorted.

"Unfortunately," said Doyle, "he won't be arriving until sometime tomorrow morning. Meantime, they'll wire the Purleigh police. The constable from the village should be here presently."

Lord Bob scowled. "That buffoon. Dubbins."

Doyle and Lord Bob had arrived together, a few minutes ago, and now they sat opposite the Great Man and me. About ten minutes before that, a uniformed servant had ferried in a crystal decanter of brandy and four balloon glasses, along with a crystal carafe of water and four water glasses. He had poured four brandies, four glasses of water, and left.

Doyle said, "A medical examiner will be dispatched from Amberly."

"Still don't get that," said Lord Bob. "What's wrong with Christie, eh? Been the family quack for years."

"In the circumstances, Lord Purleigh, my friend at the Yard feels, and I agree with him, that an outside observer would be best."

Lord Bob scowled again.

"I also mentioned," said Doyle, "the matter of Chin Soo. I explained that it was quite unrelated to the death of the Earl, but that it was a situation which required immediate attention. An additional force of police will be sent here, these to come from Amberly as well."

"More of them," grunted Lord Bob. He shook his head. "Peering and prodding. Tracking muck about the house."

"How is Lady Purleigh?" the Great Man asked.

Lord Bob sat back, raised his bushy eyebrows, sighed heavily. "Bearing up. She's a wonder, Alice. Always has been. But she's upset, of course. As I say, she was fond of the old swine." He took a sip from his brandy glass.

I asked him, "Have you told the guests about Chin Soo?"

He looked at me. "Said I would, didn't I?"

"Lord Purleigh," said Doyle, holding his pipe tilted at an angle beside his wide red face. "May I make a suggestion?"

"Certainly," he said, sitting back. "You've earned the right, Doyle. Appreciate the way you've handled things. The gun. Guarding the room. Never would've thought of it myself."

He turned back to me, frowned. "You, too, Beaumont. Owe you an apology. Got a bit shirty upstairs."

"No need to apologize," I told him. I tasted the brandy. It was older than I was. Better, too, probably.

"Pay what I owe," said Lord Bob, and sipped at his. "Even to a Pinkerton. Noblesse oblige, eh?" He turned to Doyle. "A suggestion, you said?"

Doyle took a puff from the pipe. "Yes." As he shifted slightly on the uncomfortable seat, another small quick wince flashed across his face. "I suggest to you—and I do assure you, Lord Purleigh, that I have only your best interests at heart—I suggest to you that when the police arrive, you might perhaps refrain from referring to the Earl as an old swine."

Lord Bob seemed puzzled. "Whatever for? Whole bloody county knows he was an old swine, and knows that *I* know it. He's dead, mebbe, but a swine's a swine for a' that. Eh?"

"Yes, of course. But given the unusual circumstances of the Earl's death—"

Lord Bob frowned impatiently. "You keep nattering on about the circumstances. Swine killed himself. Doesn't happen every day, grant you, but it happens. Should have done it years ago. Inevitable, in a way, you know. Inherent Contradictions of Capitalism. Historical Necessity. Swine finally realized what he was, couldn't stomach it, took the easy way out."

"But I understood that your father suffered from paralysis."

Lord Bob nodded. "Years now. Fell off a horse. Sorrel mare."

"And Mr. Beaumont has pointed out that the pistol found in his room came from that gun collection." He pointed his pipe at the guns on the wall.

Lord Bob nodded. "Got you. Worried me for a bit. How'd the old swine get hold of it, eh? Well, no mystery there. One of the servants fetched it for him."

"But why? What reason could the Earl possibly give a servant for wanting a pistol?"

"No idea. Told him he wanted to pot at pigeons, mebbe. We get them, you know. Poison doesn't work. Costs me a fortune, cleaning up after the buggers. Filthy things." He drained his brandy.

"But Lord Purleigh—"

"What is it, exactly, you're after, Doyle?"

"Not I, Lord Purleigh. The police—"

"Look here." Lord Bob grabbed the decanter, splashed some more brandy into his glass. "You're not implying that this was something more than a suicide? You're not saying, blast it, that it was *murder?*" He slapped the decanter back onto the table.

"Certainly not. But the police—"

"Bugger the police." He swallowed some brandy. "Poor Carson heard the bloody gun go off. You *saw* the door. It was locked. Barred. From the inside." He turned to the Great Man. "You're the lock-expert chap. Could *you* have nipped out of that room? Eh? In one piece? And left the locks the way we found them?"

"Of course," said the Great Man. His timing, as usual, was perfect. "There are several methods by which I could have done so. With the simplest of these, I could have prepared the door in less than a few seconds."

Doyle leaned forward, interested, and he said, "Really? By what means?"

Lord Bob sat back, scowling. "Rubbish."

"Not at all, Lord Purleigh," said the Great Man. "It is quite simple." He turned to Doyle. "The lock is an ancient one, with the warded chamber set midway between the two lock plates, one on the interior of the room and one on the exterior. The channel passes straight through, from room to room. Let us say, theoretically, that I am in the bedroom, and that the door is locked from the inside when Carson attempts to open it. As in fact it was."

My attention was wandering. The Great Man had already explained all this to me. I glanced over at the weapons on the wall. A lot of armament hanging up there.

"To deal with the bar," the Great Man was saying, "I would require only a strong piece of wire, perhaps a coat hanger—which is exactly the item, of course, with which I would have *opened* the door, had I been given the opportunity."

Up there, above an antique piece of furniture, a long dark wooden dresser, there were dirks and daggers, swords, halberds, pikes, rifles, and pistols.

"I unlock the door," said the Great Man, "leaving the key in the lock. I open the door. I raise the bar and I use the wire to support it above the restraining posts, holding the wire along the edge of the door. I am standing outside now, in the other room. As I close the door, I slide the wire from beneath the bar. The bar descends into the restraining posts, and the wire slips around the frame of the door, and out. I then use a simple lock pick to turn the key in the chamber and drive the bolt home."

Doyle laughed aloud. "Topping!"

Lord Bob said, "But how could you do all that with Carson standing right outside the door?"

"Excuse me," I said. "Lord Purleigh?"

He glared at me.

"The guns on the wall," I said. "They're not loaded, are they?"

He made a face. "What sort of blockhead puts loaded weapons on the bloody wall?"

"Where's the ammunition?"

"That cupboard there."

"Mind if I take a look?"

He waved a brusque hand. "Do as you like." He turned back to the Great Man. "Carson was standing outside the door," he said. "No way on earth you could've performed all those fancy tricks of yours without him seeing you."

I stood up, walked toward the cupboard.

"Ah, but remember," said the Great Man. "Carson left the room to summon help. He used the emergency telephone in his own quarters."

Inside the cupboard, on the top shelf, the ammunition was neatly stacked in cardboard boxes.

"When Carson leaves," said the voice of the Great Man, "I unlock the door and I prepare everything—the bar, the lock. It is a matter of seconds only. Then I slip from the room. By the time he returns to it, I am safely away."

I saw a .45 auto, 30.30 Remington, 9-millimeter Parabellum. A metal canister holding black powder. And, toward the rear, a box of .38s. I glanced at the wall.

Lord Bob: "And you're saying that's what bloody *happened?*"

The Great Man: "Not at all, Lord Purleigh. Sir Arthur asked me how it *could* have happened. I was merely explaining this."

I walked over to the scoped Winchester lever-action rifle on the wall. I leaned forward, sniffed at the ejection port.

"In my opinion," said the Great Man, "nothing like this took place. There would have been indications, you see."

"Indications?" said Doyle.

I put my right hand beneath the rifle's butt plate, used my left to grip the tip of the barrel, and lifted the weapon from its supports on the wall. I sniffed the muzzle.

"On the key, for example," said the Great Man. "The key is copper, a soft metal. Had anyone used a pick on it, he would have left marks on the key's bit."

I turned around to face them. I waited for the Great Man to

finish. Lord Bob saw me holding the Winchester, frowned briefly, looked back at the Great Man.

"The key," said the Great Man, "landed on the floor on its right side. Its left side, of course, was facing up. It is on the left side of the bit that marks would have been left, had someone used a pick. I examined it and saw that there were no marks. You will find, however, when the key is turned over, the marks *I* left when I opened the lock."

He took a sip of water. "I also examined the wooden frame of the door. Had someone used a wire to lower the bar, the wire would have left a very narrow groove in the wood. I found no such groove. It is therefore obvious to me that no one used this method. Or, for that matter, any of the other methods that might have been employed. It is perfectly clear to me that the Earl did, in fact, commit suicide."

"There you are," said Lord Bob triumphantly to Doyle. *"Suicide.* Plain and simple."

"Sorry," I said. They turned to me. "It's not all that simple."

It was Doyle who spoke. "What do you mean?"

"I could be wrong," I said, "but I think this is the rifle that was fired at Houdini today."

The three of them stared at me. Once again it was Doyle who did the talking. "Surely you're not suggesting that Chin Soo came in *here* to obtain a rifle."

"I'm not suggesting anything," I said. "I'm saying I think this is the rifle. It's been fired, and fairly recently. Probably today."

Still holding the rifle's barrel in my left hand, I jammed the butt plate against my stomach and I used the knuckles of my right hand to throw its lever open. The action was smooth and the lever moved easily, almost silently, and from the ejection port popped the long lethal shape of a 30.30 cartridge. The cartridge sailed in an arc to my right and then fell and thumped against the Oriental carpet and rolled up against the wall.

Part Two

Chapter Eighteen

IMPOSSIBLE," SAID LORD Bob, glaring at the Winchester rifle as though it had just passed gas.

Holding the rifle by its butt plate and the tip of its barrel, I carried it around the table and set it down carefully on the wooden tabletop, between Doyle and Lord Bob on one side, and the Great Man and me on the other. "Impossible or not," I said, "that rifle's been fired today."

I sat back down in my chair.

Lord Bob reached out for the rifle. Doyle said warningly, "Lord Purleigh."

Lord Bob froze and glanced over at Doyle.

"Fingerprints," Doyle told him.

Lord Bob scowled and withdrew his hand. "But damn it, Doyle," he said. "It's bloody impossible. No one could simply dash in here and grab the bloody thing!"

I said, "Harry? Could Chin Soo have gotten into Maplewhite?"

The Great Man frowned. "Get in? Yes, certainly." He turned to Lord Bob. "The locks here are very fundamental, Lord Purleigh."

"Impossible," said Lord Bob, and looked down at the rifle. He swallowed some brandy.

I asked Lord Bob, "When was the last time the gun was fired? That you know of."

Still staring at the Winchester, he said, "No idea. Spring sometime." He looked up at me. "Target practice out on the lawn. Had some guests here, they wanted to give it a go."

Doyle turned to me. "You said that you still possess the slug that was fired this afternoon. There are scientific tests that can determine whether it was fired from this weapon."

"That won't work here," I told him. "The slug was too damaged. But the caliber is right."

Lord Bob turned to Doyle. "How could he possibly have known where the guns were kept?"

Doyle puffed at the pipe, took it from his mouth. "Well, Lord Purleigh, there *are* written accounts of Maplewhite, you know. Descriptions of its rooms, its architecture."

Lord Bob's furry eyebrows shot skyward. "You mean the filthy bugger *investigated* me? Investigated my bloody *home?* Is *that* what you're saying?"

Doyle shrugged. "It's possible, I suppose."

"The *swine.*" Lord Bob snatched up the decanter of brandy, splashed a couple of inches into his glass.

Doyle frowned. "But would he've had the time to do so, I wonder?" He turned to me. "As I understand it, Chin Soo couldn't have known until this morning that Houdini would be at Maplewhite this weekend. It was this morning that the article appeared in the *Times.* Even if he read it first thing in the day, would he have had time enough to study the accounts of the house *and* appear here as quickly as he did?"

"I've been thinking about that," I said. "Maybe Chin Soo had already figured out that Harry would be here."

Doyle raised his left eyebrow. "How so?" he asked.

I asked, "How long have you known you'd be coming here, Sir Arthur? For the séance."

He stroked his mustache with the mouthpiece of the pipe as he thought about it. "Since Monday last," he said finally. "Lady Purleigh asked me then, over the telephone, whether Madame Sosostris might be available this weekend. I rang up Madame and I asked her. She was available, she said, and she agreed to come. I telephoned Lady Purleigh and accepted her invitation, on both our behalfs."

Suddenly he smiled at me. "I see. Yes, of course. There was something in the *Times* on Wednesday, an article about Spiritualism. It mentioned my forthcoming visit to Maplewhite, and the séance here. Houdini's name wasn't mentioned—" He turned to the Great Man. "I didn't discuss it with you until Thursday, did I?"

"Thursday, yes," said the Great Man. "Exactly."

Doyle looked back at me. "But it's common knowledge that he and I are friends, that we attend séances together."

"And Chin Soo knows," I said, "that Harry is in England. It'd make sense to him that Harry would show up at Maplewhite."

Doyle nodded thoughtfully. "He should have had ample time, then, to study the accounts of the building."

"Yeah," I said. "And he could've arrived here anytime over the last week, from Wednesday on." I turned to Lord Bob. "He could've been in and out of this place twenty times."

Lord Bob slammed his fist against the table. "Rotten stinking *sod!*"

Doyle asked me, "But wouldn't someone have noticed that the rifle was missing?"

"It was here Friday night," I said, "when we got here. I saw it."

"Lord Purleigh . . ." said the Great Man, and leaned forward.

"Filthy *bloody* swine," Lord Bob snarled. He tossed back some more brandy.

"Lord Purleigh?" said the Great Man.

Another voice said, "Milord?"

We all looked over to the Great Hall's entrance. Briggs stood there, and another man.

"Police Constable Dubbins," announced Briggs.

"Yes, yes," said Lord Bob. "Show him in."

The Great Man sat back.

Constable Dubbins, a tall, bulky police officer wearing a blue uniform, marched into the room behind Briggs. He held a bulky blue helmet under his left arm. Above his right shoe, a bicycle clip bunched his pants leg around his ankle. When they reached us, Dubbins stopped and stood rigidly at attention. He saluted Lord Bob, his head held stiffly forward, his stiff palm facing outward. "Good afternoon, your lordship. If I may be so bold, sir, I'd like to say that I'm dreadful sorry for the tragic loss of the Earl, sir. And I believe I speak for all the folk in the village when I say that, your lordship."

"Yes," said Lord Bob. "Yes, thank you, Dubbins. Most kind. Briggs, would you wait in the hallway, please."

"Very good, milord," said Briggs. He nodded once, turned and left. Dubbins was still standing at attention.

Lord Bob rose from the table, wavering only a little, and he shuffled behind his chair. "Dubbins, this is Sir Arthur Conan Doyle. That gentleman is Mr. Harry Houdini, and the man beside him is Mr. Beaumont, from the Pinkerton Detective Agency, in America." He was pronouncing his words carefully.

Dubbins swiveled his head stiffly, nodded stiffly. "Afternoon, gentlemen."

"Dubbins," said Lord Bob, "there's really no need, you know, for you to stand at attention."

"No sir, your lordship," said Dubbins. He relaxed his body slightly but his face remained immobile. He turned to Doyle. "You'd be the gentleman, sir, what wrote them stories about Sherlock Holmes, would you?"

Doyle smiled. "Yes, I would."

"Smashin' stories, if I may say so, sir. Smashin'. Read 'em when I was a nipper. It was them, the stories, what made me take up my career in the Law. That's the God's honest truth, sir."

Doyle smiled. "And very flattering to learn, Constable Dubbins."

"Yes sir. Smashin', sir. Boggle the mind, they do, sir."

"Dubbins?" said Lord Bob.

"Yes sir, your lordship?"

Lord Bob was leaning both his forearms against the top of the chair's back as he looked over at Dubbins. "What precisely are your orders, Dubbins?"

"Your lordship, accordin' to my orders, I am to proceed to the scene of the tragic accident and make it secure, like, sir, until I am relieved of my duties. No one is to enter or exit the scene of the accident, sir."

Lord Bob nodded. "Not very likely, anyone making an exit. In the circumstances."

"No sir, your lordship." Dubbins had noticed the Winchester on the table.

"Right," said Lord Bob. "Partridge—one of the footmen—is up there now. My suggestion, he stays there with you. Two heads better than one, eh?"

"Yes sir, your lordship." He took a step toward the table and reached for the rifle. "Would this be the weapon in ques—"

"Good lord, man!" barked Lord Bob, and Dubbins whipped back his hand and snapped to attention. Lord Bob stepped back from the chair and cleared his throat. "Fingerprints, Dubbins. Surely you know about fingerprints?"

"Yes sir, your lordship. Forgot myself for a moment. The tragedy and all, sir."

"Yes, yes," said Lord Bob. "And to answer your question, no, that is not the weapon in question. That weapon was used—was *perhaps* used, I should say—in a vile attack against one of my guests. A different incident entirely. Different swine entirely, eh? We'll let the Amberly chaps deal with it, shall we?"

"Yes sir, your lordship. Your lordship?"

"Yes?"

"Would it be permitted for me, sir, to pay my last respects to the late Earl?"

Lord Bob frowned. "Pay them how?"

Dubbins shifted slightly on his feet. "Well, you know, your lordship. Run in there, right quickly like, and say a quiet word over 'im, sir. My last goodbyes, sir."

Lord Bob took a deep breath, blinked, and focused his glance on Dubbins. "No, Dubbins," he said. "That is not, I think, an altogether splendid idea. Best, I think, that the room remain sealed for now. Eh, Doyle?"

"I think that best, Lord Purleigh."

Lord Bob turned back to Dubbins, and studied him for a moment. "Perhaps," he said, "I should come with you. Have a word or two with Partridge."

"Yes sir, your lordship."

I said, "Lord Purleigh?"

He frowned at me. "What is it?"

"Mind if I tag along? I'd like to talk to the Earl's valet."

"Carson? Whatever for?"

"Maybe it's a good idea for me to hear his story before somebody else does." I glanced at Constable Dubbins.

Lord Bob looked from Dubbins to me, back to Dubbins, back

to me. He narrowed his eyes and nodded sagely. "Got you. Better the devil you know . . ." he concentrated for an instant then waved a dismissive hand ". . . than some other bloody devil. Right. Right. Come along then." He looked at Doyle and the Great Man, nodded to the Winchester. "You gentlemen will watch over this?"

"Certainly," said Doyle.

LORD BOB LED Dubbins and me through the corridors to the Earl's suite. Lord Bob weaved a bit but he stumbled only once, on the stairwell. He said nothing to me all the way. As we came down the hallway toward the Earl's suite, he said to Dubbins, "When will your colleagues be arriving from Amberly?"

"Momentarily, your lordship. Superintendent Honniwell is with 'em, sir."

"Indeed. We can all rest easy now."

"Yes sir, your lordship. What I meant, sir, he'll hurry 'em along, the Super will."

"Yes, of course. And how *is* the villainy business these days, Dubbins?"

"Well, your lordship, Florrie Chubb's oldest, Little Tom, he smashed the window of the chemist's shop on Monday last. Old Mrs. Hornsby banged Jerry over the head with a teapot again. That was Wednesday, your lordship. And someone nicked Wilbur Dent's bicycle today."

"A veritable crime wave. We must nip that in the bud, eh?"

"Yes sir, your lordship."

"I have every confidence in you, Dubbins."

"Thank you, sir, your lordship."

When we arrived at a doorway a few doors away from the Earl's rooms, Lord Bob stopped, Dubbins and I stopped, and Lord Bob knocked on the door. A thin voice called out for us to come in.

Lord Bob opened the door. The room was small, half the size of the anteroom next door. A curtained window, a dresser, a wardrobe, a small desk that held a lighted electric lamp and the emergency telephone. Still fully dressed but with his tie loosened at his neck, Carson was trying to raise himself off the small single bed. "I do apologize, milord—"

"No, no," said Lord Bob. "Be a good fellow now, and lie down. Good. You've met Mr. Beaumont. He'll be asking you a few questions about what happened today. He's a Pinkerton, but we won't hold that against him, eh? Feel up to it, do you?"

Carson had eased his white head back onto the pillow and put his small frail hands on his chest. The hands still trembled. Maybe they always did. "Yes, milord. I feel quite useless, sir, lying here like this. I should be very happy to be of help, if I could."

"Splendid. Good man. I'll have someone look in on you later. Need anything, use the telephone and ask Higgens, eh?"

"Very good, milord. Thank you."

"Right. Dubbins? Ah, there you are. Right. Come along."

They left, Lord Bob pulling the door shut behind them.

"There's a chair, sir," said Carson, "over by the desk."

I eased the chair out from under the desk, turned it around, straddled it. I said, "I'm sorry to bother you with this now, Mr. Carson."

"No bother, sir. As I told his lordship, I'm happy to help, sir." His hands were white, spattered with liver spots. They lay on the front of his coat, trembling like a pair of small pale frightened animals.

"Appreciate it," I said. "How long have you worked here, Mr. Carson?"

"Over sixty years now, sir. Since I was a child."

"And how long have you been the Earl's valet?"

"Forty years, sir."

"You must've known him fairly well."

"I believe so, sir," he said.

"It's been a big shock to you, his death."

He blinked. His hands clenched slightly. "It has, sir, yes."

"So the Earl hasn't been acting differently lately?"

He blinked again. "Differently, sir?"

"Worried. Unhappy."

Blink, blink. "No, sir."

"You would've known if he was worried."

"I like to think so, sir, yes. But the Earl, he was a man who kept his own council."

I nodded. Forty years with the Earl. It was a relationship that was longer and maybe more complicated than most marriages. And sixty years here at Maplewhite. Wherever Carson's loyalties lay, they didn't lie with me.

"But as far as you know," I said, "he wasn't depressed. Wasn't worried."

"No, sir."

"Anything unusual happen today?" I asked him.

Blink. "How do you mean that, sir?"

"Visitors, letters. Anything that didn't usually happen."

"No, sir."

"No visitors?"

"No, sir."

"Any visitors yesterday?"

"Lord and Lady Purleigh, sir."

"In the evening." When Lord Bob and his wife had left the drawing room.

"Yes, sir."

I nodded. "No one else?"

"No, sir."

"I noticed there was a fire in the fireplace today."

"Yes, sir. There's always a fire."

"Always?"

"The Earl required it, sir."

"Required it?"

"For his circulation, sir. Ever since the accident."

I nodded. "He fell off a horse, I heard."

"Yes, sir."

This wasn't much more difficult than pulling teeth from an eel. "And when was that, Mr. Carson?"

"Three years ago, sir."

"Wasn't the Earl a little old to go riding?"

"He was a great sportsman, sir."

"Right. So the fire stayed lit all the time. Day and night."

"Yes, sir. Mornings, I raked the coals and got a new one started."

"The Earl hasn't walked since the accident?"

Blink, blink. "No, sir."

"He had a wheelchair. He could use that by himself."

Blink. "For short distances, yes, sir."

"He could get in and out of it himself?"

"On some days, sir. Some days he required assistance."

"Did you give him the gun, Mr. Carson?"

The pale hands clenched at the lapels of his coat. "The gun, sir? No, sir, I never did, sir. I swear on my life I didn't."

"You know that the gun was kept in the Great Hall."

"I heard you say so, sir, to Lord Purleigh."

"You haven't seen it there?"

"Not to notice it, sir. I know very little about guns."

"How do you think it got to the Earl's room?"

"I can't imagine, sir." He shook his white head. "For a fact, sir, I can't."

"Could the Earl have gone down the stairs by himself? In the wheelchair?"

"No, sir. When he came downstairs, I needed help with the chair. It's very heavy, sir."

"When was the last time he came downstairs?"

"Last week, sir. It was a sunny day, and the Earl wanted to see the gardens."

"Did he go anywhere near the Great Hall?"

"No, sir. Briggs helped me with the chair, getting it downstairs, and I rolled it out to the gardens myself."

"Was someone with him all the time?"

"I was, sir. The entire time. Near to half an hour. And then Briggs helped me get him back up to his room."

"Okay," I said. "What happened today?"

"When, sir?"

Bit by bit, I got it out of him. At four o'clock, as usual, Carson had brought the Earl his afternoon tea. As usual, the door between the anteroom and the Earl's bedroom was shut. As usual, Carson waited in the anteroom for the Earl to ring a bell by his bedside, signaling that he was ready for the tea. No bell rang. At a quarter after four, Carson heard the sound of a gunshot. He ran to the Earl's door, tried to open it, discovered it was locked. He tried his own key. It wouldn't work. He pounded on the door. No answer. He ran into his room, used the emergency telephone to call Higgens. A few minutes later, Higgens arrived, with Lord Bob. The two of them couldn't open the door. Lord Bob went off for help.

"Okay," I said. "When you heard the gunshot, did you know what it was?"

He blinked. "I wasn't quite sure *what* it was, sir. But a gunshot is what it sounded like. It was very loud, sir, even through the door."

"Did the Earl usually lock his door?"

"No, sir. He never did."

"Where was the other key? The one that was in the lock this afternoon?"

"In his cabinet, sir. The bottom drawer."

"And you're sure you heard the shot at a quarter after four?"

"Yes, sir. I'd just looked at my watch, sir."

"Why look at your watch?"

"It was getting late, sir. Most times, the Earl rang for tea by ten minutes past four."

"Mr. Carson, I've heard that there's been some bad feelings between the Earl and Lord Purleigh."

He blinked. The hands stirred. "Bad feelings, sir?"

"I heard that the Earl didn't like what Lord Purleigh planned to do with Maplewhite, after the Earl was gone."

He shook his head earnestly. "Oh no, sir. They had their disagreements, sir, as you might expect. It happens in every family, doesn't it, sir? But there were no bad feelings, sir."

"No arguments, no fights?"

"Oh no, sir. Nothing like that."

Just then, I heard a noise coming from the hallway outside Carson's room. The stomp of heavy feet, the mumble of male voices. I got up from my chair and went to the door.

Chapter Nineteen

WALKING OUT INTO the hallway was like walking into a Mack Sennett movie. It was crowded with people who seemed to be rushing in a dozen different directions at the same time. They all stopped rushing when I came out, and they all looked at me and I looked at all of them. There were a couple of burly uniformed cops, and two other burly men in black suits carrying a rolled-up stretcher. A short man in a gray suit held a doctor's bag. There was a tall thin man in a brown suit, with the strap from a bulky camera hanging around his skinny neck. And there was a tall man in a vested, military-looking black suit who had square shoulders and a square jaw and wavy gray hair that swept back from a nice widow's peak above a square forehead and a pair of pale gray eyes. He looked like someone who had wandered into the wrong movie, and who resented it. He was the one who did the talking.

"And what have we here?" he said to me.

"Phil Beaumont," I told him.

He nodded crisply, once. "You'll be the Pinkerton."

"I already am," I said.

After a moment, he smiled bleakly. His must have practiced that smile, because he did a good job with it. "Superintendent Honniwell," he said. "Lord Purleigh has put us into the picture. We'll carry on from here."

"Fine."

He nodded crisply toward the door I'd just closed. "The valet's room?"

"Yeah."

He nodded again. "You may go, Beaumont. I may have some questions for you later."

"Swell. There's one thing, though."

He smiled faintly, to let me know he was humoring me. Or maybe he was letting himself know. "Yes?"

"The gun. The Smith and Wesson. You'll be checking it for prints?"

"Of course."

"Lord Purleigh's prints are on it."

He pursed his lips. "Lord Purleigh and Sir Arthur have already apprised me of that fact."

"Right. Well, I don't know how good your laboratory people are, but you could tell them to look for prints under the ash."

He raised one of his handsome gray eyebrows. "Under the ash?"

"When we broke open the door," I said, "it blew ash from the fireplace all over the room. It was on the gun before Lord Purleigh picked it up. His prints will be on top of the ash. If you find any prints under the ash, they belong to whoever used the pistol."

"I expect," he said, "that our technicians are quite capable of making that determination on their own." He turned back to the rest of them. "Proceed, gentlemen. Touch nothing until I arrive."

In a jumble, the others began shambling and shuffling toward the Earl's room. Honniwell reached for the knob to Carson's door, then stopped and looked at me as if he were a little bit surprised to find out I was still in the same universe that he was.

"You may *go,* Beaumont," he told me.

"Thanks," I said, and went.

I WENT BACK to the drawing room. It was empty. Even better, no one had bothered to clean up after the tea party. There was still food lying untouched on the tables. I had just finished wolfing down my second smoked salmon sandwich, and I was reaching for the third, when two servants came into the room. They were carrying large metal trays. One of them was Briggs.

"Mr. Briggs," I said. "Could I talk to you for a minute?"

Briggs glanced at the other servant, looked back at me, and said, "Certainly, sir." He set his tray down on one of the tables and came over to where I was standing.

I said, "You've heard about the Earl?" It was probably impossible to keep it a secret from the servants.

"Yes, sir," he said. "A great tragedy, sir."

"I was just wondering, Mr. Briggs. Do you know anything about any visitors the Earl might've had in the past few days?"

For the first time, Briggs's pale, pinched face showed some expression. His glance darted over to the other servant, who was very busy being busy, and then it darted back to me. His small eyes narrowed with that slow appraising slyness that mothers and employers hate but Pinkertons love. "I'm sorry, sir," he told me. "I couldn't say." He glanced at the other servant again, in case I hadn't gotten the message.

"Okay, Mr. Briggs," I said. "Thanks. See you around."

"Yes, sir. Thank you, sir."

SUPERINTENDENT HONNIWELL WAS already in the Great Hall when I got back there. He stood facing the table, where Doyle, Lord Bob, and the Great Man were all sitting. The Winchester rifle was gone. Honniwell ignored me as I sat down next to the Great Man. His hands were clasped behind him and he was summing up.

"It was Carson, of course," Honniwell said to Lord Bob. "There's no question in my mind. The Earl ordered him to obtain the pistol."

"Absurd," said Lord Bob. He was slouched down in his chair, slump-shouldered and sleepy-eyed. On the table before him, the decanter of brandy was nearly empty.

"With all due respect, Lord Purleigh," said Honniwell, "I beg to differ. The man was literally quaking with guilt."

"Guilt?" said Lord Bob. He raised his balloon glass, drank some more brandy. "Been quaking with it, then, for seven bloody years. Bloody palsy, Superintendent."

Honniwell wasn't the kind of cop who let facts interfere with a summing up. "Be that as it may, sir, the man is guilty. If I had him alone for a few hours, I'll wager I'd shake the truth out of him."

Lord Bob looked at him for a moment. When he spoke, his

voice was sober and dangerously level. "Lay a finger on Carson, Superintendent, and you'll not believe the trouble in which you find yourself."

"But Lord Purleigh," said Honniwell, "you mistake my meaning."

"Forgive me," said Doyle, diplomatically. "Superintendent?"

Honniwell turned to Doyle and this time he raised both of his handsome eyebrows. "Sir Arthur?"

Doyle said, "I take it, Superintendent, that you don't believe Carson to be responsible for the Earl's death."

"Not responsible, Sir Arthur, no. But he did assist in the death, indirectly, by making the pistol available."

"Perhaps so," said Doyle. His hands on the table, fingers interlocked, he leaned forward. He winced faintly. "But you've no doubt that the death itself was self-inflicted."

"None at all. Powder burns at the wound. Nothing else is possible, not with the door locked and bolted as it was."

The Great Man sat up and Doyle shot him a subtle warning glance. Subtlety wasn't the Great Man's strong point, so I kicked him in the ankle. He spun his head and glared at me, then he pursed his lips and looked away and sat back. He crossed his arms over his chest, silent and sulky.

"Precisely," said Doyle to Honniwell. "And so, even if you could verify your belief that Carson provided the pistol, which I very much doubt, you're still left with a suicide."

"That's correct," said Honniwell. "And that is what my report will read." He turned back to Lord Bob. "As I was about to say, Lord Purleigh. I am merely attempting here to do what's best for all concerned."

Lord Bob scowled and waved his hand slowly, as if shooing away sluggish flies. He reached out, snared the brandy decanter, poured what was left into his glass.

Honniwell said to Doyle, "As I told you earlier, it's an utter waste of time, sending this Inspector Marsh from London. The autopsy and the examination of the pistol will establish that, of course." He turned to Lord Bob. "As to the rifle, Lord Purleigh, I shall inform you when that examination is completed."

Lord Bob nodded. "Can't wait."

I said, "You know about Chin Soo, Superintendent?"

He gave me the faint smile he reserved for Pinkertons. Or maybe he reserved it for Americans. Or maybe it wasn't reserved at all, and he gave it out to anybody he thought it was okay to smile faintly at. "Yes," he said. "Mr. Houdini and Sir Arthur have explained that situation. I think it extremely unlikely that this person could make his way into Maplewhite. I agree with Lord Purleigh that the rifle that was fired this afternoon was most likely fired by a poacher. The man is long gone by now."

He glanced at Lord Bob to see how he took that. Lord Bob didn't take it at all. He was staring at the empty brandy decanter as though it were the philosophers' stone.

"How do you explain the Winchester?" I asked him. "It's been fired recently."

"One of the servants, perhaps."

"Uh-huh. But you'll leave some police on the premises?"

Another faint smile. "I shall be posting two of my men outside. I'll see to it that they're relieved in the morning."

"Only two?" I said.

He let himself get faintly amused again. "I'm quite sure that two trained British police officers will be more than sufficient. And, in deference to Lord Purleigh and his guests, I wish to keep our presence to a minimum." He glanced hopefully at Lord Bob.

"Long as they stay outside," said Lord Bob, talking to the empty decanter. "Don't want 'em in here. Tracking muck about."

The Great Man said, "And you will not be informing the press?"

"Not as to your difficulties, Mr. Houdini. I will of course defer to Lord Purleigh's request. But, Lord Purleigh, I'm afraid the news of the Earl's death will soon reach the newspapers."

"Swine's a swine for a' that," Lord Purleigh told the brandy decanter.

Honniwell nodded crisply. "Yes. Well, then. I must be getting back to Amberly. I came here only to make certain that Lord Purleigh wasn't unduly troubled by the arrival of my men."

He looked at Lord Bob, who ignored him again.

Doyle stood up. "Perhaps you'd permit me to accompany you, Superintendent." More diplomacy.

"Certainly, Sir Arthur. Lord Purleigh." Still peering at the brandy decanter, Lord Bob scowled and waved a limp hand. "Mr. Houdini." The Great Man nodded. "Mr. Beaumont." I nodded.

He had decided, I guess, that there was no point in asking me any questions.

Doyle escorted him from the hall.

The Great Man turned to Lord Bob. "Excuse me, Lord Purleigh. I shall be going to my room for a short while."

"Bloody nincompoop," Lord Bob told the brandy decanter.

The Great Man stood.

"Harry?" I said.

He looked down at me, his face cold. Without saying a word, he pursed his lips and looked away. Then he strode off.

Lord Bob was still studying the decanter.

I got up and went after the Great Man.

Doyle was coming back from the main entrance, and he intercepted me. "Mr. Beaumont?"

Chapter Twenty

YES?" I SAID.

"Well," he said, and his wide pink forehead was creased with thought. "What did you think of our Superintendent?"

"Not a whole lot," I told him.

"No. I gathered as much. But I'd like to assure you that he's not truly representative of our police officials."

"Good."

"I've heard, for example, excellent reports of Inspector Marsh."

"Marsh is still coming tomorrow?"

"Well, I doubt, personally, that Scotland Yard will give any great credence to Superintendent Honniwell's report. He and his people spent only about ten minutes in the Earl's room."

"They took away the body?"

"For the autopsy, yes."

"You think it was a suicide, Sir Arthur?"

He considered the question for a moment. "Let me put it this way," he said. "I should like to persuade myself that if it was *not* a suicide, then all other human agencies have been entirely ruled out."

"Human agencies," I said.

"Yes."

"Uh-huh." I looked back at Lord Bob. He was still contemplating the empty decanter. I turned to Doyle. "You might talk to Lord Purleigh about moving the rest of the ammunition and locking it up somewhere."

"The ammunition? Oh yes. Yes, of course. If it *is* Chin Soo, why should we provide him any more it?"

"Right."

"An excellent idea." He glanced at Lord Bob. "Lord Purleigh is rather under the weather at the moment. But I'll have a word with Higgens."

"Thanks. I'll see you later."

"HARRY?"

Nothing.

I knocked on the Great Man's door again. "Harry?"

Nothing.

I tried the knob. The door was locked.

I rapped again at the wooden panel. "Harry. Open the door."

Nothing.

I said, "It's about Bess, Harry."

I waited. After a long moment, I heard his voice on the other side of the door. "What about her?"

"Open the door," I said, "and I'll tell you."

I waited.

Finally I heard a click at the lock. I turned the knob and the door opened. The Great Man was walking away, his back to me. He was naked except for a pair of the black briefs he ordered by the gross from France. I looked down at the lock. No key. There hadn't been one earlier.

I said, "You used a pick to lock it. And unlock it."

But where had he put the pick afterward? His hands were empty.

He turned to me and he moved his muscular shoulders in a small shrug. He wasn't going to tell me anything he didn't want me to know. He crossed his arms over his chest and he said flatly, "What is it about Bess?"

Probably he'd just thrown it across the room, behind the bed.

"The Earl's death," I said. "It's going to make the newspapers. The London *Times* for sure, and maybe the French papers, too. Bess is going to read about it, in Paris. You know she's worried about Chin Soo. She's going to wonder, maybe, if there's any connection."

He thought about that. "Perhaps," he said. He lowered himself gracefully to the floor and lay down along the rug. He didn't look at me as he locked his hands behind his head and began to do sit-ups. "I shall ask Lord Purleigh," he said, touching his left knee with his right elbow, "if I can send a wire. To reassure her." He sank back to the floor.

I walked over to the desk, sat down in the chair.

"Listen, Harry," I said. "I'm sorry I kicked you."

He grazed his right knee with his left elbow.

"Harry, I apologize. I just didn't want you saying anything to Honniwell about getting out of that room."

"The man is a cretin," he said to the ceiling.

"Exactly," I said. "And if you started explaining how someone could get out of there, he would've hung around all night."

"I was *about* to explain," he said, on the upswing, "that no one *had* escaped from the room."

"Honniwell's not a guy you want to confuse with too many theories, Harry. This guy Marsh, the one who's coming tomorrow, Sir Arthur says he's smart. He's the one you should talk to."

"I intend to." On the upswing again.

"Good. That's good, Harry. You should. He'll probably be glad to hear whatever you have to say. Look, I didn't mean to hurt you—"

He straightened out his legs and sat up, his hands against the floor, and he looked at me. "Hurt me? Pain is nothing to Houdini. You should understand that by now. No, Phil, what disturbs me is the *rudeness* of it. Have I ever kicked *you* in the ankle?"

It was an interesting conversation to be having with a semi-naked man. "No, Harry," I said, "I've got to admit you haven't."

"Surely you could have devised some other means of signaling me?"

"Probably, yeah, but nothing sprang to mind. Maybe we could work out a code."

"And, to tell you the truth, I do not understand why you are so fascinated by the death of the Earl. As I have established, this was definitely a suicide. And it has nothing whatever to do with Chin Soo. Who is, if my memory serves me, your sole reason for being here."

"Well, Harry," I said, "I'm not so sure that Chin Soo and the Earl's death are unconnected."

The Great Man frowned. "What are you saying?"

"Someone takes a rifle from the gun collection, uses it to shoot at you, and then puts it back. And then someone takes a revolver from the same gun collection, probably within a few hours, and the Earl gets shot with it."

"But no one could have shot the Earl. Except himself. As I told you, Phil, I examined that door very carefully. No one had tampered with it. And if *Chin Soo* had done so—which is totally impossible—what reason would he have for killing the Earl?"

"I don't know. But how did that revolver get into the Earl's room?"

He shrugged. "Perhaps the Superintendent is right, and the Earl's valet brought it to him."

"I don't think so. I talked to the valet."

"It was another servant, then. One of them, perhaps, who was fond of the Earl. He brought the gun at the Earl's request."

"He was fond of the Earl, so he helped him commit suicide?"

"Perhaps the Earl told him he wanted the gun for some other reason. Lord Purleigh suggested as much."

"A lot of guns were being moved in and out of that hall today."

He shook his head. "It is a coincidence, Phil. Nothing more."

"I don't like coincidences."

"Phil, I do not like being kicked in the ankle. But there are some things, apparently, that we must learn to live with."

I smiled. "Harry, I said I was sorry."

He put up a hand. "Yes, yes. I accept your apology, of course."

"Thanks," I said. "Okay. Have you changed your mind about staying here?"

He seemed surprised. "Why should I change my mind?"

"Harry. That rifle, the Winchester, I'm pretty sure it was the rifle that shot at you. If it was, and if Chin Soo fired it, that means he came into the house, took the rifle, left the house, fired the rifle, came *back* into the house, and put the rifle back."

"Yes. So you said to Lord Purleigh. But Phil, I must tell you, in all honesty, that it would be impossible for Chin Soo to run in and out of the house in this manner. I tried to say as much to Lord Purleigh, earlier. Chin Soo is simply not skilled enough. He could manage the locks, yes, perhaps. But as for lurking within the house, and scooting back and forth to the outside—impossible."

"Uh-huh."

"Phil, I believe that it was not Chin Soo who fired that weapon."

"Why?"

"Is it logical to believe that Chin Soo would go to all the trouble you describe, putting himself in jeopardy several times over, simply to obtain a rifle from the Great Hall? Why did he not merely bring along, to Maplewhite, a rifle of his own? He could have purchased one, or even stolen one."

"Good question," I admitted. "I don't know. But the fact is, that Winchester was the rifle that got fired today."

"Perhaps it was. But consider this, Phil." He crossed his legs and leaned forward, like a small boy at a campfire. He was smiling the smile he smiled on stage whenever he was about to pull off some especially spectacular stunt. "Perhaps when the rifle was fired today, it was not, in fact, being fired at me."

"Harry, the slug missed you by a few inches."

"Yes," he said, holding up a finger and smiling that smile, "but it also missed everyone else. By very much the same distance." He put his hands on his knees. "You remember that we were all gathered together beneath that tree. You have been assuming all along that the famous slug was meant for me. But how do we know this is true?"

I sat back in the chair. I thought about it. "We don't." I nodded. "That's pretty good, Harry."

He shrugged with what he probably thought was modesty, but what looked more like satisfaction. "It is merely logical," he said.

I was thinking. "It makes more sense that way," I told him. "Your way. Somebody who was already here at Maplewhite would be able to get into the Great Hall a lot easier than a stranger."

"Of course."

"But if you're right, who were they shooting at? Who was

there?" I thought back. "Miss Turner, Mrs. Corneille. Mrs. Allardyce. Lord Bob."

"Lord Purleigh," he corrected me. "The more interesting question, I believe, is—who was *not* there?"

"Right. Madame Whosis and her husband weren't even here at Maplewhite yet. Neither was Sir Arthur. So who was? Cecily. Lady Purleigh. Dr. Auerbach. Sir David."

"And a host of servants, do not forget."

I smiled. "Everybody wants to blame everything on the servants."

"But Phil, these are all cultured, wealthy people."

"Wealthy people kill each other all the time, Harry. It's what they do when they're not counting their money."

"You are a cynic, Phil."

"Or maybe Sir Arthur's right. He's beginning to think it was some goblin who did it."

The Great Man nodded sadly. "Yes. I sometimes worry about Sir Arthur."

He lay back down on the rug, raised his knees, and put his hands back behind his head. "We have established the important thing," he said, lifting his shoulders, touching his right elbow against his left knee. "That it was not Chin Soo who fired the rifle. Which means, therefore, that both of us can relax now."

"Not exactly," I said.

He looked over at me but didn't stop his sit-ups.

"We've established," I said, "that it *probably* wasn't Chin Soo who fired the rifle. Even if it wasn't, that doesn't mean that he's not hanging around somewhere."

"But there are police guards here now, Phil." Down went his shoulders.

"Chin Soo has gotten past the police before."

"In Philadelphia. These are British police." Down again.

"Could you get past a pair of British cops, Harry?"

"Of course. But Chin Soo is not Houdini." Down.

"Uh-huh. Well, listen. I'm going to go snoop around for a while. Do me a favor and put a chair up against the door?"

"It is completely unnecessary, Phil. And why do you plan to snoop around?" Up went his shoulders.

"I want to make sure you're right about the rifle."

"It is only logical, Phil." Up again.

"Right. You'll put the chair up against the door?"

He sighed theatrically. This isn't an easy thing to do while you're in the middle of a sit-up.

I said, "Humor me, Harry."

"Oh, very well. If you insist." With another sigh, he swung himself up again.

I stood.

He said, "Oh. Phil?" Down went the shoulders.

"Yeah?"

He smiled. "It was very obvious, what you were doing when you mentioned Bess. You merely wanted me to open the door." Down.

I smiled back. "It worked, though, Harry. There's more than one way to get through a locked door."

"It worked," he said, coming back up off the floor, "only because it is impossible for Houdini to hold a grudge."

As usual, he had the last word.

I went looking for Briggs.

Chapter Twenty-one

Briggs wasn't in the drawing room and neither was anyone else.

I went wandering through the corridors and after a while I found another servant who told me he had seen Briggs near the conservatory. I trudged off in that direction.

The outer door to the conservatory was open. It led onto a flagstone terrace, where a group of the guests were gathered around a circular white table beneath a tall oak tree. Sir Arthur was there, and he saw me and waved for me to join them. The others were Mrs. Corneille, Dr. Auerbach, Madame Sosostris in her wheelchair and her amazing hair, Mr. Dempsey, and Sir David. They all had drinks in front of them, so maybe a servant would be coming soon, and maybe it would be Briggs.

It had been a long day but the air was still warm and the sky was still bright. To the west, across the enormous lawn, the sun was finally sliding down through the expanse of blue. It hadn't reached the treetops yet, but its light was yellow now as it slanted from beneath the flat bottom of a small white cloud.

"Mr. Beaumont," Doyle said. "Please. Have a seat."

There was an empty white-enameled chair to Mrs. Corneille's right. I took it and I smiled at her. "Hello," I said, and breathed in the scent of her perfume. She was wearing the white dress but not the straw bonnet. Sunlight shimmered along the black gloss of her hair.

"Good afternoon, Mr. Beaumont," she said, smiling back at me. "It *is* Mr. Beaumont, isn't it? You haven't some other, cryptic, Pinkerton sort of name?"

"Just Beaumont."

She said, "But you haven't been entirely honest with us, it seems."

"Didn't have any choice," I told her.

"I sensed somet'ing," said Madame Sosostris, narrowing the dark shrewd eyes in her round white face. "Did I not, Charles? I said, t'ere is some dark deep currents in t'at man."

Grinning, Mr. Dempsey patted her hand. She wore big jeweled rings on every finger and he was careful not to hit any of them. They would have poked holes in his palm. "You sure did," he said. He looked at me proudly. "Dark deep currents, that's what she said, word for word."

"I was explaining," said Doyle, "that it was most likely Chin Soo who fired that rifle this afternoon."

I shook my head. "I was just talking to Mr. Houdini. He made a good point. I've been assuming that the rifle shot this afternoon was fired at him. But, like he says, there's no reason to assume that. It could've been meant for anyone."

Doyle frowned. "Yes," he said. "Houdini mentioned that notion to me earlier."

Mrs. Corneille said to me, "It wasn't Chin Soo who fired the rifle?"

"It makes more sense," I said, "that somebody else was firing it, and at somebody besides Houdini."

"And who," said Sir David blandly, "do you conclude it was?"

"The person doing the shooting?"

He smiled. Blandly. "Whichever. The shoot-er or the shoot-ee."

"No idea. But the police will probably figure it out. There's an inspector coming down here tomorrow morning, from London. He'll want to talk to all the people who weren't out on the lawn this afternoon. Between twelve-thirty and one o'clock. Like you, I guess, Dr. Auerbach."

Dr. Auerbach adjusted his pince-nez. "I? But I was nowhere near to Maplewhite at that time."

"And where were you, Doctor?" I said. "If you don't mind my asking."

"Of course not," he said. "Not at all. Between twelve-thirty and one, you say? Yes, I was in the village then. In the lovely little cemetery behind the church. I was making the rubbings from the tombstones. It is a hobby of mine. And this cemetery, it has some truly quite beautiful stones. Some of them date back even to the fourteenth century."

"Anyone see you?"

He nodded. "Aha, yes, I understand, for the purposes of verification. As it happens, yes, I had a long and a quite fascinating discussion with the vicar of the church. An extremely charming man. He also has an interest in these stones." He looked at me hopefully. "I have the rubbings, if you would like to examine them?"

"That's okay," I told him.

Just then a servant with a drinks tray came gliding through the conservatory door. It was Briggs. His face was expressionless again as he replaced Sir David's empty glass with a full one. I asked him for a whiskey and water.

When he glided away, I turned back to Dr. Auerbach. "Everyone went into the village together today, is that right?"

"In Lord Purleigh's motor car," he nodded. "That is correct."

"And you all came back together? In the car?"

"I did not, no," he said. "I walked back. It was a beautiful day, yes? And it remains so even now," he added, looking around happily.

"So you didn't get here until when?"

"Oh my." He turned to Mrs. Corneille. "It was at approximately two-thirty that we spoke, was it not?"

She nodded. "Shortly afterward, I believe. I'd just come from Jane's room."

"Then at two-thirty, almost exactly," said Dr. Auerbach. "I had returned a few minutes before I spoke with Mrs. Corneille. She requested that I look in on Miss Turner."

"Look in on her?"

"To offer her a brief medical examination. As you know, the young woman had fainted. I am a psychoanalyst, yes, but like most psychoanalysts I am a medical doctor also."

I nodded and turned back to Mrs. Corneille. "You came back in the car, Mrs. Corneille?"

"Yes. With Alice and Mrs. Allardyce. We arrived back here at twelve or so."

"And the others?"

"The others stayed in town. But really, Mr. Beaumont, you don't honestly believe that one of us fired that shot?"

I shrugged. "There was a Winchester rifle in the gun collection. Someone loaded it, took it from the Great Hall, fired it at someone out on the lawn, then brought it back to the hall and put it back up on the wall. Mr. Houdini is right. It probably wasn't Chin Soo who did all that."

"If you're correct," said Doyle, "in your belief that it was the Winchester which fired the shot in question."

Briggs came floating back just then with my drink. He set it on the table in front of me. I thanked him. No one else wanted anything, and he tucked the tray under his arm and floated away.

I shrugged. "Makes sense that it was the Winchester."

"Nonsense," said Sir David, and took a sip from his glass. Ignoring me, he said to Doyle and Mrs. Corneille, "It was obviously a poacher who fired the shot. It's the season. For miles around, every property in Devon is acrawl with purblind peers squinting down the barrels of rusty rifles."

"It's the grouse season, you know," said Doyle. "They'll be peering down the barrels of shotguns."

"And Lord Purleigh," said Mrs. Corneille to Sir David, "has forbidden blood sports on the grounds of Maplewhite."

I raised my drink and saw through the amber liquid that a scrap of paper had been stuck to the bottom of the glass. *Library, fifteen minutes,* someone had scrawled across the paper.

The message was easy to read. As usual, there was no ice in the glass.

Looking at Mrs. Corneille, Sir David shrugged comfortably. "Which means that the poaching would be infinitely superior here." He turned to Doyle. "For every sort of fauna. As I'm sure the poachers are well aware."

As I set the drink down with my left hand, I used my right to slip the paper from the bottom of the glass. I palmed it, crumpled it into a small damp wad.

"But the Winchester *was* fired," said Doyle.

"Perhaps," said Sir David. "But we have no way of knowing

when. Today? Yesterday? Last week sometime?"

I scratched casually at my thigh and I dropped the wad to the flagstones.

Doyle said, "Mr. Beaumont believes that it was fired today."

"Ah well," said Sir David, and smiled blandly. "Mr. Beaumont."

Doyle raised his eyebrows in surprise and looked over at me.

I said, "What about you, Sir David?"

Sir David turned. "I beg your pardon?"

"You mind if I ask you where you were this afternoon?"

"I very much mind," he said. "I can't, for the life of me, see that it's even remotely any of your business."

"David," said Mrs. Corneille. "Please. There's no need to be offensive."

"It's not I who's being offensive, Vanessa. It's Our American Friend. I put it to you—why on earth should any of us let ourselves be interrogated by some threadbare enquiry agent? After we chat with this lout, shall we run off and bare our souls to the scullery maid?"

"David," said Mrs. Corneille.

"Really, Sir David," said Doyle. "I don't think—"

"This has all suddenly become very tedious," Sir David said. He stood up without any hurry. "I believe I shall rest for a bit."

"Really, Sir David," said Doyle. The pink of his face had grown a couple of shades more red, which made the gray of his big mustache seem a couple of shades more white.

"Until dinner, then," said Sir David, and ambled away.

"My dear Beaumont," said Doyle, leaning toward me urgently with his face still red, and getting redder. "I *am* most dreadfully sorry. That was absolutely unforgivable. I've half a mind to run after the wretch and give him a damned sound thrashing. By God," he said, and he opened his eyes wide and bunched his big shoulders as he wrapped his big hands around the arms of his chair, "I believe I *will!"*

Mrs. Corneille leaned over and put her hand atop Doyle's. "No, Sir Arthur. Please."

"It's okay," I said to Doyle.

Doyle kept his shoulders bunched, as though he were still planning to leap from the chair. "But he was *unconscionably* rude."

"It's okay," I said. "Everyone's a little upset today. Don't worry about it, Sir Arthur."

Madame Sosostris said, "Mr. Beaumont is correct, Sir Art'ur. T'e Et'eric Vibrations, t'ey are very violet today. Very much so. I sense t'em. You must not to let yourself fall prey to t'ese and become violet in your own self."

"Yes," said Doyle. He sat back, plucked the handkerchief from his suit coat pocket, lightly patted it against his wide forehead. Mrs. Corneille sat back, too. I think that everyone sat back.

"Yes," Doyle repeated, to Madame Sosostris, "you're right, of course. No violence." And then, patting his forehead, he said to no one in particular, "What *is* this country coming to?"

I pulled out my watch.

"Mr. Beaumont," said Doyle.

I looked over at him.

"I wonder if you and I could have a few words."

"Sure," I told him.

Chapter Twenty-two

DOYLE AND I excused ourselves and walked in through the conservatory door. Doyle was looking for a place to talk. He found one, a small parlor to the right. We slipped in there and he glanced quickly around the room and shut the door. We sat down opposite each other on a pair of love seats. His face had gone back to its normal pink.

"First off," Doyle said, "I want to apologize again for the manner in which Sir David behaved. It was abominable."

"You don't need to apologize, Sir Arthur. It wasn't your fault."

"But the man is *English.* He's a *baronet,* Mr. Beaumont. For a so-called gentleman, I must tell you, it was an unforgivable display."

"I'm not worried about it. You shouldn't be, either."

He leaned toward me, wincing slightly. "Whenever I've traveled in America, wherever I've gone in that remarkable country, I've received nothing but the kindliest and most gracious treatment from everyone I met. Virtually everyone. I want you to know that I feel personally embarrassed that this has happened today."

"You shouldn't. But thank you, Sir Arthur. You said there was something you wanted to say?"

"Yes. Yes." He sat back with another small wince. He stuck his hand into his coat pocket, burrowed around for a while, came out with his pipe and tobacco pouch. "D'you mind?"

I shook my head.

"Well, look here," he said, as he searched for his matches, "did you really mean what you said out there? You genuinely believe that some member of the house party fired that shot?" He fiddled with the pipe.

"It makes sense to me."

"But I'm afraid that it doesn't make sense to *me,* you see." He got the pipe lit. The smell of burning potato sacks drifted across the room. He stuffed his matches back in one pocket, his tobacco pouch in another. "As I told Houdini earlier today, I simply can't credit the idea that one of Lord Purleigh's guests would do such a thing. Not even Sir David." He puffed at the pipe, looked at me with narrowed eyes through the pale blue streamers of smoke. "I've begun to suspect that something very strange, and very sinister, is occurring here at Maplewhite."

"And what's that, Sir Arthur?"

He frowned. "I really can't say as yet. But what I should like to do, with your permission, is attempt to learn something from Running Bear tonight."

"Excuse me?" From running bare?

"Running Bear. The Spirit Guide summoned by Madame Sosostris. Her control. A Shoshone Indian chieftain who died during your French and Indian War."

"Running Bear," I said. "Right."

"You've no objection to my discussing this with him?"

"Not me," I said. "Ask him whatever you want."

"Good. I thank you."

"Don't mention it, Sir Arthur." I stood up. "Well, I'm sorry, but I've got to run myself. I need to talk to Harry about something."

"As I HEAR it, sir," said Briggs, "you're one of the Pinkertons. The American detectives, sir."

"You hear it right, Mr. Briggs," I said.

We were in the library, just the two of us, and the door was shut.

Briggs glanced toward the closed door. In only a minute or so I had learned that he could put a pretty good assortment of expressions on his pale narrow face. This one, as he looked back toward the door, was furtive. The next one, when he turned back to me, was politely inquisitive. "As I hear it, sir, you Pinkerton gentlemen have access to, um, certain discretionary funds, shall we say, sir. Money which on occasion you are permitted to, um, dispense to those individuals who come forward to assist you in your enquiries."

"We sometimes pay for information," I admitted.

"And how much, if I may ask, might you be permitted to, ah, allocate, sir?"

"That depends on the information."

"Yes, sir. Of course, sir. You were enquiring, as I recollect, about individuals who might recently have visited the late Earl?"

"That's right. You know of any, Mr. Briggs?"

"Well, sir." He made a dainty cough into his balled fist. "It would be imprudent of me, wouldn't it, sir, to impart such information as I might possess without the two of us, you and I, first coming to some general category of understanding, as one might say."

I smiled. "I could see my way to a pound."

He frowned. "Oh, that *is* a pity, sir. Because, you see, I must tell you that the, um, emolument which I myself had in mind was of a rather larger order, sir."

"How much larger?"

He glanced at the door and then back at me. "Well, to be perfectly frank, sir, I was contemplating an amount which more nearly approached the figure of, oh, shall we say five pounds, sir?"

"How do I know I can't get the information from someone else, and for free?"

"Oh no, sir," he said sadly. "No, that would be quite impossible. Inconceivable, sir. I am confident, sir, entirely so, that I am the sole owner, shall we say, of this intelligence."

"You could be wrong about that."

"I could, sir, yes. Logically speaking. But I am certain, in this particular instance, sir, that I am not."

"I can go to three pounds, Mr. Briggs. That's where I tap out."

Briggs thought about that. He studied the cut of my jacket, the length of my pants, the shine of my shoes, or the lack of one. Finally he sighed. "You have the better of me, sir, I must tell you. But very well. I accept, sir." He coughed into his fist again. "All that remains at this juncture is for the actual, um, disbursement to take place, sir."

I reached into my back pocket and tugged out my wallet. If I didn't pay him now, he'd probably keep talking like that.

I gave him three pound notes and he folded them neatly and slipped them into his jacket pocket.

"Thank you, sir," he said. "Well now, sir, what you need to know, initially, is that we have a member of the household staff named Darleen, sir . . ."

He kept talking like that anyway, and it took him a while to get everything out. But what he said, basically, was that this Darleen, one of the maids, had been secretly visiting the Earl's bedroom at night for the past few months.

I said, "And no one else knew about this, Mr. Briggs?"

"No one, sir. The young woman would bide her time, you see, until after two o'clock in the morning, and by that time Carson, the Earl's valet, was fast asleep."

"So how do you know about it?"

"Well, sir, I confess to you that until rather recently the young woman and I, well, we had a certain, ah, understanding."

"The two of you were involved."

"In a manner of speaking, sir, yes."

"And she dropped you for the Earl."

He nodded sadly. "Well, sir, it does go without saying, does it not, that an individual such as the Earl would be in a better position than I, sir, to offer the young woman inducements of, um, shall we say a financial nature?"

I nodded. "And when did this all start, Mr. Briggs?"

"Several months ago, sir. Sometime in June. Carson was ill, and Mrs. Blandings—the housekeeper, sir—sent the young woman to the Earl's room with his afternoon tea. That evening—or, I should say, early the next morning—she made her first clandestine visit."

"And the visits have been going on ever since?"

"Yes, sir. Regularly, sir."

"Every day?"

"No, sir, not so often as that. Two or three times a week, I should say."

"Up until the time the Earl died?"

"So far as I know, sir. I must tell you, sir, that the young woman and I have ceased communicating."

Beyond Briggs, in the north wall of the library, surrounded by rows of books, there was a closet or a storage room with a white wooden door. The door was slightly ajar now. It had been closed when I got here.

"Okay, Mr. Briggs," I said. "Thank you."

"You're quite welcome, sir." He gave a small bow and then he turned and sailed off. He stopped at the library entrance, opened that door, and turned back to me. "Shall I leave this opened, sir, or closed?"

"Closed," I told him.

"Very good, sir," he said, and he glided through it and pulled it shut behind him.

I reached into my coat pocket and slid out the Colt automatic and I pointed it at the door. Without bending over, I slipped off my shoes. Silently, in stocking feet, I padded around the sofa until I was about six feet from the closet door.

"Okay," I said. "You in the closet. Come on out of there."

Maplewhite, Devon

August 18 (again)

Dear Evangeline,

So much has happened, and within so few hours, that I honestly don't know where to begin.

It's really a hopeless task, Evy, scribbling these letters. Life keeps overtaking my account of it. I feel like Sisyphus, but poor Sisyphus had only a single paltry boulder to fret over, and shove about. Every time I succeed in wrestling one of my boulders up the hill (and into the post), another boulder trundles down the slope, knocks me down, and rumbles over me.

Where was I? I had just fainted gothically from my horse, I believe, at the close of the last letter. According to Mrs Corneille, I should have hurtled to the gravel pathway, had Mr Beaumont not swiftly interposed himself between me and it. He is, perhaps, rather more useful than he appears to be. (And it transpires that he is not what, since he arrived, he has claimed to be. More on this later.)

It was all a dreadful bother after that, people hovering over me and coddling me and whisking me off to bed. Mrs Corneille enlisted Dr Auerbach to examine me, which he did with a dreadful bedside manner, all fumbling thumbs and darting glances. He hasn't practiced medicine for some time, he told me; and I can easily believe him. His prognosis was certainly less than accurate: he told me that "there might be some small bruising"; in fact I am turning, rather spectacularly, into an aubergine.

Like everyone else, he asked why the horse had bolted; and I told him, as I'd told everyone else, that it had seen a snake. Psychoanalysts, as perhaps you know, are invariably fascinated by snakes, and he wanted to know what sort of snake it had been. I explained that I was not on familiar terms with snakes, and that, even if I had been, my nearsightedness made me a less-than-scrupulous observer. My eye-glasses, I explained, had been in the pocket of the riding jacket. This seemed to satisfy him.

He left; Lady Purleigh visited and was, as usual, utterly charming; I wrote another letter; the Allardyce arrived and dragged me from bed to attend tea.

I really must tell you about Cecily. I'm a perfect witch to babble about it; I've actually considered not mentioning it at all. Truly I have. But, after much serious thought, I've concluded that it's simply too savory to let slip away. Have compassion for me, Evy; I'm a doomed woman.

When the Allardyce and I were leaving our room, on our way to tea, I opened the door and discovered the Honourable Cecily standing out in the corridor with Mr Beaumont. (She was, of course, looking very smart, in a drop-waist dress of burgundy silk with billowing bishop sleeves and a draped neckline.) The two of them had evidently been arguing, and she was saying—quite loudly, almost shouting it—that she *wasn't* a nymphomaniac.

Wasn't a nymphomaniac. Isn't that astounding?

After we joined them out there, she attempted to put a good face and a plummy voice on everything, but she was transparently upset.

The two of them are having an affair, Evy. The daughter of the manor is secretly cavorting about, and with an American personal secretary (except that he's not, really, and I'll be coming to this). What other possible explanation for that remarkable announcement could there be?

Cecily is nicer, certainly, than I'd originally believed (she was really quite charming in her room); but could she actually be more *interesting?*

And doesn't her heated denial suggest to you that she was, just then, refuting an accusation? And doesn't *that* suggest to you that Mr Beaumont was, in this particular chase, the pursued and not the pursuer?

If she *is* cavorting, what on earth does she see in him? He's good-looking enough, in a sullen, lumbering, American sort of way, but altogether too smirky and arrogant for my tastes.

Socially, of course, for someone like Cecily, he is hopeless, either as a personal secretary or as a private detective. (Have I mentioned that he's a private detective?) Unless, on the other hand, he's secretly a fabulously wealthy American financier masquerading as a private detective masquerading as a personal secretary. Which, given everything else that's transpired here, is entirely possible.

What's certain is that I shall be keeping a watchful eye on Cecily, to decide whether I can go back to belittling her; or whether I shall be forced, however reluctantly, to start admiring the wench.

We shall be getting to this private detective business in a moment.

Cecily was there, at tea time, having arrived (alone) shortly after the Allardyce and me. She sat at the table with us, and with Lady Purleigh, Sir Arthur Conan Doyle, the medium Madame Sosostris, and her husband, a Mr Dempsey.

Mrs Corneille, Sir David, and Dr Auerbach sat at another table, toward the far side of the room. Mr Houdini sat away by himself, scribbling something in a notebook, and occasionally looking up to smirk in the direction of Madame Sosostris.

Mr Dempsey and she look like Jack Sprat and his wife: he is tall and gaunt and cadaverous; she is round and roly-poly, fatter even than the Allardyce. Her gaudy silk robe, and her several layers of cosmetics, make her resemble a circus clown.

What a shrew I am. I should be kinder to the woman: she is crippled, poor thing, and gets about in a wheelchair.

Sir Arthur is besotted with her. Not (I think) in any sexual or romantic way; yet still besotted. He hangs upon her every banal word, nods gravely at her every dreary observation. (Even crippled people can be banal and dreary, it seems.)

He himself is a man much taller than I expected, at least six feet, four inches in height, who resembles a retired brewer more than a famous author: big and bluff and hearty, with a huge charming smile. He seems so typically English and matter-of-fact, so solid and commonplace, that his wholehearted belief in Spiritualism struck me at first as preposterous; and then, after a time, as rather sad.

The Afterlife was the subject of discussion. Sir Arthur was

telling us that Death was no ending, but instead a wonderful doorway from this world to the next; very much, evidently, like the entrance to Harrods. In the Afterlife, he said, our existence will be substantially the same as it has been here, except that There we shall be spared all petty annoyances and physical discomforts. Which is not, as you know, altogether true of Harrods.

'But what about servants?' asked the Allardyce, who can always be relied upon to raise the level of discourse. 'There *will* be servants, won't there? There are so *many* things, after all, that one can no longer do for oneself.' Such as packing and unpacking the luggage.

Sir Arthur smiled. As I said, he has an enormously charming smile. He is, I think, a genuinely kind and good man who believes everyone else to be as fundamentally decent and honest as he is. This would naturally render him susceptible to someone like Madame Sosostris, and polite to someone like the Allardyce.

'There is no need for servants there,' he said. 'All our wants and needs will be provided us.'

All of them? I wondered, and glanced at Cecily, who was, so far as I knew, the only other potential nymphomaniac at the table. She was pensive, perhaps wondering the same.

'And we ourselves,' Sir Arthur continued, 'will be cast in new forms, strong and healthy and vibrant.' He leaned toward Madame Sosostris. 'Is that not as you understand it, madame?'

'Yaas,' she said. Her accent is odd, something Middle European, but not German, I think. 'However, if ve are do-ink t'e sort of important verk dat requires us an assistant, one vill be given for us.'

I suspect that, like the Allardyce, when she dropped anchor on the Other Shore Madame S. would be expecting someone else to unpack the luggage.

Mr Beaumont arrived in the drawing room then, and Sir Arthur brought him over to the table, for introductions. The Honourable Cecily was pointedly indifferent to the American's presence. After he left, she returned to her pensiveness. Sir Arthur returned to his Afterlife.

Suddenly, Lord Purleigh arrived. He looked harried, his white hair frazzled, his splendid moustache unkempt. He apologized to us, hurriedly, for his tardiness, and told Lady Purleigh that there had been some sort of accident in the Earl's room, that the door was inexplicably locked. He would return, he said, after obtaining the assistance of Mr Houdini and trying again. He left the room with Sir Arthur, Mr Houdini, and Mr Beaumont. At this point, Mr Beaumont was still a personal secretary.

After they left, Cecily turned to Lady Purleigh and leaned forward to put her slender hand along her mother's slender arm. 'Mummy,' she said, 'Grandpère's all right, isn't he?'

This would have sounded affected and insipid, perhaps, if not for the genuine fear in Cecily's voice.

Lady Purleigh was clearly agitated herself, but she forced a small smile and she patted Cecily's hand. 'I do hope so, darling. He *must* be, mustn't he?'

Madame Sosostris spoke. 'You need not to vorry,' she intoned. 'Vatever happens, it is part of de Great Plan. It is for de best.'

'Yes,' said Lady Purleigh, rather uncertainly. 'Yes, of course.'

Lord Purleigh returned within half an hour or so, looking very grim. He nodded abruptly to us, apologized again, and asked Lady Purleigh and Cecily to come with him for a moment. Lady Purleigh made her excuses and the three of them left the room. Cecily looked, for the first time since I've been here, confused and rather lost.

After the three of them left, for several minutes a kind of social limbo prevailed.

Have I mentioned that Lord Purleigh's father, the Earl, is bedridden? I think that with all these alarums and excursions, most of us believed that something quite awful had happened to him. No one spoke; no one, perhaps, knew what to say. The Allardyce, consumed no doubt by worry, consumed a smoked salmon sandwich.

When he returned, alone, Lord Purleigh looked even grimmer than he had before. He stalked across the drawing room, spoke softly for a moment to the people at Mrs Corneille's table. They all arose and followed him over to us, everyone moving silently. Apprehension seemed to congeal in the air. Some chairs were arranged, and we were transmuted from an afternoon tea into a solemn audience, with Lord Purleigh as the solitary, somber performer.

He was still standing, very formal, his hands held tautly at his sides. "Wanted to tell all of you," he said. "Been a bit of an accident. My father, the Earl. Wounded himself. Gun went off. Potting at pigeons. Nothing serious, mind. Scratch, really. Barely broke the skin. Alice and Cecily, they're attending to it. Won't be long. Forgive them their absence, eh? Stay here, if you like. Return to your rooms, wander about. As you like. Dinner will be served at the usual time."

There was a kind of soft, general letting out of breath, as though the room itself were sighing with relief.

Lord Purleigh nodded once, briskly, and then turned away, about to leave. He caught himself and turned back. 'There is, sorry to say, one further unpleasantness.' He paused, and a shadow passed across his face. 'That rifle shot of yesterday.' He looked toward me, with what I flatter myself was kindness. 'I had believed it fired by a poacher.' He addressed the crowd. 'Turns out I was mistaken. One of my guests, Mr Houdini, is being stalked by a madman. From all accounts, he was the fellow fired the shot. But there's no cause for alarm. Some police will be arriving from Amberly shortly.'

'But Robert,' said the Allardyce, 'who *is* this man?'

A tartness came over Lord Purleigh's face. 'A stage magician. Rival of Houdini's. Fellow named Chin Soo.'

'A *Chinaman?*' exclaimed the Allardyce.

Tart became bitter. 'No, not a Chinaman,' he said. 'Chin Soo's a stage name. We don't really know much more about him.' His face softened. 'Not to worry, though. Everything's under control. Police'll be here soon. And, as it happens, Mr Houdini's secretary is actually a Pinkerton.' He said this rapidly, as though it were an embarrassment he wished to move quickly beyond.

This was not to be, of course, so long as the Allardyce was present. 'A what?' she said.

'A private detective,' he said, impatience flaring out briefly.

'An enquiry agent, from America. Assigned to protect Mr Houdini.'

I wondered if Cecily knew. Would Mr Beaumont have told her?

'Now,' Lord Purleigh said, 'if you'll excuse me.' He turned and strode away.

As soon as he was gone, the Allardyce looked around herself like an anxious walrus on an ice floe. 'Chin *Soo?*' she said.

'Gesundheit,' said Sir David.

As I said before, he can be clever; he's simply not so clever as he thinks he is. No human being possibly could be.

'Oh David,' said Mrs Corneille wearily. 'This is not the time.'

'On the contrary,' he said, smiling that infuriating ironic smile of his. 'Nothing eases tension like a bit of drollery, don't you think?' He turned to Dr Auerbach. 'This would be the ideal moment for one of your English jokes, Doctor.'

I have no idea what he meant by this. Dr Auerbach had told me no jokes, certainly, English or otherwise, while he was conducting his examination. Whatever Sir David might have meant, Dr Auerbach smiled and shook his head slightly. 'I am thinking not, Sir David.'

Sir David returned to Mrs Corneille. 'Well,' he said, 'I must say that I'm not surprised to learn about Beaumont. He always struck me as rather shifty and seedy, exactly the sort to be prying into people's private affairs.'

Mrs Corneille looked at him. 'Why should that trouble *you,* David?' she said. 'Your own affairs are seldom private.'

'Ah, Vanessa,' he said. 'I race neck and neck with my reputation. But inevitably it precedes me.' An intolerable man.

'But Sir David,' said the Allardyce, 'do you *really* think it wise for us to remain here? I mean to say, if there's a *madman* running loose in the neighbourhood . . .'

'There frequently is,' he said. 'This is England, after all.'

'Yes, but are we *safe* here, do you think?'

'Safe?' He pretended to consider this, and finally he said, with great seriousness, 'No, on balance I shouldn't think so.'

'Sir David is playing with you, Mrs Allardyce,' said Mrs Corneille. 'Of course we're safe here. Lord Purleigh shouldn't have said so if it weren't true.'

'No,' said the Allardyce, blinking. She pressed her hand against her bosom, or against that portion of it that could be covered by a single hand. 'Certainly he wouldn't. Certainly.' She blinked again, patted herself again, looked vaguely around the room. 'Oh dear,' she said, again to no one in particular, 'I suppose I must go find poor Alice. She'll be needing the comfort of her *family* now.'

And with that she got up and waddled vaguely away. I left shortly afterward, and came up here, to my room.

I'm exhausted, Evy, and sore all over. My bruises are throbbing. I'll drop this in the post box and then try to get some rest. I'll write again later, after dinner. And after the séance!

All my love,
Jane

Chapter Twenty-three

THE CLOSET DOOR swung open. Mrs. Corneille stepped out in her white dress, her sleek black hair swaying along her shoulders. She saw the gun in my hand and she smiled. "You're not going to shoot me, I hope."

I put the gun away. "You saw me drop that piece of paper," I said. "Out on the patio."

"Yes," she said. "And I read it." Her smile faded and she lifted her elegant chin. "Alice is a good friend of mine. I shouldn't want you or anyone else to harm her. It seemed to me that if you were having secret meetings with one of her servants, someone ought to be there to represent her interests."

"You think her interests are in jeopardy?"

"Not at all. But she might need looking after."

"You feel better now?"

"Not remarkably so." Suddenly she frowned. "Oh dear, what *time* is it?"

I pulled out my watch. "Twenty minutes to eight."

"I'd forgotten—dinner. I must run and change." She crossed the carpet, put her hand along my arm, looked up at me with those big black eyes. "Come to my room tonight," she said urgently. "After the séance. We'll discuss this."

"Sure," I said.

THE GREAT MAN'S door was still shut when I got back to the suite. As I crossed the room, I stripped off my jacket and flung it to the bed. I knocked on his door and tugged loose the knot of my tie. "Harry."

I pulled the tie from my neck, balled it up, threw it to the bed.

I started unbuttoning my shirt. I rapped my knuckles at the door again. "Harry?"

His voice came through the door. "Phil? Are you alone out there?"

"I brought along a tuba player. Does that count?" I tore off the shirt, balled it, fired it at the bed.

"Are you alone, Phil?"

"Yeah, Harry, I'm alone."

The door opened a notch and the Great Man stuck his head out. He glanced at me, glanced around the room like a pickpocket at a policemen's ball. He looked back at me. "She is gone," he said.

"Who's gone?"

He jerked open the door and darted into my room, his gray eyes wide. He was wearing his dinner jacket and a crisp black bow tie. He had brushed his hair back, and pomaded it, but it still cropped out from his temples like clumps of steel wool. Quickly, he glanced around again. "Where have you *been,* Phil?"

I unbuckled my belt. "I told you. Snooping around. Who's gone?"

"Cecily Fitzwilliam. She was *here.*"

I stepped out of my pants, flung them onto the bed. "What'd she want?"

"She *said* she wanted to talk to you. But she wouldn't go away, Phil. She kept pounding on the door, demanding that I open it."

I stalked over to the wardrobe. "But you didn't, right?"

"Of course not." Indignant.

"Good for you, Harry." I snatched a clean shirt from the hanger, put it on.

"Why is this woman harassing me?"

"Maybe she's still smitten," I told him. I took out the dress pants and the suspenders, both of them rented in London, and buttoned the suspenders to the back of the pants.

"Phil, you said this would not happen again."

"I'll talk to her, Harry," I said.

* * *

THE MOOD AT dinner was strained. No one was supposed to know that the Earl was dead, but I think that everyone did, except maybe Mrs. Allardyce, and maybe Miss Turner. Lord Bob never showed—Lady Purleigh said that he wasn't feeling well. She was wearing a regal black dress that could have been a mourning dress, if you wanted it to be, or just a regal black dress, if you didn't. She looked tired, but from time to time she smiled, a fragile smile, and from time to time she encouraged this guest or that one to talk. Some of them tried for a while, chattering away until they heard the sound of their own voices echo in the surrounding silence. And then they slowed down, like sightseers nearing the lip of a chasm, and then suddenly they stopped.

Miss Turner never said a word. She again only sat there and glanced around the table. Whenever she caught me catching her at it, her glance skittered away. I wondered what went on beyond that bright blue dazzle.

I think that everyone was worried that too much enthusiasm would bother Lady Purleigh.

Everyone except Mrs. Allardyce and the Great Man. The Great Man's conversations were usually monologues, even in better times, and he had never in his life worried about bothering anyone. Mrs. Allardyce kept feeding him questions, and he kept giving the rest of us his answers. He told us about his incredible dip beneath the ice in the Detroit River. He told us about his incredible escape from the prison wagon in Moscow. He told us about his incredible single-handed airplane flight in Germany in 1909, and his incredible award-winning flight in 1910 in Australia, the first ever in that country. The airplane stories were mostly true.

Almost all the guests listened politely, even Madame Sosostris and Mr. Dempsey—and both of them had to know that the Great Man was there to prove she was a fake.

But not Sir David. He scowled occasionally, or looked deliberately away. Now and then he leaned toward Mrs. Corneille, who sat beside him, and whispered something. Whatever it was, usually she frowned at it, or ignored it. Once he whispered while she was cutting a bite of roast beef, and she froze in mid-cut and turned to him with a stony look and spoke quickly under her breath. He smiled, blandly, and ate another forkful of creamed peas.

It seemed to me that trouble was coming, but I knew there wasn't much I could do about it until it arrived. If it did.

I hadn't had a chance to talk to Cecily alone. But she didn't seem very anxious to talk to me. She spent most of her time watching the Great Man. Like her mother, she smiled wanly but in all the right places.

The trouble arrived in the drawing room. We were all sitting around at different tables. Doyle, smoking his pipe, was telling me about the afterlife, and how life was better there. On Doyle's right, Sir David and Dr. Auerbach and Mr. Dempsey were sitting with Lady Purleigh, Mrs. Corneille, and Madame Sosostris. On my left, the Great Man was telling Mr. Dempsey, Mrs. Allardyce, and Miss Turner about his stomach.

"Years of conditioning," he said, "have turned Houdini's muscles into steel." He stood up and yanked open his dinner jacket. Doyle and I looked over. "Here," the Great Man said to Mrs. Allardyce. He nodded toward his stomach. "Go ahead. Hit me."

Mrs. Allardyce sat there. "I beg your pardon?" she said.

I saw Sir David put his cigar in his mouth, watching.

"Hit me," said the Great Man. "Feel free."

The others were watching, all of them. I was watching Sir David.

Mrs. Allardyce blinked again. "You want me to strike you?"

"Yes, of course," said the Great Man. "As a demonstration."

Mrs. Allardyce blinked some more. "But really," she said. "I *couldn't.*"

"But I could," said Sir David. He set his cigar in the ashtray and stood up. "With great pleasure." He was almost a foot taller than the Great Man.

"Ah," said the Great Man, still holding open his dinner jacket. He smiled. He was pleased. This was a chance to prove his superiority over someone he still thought was vermin. "Feel free to hit as hard—"

Sir David rammed his right fist into the Great Man's stomach, pivoting on the ball of his left foot, slamming the weight of his heavy shoulder behind the punch. Hissing, the Great Man doubled over and grabbed at his belly.

Doyle pushed himself up from his chair. "Now see here!"

Sir David stepped back, smiling. The Great Man hung there, bent forward, clutching himself. Sir David said to Doyle, "It was his idea, after all."

"But he wasn't prepared!" said Doyle.

The Great Man abruptly threw out his right arm and held it there, parallel to the carpet. For a moment no one spoke. Holding his left hand to his stomach, he slowly raised his torso until he was fully upright. He let both his arms fall to his sides. His face was white and shiny.

But when he smiled, his smile seemed perfectly normal. "Sir Arthur is correct," he said to Sir David. "I was unprepared."

His voice was slightly higher than normal, but no one could hear the difference unless they knew him well. "So," he said, "if you do not object, we shall not count that punch." He drew back his jacket, put his balled fists on his hips. "Now," he said.

Sir David smiled at the Great Man. "I should tell you," he said, "that I got my Blue for boxing when I was up at Oxford."

"That," said the Great Man, "is completely irrelevant."

Sir David planted his feet on the carpet like a lumberjack, drew back his right arm, and then hauled off and let go, knifing his fist into the Great Man's midsection.

The Great Man's upper body moved forward a bit, and I think that his feet skidded a few inches backward on the carpet. But he didn't move otherwise. His smile hadn't wavered. He said, "You see? Like steel."

From the women came a smattering of applause. I glanced over to see who was clapping. Lady Purleigh, Cecily, Miss Turner.

"Wunderbar!" cried Dr. Auerbach.

"Well done!" said Doyle.

Sir David frowned. He pounded his right fist into his left palm. "Once more," he said.

"Nope," I said. I stood up, and he turned to face me. The two of us were the same height. "You already had your shot," I said. "Two shots. Next time, try it with someone who might hit back."

Sir David grinned and pounded his fist into his palm again. "You, for example, Beaumont?"

"For example."

"No, no," said Doyle suddenly, and he stepped forward, putting his body between Sir David and me. He looked back and forth between us. "I won't have this. Not in Lady Purleigh's house. And certainly not on the night of a séance."

Sir David smiled blandly. "You heard him, Doyle. He challenged me."

"As any right-minded man *would've* done. Sir David, you oblige me to say that your behavior has been deplorable. I ask you to remember yourself, sir, and remember what is proper."

Sir David raised his handsome jaw. "The man has challenged me."

"There will be no violence here tonight," said Doyle.

For a moment or two, Sir David looked like a man who was thinking about taking a pop at Sir Arthur Conan Doyle. Then he nodded. Casually, he adjusted the fit of his coat. "As you wish," he said. "Not tonight. I shall be delighted to meet with him at any other time." He looked over at me and smiled. "Unless Beaumont would care to withdraw his challenge?"

"I don't think so," I said.

"Tomorrow morning, then?" he said. "At seven, shall we say?" He turned to Doyle. "And let it be a *proper* match, by all means," he said. "You may referee, if you like."

Doyle thought about that. It had caught him by surprise, but you could see that a part of him liked the idea. He looked from Sir David to me, and back again, as though he were trying to gauge our respective weights and potential skills. I think that probably, when he was younger, he'd done a bit of boxing himself. He turned to me. "Mr. Beaumont, what do you say to that?"

"Fine with me."

He looked back at Sir David. He frowned. "But of course this isn't for me to decide." He turned. "Lady Purleigh, the decision is yours. Would you object to two of your guests engaging in a brief boxing match tomorrow morning?"

Lady Purleigh didn't hesitate. She looked from me to Sir David. "Do you both wish this?"

Sir David smiled. "Most acutely," he said.

I said, "Yes."

She nodded. "I shall permit it," she said, "on three conditions. The first is that, my permission having been given, the two of you will forget about this affair for the remainder of the evening. You will dismiss it from your minds, both of you, so that we may all proceed with the séance. The second is that after the event, whatever its conclusion, this matter is ended. Both the victor and the defeated will accept the outcome. Do you agree to these conditions, Mr. Beaumont?"

"Sure," I said.

"Do you, Sir David?" she asked him.

He gave her a single small nod. "I do."

Doyle spoke. "You said three conditions, Lady Purleigh?"

"Yes." She smiled. "The third being that this competition does not take place anywhere near the garden. We have trouble enough with the flower beds as it is."

Doyle smiled. "I think we can promise you that we won't disturb the flower beds, Lady Purleigh."

"Very well, then," she said. "Permission is granted."

Doyle turned to Sir David. "Marquis of Queensberry rules?"

He nodded. "Without the gloves, of course."

"Yes," said Doyle, frowning. "Of course. We haven't any." He turned to me. "You object to their absence?"

"No," I said.

"Ten rounds," said Doyle to Sir David. "With me to decide the winner."

"Ten rounds," said Sir David. "But I doubt that deciding the winner will be an especially taxing process."

Doyle looked at me. "You agree to ten rounds?"

"Sure."

"Right, then," said Doyle. "Seven o'clock tomorrow morning." He rubbed his big hands together. "And now," he said, "for the séance."

Chapter Twenty-four

UNDER DOYLE'S DIRECTION, the men moved three rectangular coffee tables together into the center of the drawing room and then set chairs around them. Once or twice, while both of us were lugging chairs, Sir David glanced over at me and blandly smiled. Whatever he'd promised Lady Purleigh, I didn't think that he'd dismissed tomorrow's fight from his mind. But then I hadn't dismissed it from mine.

There were thirteen of us, and Lady Purleigh arranged us around the tables so that the men alternated with the women. I sat down next to Cecily. She glanced at me as if she had never seen me before and didn't expect to see me again. Sir Arthur sat to Cecily's left. To Sir Arthur's left, at the head of the table, sat Madame Sosostris and her husband, Mr. Dempsey. After Mr. Dempsey came Lady Purleigh herself, and then Sir David. After Sir David, and opposite me, came Mrs. Allardyce and then Dr. Auerbach. On the doctor's left, and at the table end opposite Madame Sosostris, sat Miss Turner and the Great Man. To the Great Man's left sat Mrs. Corneille and her perfume. I was the one sitting to her left.

Lady Purleigh had rung for a servant. The man who arrived was short and heavyset and his name was Parsons. At Doyle's request, he pulled the entrance doors shut, drew the thick curtains over the mullioned windows, and then marched across the carpets clicking off electric lights.

The séance was what we had all come here for, and no one said anything as the air grew more dusky, click by click. I looked at the Great Man. He was smiling at Madame Sosostris. I looked at Miss Turner. She had been watching me, and her glance skipped away. I looked at Mrs. Corneille. She looked back at me and smiled.

Finally there was only one lamp left, burning on a table that stood at the base of a tapestry. Shadows streamed along the floor and pooled in the corners of the room.

Doyle asked Parsons to sit down beside the lamp and wait, and then he turned to Madame Sosostris. "Madame?" he said.

Madame Sosostris's hair was the same tonight, a white thicket above her round white face, but she was wearing a different silk gown. This one was black and shiny and spangled with golden astrological signs. Her hands, small and plump and jeweled, were perched along the wooden arms of her wheelchair. Slowly, in the hazy gray, she looked around the table like a general inspecting his troops. The glance from her shrewd dark eyes met the glance of each of us, one by one, before it moved on. Her glance didn't waver when it met the Great Man's.

Finally she spoke. "T'e first t'ing you must all to understand," she said, her heavy jowls quivering, "is t'at once we have, all of us, in the circle wit' our hands toget'er joined, we must not to break t'e circle. Yas?"

Doyle translated. "Once we join our hands," he said, surveying the table, "we must not break the circle. This could be dangerous."

"Yas," said Madame Sosostris. "The second t'ing. At t'e beginning, my husband will be to asking t'e questions for Running Bear. Afterwards, others may to speak wit' him."

"Initially," said Doyle, "Mr. Dempsey will ask the questions of Running Bear, Madame's Spirit Guide. When Running Bear gives his permission, the rest of us may ask what we like."

"Yas," said Madame Sosostris. "Now. We will all to join our hands toget'er, pliss."

I took Mrs. Corneille's left hand. It was small and cool and soft. She smiled at me, then turned to the Great Man and offered him her right. He took it, but he was still studying Madame Sosostris, and still enjoying himself.

I turned to Cecily, reached for her right hand. She gave it to me and looked away. Her fingers were warm. Suddenly they made a quick squeeze against mine, and her sharp little fingernails nipped into my palm. She was still looking away.

"Yas," said Madame Sosostris. "Now we are ready."

"Parsons?" said Doyle. "The lights, please, if you will."

The light clicked off, the room was suddenly black. Cecily squeezed my hand. Her thumb stroked my little finger. Her nails nipped at my palm. It seemed to me that Cecily wasn't throwing herself into this séance business the way she was supposed to.

Then, out of the total darkness, came a droning sound. Madame Sosostris had begun to make a kind of hum. It was a drawn-out single note, low and stony and unwavering, and it went on for a long time. Then it stopped. She made a deep raspy noise, like a broken snore, and she was silent.

And then things started happening. A small bell rang, from far away. Cecily's hand clenched at mine. Something rapped at a table. Once, twice, three times. Some heavy chains clattered somewhere nearby. A sudden trumpet blared, and Mrs. Corneille's hand tightened on mine but relaxed almost immediately. Then there was a soft swishing sound, and then a quick muffled rattling, and the air was suddenly laced with the smell of flowers. Cecily jerked her hand from mine and said, *"Ouch!"*

"Parsons," called out Doyle, "the light, please."

The light clicked on. Someone hissed, sucking in a breath.

The tops of all three tables were strewn with roses, covered with them, maybe fifty or sixty flowers. Heavy blossoms, dark red and looking almost black in the muted light. Each was attached to a leafy, thorny stem about a foot long.

At the head of the table, Madame Sosostris flipped open her eyes. "Someone has broken t'e circle!"

"It *hit* me," Cecily pouted. She held up a rose as proof, and then peered at it more carefully. She raised her eyes toward the ceiling, puzzled, and then she turned to her mother. "But how could *that* be?"

Lady Purleigh smiled faintly, shook her head. "I don't know, darling." She turned to Madame Sosostris.

"Please, my good girl," said Madame Sosostris to Cecily. "You must not to break t'e circle."

I looked at the Great Man. He was smirking.

I was still holding Mrs. Corneille's hand. She was staring at the roses. She felt my glance, turned to me, arched her eyebrows, smiled.

"Now," said Madame Sosostris. "We will to try again, yas? We will all to join our hands toget'er."

Cecily made a face and tossed the rose to the table. She narrowed her mouth and she curled her fingers around my hand in a death grip.

Doyle called out, "The light, please, Parsons."

The light clicked off.

In the dark, Madame Sosostris hummed again, and snored again. The bell rang. The table rapped. The chains rattled, the trumpet blew.

Then someone said, "Ugh." A low voice, masculine, smoky, nothing like the voice of Madame Sosostris. Cecily tightened her grip around my fingers.

Mr. Dempsey spoke. "Running Bear? Are you here?"

"Ugh," said the voice. "It is Running Bear, come to speak."

Cecily squeezed. My fingers were beginning to feel like grapes in a wine press. Somewhere along the table, someone stirred.

"Greetings," said Mr. Dempsey. "We're pleased that you could join us tonight."

"Running Bear comes to the aid of those who seek."

This was pretty good English for Madame Sosostris. It was also pretty good English for a dead Shoshone Indian.

"Running Bear," said Mr. Dempsey, "is there someone present you want to talk to?"

"Ugh. I will touch her. But do not break the circle."

Suddenly Mrs. Corneille's hand jumped within mine.

Mr. Dempsey spoke. "Did Running Bear touch someone?"

"I was touched," said Mrs. Corneille. Her voice was flat.

"Don't be frightened," said Mr. Dempsey. "Running Bear is a being of great kindness. Open yourself to him now, and he'll speak to you. Open yourself."

"You worry," said Running Bear, "for many moons about the death of your brave, Gerard, who passed over during the Great Destruction. I tell you now that the worry may stop. He is at peace. He salutes you in love."

"I see," said Mrs. Corneille, in the same flat tone.

"Open yourself," said Mr. Dempsey, "and Running Bear will comfort you."

"I'm feeling quite open, thank you," said Mrs. Corneille.

"There is another loved one," said Running Bear. "Your young daughter. Esme. She of the golden hair."

Mrs. Corneille's hand clutched at mine, just for an instant.

"She is well also," said Running Bear. "She is happy, there by the banks of the Shining Water. She salutes you in love."

"Thank you," said Mrs. Corneille. Her voice was still flat. But—maybe I imagined it—it also seemed a little shaky, as though she were hammering it flat with force of will.

"Running Bear?" said Mr. Dempsey.

"Ugh?"

"Sir Arthur Conan Doyle wishes to speak."

"I greet Sir Arthur Conan Doyle."

"Good evening, Running Bear," said Doyle conversationally. They had talked before, they were old pals. "How are you?"

"Running Bear is unhappy."

"And why might that be?"

"There has been a death in this house."

Someone moved, somewhere along the table. Mrs. Allardyce said, *"What?"*

"Please," said Doyle sharply. "Don't break the circle. Running Bear?"

"Ugh."

"You know, then, of the death that took place here."

"Ugh. The Elder One has passed over. Running Bear gives much sympathy to his family."

"Thank you. Could you give us any assurances, I wonder, as to whether the Earl is at peace?"

"The Earl's *died?"* said Mrs. Allardyce.

"Please," snapped Doyle. "Running Bear?"

"Running Bear cannot do this thing."

"Why is that?"

"The spirit of the Elder One is troubled. He lived a life of greed and lust. In recent times he imposed his sick desires on an innocent young woman. Now he has seen the error of his ways. He is poisoned by guilt. His spirit is tortured."

"And was it for this reason," said Doyle, slowly and cautiously, like a hunter following spoor, "that he ended his life?"

"The Elder One did not end his life. His life was taken."

"By restless spirits?" said Doyle. There was excitement in his voice now, the hunter cornering his prey. "By elemental forces?"

Suddenly the doors to the drawing room swung open and smashed against the walls. A bar of light toppled onto the table and all at once we were blinking at each other.

A stocky figure stood in silhouette at the doorway, its right shoulder slumped against the jamb. "What *is* this?"

A commanding aristocratic voice, testy but blurred. Lord Bob.

"The light, please, Parsons," said Doyle.

The light clicked on.

"Lord Purleigh," said Doyle, and stood.

Lord Bob was looking a little testy and blurred himself. His collar was askew. His necktie drooped outside his vest, and the vest bulged where a button had hooked into the wrong hole. His eyes were puffy, his white hair and his bushy white eyebrows were rumpled. "What *is* this?" he said again, and tugged loose from the doorjamb. He overbalanced, then righted himself, tottering. He squinted toward us. "Bloody séance, is it? Bad form. Damnably bad form, I must say."

Lady Purleigh stood up. So did the rest of the men, joining Doyle on foot. "Robert, darling," she said. She spoke as though she were talking to a small child.

"But *Alice,*" he said. He scowled and shook his head. "Never do, my love. Never do. No respect. Old swine only kicked the bucket this afternoon. Not even *buried* yet." He took a step, swayed, then glared around the room. "What happened to the bloody lights? Dark as pitch in here."

"Parsons?" said Lady Purleigh. "Please see to the lights."

Parsons scurried around the carpets. Click by click the room grew brighter.

Lord Bob took another unsteady step. He was staring at the flowers scattered around the tabletops. He lowered his brow.

"Someone been mucking about in the garden? Not the bloody police, was it?"

"Robert," said Lady Purleigh gently.

Lord Bob tugged at his vest and eyed us gravely. "Terribly sorry, ladies and gentlemen. The party is over." He waved his arms up through the air and almost collapsed backward.

Lady Purleigh sighed.

"Steady as she goes," said Lord Bob, and pulled himself upright. He tugged down his vest again. "Witching hour has arrived, I'm afraid. Bedtime. No ghosts, no phantoms, no spookey-wookies. Abandon ship. Disengage. Retreat." He swept his arm toward the door, but swung too far and aimed his wavering finger at a tapestry on the wall. "Fall back, lads!"

"I apologize," said Lady Purleigh, looking around the table. "My husband is unwell."

"Far from it!" said Lord Bob, spinning to face her, overspinning, then correcting his spin. He straightened up. "I am *pissed,*" he announced. "Your husband, my love, is as pissed as a bloody lord." Suddenly he grinned proudly and adjusted the lapels of his suitcoat. "I really *am* a bloody lord, you know. I really am, now the old swine's gone belly up."

"Lady Purleigh," said Doyle softly.

Lady Purleigh shook her head wearily. "It's quite all right, Sir Arthur." She looked around the table. "As you've all just learned, my father-in-law has died today. My husband and I were hoping to spare you any distress."

"Bloody right," said Lord Bob, and waved his arm. "Didn't come here for a bloody funeral, did you? Eh?"

"I apologize to you all," said Lady Purleigh. "But, if you don't mind, I'm afraid that we should, all of us, retire just now. We shall see you at breakfast."

"Call it a night," said Lord Bob, nodding.

Lady Purleigh turned to Madame Sosostris. "I apologize in particular, to you, madame."

"Not at all, my lady," she said. She wrapped her plump jeweled fingers around the wheels of her chair and rolled herself back a few feet. "Pliss," she said to Mr. Dempsey. "We are to going now."

"Splendid to see you," Lord Bob told her merrily. "Must do this again sometime, eh?"

Doyle said, "Lady Purleigh?"

She turned to him. "Sir Arthur?"

"Perhaps we should cancel the boxing match?"

"Eh?" said Lord Bob.

"I shall explain, Robert." Lady Purleigh turned to Doyle. "I see no reason to cancel it, Sir Arthur. If you have a moment, we can discuss the arrangements." She looked around the table. "Good night to you all. We shall see you at breakfast."

"Boxing match?" said Lord Bob.

Beside me, Mrs. Corneille stood. She leaned toward me and whispered. "Twelve-thirty."

People were moving. From across the table, Sir David called out, "Beaumont."

I turned.

He smiled. "In the morning, then."

"See you," I said.

The Morning Post

Maplewhite, Devon

August 19 (early morning)

Dear Evangeline,

A few more boulders have landed.

First off, the Earl of Axminster, who was merely wounded at tea time, was dead at dinner.

I shouldn't make light of it, I know; Lord and Lady Purleigh were apparently keeping the death secret as a kindness to their guests. I do feel badly for both of them. They're such wonderful people, admirable in every way. Why is that tragedy always slashes out at those who will most intensely feel it, and ignores those who would be insensible to its presence if it toppled onto them from the roof of a barn? Or is this, as Mrs Applewhite would have said, one of those foolish questions which contain their own answers?

From what the Allardyce was able to pry out of Lady Purleigh, after the séance, the Earl committed suicide, but Lady Purleigh cannot imagine why. Perhaps the schedule of events here at Maplewhite was simply too much for him.

Dinner was dreadful. Neither the Allardyce nor I knew, at the time, of the Earl's death; but I suspect that all the others did. No one said much of anything, except for the Allardyce, who flirted shamelessly with Mr Houdini, and for Mr Houdini, who regaled us with several seemingly endless stories the hero of which was invariably himself.

Things rather livened up afterward, however, in the drawing room. Sir David stuck Mr Houdini in the stomach, and then very badly wanted to strike Mr Beaumont, almost anywhere on his person, I expect; but Sir Arthur intervened. Sir David and Mr Beaumont will battle it out tomorrow morning. Fisticuffs at dawn. Sir Arthur will act as referee.

As to the séance, it was moderately interesting as well, until Lord Purleigh appeared and made a terrible scene. The poor man was clearly deranged with shock, and not a little inebriated.

It was at the séance that I learned of the Earl's death. Roly-poly Madame Sosostris, masquerading as her Red Indian Spirit Guide, revealed the truth. No doubt she bribed it loose from one of the servants.

You'll notice that I've become rather blasé about all this. I am becoming a woman of the world, Evy. Death, deceit, ghosts, goblins, boulders, maskings and unmaskings: they bounce off my back like water off a burnished duck.

Madame Sosostris did say something curious this evening, during the séance, and it has given me an idea. I am going to investigate.

The time is nearly one o'clock; the house is hushed, no one is moving.

It's unmannerly of me, I know, to go prowling about Maplewhite in the dark, on my own. But already, and especially after today's spectacular display of horsemanship, my reputation is so crippled that no additional eccentricity could possibly maim it further. Moreover, I'll be bringing along this letter, enveloped and addressed and stamped. Should someone be lurking in the hallways, I shall simply explain that I was swept from bed by an urgent need to plump this into the post box.

It isn't much of a plan, I realize; but then I'm not much of a planner. I *am* exceedingly weary of being acted upon. And tonight I will act.

So, Evy: the game is afoot!

All my love,
Jane

Chapter Twenty-five

FRAUD ALWAYS BROUGHT out the best in the Great Man. Back in my room, he was in dandy form. For nearly an hour he sat on my bed and laughed and snickered. Now and then he waved his arms. He explained all the tricks that Madame Sosostris had performed during the séance, and then he explained them all again.

"She is an *absolute* amateur, Phil," he said. He was still wearing his dinner jacket but he had taken off his shoes. His legs were crossed like a yogi's and he was tilted cheerfully toward me. "A twelve-year-old child could produce more spectacular effects."

"Right," I said from my chair by the desk. I hauled out my watch. Quarter to twelve. "Harry," I said. "Look, I'm sorry, but I'm exhausted."

"That bell!" he said, and laughed. "And those chains!" He waved his arms. "Clanging chains! Phil, over thirty years ago, when I gave my own performance as a medium, I refused to use the clanging chains. Imagine, Phil. They were passé even then."

"Right, Harry. But—"

"And did you like her Spirit Guide?" He lowered his head and lowered his voice—"Running Bear, him come to aid of those who seek. *Ugh.* Ha!" He curled up his body and slapped at his thigh.

I smiled. "Harry, listen . . ."

"I cannot wait," he said, "to tell Sir Arthur what I think."

"Maybe Sir Arthur won't be as thrilled as you are."

He looked at me and he frowned. "No. Perhaps not." He raised his head. "But the truth must prevail, Phil."

"Uh-huh. Meantime, Harry, I need some rest. I've got a big day tomorrow."

"What?" He sat up. "Oh yes, yes, of course! Your famous boxing match with Sir David! Phil, I must tell you, you were very impressive, standing up to that man for my sake."

"Doing my job, Harry. Guarding the body."

"But it was unnecessary, you know. I was suffering not at all."

"You, maybe. I was getting a pain in the neck."

He grinned happily. "The man is a pig, is he not, Phil? Tomorrow, when you fight your great battle, you must teach him to mind his manners." Sitting there on the bed he mimed a prize-fighter, fists jabbing at the air. "Pow, pow," he said. "Take that, Sir David! Ha ha!"

Suddenly he raised a finger in the air. "Phil," he said, "I have it!"

"Have what?"

Excited, he clasped his hands over his knees and he leaned forward. "Tomorrow morning, when you go to the scene of the combat, I will come along as your—how do they call it? Yes, your *second*. How would that be, Phil? *Houdini* will be your second!"

He said this as if it were the biggest favor he could possibly do for me. Maybe it was. The Great Man was never second to anyone, in anything.

"That'd be great, Harry," I told him.

Smoothly, in what looked like a single movement, his legs untied themselves and his hands slapped against the mattress and he bounded off the bed. "But now you must conserve your strength, eh? You must sleep, Phil. Would you like to borrow some ear wax?"

I smiled. He meant the beeswax he used as plugs. "No thanks."

"You are sure? Perhaps a blindfold?"

"No thanks, Harry."

He bent over and scooped up both his shoes in his right hand, fingers hooked beneath the tongues. He padded lightly across the room and clapped me on the shoulder. "Very well. But you must rest, Phil. It is an important business, this fight. Everyone will be there."

"My audience," I said.

"Exactly, yes!" He squeezed my shoulder and then dropped his arm, beaming at me like a proud father.

"Everyone but Lord Bob, probably," I said.

"Lord Purleigh," he corrected, sadness in his voice. "Poor Lord Purleigh. The death of his father has affected him deeply."

"Yeah."

"Tomorrow, no doubt, he will feel terrible about his behavior tonight."

"He'll feel terrible anyway. He put away a quart of brandy this afternoon. And more, maybe, later on."

"Alcohol," he said, and shook his head. "It destroys muscle tissue, you know. Eats it away, like sulfuric acid."

"I've heard that, yeah."

"Well," he smiled, and clapped me on the shoulder again. "To bed then, eh? Pleasant dreams, Phil."

"You too, Harry."

"Ugh," he said. "Ha ha." Cackling, shaking his head, he padded from the room.

I waited on the bed. In ten minutes, I heard him finish in the bathroom. In another fifteen, I heard his snoring start in the bedroom. At twelve-thirty, I got up and left.

"COME IN," SAID Mrs. Corneille. I stepped in and she shut the door.

I was still wearing my rented dinner jacket. She was wearing her red robe, its dark silk looking sleek and bright below the bright sleek spill of black hair. Between the scarlet neck of the robe and the marble neck of Mrs. Corneille, on both sides, ran a slender frill of black lace nightgown. She wasn't wearing a corset beneath the nightgown, or much of anything else.

"Please," she said, "do sit down." She indicated a small love seat along the wall, braced by two end tables. "May I pour you a brandy?"

"Sure," I said. "Thanks."

I sat.

This room, which was a bedroom in the suite I shared, and in the suite shared by Mrs. Allardyce and Miss Turner, was a kind of parlor here. Off to the left was the door that led to her bedroom.

The furniture here was just as old as the furniture in mine, but it was light and feminine, with a lot of fluffs and flounces and floral patterns. There were old paintings on the walls—misty landscapes and pictures of vases filled with flowers. There were more flowers, maybe just as old, embroidered into the carpets on the floor. And more of them, older still, embroidered into the scent of her perfume.

She poured brandy from a pale green bottle into two snifters that sat on a dark wood sideboard. She set down the bottle, lifted the snifters, and carried them over. She stepped lightly around the coffee table and she handed me a snifter and sat down on my left. She moved like someone who had practiced moving, years ago, until she got it exactly right and then never needed to think about it ever again.

She sat with her body leaning slightly toward the room and her knees together beneath the robe. "To the late Earl," she said, and raised her glass.

I raised mine. "To the Earl." I sipped at the brandy. "You knew he was dead," I said. "Before the séance."

"Alice told me." She lowered the snifter to her lap and held it with both hands. "Are you really planning to fight with David tomorrow morning?"

"Looks like it."

"You feel that this is absolutely necessary?"

"It is now."

"I've heard that David's a very good boxer."

"He probably is."

"And what does Mr. Houdini think about this?"

"He thinks it'll be a swell performance."

She raised an eyebrow. "He isn't concerned for you?"

"Everything Harry does, he does better than anyone in the world. He probably thinks that I wouldn't have gotten into this unless I could pull it off."

"And can you?"

"I guess we'll find out."

"You aren't concerned for yourself?"

"Wouldn't help any."

She sipped at her brandy, eyed me over the snifter. "Is that bravery speaking, or stupidity?"

"Stupidity, probably."

She smiled. "But just now, shouldn't you be getting some rest? I know I asked you here, but that was before this bout of yours was arranged. I shouldn't be offended if you wish to leave."

"Thanks," I said, "but I'm not tired. What did you think about the séance?"

"We're changing the subject, are we?"

"Yeah."

"Well," she said. She looked down, smoothed the robe along her thigh, looked up again. "I thought it was a charming piece of theater. I understand how they did most of it, I think. They're working together, of course. Madame Sosostris and her husband."

I nodded, sipped at my brandy.

"The roses," she said. "They were in her wheelchair, beneath that gown of hers. Mr. Dempsey released her hand and she simply reached down and retrieved them. And then tossed them onto the table."

I nodded again.

"And the bell and the trumpet," she said. "She keeps them beneath her gown as well."

"The chains, too." I had figured most of this out, too, even before the Great Man explained it all.

Her red lips tightened thoughtfully. "That *thing* that touched me on the shoulder. Could that've been one of those extending tools that shopkeepers use? Do you know what I mean? To reach something on an upper shelf?"

"Probably."

"When Running Bear—" She smiled suddenly, amused at herself. "When Madame Sosostris was talking about the Earl, she said that he'd imposed his sick desires upon an innocent young woman. Presumably she meant the kitchen maid, the woman that Briggs mentioned to you in the library."

"Darleen."

"Yes." She frowned. "Briggs is a bit of a cad. Telling tales on his employer. And on a former sweetheart."

"Not a very nice guy," I agreed.

"He must've given the same information to Madame Sosostris. And told her of the Earl's death."

"If it was Briggs, he didn't give it to her."

She smiled. "He sold it, you mean. I'm sure you're right." Her face went serious again. "But what did she mean, do you think—Madame Sosostris—when she said that the Earl hadn't ended his life? She said that his life had been taken."

"I don't know," I said. "That was when Lord Purleigh showed up."

"Yes." She sighed, softly shook her head. Lamplight shimmered along the black sheen of her hair. "Poor Robert. For years he's been telling people he wanted his father dead. Now that it's actually happened, I think he's rather at a loss. I feel terribly for him. He's such a sweet man."

"What does Lady Purleigh think?"

"Regarding the Earl's death?"

"Yeah. Was she surprised?"

"Surprised? Yes, of course. Wouldn't anyone be?"

"Sometimes people see it coming."

"But Alice didn't. She was shocked. She told me she couldn't imagine why he'd do such a thing."

Just then, I think, she realized she was talking about friends of hers, and to a stranger. Smiling, she changed the subject. "But the two of them are quite good, aren't they? Madame Sosostris and her husband. It was quite an accomplishment, I thought, producing all those apparitions without giving themselves away. And with people sitting on either side of them, holding their hands."

"Practice," I said.

She cocked her head. "But in a way, you know, I was . . . rather disappointed." She moved her shoulders in a small, dismissive shrug. "I'd been hoping for something more, I suppose."

"Real ghosts?"

"Something with a less obvious explanation. A more persuasive apparition, perhaps. Something surprising."

"You seemed a bit surprised there, for a second or two."

Her face was calm but those black, almond-shaped eyes were watchful. "Oh?"

"When your daughter was mentioned."

"Yes," she said.

"It caught you off guard," I said.

"Yes." She looked down, lightly ran the tip of her finger along the rim of the snifter. "Not everyone knows about my daughter." She looked up at me. "But Alice does, which no doubt means that her servants know as well. Including Briggs, I imagine."

I nodded.

"But why should they bother learning about my daughter?" she asked me. "Why choose me?"

"You have money."

She blinked her long black lashes. Money was something that wasn't discussed in polite conversation. Then she understood what I meant and her eyebrows lowered. "You're saying that they found out about Esme, and they deliberately used the information to impress me, to bring me into . . . To . . ." She frowned impatiently. "What *is* the word I'm looking for?"

"Enlist?"

"To *enlist* me as one of their followers?"

"Probably."

She stared at me for a moment, her wide red mouth open, her black eyes narrowed. Finally she said, "But that's *filthy.*" She looked off, her mouth grim now. "That's *vile.*"

"Yeah."

She drank some more brandy.

"How old was your daughter?" I asked her.

Still looking off, she said, "Five."

"When did she die?"

"Six years ago." She turned to me. "I'd prefer not to talk about her, if you don't mind."

"Fine."

"Tell me something," she said. I think she heard her own voice, heard how curt it sounded. She added, "Would you?"

"Sure."

"Why were you asking Briggs all those questions?"

"That's what I do for a living."

"Yes, but why those questions, and why Briggs? The Earl committed suicide. It's a tragedy, of course, a terrible tragedy, but it has nothing to do with this magician you're after, this Chin Soo."

"Probably not. I'm just basically nosy."

"Tell me about this Chin Soo."

I told her. It took a while but she listened well. When she asked a question, which wasn't often, it was a good question. From time to time her glance dipped down toward my mouth and then slipped back up. It made me very conscious of my mouth. And very conscious of hers—I realized that my own glance was doing pretty much the same thing, sliding down along her cheekbones to flick against her wide red lips, then darting back up to her almond-shaped eyes.

When I was finished, she said, "You no longer believe that it was Chin Soo who fired that rifle this afternoon." She looked at the clock on the end table, looked back at me, smiled. "Yesterday afternoon."

"No," I said.

"You believe that it was one of us. One of the guests."

I nodded. "Yeah. There were four guests who weren't on the lawn. Four guests who could've fired the rifle. Lady Purleigh, Cecily Fitzwilliam, Dr. Auerbach, and Sir David. Can you think of any reason why one of them would want to shoot at anybody? Shoot at you, for example?"

"Me?" She laughed. "You can't really think that someone was shooting at *me?"*

"Someone was getting shot at. If it wasn't Harry, it had to be one of you."

"But it couldn't possibly have been me. It couldn't have been *any* of us, but who on earth would shoot at *me?"*

"I don't know," I said. "I don't really see Lady Purleigh or Cecily using a rifle. Dr. Auerbach has an alibi, or says he has. Besides, you never met him before this weekend. Or did you?"

"No. He's a friend of a friend of Alice's. He learned about the séance and asked Alice if he could attend."

"That leaves Sir David."

She laughed again. *"David?* Why would David want to shoot me?"

"I don't know."

"Really, Mr. Beaumont, the idea is ridiculous. I've known David for years. He can be unpleasant, he often *is* unpleasant, as you saw for yourself, but he'd never shoot anyone. And he certainly wouldn't shoot me."

She leaned slightly toward me and gave me a martini smile—dry, with a twist of lemon in it. The scent of her perfume grew stronger. She said, "I think you've been letting your imagination get the better of you."

"Maybe. That happens."

She leaned away but her perfume hung there in the air between us like an invitation, or a promise. She said, "And why are you so concerned about the gunshot in any case? If, as you say, it wasn't fired by Chin Soo?"

"Habit."

"Ah," she said. "You told me in the garden that smoking cigarettes wasn't one of your bad habits. Is this one of them?"

"Which?"

"Asking these questions."

I shrugged. "Like I said. It's what I do for a living."

She eased herself comfortably back against the love seat and she looked over at me. "What *are* your bad habits?"

"Is that why you asked me here? To find out about my bad habits?"

"Among other things." She raised the snifter to her mouth, sipped at it.

"Which other things?"

"I told you in the library. Alice is a friend of mine. If you're asking questions about her household, I'd like to know why."

"And like I said then, do you feel better now?"

She smiled. "Not remarkably so. Not yet."

"Not yet?"

The black eyes were staring steadily into mine. She was holding the brandy snifter lightly in both hands, the index finger of her right hand pointed upward. The polish on her long nail was the same bright red as her lips.

She said, "Are you quite certain you don't feel like resting?"

I could hear the ticking of the clock on the end table. I took in a breath. It seemed to me that all the air in the room had been replaced by the scent of her perfume. "Not yet," I said.

"Then don't you think," she said, "that you're a trifle overdressed?"

I smiled. I turned, set my brandy on the end table, turned back to her. I reached for her glass and she handed it to me. I set it beside my own. When I turned back again, her head was back and her black hair was fanned across the cushion of the love seat. The black eyes were staring up at me, the wide red lips were parted in another smile.

I leaned toward her.

Someone knocked at the door.

It had a tentative sound, two or three light raps, as though the knocker, whoever it was, didn't really want to bother anyone this late at night.

I sat up.

Without moving her head from the cushion, Mrs. Corneille reached out and put her hand on my arm. "They'll go away," she said softly.

The knocking came again, harder.

"I don't think so," I said.

She sighed, lightly squeezed my arm, and stood up. "Don't move," she said.

She waltzed around the coffee table and across the carpet to the door. She opened it a few inches, craned her head around its edge, and suddenly she said, "Jane!"

She opened wide the door and stepped out into the hallway, then stepped back into the room with her arm around Miss Turner's shoulders.

Miss Turner's brown hair was loose, tumbling to her shoulders. She was wearing her gray robe. It was streaked with dust and spotted with clumps of what looked like fur. Her arms were hanging limply at her sides and in her right hand she held a shiny double-bladed dagger.

Chapter Twenty-six

I STOOD UP.

Miss Turner saw me and she said, "Oh!" Her blue eyes flew open as she wheeled to face Mrs. Corneille. She put her hand to her chest, the hand that held the dagger, its bright blade aimed toward the floor. "I didn't know, I didn't realize you had a guest. I'm so sorry!"

"It's quite all right, Jane," said Mrs. Corneille, and led her to the love seat. "Mr. Beaumont and I were just talking. Here. Do sit down."

A gentleman might have offered to leave the parlor right about then. I took a few steps sideways, to give Miss Turner room on the love seat. Still gripping the dagger between her breasts, her knuckles white, she sat down and she leaned forward, balancing herself on the edge of the cushion. She looked up at me and suddenly her face and her throat went red. It made the blue of her eyes seem deeper and brighter. She looked away and then looked back, her lashes fluttering. "I'm sorry," she told me. "I truly am. I didn't mean to disturb anyone."

She looked up at Mrs. Corneille, who stood bending over her, her hand on Miss Turner's shoulder. "I think it would be best if I left," Miss Turner said.

"Jane, really, don't be silly," said Mrs. Corneille. She looked at me. "Please, Mr. Beaumont. Sit."

I sat.

Miss Turner said, "I . . ." She looked down at the dagger. She held it out, away from her, and she stared at it as if she couldn't understand how it gotten there.

"Why don't I just take that," said Mrs. Corneille. I didn't say anything—if there had been any other fingerprints on the knife, they were gone now, smeared by Miss Turner's. Mrs. Corneille reached out and Miss Turner surrendered the weapon, then winced and wiped her hand on her thigh as if her palm were bloody.

Standing upright, Mrs. Corneille examined the knife. Both the blade and the ornately carved handle were silver. "It's very pretty, Jane," she said. "Wherever did you find it?"

Miss Turner's hands clutched at each other on her lap. She looked up said, "It was in my bed. I think someone tried to kill me." She turned to me. "Does that sound utterly insane?"

I said, "Not if they used that knife."

"You were in bed," said Mrs. Corneille, "and someone tried to kill you?"

Miss Turner shook her head. "No, no. I was in the Earl's room when it happened."

Mrs. Corneille looked at me, looked back at Miss Turner. She nodded. "This sounds as though it may take a while. Would you like a brandy, Jane?"

"Yes," said Miss Turner. "Please. Very much."

"You sit back," said Mrs. Corneille. "Relax. No one will harm you here."

"Yes," said Miss Turner. She sat back, glanced quickly around the room again. She took a long deep shuddery breath. "Yes," she said.

She peered down at herself and she sat forward. "Oh dear," she said. Her voice was higher now, and it sounded as if it might crack. "What a *fright* I look." She brushed at the front of her robe and then plucked away a tuft of what I'd thought was fur. It wasn't fur. It was a flattened dustball, the kind that grows underneath sofas and beds if you don't sweep often enough. Wincing again, her mouth twisted, she shook it from her hands, then quickly rubbed her fingers on the robe.

Those sapphire eyes were a bit wild and I thought she might leap up and run away. Out the door, maybe out the window.

She didn't. The eyes closed and she took another deep breath. She set her mouth in a firm straight line. Then she opened her eyes and looked over at Mrs. Corneille, who was pouring brandy into another snifter. With only a thin ribbon of strain left in her voice, she said, "I feel as though I've been pestering people and making a fool of myself all weekend."

She was a real surprise, Miss Turner. A stronger woman than she seemed.

"Not at all," said Mrs. Corneille. She set down the bottle and carried the snifter over to Miss Turner. She had left the dagger beside the brandy bottle on the sideboard. "Only a fool," she said, "can actually make a fool of herself."

Miss Turner smiled with a kind of tentative irony. "Perhaps that's why I've succeeded so well."

"Nonsense," said Mrs. Corneille. "Here you are. Have a big swallow now."

"Thank you," said Miss Turner. Her right hand was unsteady and the brandy shivered against the curved walls of the glass. She put both hands around the snifter and raised it to her mouth and she took a swallow that would've done Lord Bob proud. She sat back and closed her eyes and screwed up her face.

Mrs. Corneille smiled. "You needn't swallow like that again. Unless you want to, of course. I'll fetch a chair."

I stood, but she waved me back down. She stepped over to a spindly wooden desk, lifted the spindly wooden chair from beneath it, carried it over to us and placed it a few feet from Miss Turner.

She picked up the two brandy snifters from the end table, leaned around Miss Turner to hand me mine, and then she sat down, her back straight. "Now," she said to Miss Turner. "Do you feel better?"

Her lower lip caught between her teeth, Miss Turner had been staring at the snifter on her lap as though there were a message floating across the surface of the brandy. She looked up at Mrs. Corneille. "Yes," she said. Her voice was small. "I think I do. Thank you."

"Not at all. Now. You must tell us all about it."

Miss Turner moved her shoulders in a frail shrug. She smiled hopelessly. "I'm not at all sure where to begin, really."

"Well," said Mrs. Corneille. "We tried starting in the middle and that didn't work terribly well. At the risk of sounding obvious, why don't we try starting at the beginning. Why did you go to the Earl's room?"

Miss Turner took another swallow of brandy. "Because of something Madame Sosostris said. At the séance." She looked at me.

I smiled and I nodded. That was supposed to encourage her.

"Madame Sosostris?" said Mrs. Corneille.

"Yes. She was talking about the Earl—she was Running Bear then, do you remember?"

"Yes?"

"She was Running Bear—playing the part, I mean—and she was talking about the Earl. She said that the Earl felt guilty now, because he'd imposed his sick desires on an innocent young woman. He felt tortured about it, she said. Well, it occurred to me that I was the woman Madame Sosostris meant."

Mrs. Corneille smiled as though she hadn't really followed all that. "You?"

"Yes," said Miss Turner. She leaned toward Mrs. Corneille. "Don't you see? The ghost. Lord Reginald. The ghost that came to my room last night. That was no ghost. It was the Earl." She looked at me. I remembered to smile and nod some more.

Mrs. Corneille glanced at me and then looked back at Miss Turner. "But Jane," she said. "The Earl was bedridden. Paralyzed."

"Yes," said Miss Turner, nodding, excited now, "that's what I told myself. But then I thought, what if he weren't? What if he were only shamming? He knows Maplewhite. He's lived here all his life. It would've been so easy for him to sneak into my room, and then run out again, while I was behaving like an hysterical schoolgirl. He could've slipped right past Mrs. Allardyce. It takes her forever to wake up."

I said, "Mrs. Allardyce said she woke up when you screamed the first time."

Miss Turner shook her head. "But that's not possible. He *had* to run past her, in order to leave the room. I'm sure he must have done. I've been going over it tonight, trying to remember."

"You told me," I said, "that you weren't sleeping when it all happened."

"No." She drank some brandy. "I was just lying there, in the darkness. And then, as I told you, I heard a sound, a sort of clicking noise, and I rolled over and switched on the light. And he was standing there. At the foot of the bed. Wearing an old nightgown. He had long white hair and a long white beard—I mentioned that, didn't I?"

I nodded. "And you screamed?"

"No," she said. "No, not then. I think I was too frightened. To do anything, really. And then he . . ." Her eyelashes fluttered. "And then *he* did something. And said something."

So she hadn't told me the truth before, or all of it. "Did what?" I asked. "Said what?"

She took another deep breath, and I got the feeling that she was steeling herself to get through this. It was the same feeling I'd gotten this afternoon, when she thanked me in the hallway.

But she didn't talk to me this time. She turned to Mrs. Corneille. "He pulled up his nightgown," she said, her voice flat and deliberate, "and raised it to his stomach. He was . . . naked. And he said"—she swallowed—"he said, 'Want a nice little piece of this, dearie?' "

She was trying to be cool and detached, but the skin of her face had gone pink. I hadn't noticed before, but it was very nice skin. It was a very nice face.

Mrs. Corneille frowned, looked at me, looked back at Miss Turner. "You honestly believe that the Earl of Axminster did *that?"*

"Yes," said Miss Turner, leaning toward her over the brandy snifter, as if trying to convince her by intensity alone. "It *must* have been the Earl."

"Okay," I said. "What happened then?"

She swallowed again and sat back. "He made a move toward me, as if he were going to climb onto the bed. He was still holding up his nightgown. That was when I screamed. I screamed once, and he stopped moving. He seemed rather alarmed himself, actually."

She smiled faintly. "In a different context, I suppose, it might have been almost comical. He dropped his nightgown and he looked around the room as though he were afraid that someone had heard me. And then I screamed again and I snatched up a pillow and threw it at him. Then I rolled off the bed, to the floor."

She took a breath. "I don't know what I was thinking to do down there—simply trying to get away, I expect. I scrambled across the carpet to the wall. And then I turned around, and he was gone. Vanished. I pulled myself up from the floor and I looked all around and I couldn't see him. That was when I ran into the other room. The—Mrs. Allardyce was just getting out of bed."

"So there was time," I said, "for the ghost, or whoever, to get past her."

"There must've been," she told me. She looked back at Mrs. Corneille. "Don't you see? It was the Earl."

"Jane," said Mrs. Corneille, and her voice was kind. "You said at breakfast this morning that you'd dreamed the ghost."

Miss Turner shook her head. "I was embarrassed. And *confused.* I didn't want to believe that I'd actually seen . . . what I'd seen." She turned to me. "You suggested as much, when I saw you on the lawn this afternoon. You said that I sounded as though I were trying to persuade myself. And you were right."

"But Jane," said Mrs. Corneille, "do I understand you correctly? Are you saying that the Earl's *ghost* is actually feeling guilty about this attack on you, and that somehow that Spirit Guide of Madame Sosostris—"

"No, no, no." Miss Turner shook her head so vigorously that her hair whipped back and forth. "No, I don't believe in any of that. Spirit Guides, the afterlife. But I've read about mediums, people like Madame Sosostris. They obtain their information from whatever sources they can find, don't they? From newspapers, from servants, wherever. And that's what she must've done, don't you see? One of the servants must've known it was the Earl in my room last night, and he told Madame Sosostris."

"But Jane," said Mrs. Corneille. Then she frowned, as if reconsidering what she'd been about to say. Her cigarette case and a box of matches lay on the coffee table. She set her snifter on the table and picked them up.

"Okay," I said. "So you went to the Earl's room. You were looking for proof."

She nodded to me and then turned to Mrs. Corneille. "It was wrong of me, I realize. Sneaking about at night. But I could hardly go to Lady Purleigh and ask her about it. And I simply had to know. Can you understand that? I'd been thinking I was going mad."

Mrs. Corneille smiled at her. "I told you last night, Jane. You're probably the sanest of us all." She had one of her brown cigarettes free now. She put it between her lips.

"I very much doubt that," said Miss Turner, and smiled another weak smile. "But thank you."

I leaned toward Mrs. Corneille, reaching for the matches, but she shook her head. She struck a match herself and held the flame to the cigarette.

Miss Turner turned to me. "So, yes," she said, "after the séance I asked the footman, Parsons, where the Earl's room was located. And then later, after midnight, I went up there." For some reason she blushed again. Again it deepened the blue of her eyes. She looked away from me.

Mrs. Corneille had blown out the match. She sat there, immobile, holding it over the ashtray, watching Miss Turner. She said, "But you didn't find anything?"

"Not at first."

Mrs. Corneille arched her eyebrows and dropped the match into the ashtray.

She looked everywhere, Miss Turner said. In the wardrobe, in the bookcase, in drawers of the cabinet. She had no idea what she was looking for—but whatever it was, she didn't find it. After a while she gave up. She had closed the door before she turned on the overhead light. Then she walked over to the entrance, turned off the light, and opened the door a crack to peek out.

She saw candlelight moving toward her in the darkness, through the parlor.

"Who was holding the candle?" I asked her.

"I don't know. I couldn't tell. All I could see was the light, coming closer."

"What happened?"

"I closed the door," said Miss Turner, "and I fumbled about in the darkness until I found the bed. And then I crawled beneath it."

She waited there, lying on the hard wooden floor amid the dust and the bits of fluff. The door opened and the thin wobbling light of the candle moved through the room. Miss Turner tried not to breathe.

From beneath the bed, in the dimness, she could just make out the feet of the person holding the candle. It was a woman.

I said, "What kind of shoes was she wearing?"

"Boots," said Miss Turner. "A woman's boots. And a long dress or skirt. Black. It came down to her ankles."

Mrs. Corneille took a drag from her cigarette.

"Okay," I said to Miss Turner. "Then what happened?"

The woman sat down on the bed, said Miss Turner. Just sat there. Said nothing. Did nothing. Miss Turner kept herself frozen in position. Pale yellow light trembled around the room.

And then she realized that the woman was crying.

"Not loudly," she said. "Not sobbing or wailing. Just a small, quiet sort of private weeping. The way people sometimes do when they're alone, remembering someone."

Mrs. Corneille pursed her lips and sighed out two small silent streamers of smoke.

Miss Turner turned to her. "I felt badly for her," she said. "Isn't that absurd? I was lying there under the bed like a spy, and I had virtually no idea who she was or why she was crying, and I felt badly for her."

Mrs. Corneille smiled. "It isn't absurd at all, Jane."

"How long was she there?" I asked her.

"Five minutes," she said. "Perhaps longer. I don't know, really. It seemed like years."

Finally the woman got up from the bed and walked out, closing the door behind her. Miss Turner waited a few moments, and then began to move out from beneath the bed. As she did, her hand plunged through the floorboards, down into a kind of hole. She felt something inside there.

"At first," she said, "I thought it was a *rat,* something alive, and I nearly screamed."

But whatever it was, it didn't move. Miss Turner slid away from the bed, turned on the end table's electric lamp, and looked more closely.

One rectangular section of planking had been sawed free and made into a kind of lid for a box built under the floorboards.

"And it wasn't a rat I'd found," she said, and there was a small light of triumph in her blue eyes. Miss Turner was coming to her proof. Holding the brandy snifter in her right hand, she reached into the left-hand pocket of her bathrobe and pulled something out. "It was this."

It looked pretty much like a dead white rat. About eight inches long, dense and furry. Then Miss Turner bent forward, set down her brandy, and spread the thing out along the coffee table.

It had scraggly white sideburns and, in its middle, an opening for a mouth.

A false beard.

"There was a wig in there as well," said Miss Turner. "Made of the same material. And these." She shifted the snifter to her left hand and reached into the right pocket of her robe and pulled out a handful of small items. She dumped them onto the table.

"Jane!" said Mrs. Corneille, sounding surprised. "You took them from the Earl's room?"

"He took them first," she said. She set down the brandy snifter and she picked up one of the items. "This is my comb. Here on the back, you can see where I've scratched my initials into the tortoise shell. It went missing sometime today. I didn't think much about it—so much else has happened. But it was taken from my room. And it was taken by the Earl."

Mrs. Corneille stubbed her cigarette into the ashtray and looked up at me.

I looked at the knickknacks scattered across the table.

An inexpensive metal watch fob. A pencil stub. A copper button. A metal nail file with an ebony handle. A shaving brush. A small key.

"My goodness," said Mrs. Corneille. She reached forward, picked up the file, examined it. "But this is *mine,*" she told me. "I hadn't even realized it was gone."

I leaned forward and lifted the key from the table. A simple key, base metal. I could just make out, stamped along its shaft, tiny letters that spelled out *Mueller and Kohl.*

"Is it yours?" asked Miss Turner.

"No," I said. "But I know what it opens."

"And what's that?" asked Mrs. Corneille.

"A pair of handcuffs."

Chapter Twenty-seven

THE HANDCUFFS BELONG to Mr. Houdini?" Mrs. Corneille asked me.

"In a way," I said. I slipped the key into the pocket of my dinner jacket. I said to Miss Turner, "Tell me about the knife."

She sat back. She was a bit breathless again, as though she had just physically relived the whole thing. She drank some brandy.

"Well," she said, and she inhaled deeply once more. "I wanted to tell someone. Show someone what I'd found." She looked over at Mrs. Corneille. "I thought about coming to you, to discuss it. But it was late, and there didn't seem to be any real urgency. I told myself that it could wait until tomorrow morning. So I returned to my room."

She paused to sip her brandy. "Mrs. Allardyce was still asleep, and she didn't wake when I tiptoed past her. She's a very sound sleeper." She blinked. "But I've said that." She turned to me. "Haven't I?" I think she was beginning to feel the brandy.

I nodded.

"Yes," she said. "Well. I'd put a bolster on the bed, under the blanket, when I left, and I'd arranged it to look like someone sleeping. To look like me sleeping, on my side. I didn't really expect Mrs. Allardyce to come into my room, but I wanted to make certain that if she did, she'd think I was still asleep. When I came back and switched on the light, the bolster and the blanket were just as I'd left them. But the knife was . . . sticking out. I stood there and I went through one of those incredibly stupid moments, telling myself, But I didn't leave *that* there. It seemed so strange—the knife, I mean—so bizarrely *out of place.* And then I understood what must've happened, and I started to shake. The knife was in exactly the spot where my chest would've been."

She turned to Mrs. Corneille. "It was extraordinary, really. You read about people shaking when they're frightened, and you think it's a figure of speech. But I was literally quaking." Her voice was level, but she used both hands again when she lifted her brandy to her lips.

Mrs. Corneille touched her knee. "But it's all over now, Jane. And you removed the knife and you brought it here."

"Yes. And I apologize for—"

"Hush, dear," said Mrs. Corneille. "You did absolutely the right thing. You've been terribly brave." She sat back and looked at me. She said, "Who could've done that?"

"The knife?" I said. "I don't know."

"But it's *horrid.*"

I nodded.

"Someone meant to *kill* her?" she asked me.

"Sounds like it."

"But that's insane," said Mrs. Corneille. *"Why?* Why would anyone want to harm Jane?"

I looked at the young woman. "Miss Turner? You have any ideas?"

She widened her eyes and arched her eyebrows, surprised—at the question itself, or maybe at my asking it. Then she smiled another small smile that was both tentative and ironic. "Well," she said, "Mrs. Allardyce wasn't altogether pleased with the way I packed the luggage."

I grinned. A real surprise, Miss Turner.

"Anyone else?" I asked her. "Anyone angry with you?"

"No." She shook her head. "No, no one." But for an instant her eyes widened again. Then she narrowed them, shook her head once more. "No."

"What?" I said. "You remembered something."

"It's ridiculous."

"What?"

She inhaled again. "It's nothing, really. Sir David . . . This morning . . ." She turned to Mrs. Corneille. For the first time in a while, she seemed unsure of herself. She didn't like doing this. "Before all of you motored into the village." She turned back to me. "This morning, Sir David made . . . well, a kind of advance, I suppose. And I rejected it. And he did seem upset at the time. But I can't believe that he was upset enough to harm me."

I nodded. "Sir David."

"But really, Mr. Beaumont," she said. "I shouldn't want you to think that it was anything more than it was. He made an advance, I rejected it, and that was the end of it." But she frowned then, as if she weren't so sure.

"And you were out there on the lawn," I said. "This afternoon, with the rest of us. When the shot was fired."

Mrs. Corneille said, "You can't be thinking that the shot was meant for *Jane?*"

"The knife was," I said.

"But—" She stopped herself. She pressed her lips tightly together and she reached for her cigarette case and the box of matches.

I said, "And Sir David wasn't out there this afternoon."

She sat back, holding the case and the matches in both hands. "Mr. Beaumont," she said. "If David killed every woman who rejected his advances, the streets of London would be piled high with female bodies."

She opened the cigarette case. She shook her head. "It's all just too absurd." Suddenly she looked up at me. "What of the knife? Wouldn't it be possible to learn who owned it?"

"It probably came from the collection in the Great Hall," I said. "Like all the other weapons floating around here."

Mrs. Corneille put a cigarette in her mouth, struck a match, held it up. The flame flared, the tip glowed. With the fingers of her left hand, she took the cigarette from her lips. She blew the match out with a streamer of smoke and she dropped it into the ashtray.

"You know," she said, "there *is* something we all seem to be forgetting."

"What?" I asked.

"The Earl," she said. "The Earl of Axminster." She pronounced the name as though it were heavily salted. "And *those* things." She nodded to the table. "And the wig Jane found. She *must* be right about him." Suddenly she frowned. "You don't suppose that Alice and Robert know?"

"I don't know," I said.

"No," she said firmly. She shook her head, inhaled on the cigarette. "They couldn't possibly." It seemed to me that I wasn't the one she was trying to convince.

WE TALKED FOR a while. We made some decisions. For one thing, we decided that Miss Turner would stay in Mrs. Corneille's suite for the rest of the night.

Maybe half an hour later, I left. It was nearly two in the morning. I had an appointment with Sir David in another five hours.

Out in the hallway, I thought for a minute about slipping into Miss Turner's room and taking a quick look around. I decided against it. No matter how soundly Mrs. Allardyce slept, I didn't want to take a chance on her waking up while I was creeping through there. I wasn't sure that either one of us would survive.

I could take a look in the morning. Before the boxing match.

AFTER ALL THE excitement today—the rifle shot, the Earl's death, the séance, Lord Bob's performance, the rendezvous with Mrs. Corneille, Miss Turner's story—I was exhausted. I was yawning when I opened the door to my room and turned on the overhead light.

Cecily Fitzwilliam sat on my bed, her back propped against the headboard, her legs stretched out and crossed along the covers. She was wearing the white silk robe she'd worn last night. Her arms were folded beneath her breasts and she was trying to scowl. The scowl wasn't working very well because she was also blinking against the brightness of the light. "Where have you *been?*" she said.

"I'm glad you're here, Cecily," I said, as cheerfully as I could. "I need—"

"It's nearly *dawn.*"

"I need to talk to you. Something's come—"

"Where *were* you?" She was pouting now. She pouted better than she scowled.

"Outside. I went for a walk. Listen, Cecily, it's about your grandfather."

She threw her arms down along the bed. "Isn't it terrible?" she said. "He was ancient, of course, but no one expected him to go and *die* on us."

"That's what I want to talk about," I said. I hooked my hand around the back of the writing chair, swung it out, turned it around and straddled it. Keeping the wooden back between me and Cecily.

"And why on earth would he commit suicide?" she said. "He did, you know. Mother told me. *Because* he was so ancient, do you think?" She was speaking more quickly than she usually did, and her face was more animated. Her eyes were shiny. I wondered if she'd been playing around with her father's brandy.

I said, "That's one of the things—"

"Mother's heartbroken," she said, "and Daddy's . . . oh, well, you've seen Daddy, of course. At the séance." She rolled her eyes. "God, *everyone's* seen Daddy. It was mortifying, utterly. I've never been so humiliated in my entire life. That's not at all like him, you know. He's very proper. For a Bolshevist, I mean. He's an absolute stickler, really. He always dresses beautifully, and he's always on time for every single one of his appointments. Mother says he's in shock now."

"Probably. Listen—"

She was pouting again. "But they're all so wrapped up in themselves that no one's bothered to ask me how *I* feel. Not even Mother. I'm miserable, too, you know. I loved him just as much as everyone else did. Even if he *was* ancient and strange sometimes."

"Strange how?" When you're swept away by a river, you go with the flow.

She waved a hand. "The way old people get. Forgetful. Mumbling to himself." She made a face. "And drooling all over himself sometimes, too, which was a bit sick-making, really." She raised her chin. "But I loved him regardless. He was my grandfather, after all. And he wasn't always like that. Sometimes he was perfectly normal."

"You spend much time with him?"

"Of course I did," she said. "I mean, I wasn't up there every waking hour of every single *day*. That would've been completely impossible. I've masses of chores and things to do, you can't imagine, and most days there simply wasn't time. But I saw him in the afternoons, sometimes. As often as I could. Quite often, actually."

"What did you—"

She smiled suddenly and pushed herself up. "But that's not important. Let me explain why I've come. I wanted to apologize!"

She said this as if she were talking about a Christmas present she'd made with her own hands. Lately, more and more often, more and more people were reminding me of the Great Man.

"Apologize," I said.

"Yes. I realized afterward that I was rude to you. This afternoon. In the hallway? Before tea?"

"Yeah?"

"Yes! I realized that it was rude and utterly immature of me to say all those dreadful things. About you being a servant, I mean. They would've been rude and immature, of course, even if you actually *were* a servant, which you're not, thank goodness." She cocked her head. "But in a way that makes it *doubly* rude and immature, doesn't it?"

"Don't worry about it, Cecily."

She didn't. "I came around earlier," she said. "before dinner. To apologize. And to talk to someone. I was so upset about Grandpère. But you weren't here and Mr. Houdini was hiding in the other room." She put her hand to her mouth to hide a giggle. "I was awful, I'm afraid. I teased him terribly. I kept knocking on his door and I wouldn't go away. But he was being so *silly*. Does he always get so frantic when there are women about?"

"He's shy," I said.

She lowered her head and tilted it slightly to the side and she eyed me obliquely from beneath her blond bangs. "It's not because he thinks I'm a nymphomaniac?"

"No. Listen—"

"You're certain?"

"Yeah. Cecily—"

"Because I'm not, you know."

"Yeah. I—"

She took a breath. "Anyway, after that horrible séance, Mother went off with Daddy and it was obvious that no one cared in the least what happened to *me.* So I came around again and I waited. And I've been waiting for *hours,* all by myself, just sitting here, while you've been God knows where. And you haven't even noticed that I've picked up after you." She plucked invisible bits of something out of the air. "Pick, pick, pick. Like a pickaninny." She giggled, then covered that over with a stern frown. "You left this place a terrible mess, you know. There were clothes and things scattered everywhere."

She sounded like a tipsy young girl playing house, but that was pretty much what she was. She was working herself back into a pout, or maybe even another scowl.

"Thanks, Cecily. But—"

"Do you have something to drink here?" she asked me, looking around the room. "Whiskey or brandy or something?"

I had kept my bag locked since the first night here. Probably, if I hadn't, she would've found the bottle of bourbon inside it.

"Only water," I told her. "Sorry."

She made a face. Then she glanced toward the Great Man's door, turned back to me, and smiled. "Why don't you come over here?" she said, and patted the bedspread.

"In a minute. But first, tell me something about your grandfather."

Her brow furrowed. "My grandfather?"

"He fell from a horse, what was it, three years ago?"

She nodded. "From Rosebud, his mare."

"He's been paralyzed ever since?"

"Yes." She tilted her head to the side. "But why do you want to know about my grandfather?"

"I'm curious. He broke his back?"

"Not his back. The nerves got all twisted. Or torn or something. Some sort of complicated medical thing." She waved a hand vaguely. The gesture reminded me of her father.

"Was there any chance he'd be walking again?"

She shook her head. "The doctor said it was impossible. Dr. Christie."

"He's a specialist, Dr. Christie?"

"He's the family doctor. Grandpère didn't trust anyone else. Daddy and Mother wanted to bring in someone from London, but Grandpère refused." She frowned. She said, "Do you think it just finally become too much for him? Not being able to walk? Trapped in that room all day?"

"Did he seem depressed?"

"No. Not at all, really." Her brow furrowed again. "In fact, sometimes, you know, I thought he actually enjoyed it. Lying there, reading his books, having people waiting on him hand and foot." She made a face. "I'd hate it. It would drive me utterly mad."

"There's a maid here named Darleen."

"In the kitchen." Her face clouded. "What about her?"

"Her name came up. I just wanted—"

She was frowning. "Do you like her?"

"I've never met her."

"Why are you asking all these questions?"

"That's my job."

"You haven't asked me any questions about *me.*"

"Okay," I said. "Where were you this past afternoon?"

She blinked. "I beg your pardon?"

"Yesterday afternoon, between twelve-thirty and one o'clock. Where were you?"

"Why?"

"I'm an investigator. I'm investigating."

"But what *is* it you're investigating?"

"The rifle shot that was fired this afternoon. Where were you when that happened?"

She looked at me blankly. "But what difference would that make?"

"Maybe you saw something. Or heard something. Something that could help me figure out who fired the shot."

"I haven't the faintest idea who fired the shot. I was in the village."

"Where?"

She rolled her eyes, exasperated. "Does it really matter?"

"Yeah."

She sighed heavily, to prove how bored she was. "I was at Connie's house."

"Who's Connie?"

"She was my nanny. *Ages* ago."

"You were there between twelve-thirty and one?"

"Yes," she said, leaning toward me. She sat back and smiled. "Now. That's settled." She patted the bedspread again. "Aren't you coming over here?"

"Nope. Time for you to leave, Cecily."

She stared at me. "Pardon me?"

"Time to go."

She frowned. "You're joking."

"Nope."

"But I came to see you. I waited for hours. I *apologized."*

"Yeah. I appreciate it. But you've got to go."

"But I don't *want* to leave."

"Sorry, but that doesn't matter."

She shook her head. Once again she crossed her arms. "I won't leave. You can't force me."

"So I'll go. And find someone who can carry you back to your room. Your mother, maybe."

She hardened her face. "I'll scream. People will come. I'll tell them you attacked me. You *raped* me." She raised her chin. "I'll do it, I promise you I will."

"Swell. When they come, you can explain what you were doing here at two o'clock in the morning."

She put her hands on the bed and she leaned toward me. "I'll tell them . . ." Her face was growing red and she was nearly sputtering. "I'll . . ."

"Come on, Cecily. It's time to leave."

She stared at me again. She widened her eyes. "You only let me stay so you could ask all those boring stupid questions of yours. Didn't you? You don't care about me at all!" She narrowed her eyes and she slapped at the bed with both hands. "You . . . you *took* what you wanted and now you're *throwing* me out!"

"Yeah," I said.

"You were *toying* with me!" Her eyes were slits now. She swung around and tore away the bedspread and grabbed a pillow with both hands. Her mouth open, her teeth clenched, she spun back and hurled it at me. I caught it.

"You *used* me!" She jumped off the bed. "You . . . filthy rotten *bastard!*"

She stalked around me, her shoulders hunched, keeping as much distance from me as the bed allowed. At the door she turned around. Her face twisted into a snarl and she said, "I hope David beats you to a *pulp!*"

She turned back, grabbed the doorknob, ripped open the door, and stomped out, slamming the door shut behind her.

Chapter Twenty-eight

"PHIL?"

My eyes fluttered open. Slowly. Reluctantly. While I was asleep someone had pried out my eyeballs, dipped them in sand, then hammered them back into their sockets.

"Phil?"

The Great Man. He stood beside my bed, wearing a dark gray three-piece suit. He looked fresh and chipper and eager. If I'd had the Colt in my hand I would have shot him.

"Phil," he said, "it is a quarter after six."

"Uh-huh."

"It is time. Sir David." He grinned at me and clapped his hands together. "Up and at him, Phil!"

"Yeah." I closed my eyes. "Yeah. You go ahead, Harry. I'll meet you downstairs."

"But Phil. I am your second. We must arrive together."

I opened my eyes again and looked up at the ceiling. It hung over me like a huge white anvil about to fall. "Right. Right. Okay."

I rolled out of bed, groaning, and I cranked myself upright. My muscles were stiff, my joints were grainy.

Sunlight was trembling throughout the room. England is only a few miles south of the North Pole and in summer the days are longer, at both ends, than they have any right to be.

I staggered past the Great Man into the bathroom. I stripped off my pajamas, stepped into the bathtub, got down on my hands and knees, and turned on the cold water. I leaned my head into the stream. It hit me like a sledgehammer.

* * *

"HOLD ON, HARRY," I said. I was dressed and we were in the hallway outside the suite of Mrs. Allardyce and Miss Turner. The door was shut. I knocked on it. Waited. Knocked again.

"We will be late, Phil," said the Great Man impatiently.

I tried the door. Locked. I turned to the Great Man and nodded toward the lock. "Do your stuff, Harry."

"Phil!" He looked at me as if I'd just told him I carried the plague.

"It's important," I said. "We need to get in there. Before the maid does."

"Whatever for?"

"I'll tell you later. Come on."

The small white card with the names of Mrs. Allardyce and Miss Turner was still thumbtacked to the door. The Great Man peered at it.

I had forgotten that he didn't know who was staying in each room. He knew which room was his, and that was all he needed to know, or wanted to.

He looked at me. "The two women, they are in danger?"

"Maybe."

"But you are not certain?"

"It's important, Harry."

"But Phil!"

"We'll be late, Harry."

Frowning the whole time, he tugged his wallet from his back pocket, opened it, plucked out a pick, bent forward, slipped the pick into the keyhole. Click. He stood up, still frowning, and he turned the knob and opened the door. He stepped back. I stepped into the room.

Mrs. Allardyce's bed was empty, the sheets and the blanket thrown back. There was a depression in the mattress deep enough for a yak's nest.

I walked into Miss Turner's room, the Great Man trailing behind me. Frowning, probably.

The bolster still lay beneath the blanket. Miss Turner had done a good job with her dummy—even in daylight it looked like a sleeping form. I put my knee on the bed and leaned forward to examine the blanket. About a foot down from the pillow, there were eight narrow holes in the fabric, each an inch wide, all within two or three inches of each other.

"What is it, Phil?"

"Just a minute."

I tossed back the blanket and the sheet and I took a look at the bolster. It was plump and soft, covered with satin and stuffed with down. There were eight narrow holes in the cover, identical to the holes in the blanket. I stuck my finger into one of them. When I pulled it back, a small white feather came puffing out. It floated briefly in the air and then settled back against the bolster, quivering.

"What, Phil?"

"Someone stuck a knife into this thing last night."

"A knife?"

"While Miss Turner was out." I pushed myself off the bed.

"A knife?"

"Yeah." I glanced around the room. Nothing.

"But for what purpose?"

"To kill Miss Turner, it looks like."

He looked from me to the bed, looked back at me. "Are you joking with me, Phil?"

"I'll tell you about it on the way downstairs."

A SERVANT—A new one, for me—told us that everyone was waiting out on the patio, by the conservatory. When the Great Man and I arrived, I saw that everyone was.

Even Lord Bob was there.

During the night, or sometime this morning, someone had used a white powder—lime, maybe—to mark off a neat square on the grass, beyond the flagstones of the patio. The square looked to be the size of a standard boxing ring, about twenty-four feet on a side. There were no ropes and no posts, but two wooden stools squatted in opposite corners. Beside each stool was a straight-back wooden chair and, beside that, a small table supporting a heavy glass goblet, a crystal decanter filled with water, and a thick stack of white towels.

People were sitting in chairs arranged around three sides of the square and set back from it by a couple of yards, behind low tables that held big pots of tea and coffee. Nearly everyone was dressed in black, but most of them were chatting and sipping at china cups, and the whole thing seemed very jolly.

Miss Turner, Mrs. Corneille, and Mrs. Allardyce sat in a group to the left, on the south side of the ring. Lady Purleigh, Cecily, and Dr. Auerbach sat directly ahead, on the west side. On the coffee table in front of them, beside the teapot, was a large copper cowbell.

Sir Arthur stood next to Lady Purleigh, behind an empty chair, and he was bending forward, listening carefully. Madame Sosostris and Mr. Dempsey sat to the right, on the north side. Between these last two groups, Lord Bob stood talking to Sir David Merridale. Sir David was in shirtsleeves, his collar open, his cuffs rolled back. His black mustache and his wavy black hair glistened in the early morning sunlight and he looked very fit.

When Lord Bob saw the Great Man and me, he muttered something to the other two and then bustled over to us.

"Houdini! Beaumont! Good to see you!" His black suit and white shirt were neatly pressed this morning. All the buttons were in all the right holes and his tie was firmly trapped inside his vest. He sounded as brisk and lively as ever, maybe more so. But the ruddiness had drained from his face and left most of it waxy and pale. On his cheeks, beneath the pallor, purple veins were coiled like tiny snakes. Below his bloodshot eyes the skin was the color of fried liver. He turned to me and proudly waved a hand at the ring. "Look all right, does it?"

"I'm impressed," I told him.

He beamed. "Sir Arthur and my wife. Up at the crack of dawn with the servants. Damned ambitious, eh?" Stroking his mustache, he turned to the Great Man. "Eh? What d'you think?"

The Great Man nodded, smiling. "*Most* impressive, Lord Purleigh."

Lord Bob grinned. "Alice explained it to me last night. A boxing match. You and Merridale. Splendid idea, I thought. Symbolic, in a way, eh? The bourgeoisie versus the aristocracy, New World versus the Old. And a rousing bit of sport for the guests, eh? Get their minds off the old swine and the ghosts and whatnot. Ah." He frowned suddenly, as if he'd just remembered something.

He glanced quickly over at the others, then back to us. "About last night." He frowned, shook his head. "Disgraceful performance on my part. Scandalous. Made my apologies to all the rest, owe one to both of you. Damn sorry it happened. Don't know what came over me. Quart or two of Napoleon brandy, eh?" He chuckled, but the chuckle sounded empty and forced, and beneath the bushy eyebrows he was watching us. I think he was embarrassed, and I think that embarrassment was something he didn't experience very often.

The Great Man said, "No apology is necessary, Lord Purleigh."

Lord Bob grinned. "Good of you to say so. But it's Bob, eh?" He turned to me, the eyebrows raised. "Hale and hearty, are we? Ready for the main event?"

"Yeah."

"Good man." He leaned toward me and gave me a wink. "Got a fiver riding on you. Don't let me down, eh?"

He was a lot happier with me today than he'd been yesterday. Or maybe he was just unhappy with Sir David. "Who took your bet?" I asked him.

"Madame Whatsis's husband. The skinny chap. Tunney, is it?"

I smiled. "Dempsey."

"Whatever. In any event, good luck, eh?" Grinning, he moved into a boxing stance. "Keep up that left, eh?"

"I'll try."

"Good fellow. Ah, Doyle, there you are. About ready to begin, are we?"

Towering over us all, Doyle nodded his big pink head. "Very nearly, Lord Purleigh. But I must speak briefly with Mr. Beaumont."

"Right you are," said Lord Bob. "I'm off." He turned back to me, grinning again, and he held up his left hand, balled into a fist. "The left, eh?"

I smiled and nodded, and he bustled away.

"Now," said Doyle. "Mr. Beaumont, do you still wish to go through with this?"

"Yeah."

For a moment his glance traveled around my face like the beam of a searchlight. "Are you really quite sure, Beaumont? No offense, but you do look a trifle"—he frowned—"*worn* this morning."

"I'm fine."

He nodded. "Very well." He smiled slightly. "But I dare say you'll be a shade more mobile without your coat and tie."

As I pulled off the coat, Doyle turned to the Great Man. "You'll be in Mr. Beaumont's corner? Acting as his assistant?"

"As his second," corrected the Great Man.

"Yes," said Doyle. "Here, permit me to take that." He took my coat, draped it over his arm, took my tie, draped that over the coat. "You're ready, then?" he asked me.

"Yeah." I unbuttoned my left shirt cuff.

"Very well. Houdini, you and Beaumont will have that corner." He nodded toward the southeast. The Great Man gave me one of his wide smiles and then capered off to the corner.

He'd already forgotten about Miss Turner and the Earl and everything else I'd told him when we tramped down the stairs. He was genuinely excited, I think. Maybe because, for a change, he got to be part of the audience, and he wasn't in any kind of competition with the performer.

Doyle called out, "Sir David?"

As I rolled back my sleeves, Sir David strode toward us along the grass, tall and lithe. He moved well for someone as big as he was. His eyebrows were raised as he smiled at me. I nodded to him. Without lowering his eyebrows or nodding back, he turned to Doyle. "Yes?"

"I should like to be quite certain," said Doyle, "that we all understand the rules." As he spoke, he looked back and forth between me and Sir David. "The rounds will be of three minutes duration, with a rest period of one minute between each. Any man who falls during the course of a round will have ten seconds to get up, unassisted. A man on one knee is considered down, and if struck wins the match by forfeit. There will be no wrestling or hugging. No hitting below the belt, no hitting over the kidneys or the back of the neck. No kicking, gouging, or biting. Is that clear?"

Sir David smiled. "Quite."

"Mr. Beaumont? Clear?"

"Yeah." But it took away a big chunk of my repertoire.

"Good," said Doyle. "To your corners, then, gentlemen."

I walked over to my stool. The Great Man was dancing around beside it, grinning and rubbing his palms together. I turned and looked over at Sir David. His second was Dr. Auerbach.

"Ladies and gentlemen," announced Doyle, his big voice booming out across the lawn. "Welcome to the contest. This is to be a boxing match of ten rounds, fought by modified Marquis of Queensberry rules. Each round will last for three minutes. Lady Purleigh will be acting as timekeeper. The round will end when she rings the bell. Lady Purleigh, could you demonstrate, please?"

The copper cowbell on the table was attached at the top to a strip of ribbon. Lady Purleigh smiled and then raised the bell, using the ribbon as a handle. She tapped the bell with a small metal hammer. It made a sharp pleasant ring that faded off across the wide empty lawn.

"Thank you," said Doyle. He turned to the others. "I shall be acting as referee, and my decisions are final."

"Here, here," said Lord Bob loudly, and clapped his hands. The rest of them applauded.

"In this corner," announced Doyle, "we have Sir David Merridale, from London."

People applauded politely. Behind me, the Great Man hollered, *"Boooo!"* Heads swung, stiffly, in his direction. Most of the clapping seemed to be coming from Cecily Fitzwilliam. Lady Purleigh leaned toward her.

Smiling, Sir David nodded in the direction of each table.

Just in case they hadn't heard it the first time, the Great Man hollered it again—*"Boooo!"*

The applause had stopped. Doyle was frowning at us. "And in this corner," he said, "we have Mr. Phil Beaumont, from America."

Behind me, the Great Man beat his hands together wildly. *"Hooray for Phil!"* he called out. The guests applauded politely again. Except for Cecily Fitzwilliam, who sat with her arms locked across her chest. Lady Purleigh leaned toward her.

"Hooray!" the Great Man shouted. I turned to him and under my breath I said, "Easy, Harry."

He leaned toward me, grinning. Over the sound of his own clapping, he said, "It is the show business, Phil!"

He had been the first to start clapping and he was the last to stop.

"Gentlemen?" said Doyle, and waved Sir David and me into the ring. "Shake hands, please."

Sir David offered his hand. I took it. He showed off his grip, but I'd been expecting that. He smiled at me. Blandly. "Any last words, Beaumont?" he asked me.

"I hear Miss Turner turned you down yesterday. Too bad."

He didn't stop smiling, but the skin at the corners of his eyes tightened up. He didn't look at Miss Turner either, but I think he wanted to.

"Back to your corners, gentlemen," said Doyle. "When the bell rings, come out fighting."

I went back to my corner. The Great Man grinned and pounded me on the shoulder.

Overhead, the sky was pale blue, not a cloud anywhere. The bright clear air smelled of warming earth. Far off across the broad green lawn, one red squirrel went bounding after another.

Doyle had moved to the north side of the ring, close to Lord Bob and Lady Purleigh. I glanced around the crowd. Mrs. Corneille was watching me. So was Miss Turner. So was Cecily. Cecily looked away.

Lady Purleigh raised the cowbell and struck it with the hammer.

I stepped out into the ring.

Sir David held himself upright, his handsome head and his broad shoulders thrown back, his arms up, the left arm forward, the left fist making small, tight, controlled circles. His right fist was cocked back under his chin. He advanced on his left foot, his right foot perpendicular to it, his weight balanced. He moved flatfooted but he still moved well. He had done this before.

I went to him in a crouch, shoulders down. We circled each other slowly. I smiled at him. Keeping my voice low, I said, "She must've hurt your feelings, hey, Davey?"

He jabbed his left at me and I slipped it. He followed me and jabbed again, off balance. I weaved right, faked a left at his jaw, hooked a right to his heart. He was backing off but I connected. He swung a right at my head. I caught it on my left forearm, and he pitched a left and I caught that on my right forearm and I jabbed two quick lefts at his nose. He brought up his arms and I got him with a combination, left, right, left, in the stomach. His nose was bleeding. He opened his mouth and dropped his arms and I went over them and I hooked another left at the nose. His head jerked back and his chin stuck out and I brought up my right with everything I had, brought it up at an angle from my hip, going for the ridge at the back of his jaw. I hit it and I felt a knuckle pop in my hand.

Staring up at the sky, Sir David took a step back and then his legs buckled beneath him and he dropped. He landed heavily on his back, his arms flopping out along the grass. His head rolled to the side.

I stood over him beneath that blue sky in the center of a huge silence. Nothing moved.

Suddenly Doyle was there and I eased back. He glanced at me, his expression unreadable, and then he turned to Sir David and bent slightly forward and started counting aloud, swinging his arm down through the air to mark time. *"One,"* he said. *"Two."*

I snapped my knuckle back into place. If you wait too long, the swelling starts and then you're stuck.

"Five. Six." Doyle was calling out the numbers louder now, maybe hoping that if he shouted, Sir David would hear them. And maybe Sir David did. His leg moved slightly. But he didn't get up.

No one in the crowd had said anything. Not even the Great Man. I looked out there. Mrs. Corneille glanced away. Miss Turner was staring at me with the corners of her mouth turned down.

"Nine," said Doyle. "And *ten.*" Sir David hadn't moved again. "And the winner is Mr. Beaumont." Grimly, Doyle wrapped his big hand around my wrist and raised my arm over my head. I had the feeling that if he wanted to, he could've plucked me from the ground like a dandelion.

Suddenly the Great Man was at my side, jumping from foot to foot, slamming gleefully at my shoulder. *"Hip, hip, hooray! Hip, hip, hooray!"*

The others were less enthusiastic. They applauded, but briefly and lightly. Some of their hands, probably, never made contact with each other. Even Lord Bob, who had just won five pounds, looked like a man who would rather be somewhere else. Cecily turned to her mother and said very clearly, "But is it *over?*" Her mother leaned toward her.

Doyle dropped my hand and slowly went down onto his knees beside Sir David. I could hear him exhaling with the effort.

Cecily backed away from her whispering mother and complained, "But there were supposed to be *ten* of those things. And he said they were supposed to last three *minutes.*"

On the ground, Sir David moved his leg again. Doyle looked up at me. "He's coming around. I believe he'll be all right."

I nodded. "Good."

"Excuse me," said an unfamiliar voice behind me.

I turned. So did Doyle and the Great Man.

There were three people standing on the flagstone patio. One of them was Briggs, and he was wearing his black uniform. Beside him stood two men wearing suits. One of the men was bulky in the shoulders and taller than I was. The other was shorter, and he was the one who smiled pleasantly. "Good morning to you all," he said. "And it *is* a lovely morning, isn't it? *Jocund day stands tiptoe on the misty mountain tops.*" He smiled again. "Allow me to introduce myself and my associate. I'm Inspector Marsh. This is Sergeant Meadows. We're from London. The C.I.D."

Part Three

Chapter Twenty-nine

"WELL NOW, MR. BEAUMONT," said Inspector Marsh. "You've been at Maplewhite for a while now. A houseguest since Friday evening, I take it. And you're a Pinkerton, a trained investigator, hmmm?" He smiled. "Really a stroke of luck for us, our having you here."

I wondered if he were pulling my leg. It was something I wondered the entire time I talked to him.

He turned to Sergeant Meadows. *" 'Tis a lucky day, boy, and we'll do good deeds on't."* Sergeant Meadows nodded, without taking his eyes off me. Marsh turned back to me. "The Winter's Tale. You know Shakespeare, do you, Mr. Beaumont?"

"Not personally."

He chuckled. "Lovely. We'll get along famously, you and I." He smiled. "So you've been rattling about the manor house for two days now, in the very midst of all these mysterious goings-on. And no doubt you've kept your eyes open? Asked a question or two, have you? Confess now." He smiled slyly, narrowing his eyes, and he waved a slender finger at me. "I see a strange confession in thine eye, do I not?"

I smiled. "Yeah. A question or two."

"Well of course you have. Leopards and spots, eh? I couldn't expect anything else." He sat back comfortably, adjusted his pants legs to spare the crease, and he crossed his legs, right over left. "Well then, if you don't mind, why not put the good sergeant and me into the picture."

The three of us were in the library. Marsh and Sergeant Meadows sat on the sofa, across from my chair. The sergeant sat on Marsh's left, a small notebook in his ample lap. In his late thirties, wearing a black suit, he was a big man, nearly as tall and as broad as Doyle. From a sharp widow's peak, his black hair ran slick as a coat of lacquer back along his wide rectangular skull. His heavy jaw was sheened with blue—he had the kind of beard that probably grew back while he was rinsing the soap from his razor. There was a small scar, shaped like a comma, running vertically through the center of his thick left eyebrow, and his nose had been broken at least once and then badly reset. Police sergeants in England, it looked like, didn't have any easier a life than police sergeants in the U.S.

Inspector Marsh was in his forties. His nose had never been broken. It was a narrow, aristocratic nose in a narrow, aristocratic, mobile face. The nose was delicate, like almost everything else about him—his fine brown hair, his eyebrows, his cheekbones, his pointed chin, his small chiseled mouth. The gray wool suit he wore, delicately pin-striped, had been delicately tailored to his slim athletic body. The point of a powder-blue handkerchief peeked delicately from the breast pocket of the coat. He looked so delicate that I was afraid he might float off the ground and sail away.

But delicate cops don't last very long. And Marsh's eyes—hazel, almost green—weren't delicate at all. His face seemed open and without guile. He smiled as he bantered at me, and he pursed his lips together, or nibbled the lower lip between small white teeth. Every so often he wiggled his eyebrows, or dipped them, or raised them in surprise or amusement. But whenever he looked at me his eyes were always the same—cool and shrewd and watchful.

It had been his idea to talk to me alone. Out on the patio, Lord Bob had introduced himself to the Inspector, and then introduced everyone else. Lady Purleigh, Cecily, Sir Arthur, the Great Man. And Sir David, who was up off the ground now but still a little blurry. Lord Bob had introduced me last, as "Houdini's Pinkerton bodyguard."

Marsh had smiled at me and said, "Lovely! A Pinkerton. In the flesh. Wonderful!" He had turned to Lord Bob and his thin, mobile face had suddenly gone grave. "Lord Purleigh, permit me to offer you my condolences. *Irreparable is the loss, and patience says it is past her cure.* The Tempest."

Lord Bob blinked. "Yes. Well. Thank you very much."

Marsh leaned toward him. "Now, you'll think me terribly rude, I know, and I do beg your forgiveness, but is there some secluded little corner into which I can tiptoe with Mr. Beaumont? We've things to discuss." He lowered his voice and his eyebrows. "Rather important matters, you understand. Hush hush."

Lord Bob had seemed a bit surprised. By the request, or maybe by Inspector Marsh himself. Inspector Marsh would surprise almost anyone. But Lord Bob was a gentleman, and he said, "Well, yes. Yes, of course. There's the library."

"The library!" said Marsh, eyes wide with pleasure. "Perfect!" He cocked his head. *"Come and take choice of all my library, and so beguile thy sorrow.* Titus Andronicus."

Lord Bob stared at him. Marsh turned to me. "Do you know the library's location?"

I nodded.

"Lovely. Lady Purleigh. Lord Purleigh. Ladies and gentlemen. I hope you'll all forgive this intrusion. Police, officialdom, nasty business you'll be thinking, and I couldn't agree with you more. But I do hope you'll all bear with me whilst I briefly huddle with Mr. Beaumont. I do so much look forward to chatting with each and every one of you."

Lord Bob wasn't the only person staring.

And Marsh had turned to me, smiling. "Lead on, MacDuff."

Now, as I sat there in the library, still in my shirtsleeves, I asked him, "Shall I start at the beginning?"

He smiled as if that was an idea he wouldn't have thought of himself, and one he kind of liked. "Yes, at the beginning. The very commencement of things. Mr. Houdini hired you in the United States, did he?"

"Yeah." I told him the whole story, the Great Man and Chin Soo in Buffalo, the failed attack at the Hotel Ardmore in Philadelphia, our trip to Paris and then to London, the wire from the agency telling me that Chin Soo had probably sailed from New York to Rotterdam.

After a while, March listened with his head resting against the back of the sofa, his eyes watching the ceiling. His right elbow was perched on the sofa's arm, his forearm was raised and his index finger extended, its tip resting against the delicate hollow of his right cheek.

"Hmmm," he said, still staring at the ceiling. He pursed his lips thoughtfully. "So, really, you've no evidence that this other magician ever arrived in England at all."

"No," I said. "But Houdini's itinerary was published in the American newspapers before we left. And there was the wire from my agency. I had to assume that Chin Soo knew where to find him."

He lowered his head and smiled at me. "But my dear fellow, of *course* you did. I'm in no way criticizing, I assure you. I've the utmost respect for your organization, and I'm confident you've acted with complete propriety. Absolutely certain of it. I'm merely organizing my thoughts." He smiled and waved his hand. "*Unbridled children, grown too headstrong for their mother.* Troilus and Cressida."

I nodded.

"So," he said. "You arrived here on Friday night, yes?"

"Right."

"At what time would that've been?"

I told him. I told him about meeting the other guests, and about leaving the drawing room to return to the suite I shared with the Great Man. Told him I'd discovered that someone had gone through my bag, told him the Great Man had discovered that someone had tried to go through his.

"Aha," he said. "The plot thickens. Was anything taken?" he asked me.

"No."

"Didn't you find that just a trifle curious?"

"No. There wasn't anything worth taking."

He smiled at Sergeant Meadows. "*They are but beggars who can count their worth.*" To me he said, "Romeo and Juliet."

"Uh-huh."

"And you did—what exactly? Reported the attempted theft to anyone? To Lord Purleigh, perhaps?"

"No. Everything was still there. I went to bed. During the night I heard someone screaming."

Marsh looked at Sergeant Meadows. "Thicker and thicker, eh, Sergeant?" He looked at me. "And did you make any attempt to discover the cause of this screaming?" He smiled his sly smile and waved his finger again. "If I know my Pinkertons, I'll wager you did."

"Yeah. It was Miss Turner, next door." I didn't mention that I was awake at the time, and talking to Cecily Fitzwilliam. I told him about the scene with Miss Turner and Mrs. Allardyce, Mrs. Corneille and Sir David.

"Wonderful!" he said, smiling brightly and raising his hands. "A ghost! I adore ghosts. Lord Reginald, you say."

"She said. I didn't."

"No," he agreed. "So you didn't." He leaned back. "And what sort of ghost was he, exactly? He wasn't, by any chance, the sort who hobbled about with his head tucked beneath his arm?"

"No."

"Rattling his chains?"

"No," I said. "You want me to skip ahead? To what I found out about the ghost?"

He waved his hand quickly. "No, no, no. Please. I much prefer a straightforward narrative. *An honest tale speeds best being plainly told.*" Even when he didn't tell you what play the quotation came from, you could still tell it was a quotation. His voice got more precise and even more delicate. "Tell me," he said. "Was Miss Turner in any way harmed by this . . . visitation?"

"No. Shaken up. Frightened. Not harmed."

He nodded. "And what then?"

"I went back to my room and back to sleep."

"No more ghosts?"

"Not that I know of."

"Pity. And the next day? Saturday?"

Someone knocked at the library door. "Come in," Marsh called out.

The door opened and Briggs stepped in. He had no expression

on his face this morning, but now he was carrying my coat and tie draped over his left arm. "Excuse me, gentlemen. Mr. Beaumont, sir, Lady Purleigh desired me to convey your clothing to you."

I stood up. "Thanks, Mr. Briggs." He crossed the room and handed me the tie—formally, as if it were a national flag. Then, just as formally, he handed me the coat. I said, "Thank you. And tell Lady Purleigh thanks for me." I swung the coat and tie over the arm of the chair and I sat back down.

"I shall, sir. She also desired to know, sir, whether you might wish to have your breakfast delivered here."

"Yeah. That'd be fine, Mr. Briggs. Tell her that's kind of her."

"Yes, sir." Briggs turned to Marsh. "And she requested that I ask you, sir, whether you and the other gentleman would care for something as well."

Marsh smiled. "What a lovely idea." He turned to me and confided, "We're both ravenous. Not a bite since London. *Though the chameleon Love can feed on the air, I am one that am nourished by my victuals.*" He turned to Briggs. "Two Gentlemen of Verona."

Briggs nodded. Maybe he already knew that. "Yes, sir," he said. "I'll tell Higgens, sir, and someone will be here shortly."

"Lovely. Oh and—*Briggs,* is it?"

"Sir?"

"Briggs, would you please ask Lord and Lady Purleigh whether it might be convenient for them to join us here in, oh, say an hour?"

"Yes, sir. I shall, sir."

"Thank you so much."

Briggs turned and left. He closed the door behind him.

I hooked my tie over my head, slipped it beneath my collar. "You want me to take off when Lord and Lady Purleigh get here?"

For the first time Inspector Marsh seemed genuinely puzzled. "Take what off?"

I smiled. "You want me to leave? Go away?"

"No, no. Of course not, my dear chap. We're colleagues, aren't we. Allies to the end. *And here being thus together, we are an endless mine to one another.* The Two Noble Kinsmen."

"Right." I finished tying my tie.

He pursed his lips. "Of course, scholars disagree as to precisely how much of that particular work was actually written by the Bard."

"Uh-huh."

"Now," he said. "We were about to review the events of Saturday."

"Yeah." I told him about breakfast with Lord Bob and about strolling with the Great Man along the gravel walkway. About the meeting with Miss Turner and her horse. I told him about sitting under the bronze-red tree with Mrs. Allardyce and Mrs. Corneille, and about Lord Bob arriving on his motorcycle. Told him that Miss Turner and the horse had suddenly come bolting from the forest, and that she had reined it in before she reached us.

Marsh had been staring at the ceiling but now his glance swung down to me once more. "What caused her to bolt from the forest? Do you know?"

"A snake, she said. It frightened her horse."

"I see. And then what?"

Someone knocked at the door. "Come in," called out Marsh.

It was a servant, pushing a wheeled cart. He arranged a low table in front of my chair, then slid a plate, covered with a silver lid, from one of the shelves of the cart and he placed it on the table. He arranged silverware and a linen napkin and a cup and saucer and a small pot each of tea and coffee. Then he did the same thing for Marsh and Sergeant Meadows, on the coffee table. Then he pushed the cart off into a corner, turned, and asked us, "Will there be anything else, gentlemen?"

Marsh smiled up at him. "No. Thank you very much."

The servant said, "Very good, sir," nodded, and marched from the room.

"They set a lovely table, Lord and Lady Purleigh." Marsh nodded to my food. "Please. Eat. Enjoy your meal. *Unquiet meals make ill digestion.*"

I lifted the lid from my plate. Fried eggs, bacon, sausage, fried tomatoes, buttered toast, a dead fish. I picked up the fork.

With his knife and fork, as precisely as a surgeon, Marsh cut a geometrically perfect square of egg white. He dipped the tip of his knife lightly into the bright yellow yolk, carefully spread yolk along the surface of the white, and then placed the result neatly in his mouth. He kept the fork in his left hand, the way English people do. He chewed with small even bites. Thoughtfully. Delicately. He swallowed and looked up at me, dabbing at his mouth with his napkin.

"Miss Turner had just arrived," he said. "What happened at that point?"

I swallowed some sausage. "Someone fired a rifle."

Marsh raised his eyebrows. "Fired a rifle. From where?" He cut off another perfect square of egg white.

Sergeant Meadows had set aside his notebook and he was eating as though he hadn't eaten since the War. He was bent over his eggs and his heavy elbows were flapping like wings.

"From the forest," I said. "About a hundred and fifty yards off. At the time, I thought he was aiming at Harry." I cut off a piece of bacon, ate it.

Marsh carefully spread some yolk along the square. "You believed it was—what was the name? The magician?"

I swallowed. "Chin Soo."

"You believed it was Chin Soo who fired the rifle." He put the morsel of egg into his mouth.

"At the time, yeah."

He chewed. Neatly. Regularly. He swallowed. He dabbed at his mouth. "You're implying, of course, that you've since changed your mind."

"Yeah."

"Refresh my memory, would you? Which of the guests, exactly, were out gamboling on the lawn?"

Someone knocked at the door again.

"Rather like Victoria Station, isn't it?" Marsh smiled. He called out, *"Come in."*

The door burst open, banged against its stop, bounced back. The Great Man caught it with his left hand as he stepped into the room, and he held it. "Phil," he said. "We must leave."

Chapter Thirty

I SWALLOWED SOME egg. "Why's that, Harry?"

His brow was furrowed. "Bess." He let the door swing shut and he walked into the room. "I spoke with her on the telephone just now. She rang from Paris. She intends to leave tonight. She will be in London tomorrow morning. Tomorrow morning, Phil. I *must* be there when she arrives."

I looked at Inspector Marsh. He was smiling pleasantly up at the Great Man. "Forgive me," he said. "Mr. Houdini?"

The Great Man turned to him, frowning impatiently.

Marsh said, "Who might Bess be, exactly?"

I kept eating. I had a feeling that breakfast would be over pretty soon.

"My dear wife," said the Great Man. "She has been deathly ill in Paris. Her stomach. That awful food, all those sickening French sauces. She is better now, thank goodness, well enough to travel now. It has been a huge pleasure to meet you, Inspector, and I am sorry we shall have no opportunity to talk. But Mr. Beaumont and I must leave Maplewhite."

I finished off my egg.

"Yes," said Marsh. "So you said. You do understand, don't you, Mr. Houdini, that this is a police investigation?"

Sergeant Meadows was pouring himself a cup of coffee. It looked like a good idea, so I did the same thing.

The Great Man was frowning. Impatiently. "Of course I understand. But I am merely a guest here. The investigation has nothing to do with me. Phil, will it take you long to pack?"

I sipped at my coffee. "Well, Harry," I said.

"I imagine," said Marsh, "that it shouldn't be difficult for you to arrange for someone in London to meet your wife. I—"

"Impossible," said the Great Man. "Bess expects *me* to be

there." He raised himself fully upright. "In all our married years together, I have never disappointed my wife, Inspector."

Marsh smiled. "That does you great credit, Mr. Houdini," he said. "But I regret to tell you that no one will be permitted to leave Maplewhite until such time as the preliminary investigation has been concluded."

Impatience had become disbelief. *"Permitted?"*

"Harry," I said.

Marsh said, "Sergeant Meadows and I—"

"Inspector," said the Great Man. "You fail to understand the situation. My wife is arriving. In London. In the morning. I *will* be there."

"Mr. Houdini," said Marsh.

The Great Man spoke slowly, to make sure that Marsh understood. "Inspector, do you know who I *am?"*

"Oh yes," said Marsh, smiling brightly. "I could hardly fail to understand *that,* could I? Not a day goes by that I don't admire those colorful advertisements of yours. They're posted all over London, aren't they? Ubiquitously, one might say."

"Then perhaps it has occurred to you," the Great Man pronounced, "that I am not without influence, even here in England. I feel I must warn you—"

"Harry." I stood up. "Come on, Harry. Outside. Let's talk. We'll be back in a minute, Inspector."

He turned to me. "But Phil—"

"Come on." I took him by the arm. He resisted, his muscle bunching under my hand. He held his head up, his gray eyes glaring at Marsh. Marsh was smiling up at him, pleasantly.

I tugged at the arm. "Harry, come on. We'll get this straightened out."

Reluctantly, his head high, he came along.

"THE MAN IS insane, Phil!"

"He's a cop, Harry."

"He is an imbecile!"

"I don't think so."

"But you heard me explain. He refuses to listen!"

"Harry, he's just doing his job."

"But *permitted!* How *dare* he? Bess will be in London *tomorrow!"*

We were in the hallway outside the library. The Great Man was pacing up and down the parquet floor, waving his arms. I was leaning against the wall. My own arms were crossed.

"Why not call her back?" I said. "Ask her if she can take a later train. Tomorrow, maybe."

He stopped pacing and turned to me and put his hands on his hips. "I refuse. Absolutely. I have given my word." He stood upright again. "And Houdini never goes back on his word."

"Harry, you're just being stubborn. You're angry at Marsh."

"I have every reason to be angry."

"Marsh needs to talk to everyone. He needs to figure out what's going on."

"What?" He leaned toward me. *"What,* Phil? What is this oh-so-important thing he needs to 'figure out'?"

"Harry, I told you." You had to be patient with him. "Someone tried to stab Miss Turner last night. Maybe it was the same person who fired that shot yesterday. And maybe he'll try again—Miss Turner is in danger, Harry, until someone finds out what's happening. And maybe all that—the rifle shot, the knife—maybe it's all connected to the Earl somehow. To the Earl's death. I still don't like the idea of suicide."

He shook his head. "We have discussed this, Phil. It must have been suicide. No one could possibly have opened that door. I examined it with the utmost care."

"And what was going on with the Earl? Why was he wandering around, playing ghost in the middle of the night?"

He shook his head. "The Earl was paralyzed, Phil."

"He said he was paralyzed. He acted like he was paralyzed. But I told you, Harry, Miss Turner found those things in his room."

"Someone placed them there, of course."

"Why?"

"To discredit him."

"She found them by accident. And what's the point of discrediting the Earl?"

"I have no idea."

"Yeah. Neither do I."

He opened his mouth and then shut it. He took a deep breath. He looked out the casement window and he frowned. He cocked his head to the side. "I could simply leave," he said suddenly. He was talking more to himself than to me. "Who would stop me?"

"Marsh would," I said. "He'd call ahead, he'd set up roadblocks. That Lancia is a hard car to miss, Harry. You'd be arrested. And then you'd be in jail. Bess would love that."

He turned to me, his back stiff. "No jail in the world can hold Houdini."

"Swell. You escape from jail. Then they shoot you. And then you're catching bullets, like Chin Soo. But not with your teeth."

He frowned again and turned away. He took another deep breath and then he pounded his fist against the stone of the window sill. "I *refuse* to be trapped here." Shoving his hands into his pockets, he glared out through the panes of glass at the grounds of Maplewhite. In the sunlight, the lines around his mouth seemed deeper and darker.

"Harry," I said, "it probably won't take all that long. Let Marsh poke around, ask his questions. Let him get a grip on all this."

He snorted. "If we wait for Marsh to get a grip, we will be here until the snow falls." He shook his head. "Absurd," he told the windowpane. "Houdini, *imprisoned.*"

"Give him a chance, Harry. Maybe it won't take more than a couple of hours."

He turned back to me, his eyes narrowed. "Aha," he said.

"Aha?"

He nodded sagely. "Now I understand."

"What?"

"You wish to 'get a grip' on this yourself, do you not, Phil?" He slid his hands from his pockets and he crossed his arms. "You are curious, are you not? As a Pinkerton, you are intrigued. And you are concerned, perhaps, about Miss Turner."

"Naturally I'm curious, but—"

"But Phil. You were not hired to be curious about Maplewhite. Is that not the truth?"

I sighed. "Yeah."

"Nor to be concerned about Miss Turner."

"No."

"Tell me this, Phil. Let us say that I was allowed to leave. *Permitted* to leave. Within half an hour, let us say. Would you come with me? Back to London?"

"Yeah."

"Even though, by leaving, you might never 'get a grip'? Even though Miss Turner might remain in danger?"

"I signed on to do a job."

"But—and be honest with me, Phil—you would not be happy about leaving now."

"I'm not paid to be happy."

He shook his head. "Honestly now, Phil."

"Honestly, Harry?" I shrugged. "I'd try to talk you out of it."

"As you are doing now."

"Yeah." I smiled. "A lot like that."

He nodded gravely. "I appreciate that, Phil. Your honesty. And your personal loyalty to me. I am grateful."

He reached out and put his left hand on my shoulder, like a priest about to bestow a blessing. "Very well, Phil. *I* will get to the bottom of this. For your sake, *I* will discover what has been going on at Maplewhite."

He let go of my shoulder and pulled out his watch. "Eight-thirty now." He looked off, thoughtful. "It may take me a few hours. I have many questions to ask, of many people." He turned to me. "But if we leave, let us say, after tea time, we shall arrive in London before midnight. Time enough for us to get some rest before we proceed to the station and meet Bess."

"This is for my sake," I said.

He slipped his watch back into his vest. "For both our sakes, Phil. And for the sake of Bess, as well."

"How do you plan to do all this, Harry?"

"I shall ferret out the truth. I agree with you, Phil. Something is happening at Maplewhite. Yes. You have, just now, clarified my thinking. Something mysterious is going on here. It will take a very special mind to penetrate this. A subtle mind, a mind trained since childhood to recognize chicanery and sleights of hand. Inspector Marsh obviously has no such mind. But as you know, Phil, Houdini *has*. Trickery, deceit, bamboozlement, they are as wisps of straw to me."

"Uh-huh."

He gave me the wide, wild, charming smile. "By tea time, Phil," he said, and he clapped me on the shoulder and then he turned and strode away.

INSPECTOR MARSH LOWERED his coffee cup and smiled at me as I came back into the library. "Mr. Houdini has left?"

"For a while," I said.

I sat back down. Sergeant Meadows picked up his notebook.

"He won't be wandering off the grounds of Maplewhite, I trust," said Marsh.

"No. He's decided to solve the case for you."

Marsh raised his eyebrows. "Which case would that be?"

"Both of them. All of them."

"How exceedingly kind of him."

"That's the sort of guy he is."

"And how, dare I ask, does he intend to do that?"

"No idea."

"And how much time does he expect he'll need to accomplish this?"

"He figures he can get it done by tea time."

"Indeed. Well then. Onward. You were speaking about the guests who were present on the lawn when the shot was fired."

I told him that. I told him everything. Chasing after the sniper. Explaining my job to Lord Bob in his office and then later, here in the library, to Sir Arthur. The tea party in the afternoon. The news about the Earl's door being locked. Breaking down the door, finding the body. Lord Bob grabbing the Smith & Wesson, then setting it back down on the floor. My finding out, in the Great Hall, that the Winchester had been fired. My talking to Carson, the Earl's valet. Talking to Superintendent Honniwell about the ash on the floor.

"It sounds," said Marsh, "as though the Superintendent wasn't as appreciative of your help as he might've been."

"He probably had a lot on his mind."

"Doubtless," said March dryly. He waved a delicate hand. "Please. Carry on."

I told him about my conversation with Briggs and my learning about the nighttime visits of Darleen, the kitchen maid.

Inspector Marsh raised his eyebrows. "Briggs?" He smiled. "The faithful footman? *Served without grudge or grumblings.* The Tempest. And have you consulted with the peripatetic Darleen?"

"Not yet."

He nodded. "Please. Continue."

I told him about dinner. About the séance and Lord Bob's arrival there. About going to Mrs. Corneille's room.

"You went to her room, of course, solely to discuss the events here at Maplewhite."

"Right. And then Miss Turner showed up."

"Miss Turner of the apparition?"

"Yeah."

I'd just finished telling him what Miss Turner had found in the Earl's room, the stolen knickknacks, the beard and wig, when someone knocked at the library door.

"Come in," Marsh called out.

A servant stepped in and held the door stiffly open. Lord Bob and Lady Purleigh paraded into the library.

Chapter Thirty-one

MARSH AND MEADOWS and I stood up.

"Thank you both so very much for joining us," said Marsh. "I do realize, of course, that my presence in your lovely home is a terrible imposition."

"Got a job to do, haven't you," said Lord Bob. His color had come back and his face was florid again. Maybe the breakfast eggs had buffed it back to normal. Maybe the breakfast fish. "Couldn't stomach it myself," he said. "Prying, snooping about, tracking muck everywhere. But that's the job, isn't it. Duty. Responsibility. Understand completely."

He escorted Lady Purleigh to a high-back chair, held it while she sat. She was wearing black again, and looked as regal as she always looked. Her ash blond hair was swept above her ears and it glistened up there like a crown. She smiled at Lord Bob, then turned and smiled at us.

Lord Bob sat down in the chair beside hers. Marsh and Meadows and I found our seats.

"Can't stay for long, though," said Lord Bob. "Either of us. Services down in the village. Ten o'clock. Don't usually go myself, of course. Opiate of the people, eh? And the vicar's a nincompoop. Still, in the circumstances. Death in the family, et cetera. No choice, really."

"No, of course not," said Marsh. He turned to Lady Purleigh. "Lady Purleigh, permit me to say how sorry I am for your loss. And I apologize to you, as I have to his lordship, for imposing myself at such a time. It is, I'm afraid, a necessary evil."

"I do understand, Inspector. And I thank you."

Marsh nodded. "And as perhaps, you know, *honest plain words best pierce the heart of grief.* Love's Labour Lost."

In the background, the servant glided discreetly around the

room, picking up the breakfast dishes, marching them over to the cart in the corner with great care, as if they were the relics of a saint.

"Oh, Beaumont," said Lord Bob. "Haven't had a chance to congratulate you. Did a crackerjack job on Merridale. Very cool. Know your onions, no question. Looked like an expert out there." He leaned forward, narrowed his eyes. "Don't suppose you've ever boxed professionally, eh?"

I nodded. "Before the War."

He slapped his thigh and turned to Lady Purleigh. "Hear that, Alice? What'd I tell you?" He turned back to me, frowning. "Never mentioned that to Merridale, though, did you?"

"He never asked me," I said.

He frowned again, unsatisfied. "Still. Fellow owes it to the other chap. Let him know these things."

Lady Purleigh put her hand on her husband's forearm. "It's over now, Robert. It's finished. And the boxing match wasn't Mr. Beaumont's idea. Sir David insisted."

Lord Bob didn't want to let it go. "Yes, well," he grumbled. "Still."

Lady Purleigh squeezed his arm, turned to Inspector Marsh. "You wished to ask us some questions, Inspector?"

Finished with the dishes, the servant wheeled the cart from the room.

"Yes, milady," said Marsh. He turned to Lord Bob. "And I assure you I shall ask them with alacrity, Lord Purleigh. *The spirit of the time shall teach me speed.* The Life and Death of King John."

"Is it?" said Lord Bob, sitting back. "Take your word for it. Don't read as much as I should. The occasional *Punch.* And Marx, of course."

Marsh smiled a small swift smile. "Yes. Now, Lord Purleigh. Concerning the death of the Earl. Before the event, had he given you any reason to believe that he might be . . . despondent? Depressed?"

Lord Bob shrugged. "Well, he was mad, you know. And one never knows what a madman will do. Definition of madness, really, isn't it?"

"Mad in what way?" asked Marsh.

"Still living in the nineteenth century. Sixteenth century, more like it. Complete reactionary. One solution for every problem. *Flog 'em!* Tenants behind on the rents, *Flog 'em!* Workers rallying, *Flog 'em!* Two million unemployed in this country, Inspector. And yet the bankers, the capitalists, done damn well off the War, haven't they? Snatched the oil fields from the Arabs—Lawrence's lot. Took over the Suez. German reparations pouring into the treasury." He shook his head. "Damn criminal, you ask me."

"Yes," said Marsh. "But getting back to your father, Lord Purleigh. Had he changed recently, in your opinion? Had he evidenced—?"

"The old—"Lord Bob glanced at me. "The old man wouldn't change, Inspector. *Couldn't.* Stuck in his ways. Made Metternich look like a radical."

"Thank you," Marsh said. Sergeant Meadows made a note in his notebook.

"And what of you, Lady Purleigh?" said Marsh. "Had you perhaps detected any recent changes in the Earl?"

She shook her head. "No I hadn't, Inspector. He seemed to me as vital as he'd always been."

"So this came as a shock to you?"

"Utterly. I can't think how it could have happened. Unless, as Robert suggests, it was some sort of tragic accident."

"Oh?" Marsh turned to Lord Bob. "You believe your father's death was accidental, Lord Purleigh?"

"Possibility, isn't it," said Lord Bob. "Been mulling things over, you know. Gives a man pause, something like this. Makes him think, eh?"

Marsh nodded soberly. "Certainly. *What is pomp, rule, reign, but earth and dust?"*

"That sort of thing, yes. Try to be a bit less morbid, though, myself."

"Yes, but tell me, Lord Purleigh. How might the death of your father have been an accident?"

"Easiest thing in the world," said Lord Bob comfortably. "Say he sends one of the servants to fetch him the pistol. Wants to pot at pigeons. Place is crawling with 'em—told Beaumont that. Say he loads the gun, keeps it ready. No telling when they'll show up, pigeons. Wily birds. Unpredictable. But say he spots one at the window. Suddenly, eh? Might get excited, mightn't he? Might pull the trigger? Eh? And then, bang, Bob's your uncle."

Marsh nodded. "Pull the trigger while the gun was pointed, by happenstance, at his head."

"Exactly. Getting on, you see. Past his prime."

"But I understood from Mr. Beaumont that the bedroom window was closed at the time. If the Earl were of a mind to shoot at pigeons, wouldn't he have opened it?"

"Ah. But he was mad as well, remember. To a madman, what's a window or two, eh? Follow me?"

"Yes, of course. Had he ever shot at pigeons before? To your knowledge?"

Lord Bob shrugged. "First time for everything, though, isn't there."

"Yes. So there is." Marsh nodded. "Thank you, Lord Purleigh. This is a possibility we shall certainly wish to consider."

Sergeant Meadows wrote something in his notebook.

"Only a theory, mind," said Lord Bob. "No proof, of course. And other possibilities exist. Incline toward suicide myself, though. Contradictions of Capitalism, Historical Necessity. Explained all that to Doyle and Beaumont."

"Yes," said Marsh. "Now about this pistol. The American Smith and Wesson. It was taken, I understand, from the collection in the Great Hall."

"Yes."

"The collection is yours?"

"The Earl's. My father's. Don't much hold with guns myself. No shooting allowed at Maplewhite. Not since my father's accident. Fell from a horse, you know. Paralyzed. Years ago."

"I see. Is it fair to say, your lordship, that anyone in the house would have had access to the weapons, and to the ammunition for them?"

Lord Bob shook his head. "Higgens—that's the butler—hid all the ammunition yesterday afternoon. Locked it away. Doyle's suggestion. But the idea was Beaumont's." He turned to me, nodded once. "Credit where credit's due."

"Yes," said Marsh, "but previous to that time. Anyone at all could have removed that pistol. Or the Winchester repeating rifle."

"Beaumont told you about the rifle, did he?" He glanced at me, disapproving. "Still some question in my mind about that," he told Marsh. "It being fired, I mean. But your chaps have it now. Honniwell took it."

Marsh smiled. "Yes. And before he did, anyone at all could have removed it, or the pistol, at his leisure. Is that substantially correct, Lord Purleigh?"

"Could've done, I suppose. Have my doubts, though."

"Thank you. Now, Lord Purleigh. You do understand, I hope, that in order for me to come to some glimmer of an understanding about your father's death, I must determine, first of all, where everyone at Maplewhite was situated at precisely the time it occurred."

"That right?" said Lord Bob. "As I say, not my line, police work. Makes perfect sense, though. How can I help?"

"My Lord, Mr. Beaumont has disclosed to me that all the guests, and Lady Purleigh, were present in the drawing room when the shot occurred. But evidently you were not. Might I ask where you were?"

Lord Bob nodded in agreement. "Got you. Good question. What time would that be, exactly?"

Marsh turned to me. "You said the valet heard the shot at a quarter past four?"

"Yeah."

His eyebrows raised, Marsh turned expectantly to Lord Bob.

Lord Bob frowned. "A quarter past four." He thought for a moment and then he nodded. "Right. Got it. Just returning from MacGregor's. The gamekeeper. Had an idea, you see. Told Doyle about it, and the others. Houdini, Beaumont. This Chin Soo chap, running loose, hot and bothered. Miffed at Houdini. Know about him, do you?"

"Yes."

"Well, what I thought, why not ask the tenants, keep an eye peeled, eh? Scout the area. If the sod's anywhere nearby, they'll flush him out, won't they. Spoke with MacGregor about it, asked him to sniff up some volunteers."

"But from what Mr. Beaumont tells me," said Marsh, "you had at that point already agreed to alert the constabulary to Chin Soo's presence."

"Well, yes," said Lord Bob. "But I wasn't entirely sure that the local constabulary were up to it, you see. Nothing personal, mind. But better safe than sorry, eh? Spoke to my wife about it. She agreed." He turned to Lady Purleigh and smiled. She smiled back.

He turned back to Marsh, pursed his lips. "Now. Where was I?"

"You were asking Mr. MacGregor to sniff up some volunteers."

"Right. He agreed. All arranged. I left. Just getting back here when Higgens came running after me. Couldn't open the door to my father's room, he said. Locked, Carson unhinged. A shot fired, he said. Went up there at a gallop, don't mind telling you. You know the rest?"

"Yes," said Marsh. "Thank you. And you were where, exactly, when Higgens found you?"

Lord Bob thought. "In the west wing. The hallway. On my way to the drawing room."

"But that must have been," said Marsh, "sometime *after* a quarter past four, mustn't it? If Higgens were already aware that the shot had been fired?"

"Must've been, absolutely right. Higgens had already spoken with Carson, of course. So four-twenty, let's say, four twenty-five. Promised my wife I'd be back at four-thirty."

Marsh nodded. Sergeant Meadows wrote something.

"Do you think, Lord Purleigh," Marsh said, "that you could estimate the time of your arrival at Mr. MacGregor's, and the time of your departure?"

"Arrival? Three-thirty, thereabouts. Departure? Four o'clock, I'd say. Spent half an hour there. Chatting and what not." He paused. "Sounds about right."

"Thank you. Now. As to the other incident of yesterday. That mysterious rifle shot, out on the lawn. Have you any idea who might have been responsible for that?"

"But that was Chin Soo." Lord Bob looked at me, puzzled. "We'd agreed on that, I thought."

"I thought it was," I said. "I don't think so now." I explained what I'd already explained to Inspector Marsh, what I'd explained earlier to Doyle. "So it makes more sense," I said, "that whoever fired the rifle was someone who was already here at Maplewhite."

"Rubbish," said Lord Bob. "One of my guests, you mean? Rubbish. Why should the guests start potting at each other? This isn't Afghanistan. No bloody Pathans on the guest list here." He turned to Lady Purleigh. "Sorry, my darling."

He turned to Marsh. "Not that I've anything against Pathans, mind. Resourceful chaps, I hear."

Marsh gave him another quick smile. "Yes," he said. "So. Given the assumption that the individual firing the rifle was *not* in fact Chin Soo, you have no idea who he may have been. Or at whom he may have been firing. Is that correct?"

"Not a clue," said Lord Bob. He turned to me. "Where's this bloody Chin Soo then? Sorry, my love. You saying it was all a false alarm? Eh? Made a compete arse of myself in front of the guests—sorry—babbling about some lunatic magician doesn't even *exist?* That what you're saying?"

"He exists," I said. "But maybe not in the immediate vicinity."

He stared at me. "That's pretty thick, Beaumont. Sent the tenants out for nothing, did I? Made the poor devils go tromping through the forest for no reason at all?"

Lady Purleigh patted her husband's forearm. "Robert. Mr. Beaumont was merely doing his job."

"And he had to do it here, did he?" He scowled at me and crossed his legs. He put his elbow on the arm of the chair and his chin on his fist and he looked away. Beneath the bushy white mustache, his mouth was as thin as a razor scar.

"Excuse me," said Inspector Marsh. "Lady Purleigh. Returning for a moment to that rifle shot. Do you happen to recall where you might have been at the time it was fired?"

"Hang on," said Lord Bob, turning to Marsh. His beetle eyebrows were lowered. "You're not suggesting my *wife* fired the damn thing?"

"Certainly not. But as I told you, I must determine where everyone was situated at the time of the events in question."

The beetles danced upward. "Wanted to know about my father's death, you said."

"And so I do." Marsh smiled. "But a rifle was fired on the same day that the death occurred. This seems to me to be at the very least curious. I shouldn't be doing *my* job properly, my Lord, if I didn't make some attempt to account for it."

"Hmph," said Lord Bob. He uncrossed his legs, then crossed them again the other way. "Rum sort of job," he said. He glanced from me to Marsh. "Both of you."

"And perhaps," added Marsh, "Lady Purleigh saw something at the time which might help us determine the individual responsible."

"I'm afraid I shall disappoint you, then, Inspector," said Lady Purleigh. "I saw nothing. Nothing that might help you, at any rate. I was in the conservatory with Mrs. Blandings, the housekeeper, going over the arrangements for dinner. We heard the shot, both of us—it was quite loud—and we crossed over to the window. It surprised me, the shot. As Robert has told you, shooting is no longer allowed here."

Marsh nodded. "And what did you see, milady?"

"I saw Robert riding his motor bicycle toward the garden. Everyone else was still under the copper beech tree by the walk, gathered around one of the benches. I learned later, of course, that Miss Turner had fainted. And then one of the men began running down along the lawn, in the same direction Robert had gone, toward the rear of the garden. I recognized him as Mr. Beaumont. He disappeared into the woods as well, and I rang for some servants and asked them to run down to the copper beech. To make certain that no one had been hurt."

Marsh asked her, "What did you think had happened?"

"I hadn't the faintest idea, really. I *did* wonder about poachers, because of the shot. But they've never dared come so close to the house before. Even so, I was concerned."

"I thank you, Lady Purleigh," said Marsh. "And I thank you, Lord Purleigh. I think that should do us for the moment. I *am* most grateful for your help."

Lord Bob looked surprised. "That it, then?"

"For the moment," said Marsh. "I really must beg your forbearance, both of you. These things inevitably take longer than anyone would wish them to. But I assure you that I'll attempt to finish it as quickly as I can. And it will, I promise you, be finished. *Come what come may, time and the hour runs through the roughest day.* Macbeth."

"What about the others?" said Lord Bob. "The guests. They're all roaming about, wondering what's happening. You wanted to speak with them, did you?"

"Very much so, yes. I should be very grateful, Lord Purleigh, if you'd ask Miss Turner to join us for a few moments."

"Miss Turner?" said Lord Bob. "Why Miss Turner?"

Marsh smiled. "No particular reason," he said. "I select her entirely at random. *So we profess ourselves to be slaves of chance, and flies of every wind that blows.* The Winter's Tale."

Chapter Thirty-two

WHEN LORD BOB and Lady Purleigh had gone, and the three of us had sat back down, Marsh turned to me and smiled and said, "So. Beaumont. What are your thoughts?"

"I don't buy the pigeons," I told him.

He chuckled. "Lovely. You Americans. And what are your feelings regarding Lord Purleigh himself?"

"I like him. But he inherits."

"Yes. *The old bees die, the young possess their hive.*"

"There's no son," I said. "What happens to this place when Lord Purleigh goes?"

"Maplewhite, you mean? It would be held in trust somehow, I imagine. Depending, of course, on the marriage settlement between him and Lady Purleigh. But most of it, I expect, and possibly all of it, would ultimately go to the daughter. And ultimately, on her death, to her children, should she have any. With a life interest, perhaps, to her husband."

"It all goes to Cecily."

"Cecily?"

"To Miss Fitzwilliam, yes." He smiled. "You don't suspect Cecily Fitzwilliam of murder, do you?"

"Not yet."

He smiled. "And Lord Purleigh?"

"Not yet. What about you?"

Another smile. "Oh, it would be foolish of me to venture an opinion at this stage, don't you think? *Opinion's but a fool, that makes us scan the outward habit by the inward man.* Timon of Athens. But I do hope that Lord Purleigh was *not* responsible."

"Why?"

He looked at me. "Yes, of course. As an American, you wouldn't know, would you? Well, things become rather complex in that event. He's a lord now, you see. A peer. And, as such, he cannot be tried in a normal court of law. If an inquest returns a verdict of wilful murder, he can be tried only by the entire House of Lords, in special session. An elaborate procedure. The King himself becomes involved."

"Messy."

"Very. If in fact he *is* guilty of murder, it would be far better for everyone concerned, and doubtless more easily accomplished, for him to be declared insane, and then tucked away somewhere warm and cozy."

"I don't think he's insane."

Marsh smiled. "He is, you know, if he expects me to believe that his father mistook his own head for a pigeon."

"It could still be suicide. Maybe he's right. Maybe the Earl was crazy. The guy was running around in his pajamas, remember, pretending to be a ghost. And he was stealing junk from people's rooms and hiding it away like a pack rat."

"According to Miss Turner." He smiled. "And, even if she's telling the truth, none of that constitutes evidence of a predisposition toward suicide."

"I notice you didn't mention Miss Turner's theory to Lord Purleigh."

"Naturally not. I must speak with Miss Turner first.

"There's something else about Miss Turner you should know."

"Yes? And what might that be?"

"Someone tried to kill her, it looks like."

He raised his eyebrows. "Indeed." He turned to Sergeant Meadows. "Thicker and thicker grows our plot, eh, Sergeant? We have a proper vichyssoise here."

The sergeant said nothing, which is what he'd been saying all along. He looked down and wrote something in his notebook. Maybe *vichyssoise.*

Marsh turned back to me. "And when did this happen?"

"While she was in the Earl's room last night." I told him about the knife she'd found in her bed, told him about my checking the bolster this morning.

"A knife," said Marsh, nodding thoughtfully. "Purloined, you think, from the Earl's collection of weapons. Not a rifle, not a pistol."

"The ammunition's been locked up."

"Since yesterday afternoon, Lord Purleigh said. Intriguing. That would suggest that the knife was stolen from the collection at some time afterward."

"Or before, by someone who likes knives better than guns."

"Of course," said Marsh. He made a sour face. "Not vichyssoise. Lamb stew. Carrots and celery and onions, and a gravy like cement. Thickness is all. How I should have preferred a simple, unadorned broth, limpid and clear." He looked at me. "You haven't told Lord Purleigh of the knife."

"I wanted to talk to you first."

Someone knocked at the door.

"Miss Turner, no doubt," said Marsh. "A turnip for the pot." He looked toward the door. "Come in," he called out.

MISS TURNER TOLD her story well. She was calm today, and straightforward. Her voice was level and detached even when she described her visit from the ghost on Friday night, and when she described finding the knife in her bed last night.

"Can you think of anyone," Inspector Marsh asked her, when she finished, "who would have reason to harm you?"

"No," she said. "Not harm me. Not really."

She was wearing the gray dress she'd worn when I first met her. Her hair was drawn back. She seemed less stiff now than she'd been that first time, in the drawing room. But she'd gone through a lot this weekend—a lecherous ghost, a snake, an advance from Sir David, a visit to a dead man's room, a dagger in her bed. After all that, talking to a London cop and a Pinkerton man in broad daylight was probably pretty small potatoes.

But now Inspector Marsh had seen her hesitate. He might be delicate, but he didn't miss much. "Not harm you, you say. *Not really*. Please, Miss Turner. Has anyone displayed any sort of hostility toward you? Any sort at all?"

She glanced at me again, then looked back at Marsh. "Well. As

I told Mr. Beaumont, there was an incident yesterday morning. Involving Sir David Merridale."

"Yes?"

She told him pretty much the same thing she'd told me last night, in Mrs. Corneille's room.

Marsh nodded. "And do you believe that Sir David was so frustrated by this rejection that he crept into your room? And plunged a knife into what he believed to be your sleeping form?"

"No," she said quickly. "I don't really." She sat slightly more upright in her chair. "You asked me about hostility, Inspector. I was merely answering your question."

"For which I thank you. Now. Has anyone else evinced hostility toward you? At Maplewhite?"

"No."

"Getting back to this apparition you witnessed on Friday night."

"Yes," she said. "The Earl."

"Miss Turner, have you ever actually seen the Earl?"

"Not before Friday night."

"Disregarding Friday night. Had you ever visited the Earl in his quarters? Had you ever met him?"

"No."

"Did you perchance see him *after* he died?"

"No."

"Then how can you be so certain that the figure in your bedroom *was* the Earl?"

"I've seen his portrait."

"His portrait," said Marsh.

"This morning," said Miss Turner. "I asked one of the footmen whether a portrait of the Earl existed. One did, he told me. In the Great Hall. I went there and examined it. It was dated 1913, only eight years ago. It was the same man. If you placed a wig on him, and a false beard, he would be indistinguishable from the figure in my room."

Marsh smiled. "But so, I daresay, would anyone in a wig and a false beard. Sarah Bernhardt, say."

"And had I discovered a wig and a false beard under Sarah

Bernhardt's bed, then I should be persuaded it was she, and not the Earl, who visited me on Friday."

"And you are willing to testify—in a court of law, for example, under oath—that you did discover the beard and the wig under the Earl's bed?"

"Yes."

"Where are these items now?"

"In Mrs. Corneille's room. Mr. Beaumont suggested, last night, that Mrs. Corneille keep them there."

"Have you discussed them with anyone besides Mrs. Corneille and Mr. Beaumont? With Lord and Lady Purleigh, for example?"

"No," she said. "Mr. Beaumont suggested that we should not do so."

"Mrs. Corneille is a good friend of Lady Purleigh's, so I understand."

"I believe she is, yes."

"And she agreed to this."

"Yes."

Mrs. Corneille hadn't wanted to, and she hadn't agreed until I reminded her that the servants seemed to know about everything that went on in Maplewhite. Someone had already tried to kill Miss Turner, I pointed out. I told her it would probably be safer for everyone, including Lady Purleigh, if we kept a secret or two for a while.

Marsh nodded. "What of this knife you found in your bed? Where is that at the moment?"

"Also in Mrs. Corneille's room."

He nodded again. "All right. Tell me this, Miss Turner. Do you often receive ghostly visitations?"

"No."

"Ever had one before?"

"No."

"This was your very first?"

"It wasn't a ghostly visitation, Inspector. As I've explained, it was a man. It was the Earl."

"And yet Mr. Beaumont tells me that when he and Mr.

Houdini met with you on the following midday, while you were riding, you denied having seen any ghost whatever."

She glanced at me. Her face flushed slightly. It could have been anger, it could have been embarrassment. "Yes," she said. "I did."

"You told him, in fact, that you'd dreamed the ghost, did you not?"

"Yes."

Marsh raised his eyebrows. "Could you explain to me, then, exactly why you said that?"

"I was confused. I hadn't slept. I knew that I'd caused a disturbance, and I felt that the best thing I could do was ignore it and move forward."

"Deny that it had ever happened, in fact. Claim that your ghost had been a dream."

"Yes."

"And yet now you claim that he was not."

"No. No more a dream than the false beard and the wig."

"Excuse me," I said.

Marsh turned to me. "Yes?"

"Could I ask a couple of questions?"

"But my dear chap, of course. We're confreres, are we not? Lead on."

"Miss Turner, did you know any of these people before you came here? Any of the guests?"

"No."

"The Earl? Lady Purleigh? Lord Purleigh? Anyone except Mrs. Allardyce?"

"No. None of them."

"Did you ever hear anything about this ghost? Before you came here?"

"No."

"Then you really don't have any reason to make all this up, do you? No reason to bring along a phony beard and a wig from London, and then plant them in the Earl's room?"

"No," she said to me. For the first time this morning, something like a smile moved quickly across her lips. It disappeared in an instant. "No reason at all," she said to Marsh.

Marsh was smiling at me, and his smile was more permanent. "Thank you, Beaumont, for eliciting that valuable piece of information. And I thank *you,* Miss Turner. I do very much appreciate your candor. You've been both forthright and most lucid." He stood up.

Miss Turner glanced at me and then stood. And then it was my turn to stand.

Miss Turner said to Marsh. "Did you wish to speak with any of the others?"

"Not as yet, thank you. Please inform all of them that I look forward to meeting with them shortly."

She nodded to him, nodded to me, and then turned and walked away. When she left the room, Marsh said, "Time to take a peek at the Earl's room, I think."

I LED THE way, through the halls and up the stairways. Marsh walked along beside me. His hands behind his back, he held his head upright and he peered curiously, left and right, at the furniture and the bric-a-brac as we passed. Sergeant Meadows followed behind, his notebook and pen at the ready.

Marsh didn't say anything until he started climbing the last set of stairs. Then he turned to me and he said, "You're fond of the girl. Miss Turner."

"I think she's telling the truth," I said.

"Obviously you do." He smiled. "But which is cause and which is effect? Are you fond of her because she tells the truth, or do you believe she's telling the truth because you're fond of her?"

"I think she's telling the truth," I said.

"Ah," he said. "Well, she'll make a lovely witness, to be sure. Although I must confess to the tiniest sliver of unease concerning her reason for going to the Earl's room last night."

"She explained that."

"She excused it," he said. "I'm not altogether convinced that she explained it."

"She's read about mediums. She knows they pick up information, and she knows that sometimes they pick it up from servants."

"Assume she's right," said Marsh, "and that it *was* the Earl prancing through her room last night. We haven't established, as yet, that the servants knew of this."

"But Briggs knew about Darleen's visits to the Earl's room. The kitchen maid. Maybe he told Madame Sosostris. And maybe that was what she was talking about at the séance. Maybe Miss Turner came to the right conclusion for the wrong reasons."

We were in the final corridor now. The Earl's rooms were up ahead. "Thicker and thicker," said Marsh. "Peas and parsnips, a sprig of parsley, a dash of sage."

"This is Carson's room," I told him, and I nodded toward the closed door.

"The valet. Yes."

"And this is the Earl's suite."

I turned the knob and pushed open the door, then I stood back to let Marsh go in first.

He looked around the sitting room, at the bare stone walls and the heavy oak furniture and the Oriental carpet.

"Somewhat spartan," he said. "But, good Lord, that *is* a magnificent rug." He glanced at me. "Kurdish. A Senneh." He admired the rug some more. "And seventeenth century, unless I miss my guess. Priceless. Sheer blasphemy to leave it lying about like that."

He stepped delicately around the thing and walked along the wooden floor. I followed him and Sergeant Meadows followed me. Marsh took a last glance at the carpet and then opened the door to the Earl's room.

He stood in the doorway, closely peering at the wooden jamb. He reached out and ran his fingers along the wood.

"According to Houdini," I said, "no one gimmicked the door."

"Hmmm," he said, without looking at me. "So you said." He stepped into the room and examined the broken support for the door's bar. He took a careful look at the edge of the door itself, running his slender fingers along that. He nodded to himself and then he stepped into the room. Sergeant Meadows and I followed.

The fire in the fireplace had gone out and the air in the room was cooler. I could still smell gunsmoke but it was very faint now, wavering weakly behind the smells of dust and age.

"Where was the pistol?" Marsh asked me.

I showed him. "About there. And you can still see the ash. Along the floor."

Sergeant Meadows had gone to the window and he stood there craning his neck to look down at the ground beneath.

"Hmmm," said Marsh. "Yes." He bent at the waist and studied the floor. "Footprints. A herd of wildebeest were apparently frolicking in here."

"We were all here. Doyle, Lord Purleigh, Houdini. And then Superintendent Honniwell and his men."

Marsh was still bent at the waist. "Did you examine the ash when you first arrived?"

"Yeah. No prints. There wouldn't have been. The ash flew out when we broke open the door."

"Hmmm." Bent forward, shuffling his feet, Marsh inched along the floor, toward the far wall. "This is rather intriguing," he said.

"What?"

"Here's a set of footprints that proceed directly to the wall. And then muddle about for a bit." He stood up, looked at me. "But don't return."

At that moment, the stone wall silently swung open, a door-shaped section of it, and the Great Man stepped out of the darkness beyond. He held a glowing railroad lantern in his hand and he was smiling that wide charming smile of his. "The footprints," he announced, "are mine, naturally."

Chapter Thirty-three

THE GREAT MAN knew how to make an entrance.

Inspector Marsh knew how to stand there and smile delicately. "Mr. Houdini," he said. "What a pleasant surprise."

The Great Man ignored him and he aimed his grin at me. "You see, Phil? Already I have discovered something absolutely crucial."

"I see that, Harry. Where does it go?"

"There is a stairway here." He held the lamp up to the opening in the wall. Inside, a narrow stone stairway led down into the blackness. He turned back to me. "It goes down to a kind of tunnel which seems to encircle all of Maplewhite. From this tunnel, additional stairways lead upward to various rooms of the house."

"How'd you find it?" I asked him.

"Simple logic," he said. He turned to Marsh. "May I explain?"

"But of course," said Marsh. "I swoon to hear it." He turned, dusted off the bedspread with a delicate hand, and sat down on the bed as if it were a theater seat. He put his hands on his lap and looked up at the Great Man with his eyebrows raised in attention, or maybe an impersonation of it. Sergeant Meadows was still looming with his notebook over by the window. He crossed his arms over his thick chest and leaned back against the sill.

The Great Man set the lantern on the floor. He rubbed his hands together. "Well," he said. "We have been presented here at Maplewhite with a series of totally baffling events. Even Houdini was, for a while, baffled by these. But then it occurred to me that all of them were very similar, in form, to simple magic tricks, of the sort performed by mediocre magicians." He looked at me. "And what do magic tricks require, Phil?"

I smiled. "You tell me, Harry."

Inspector Marsh had lowered his eyebrows and his head, and he was carefully studying the manicured fingernails of his left hand.

"Timing," said the Great Man. "Misdirection. And, of course, gimmicked props." He shoved his hands into his pockets and he began to pace up and down as he talked. He spoke seriously and slowly, like a professor at a college for dimwits. "Now. In order to understand the mechanics of a successful trick, we must begin with no preconceptions. None whatever. But in the case of the Earl's death, even Houdini had in fact entertained some of these. I had believed that the Earl was paralyzed and bedridden. So had all of us believed. But Miss Turner's story—of the Earl coming to her room, disguised as a ghost—clearly cast some doubt on this."

I said, "I thought you didn't believe her story."

"Aha," he said. "That was *before* I pondered my preconceptions. But suppose, I told myself, suppose Miss Turner's story were true. Suppose that the Earl were, in fact, mobile. If he had actually invaded the privacy of her room on Friday night, how had he done so without being seen?"

Marsh looked up from his fingernails and he frowned. "It was the middle of the night. There was no one about to see him."

"But could he be certain of that? A single witness would have given away his game. *And,* assuming that the Earl did, in fact, commit suicide on the following day, how did he obtain the pistol from the hall without being seen?"

Marsh held up his hand. "Yes, yes, all right. There are other means by which he could have accomplished that. But quite clearly there's also this stairway you've stumbled upon."

The Great Man drew back his head. "Stumbled upon? Hardly, Inspector Marsh. I worked it out, with complete logic. As to the Earl, you see, and his death, I considered the other possibility—that he had *not* committed suicide. That he had been murdered. In such a case, how had the murderer escaped? I have examined that door very carefully, and I knew—"

"Yes," said Marsh. "Mr. Beaumont has informed me. So you deduced there was another entrance to the room."

"I *deduced,* yes, exactly! And I obtained this from the housekeeper, Mrs. Blandings!" He reached into his coat pocket and plucked out a cloth tape measure. He waved his arm through the air in a theatrical circle, so the length of yellow tape streamed into a single hoop. "And I came up here."

He stalked to the door to show us, the tape rippling in the air behind him. On the bed, Marsh turned to follow him. The Great Man spun around. "I examined the room visually. Then I walked to the window."

He strode to the window. Sergeant Meadows stood there watching him, his arms crossed, his face blank. "Excuse me," the Great Man said, and reached out and took hold of Meadow's hips, as though he were going to pick him up and drop him somewhere. Maybe he would have. But Sergeant Meadows looked at Inspector Marsh, who nodded once, and Meadows stepped aside.

"I examined the window very carefully," said the Great Man. "Measuring, measuring." Bending over, he showed us. He stood up. "Then I went all around the room, measuring its dimensions. All of its dimensions." He waved the tape measure through the air. "Then I went to the room next door."

For a second I thought he was going to stalk over there, expecting us to follow him. He didn't.

"I examined *its* dimensions," he said. "I—"

"Yes," said Marsh. "I do believe I follow. You determined where the passage must have been."

"Exactly! And then, when I rushed back here, I set about finding it. And, of course, I did."

He went over to the opening in the wall. "It is an ingenious mechanism. You see." He pushed shut the rectangle of stone. It moved back into place, silently and smoothly. The wall seemed completely solid now. "Counterweighted. Simple but effective. The key is here."

He pressed one of the stones to his left. Silently and smoothly, the rectangle swung open.

Smiling widely, the Great Man turned back to us. "You see? Houdini succeeds before others even attempt."

"How very enterprising of you," said Inspector Marsh.

"Yes," said the Great Man. "Thank you."

"And have you by any chance examined this tunnel?"

"Only a small portion of it." He folded up the tape measure. "I climbed up one of the stairways. It leads into another room. Not a bedroom. A small parlor." He stuffed the tape back into his pocket. "But there are many of these stairways. I feel certain that one of them leads into Miss Turner's room."

"But you haven't actually established that," said Marsh.

"There is no question in my mind," said the Great Man. "And no doubt one of the stairways also leads to the Great Hall." He turned to me. "And so, Phil. The Earl *could* have removed the gun from the collection with no one being the wiser."

"Or somebody else could've taken it," I said. "And used that stairway to come up here and kill him."

"Yes." He nodded. "Both are possible, of course."

"Oh?" said Marsh. He was smiling. "You don't mean to say that you still remain baffled by something?"

The Great Man raised his head. "I shall determine the truth. And very shortly, I believe."

Marsh nodded. "Yes. Mr. Beaumont has apprised me of your plan. By afternoon tea, isn't that right?"

"Yes. That is correct."

"He that is proud eats up himself. Troilus and Cressida."

"Pride is irrelevant," said the Great Man. "What Houdini sets out to do, he does."

"By tea time."

"Exactly."

"You *will* permit me to harbor a stray doubt or two?"

"Harbor as many as you like. Harbor a fleet of these. I shall succeed, nonetheless."

"Are you a betting man, Mr. Houdini?"

The Great Man drew himself up. "Houdini never wagers."

"No," said Marsh. "I shouldn't have thought so."

"But," said the Great Man, "Houdini has been known, on occasion, to accept a challenge." He looked at Marsh. "Are you offering a challenge, Inspector Marsh?"

"I prefer to think of it as a wager. A gentleman's wager, if you like. With no money passing hands. I'll wager that you will *not* solve this case by the time of afternoon tea."

"And that *you* will?"

"Oh," said Marsh, smiling, "I fully expect to solve it long before then."

"Oh yes?"

"Oh yes."

The Great Man studied him for a moment. "Very well," he said. "I accept." He stepped forward holding out his hand. Marsh rose from the bed and took it.

The Great Man dropped Marsh's hand, took a look around the room, and then drew himself up. "I must go," he announced, and then he did, stalking out the door.

Marsh looked over at me. He smiled wryly. "Silly of me. But your employer has rather a way of getting under one's skin."

"Yeah."

Marsh reached into his pants pocket, eased out a watch, glanced at its face. He nodded, slipped it back. He turned to Sergeant Meadows. "Grab that lantern, will you, Meadows, and take a look at the tunnel. Follow all the stairways. Determine into which rooms they lead. Discreetly, of course."

Beneath his heavy brow Sergeant Meadows glanced at me. He looked back at Marsh. For the first time he spoke. "And you, sir?"

"Oh, I'll muddle along on my own for a while." Marsh turned to me. "Unless you'd care to come along?"

"Wouldn't miss it," I told him.

TALKING TO THE Great Man, Inspector Marsh had seemed very sure of himself. And he seemed sure of himself for the next few hours, but I noticed that we were moving pretty quickly through the house.

First we went to the room of Carson, the Earl's valet. Carson was in bed, wearing a white nightshirt, but he was willing to talk. He looked worse than he had yesterday. His face was paler and his eyes were more dull. The trembling of his hands was more intense.

Marsh sat in the chair, I stood leaning against the wall. Marsh asked Carson pretty much the same questions I'd asked yesterday and Carson gave pretty much the same answers.

Then Marsh said, "I understand that Lord and Lady Purleigh made a visit to the Earl's room on Friday night."

"Yes, sir," said Carson. "They did, sir." His shaking hands moved vaguely along his chest.

"Were you present at the time?"

"No, sir."

"Do you have any idea what the three of them discussed?"

"No, sir, I don't."

"How did you know, Carson, that Lord and Lady Purleigh came to visit the Earl?"

"I saw them, sir. Passing by in the hallway. I was in my room, sir, and generally I keep my door open."

"Do you indeed. At all times?"

"Until I'm ready to sleep, sir. In case the Earl calls for me. Usually, around twelve, I go in to check on him, sir." He frowned, took a ragged breath. "*Went* in to check on him, sir. Before I went to sleep."

Marsh nodded. "You could hear the Earl calling, all the way from his bedroom?"

"Yes, sir. There was nothing wrong with the Earl's voice, sir." He made a feeble smile.

"You could hear him when the doors were shut? *His* doors?"

"No, sir. During the day, sir, we left all the doors open, my door and the Earl's. Except when he took his nap, sir, before tea. I always shut his bedroom door then. It helped him to sleep."

"So your door was open yesterday afternoon, before you brought him his tea."

"Yes, sir."

"Did anyone pass by?"

"No, sir. No one, sir."

In the same conversational voice he'd been using all along, Marsh asked him, "You know the kitchen maid, Darleen?"

Carson blinked. "Yes, sir."

"Have you ever seen Darleen pass by your room?"

"No, sir." He blinked again. "Why should I, sir?"

"I've heard that this Darleen made an occasional visit to the Earl's room. Late at night."

Carson shook his head. "Oh no, sir. Why should she, sir? Oh." Carson opened his eyes wide. "Excuse me, sir. I tell a lie. Once, several months past, sir—I was ill, sir, my stomach, and I couldn't perform my duties. And I believe it was young Darleen, sir, from the kitchen, who helped the Earl then."

Marsh nodded. "Tell me, Carson. How long have you known of the secret passageway in the Earl's room?"

Carson's hand jumped and he frowned, puzzled. "Secret passageway, sir?"

"Come now, Carson. It's been there for years. Centuries, I expect. You *must* have known."

Carson shook his head. "But I didn't sir, I swear." He tried to rise up from the bed, gasped out a small cough, and he lay back down. His hands moved along his chest. "A secret passageway, sir? In the Earl's room? Where, sir?"

Marsh smiled. "Carson, do you know the penalties for perjury?"

Carson's eyes were frantic. "Sir, I swear to you, I know nothing of a secret passageway. Nothing, sir. I swear it!"

Marsh stared at him for a moment. Then he stood up, reached into his pocket, took out his watch, glanced at it, slid it back into his pocket. He turned to me. "We're for the kitchen, I think."

The Morning Post

Maplewhite, Devon

August 19

Dear Evangeline,

More boulders. *Many* more of them. *Large* boulders.

And no genteel rolling down the hillside for this pack; no. All at once they coughed from the clouds and smashed to earth at precisely that piece of it upon which I, wide-eyed and well intentioned, happened to be dawdling. I still lie here, flattened, beneath them.

Mr Beaumont is the largest of these.

An arresting image, don't you think? Me lying flattened beneath Mr Beaumont?

If such a position ever actually befell me—somewhere outside the chaste confines of metaphor—I should be far from the only woman at Maplewhite who had, shall we say, enjoyed it.

It appears that I've been mistaken about Mr Beaumont. In several ways.

Last night, you'll recall, I was about to go slinking through the dark silent halls of Maplewhite, in the hope of learning something—

Which I did; and, Evy, you won't believe me—

You recall the first ghost, the one I promised to explain but never did, really? It transpires that *that* ghost was no ghost at all. He was Lord Purleigh's father, the Earl of Axminster.

I do not invent. Apparently, whenever the whim took him, the late Earl would don a wig and an artificial beard and go bounding through the rooms of astonished paid companions, giggling obscenities and waving that organ which Mrs Applewhite once characterized as "the progenerative member". (*Member of what?* I remember you asking her; you were so heartless, Evy.)

Today the entire episode strikes me as more pathetic than terrifying. I honestly feel rather sorry for the old man. How very sad to advertise one's needs, and one's means, to total strangers. How very sad, really, to feel compelled to do so.

My aplomb of today, however, may in some way be a result of the Earl's recent death. He won't, ever again, be brandishing his endowments (which were considerable, by the way); not for me, and not for anyone else, poor soul.

But to return to the equally astonishing Mr Beaumont. Last night, at a few minutes before one o'clock, after sealing your letter, I switched off the light and eased open my bedroom door and peeped out. I looked to the left. I saw nothing. I looked to the right. I saw Cecily Fitzwilliam, sheathed in a filmy silk robe, slide into Mr Beaumont's darkened room as easily and as comfortably as a powdered foot slides into a familiar slipper.

I'd known about them, of course, about their affair. Still, I was rather shocked (and not a little envious, I confess) at the brazenness of the woman—promenading semi-naked through the hallways, where anyone might see her, even a slinking, spiteful paid companion.

I waited. I listened for the silence that would signal safety. This I heard, and I opened the door, closed it quietly behind me, and then galloped down the corridor to the post box. I slipped your letter inside and then I cantered down the stairs and through another hallway and up some more stairs and down another corridor to the Earl's room, where I found the wig and the beard beneath his bed.

Why the Earl's room?

Why must you pester me with questions?

I was beneath the bed myself at the time, or I shouldn't have discovered the beard and the wig.

Oh, it's an impossibly long story, Evy, and I'll relate it to you one day, I promise, but just now I want to get to the knife and to Mr Beaumont.

The knife was a silver dagger—an antique, and quite handsome, really—and it was thrusting out of my bed like a wicket when I returned to my room. I'd created a Sylvia—you remember the Sleeping Sylvias we fashioned from pillows and bolsters before we crept out the window of Miss Applewhite's? I'd constructed a Sylvia before I set off for the Earl's room, and this one had been impaled.

I became an imbecile for a moment or two, wondering how on earth the knife had got there. And then I realized that of course someone had *put* it there, deliberately, *stabbed* it there, having mistaken Sylvia for myself; and I promptly came down with a very bad case of the collywobbles.

No, I don't know who did it. And I can't imagine why.

After a few moments, in a sort of daze I snatched up the knife and went stumbling off toward Mrs Corneille's room.

I knocked on the door. She opened it and I staggered in. And who should be there, lurching up from a small rococo sofa, but Mr Beaumont.

He was fully dressed. Perhaps he'd clothed himself again, after the earlier rendezvous with Cecily. Or perhaps, back in his room, Cecily had lunged upon him like a panther while he still wore them, and the two had toppled to the floor, and there, without wasting a moment, in the hurried lunge and thrust of passion, they . . .

Oh dear.

It's the weather, Evy. Another day hot and sultry, and the sweetness of the sunlight sprawling across the green lawn. Everyone else has gone to Sunday services and I'm writing this out of doors, on the patio beside the conservatory. Squirrels are leaping about, and so, I fear, is my fancy.

Whatever the explanation, there was Mr Beaumont looking dark and rather dashing in his dinner jacket (and trousers, etc.).

This might have been, you may say, an innocent meeting, his engagement with Mrs Corneille. I might (almost) have believed so myself if I hadn't, while sitting down, happened (by the purest chance) to glance into the front of the standing Mr Beaumont and discover that he was in a state that your Mrs Stopes describes as "masculine readiness."

Perhaps—and this occurs to me only just now—making love while clothed is another of those perplexing American innovations, like the Charleston. Perhaps *this* is what is actually meant by "get up and go". Perhaps when I knocked at the door he and Mrs Corneille, both fully dressed, were tumbling wildly across the floor.

No. I can—and with a vividness that is not at all unpleasant—picture Mr Beaumont so performing; but not the elegant Mrs Corneille. And yet I suspect that had I not knocked at the door, *someone's* clothing would have been, at the very least, profoundly rearranged.

Mr Beaumont is indefatigable, it seems.

In any event, I was flustered when I began the conversation with the two of them; and, throughout the course of it, I could feel my face flushing idiotically whenever I looked at him.

He isn't as self-absorbed as I've portrayed him in these letters, Evy. He was most charming, really—both last night, when I spoke with him and Mrs Corneille, and today, during my interrogation by the pompous Inspector Marsh of Scotland Yard. He even went so far as to defend me.

But I get ahead of myself.

I told them the entire story last night. Mr Beaumont and Mrs Corneille.

Very nearly the entire story. I didn't mention the other ghosts, the mother and the young boy I'd seen down by the mill. The more I consider them, the more I begin to believe that they were a product of my imagination. My nerves were stretched taut, the light beneath the willow tree was thin and gray. And, moreover,

My goodness. I've just had quite the most bizarre and disquieting conversation with Mr Houdini. I'm at a loss. If what he seems to be suggesting is true—

Let me see if I can structure this.

He came strutting down the walkway, greeted me with a cheery 'Good day!,' plopped himself beside me on the bench, and declared that he was planning to resolve everything.

I closed my notebook—hiding this page, with its tumbling speculations—and I said, 'I beg your pardon?'

He waved his hand quickly back and forth as though chasing away flies. 'All this confusion, Miss Turner. Rifles and pistols and dying Earls. *Ghosts.* It has gone on for far too long, and I intend to resolve it.'

'I see,' I said. That was rather an exaggeration.

He said, 'I have been speaking with my associate, Phil Beaumont, and that policeman from London. Phil has told me of your encounter with the Earl. I sympathize completely, Miss Turner. I realize that to a demure young woman such as yourself, the Earl's behaviour must have seemed monstrous.'

I nodded demurely and looked down at my notebook. And blushed demurely, thinking of the things I'd written there.

'I should tell you,' he said, 'that I have discovered the means by which he effected his invasion of your room.'

'The means?' I said stupidly.

'Yes. By a careful examination of the Earl's room, I was able to locate a secret passageway behind the wall. This leads down a narrow stairway to a kind of tunnel which encircles all of Maplewhite. From this tunnel, additional stairways lead upward to the various rooms of the house. One of them, no doubt, leads into your room. No doubt the Earl used this on Friday night.'

'A secret passageway? I was beginning to feel rather like a parrot.'

'Correct.'

'But I thought he simply came in through the door.'

He shook his head like a prim headmistress. 'He has lived here all his life, and so must have known about the passageway. And why should he take a chance on being seen in the hallways? But, Miss Turner, a moment's thought will tell you that if the Earl used the passageway, then someone else might have used it, at some other time.'

'Yes?' I said. I was still rather lost in visions of the Earl gliding in his long nightgown through dark vaulted passageways, torchlight flickering along stone walls, bats fluttering, rats squeaking.

'Phil has also told me of the knife you found in your bed, last night,' he said. 'Whoever put it there may also have used the passageway.'

'Yes,' I said. 'I see.'

'You comprehend what this means?'

And I did, Evy. It meant that if the passageway had been used last night, it had been used by someone familiar with Maplewhite. Someone other than the Earl, who was no longer among us. 'Yes, but—'

'I have been pondering my preconceptions, Miss Turner,' he said. 'Someone attempted to kill you last night. This, I believe, was an attempt to silence you. I believe that you have heard something, or seen something, that will provide me the explanation for the mysterious events that have occurred here.'

'But what?'

He smiled. 'It is precisely to determine this that I have tracked you down.' He pulled a gold watch from his vest pocket, glanced at it, frowned, and looked at me. 'Now, Miss Turner, I would be very grateful if you will tell me everything that has happened to you since you arrived at Maplewhite.'

And, Evy, finally, I did so. I told him everything, including the tale of the two ghosts at the mill. I hadn't told anyone of this, not Mrs Corneille, not Mr Beaumont, and certainly not the imperious Inspector Marsh. I felt that I should be unable to convince them of the first ghost's identity if I complicated the story by mentioning a second ghost, and then a third. One truth, I felt, would have blemished the other. And, as I said, I had honestly begun to doubt their existence.

I nearly *did* mention them to Inspector Marsh. But the man was so accusatory, so vain and self-satisfied, so prissily officious—how he ever managed to become a police officer I cannot imagine. The London underworld and its denizens must be a good deal less robust than the press accounts suggest. Inspector Marsh would survive for perhaps five minutes in Sidmouth.

Mr Houdini possesses a certain smugness of his own, but he listened carefully to everything, paying especial attention to my chronicle of the mother and the young boy. He asked countless questions, nodding thoughtfully all the while, and then asked to hear the rest of my tale.

I gave it to him, eliminating only the story of Cecily and Mr Beaumont, which is no one's business, I think, but theirs. At the end, he began asking me a series of really quite remarkable questions. From the gist of them—no, I can't tell you even that, Evy. I'm not being coy, honestly. I promised him; I swore I would tell no one what he asked me.

'And what shall I tell Inspector Marsh,' I asked him, 'if he asks about the ghosts?'

He raised his head, like a Caesar. 'Then you must tell him. Houdini always plays fair.'

And with that, he stood up, thanked me, and set off quickly back into the house.

I really don't know what to do, Evy. This is all extremely distressing. If the ghastly things that Mr Houdini suspects are true, then—

I cannot.

I shall post this. And then I shall sit down and think everything out.

All my love,
Jane

Chapter Thirty-four

MRS. BLANDINGS WAS a tall thin woman with a narrow mouth and a narrow chin and permanently narrowed brown eyes glinting from either side of a curved, narrow nose. She had been a handsome woman once, but time and care had deepened the hollows of her face and hardened the edges. Her hair was white and it was curled so tightly that patches of pink scalp glistened between the coils. She wore a long black cotton dress so heavily starched that it rustled like dead leaves whenever she breathed.

She kept her hands on the kitchen table, her fingers interlaced. The hands were thin and almost elegant but her knuckles were red, as though she'd been pounding them against bricks.

"I will not dally," she told Inspector Marsh grimly. "I am incapable of dallying. Constitutionally."

"We won't take much of your time, Mrs. Blandings," Marsh assured her. He hadn't been doing much dallying himself. We'd come down here at nearly a run and he hadn't quoted Shakespeare once.

We were sitting down at a table in the corner of the kitchen. It was a huge room, maybe thirty feet high. Fireplaces and ovens were built into the stone walls. There were five or six big wooden cupboards and six or seven long wooden shelves sagging beneath rows of heavy porcelain canisters. Four big sinks were built into the marble counter. Hanging on the walls were pots and pans and saucers and colanders and bowls and caldrons. There was a big metal drain in the floor, so you could hose everything down after you butchered your whale.

"Lady Purleigh tells me," said Marsh, "that the two of you were together yesterday when you heard the rifle shot."

"Poachers," she said. "No respect at all these days."

"And where were you, exactly, when you heard the shot?"

"In the conservatory. Discussing dinner with her ladyship."

"How long have you been employed here, Mrs. Blandings?"

"All my life."

"So, doubtless, you know the family well."

"Yes."

"Would you say it was a happy family?"

"Certainly."

"No arguments, no dissension?"

"None."

"But even in the best of families, surely—"

"It isn't my place to speak of other families. You asked about this one. Was it happy. Yes, I said."

Marsh nodded. "So you did. Are you prepared to speak about ghosts, Mrs. Blandings?"

She eyed him skeptically. "Ghosts?"

"Were you aware that one of the guests, a Miss Turner, claims to have been visited by a ghost on Friday night?"

"Nonsense. The woman must be hysterical."

"You don't believe in ghosts."

"Of course not. But what I believe is hardly your concern, is it?"

Marsh smiled. "Do you believe, Mrs. Blandings, that the late Earl committed suicide?"

"I have no opinion on the matter."

"None?"

"None."

"The Earl had been infirm for some time," said Marsh.

"For three years."

"Had you been given any reason to believe that his condition might have been improving?"

"Improving? He was paralyzed."

Marsh nodded.

Mrs. Blandings glanced impatiently around the room, looked back at Marsh. "Are we finished? I've things to do."

"Yes. For the moment. But I should like to speak to one of the kitchen maids. A young woman named Darleen."

"The O'Brien girl? Why?"

Marsh smiled. "Forgive me, Mrs. Blandings, but that's hardly your concern, is it?"

She blinked, and then she pursed her lips and stood. "I'll send her in," she said, and left.

Marsh turned to me and smiled. "Not exactly forthcoming, was she?"

"Maybe Darleen will be different."

DARLEEN WAS DIFFERENT. She wore black patent leather shoes and white cotton stockings and a black button-up cotton dress printed with tiny pink fleurs de lis. It was a conservative outfit, or it was supposed to be, and probably she'd worn it to church this morning. I felt sorry for the minister.

She was in her early twenties and her body was so lush and ripe beneath the dress that she might as well be naked, and she knew it. She swept into the kitchen flickering like a colt and she tossed back her thick red hair and grinned at us. "And what've you done to poor Mrs. Blandings, you two? The poor old dear is givin' off more steam than an express train."

Both Marsh and I had stood. "Miss O'Brien?" he said.

"That's me," she said, and she cocked her head and smiled. Her eyes were green and bright and her cheeks were dusted faintly with freckles, cinnamon on cream. "And you're the police, I hear. Come all the way from the great city of London."

"I'm Inspector Marsh. This is Mr. Beaumont. Please, Miss O'Brien, be seated."

She plopped down into the same seat Mrs. Blandings had used. She stretched out her long legs and she crossed them at the ankles and slapped her hands into her lap, like a little girl playing at being a grown-up. She smiled at me and then at Marsh.

Marsh and I sat down. "Miss O'Brien," he said, "I intend to be straightforward with you."

"Sure," she said, and she sat back and opened her eyes in mock innocence, "and haven't the police always been straightforward?"

"You've had some experience of the police, have you, Miss O'Brien?"

"Haven't all the Irish? Experience of the Garda *and* the English." She smiled. "But that's over now, isn't it? Home Rule has come—finally, but better late than never."

"Yes," said Marsh, "to be sure. Miss O'Brien, we know about your late-night visits to the room of the late Earl. We know that these have been going on for some time."

She smiled again. "Briggs. He'll be the little bird that sang. Nasty pommy poof."

"So you don't deny it."

She shrugged. "And what would be the point?"

"No point whatever."

"There you are, then. And now you'll be runnin' off to her ladyship with the story. And young Darleen is sacked again. Well, fair enough. It's back to Ireland for me anyway. We kicked out the ruddy English, and once we kick out the ruddy priests we'll have a paradise on our hands."

"Miss O'Brien, so long as you cooperate, I see no need to apprise Lady Purleigh, or anyone else, of your relationship with the Earl."

"Cooperate, is it?" She grinned and put her elbow on the table. "And just what sort of cooperation was it you had in mind?"

"Merely the answers to a few questions."

"Well, get on with them then. Always a treat to answer questions from the police." She looked at me, looked back at Marsh, jerked her head toward me. "He doesn't have much to say for himself, this one, does he?"

"Mr. Beaumont is acting as an observer."

"And he's a demon at that, isn't he." She smiled at me.

Marsh asked his questions. Yes, she'd visited the Earl once or twice a week over the past four months. She couldn't get away more often than that. Yes, she visited only at night. Yes, she'd waited until Carson, the Earl's valet, was asleep, so she could creep past his room. Yes, she'd heard from other servants that the Earl had often argued with his son, Lord Purleigh, but she and the Earl had never spoken about his son. "Or much of anything else," she smiled. And, no, she didn't believe that the Earl had committed suicide.

"How, then, did he die?" Marsh asked her.

"An accident, wasn't it? They say the door was locked when the gun went off."

"How do you suppose he obtained the pistol?"

"One of the servants?"

"You seem to be doing an admirable job of containing your grief at the Earl's death, Miss O'Brien."

She glared at him for a moment. Then she said, "Listen to me, Mr. Inspector Marsh from London. I liked the poor sweet man. That toad Briggs, he's told you about the money, I don't doubt. And you'll not hear me denyin' the old man slipped me the odd crown or two, now and again. And why shouldn't he? He wanted me to buy some lovely new dresses for myself, didn't he, and nice handmade shoes, and silk stockings, so I could come to him looking like a lady. And who was I to tell him no? The good Lord knows he could afford it. But I liked him. He was dear with me, and he was as grateful for my bein' with him as a wee young boy. Well, he's dead now, and I'm sorry. I hope he's happy as a lark wherever he is, that's the God's honest truth, but if you're waitin' for me to start wailin' and weepin' for *your* sake, then you're in for quite a wait, Mr. Inspector."

Marsh smiled. "But then you've already done your grieving, haven't you? In the Earl's bedroom. Last night."

She stared at him. She turned and stared at me.

"You were seen, Miss O'Brien," said Marsh.

"But who—" She lifted her chin. "Well, what of it? No crime, is it?"

"No. Tell me. Had the Earl ever given you cause to believe that he was recovering from his paralysis?"

"But, Inspector sir, it was only his legs that didn't work proper. The rest of him worked perfectly fine."

"But he was still unable to use his legs."

She grinned. "He didn't need them, did he."

Marsh sat back and nodded. "Thank you, Miss O'Brien. I may speak with you again later."

She shrugged as if she didn't really care, one way or the other.

* * *

AFTER SHE LEFT, somehow the kitchen seemed even larger.

I turned to Marsh, who was staring down at the floor. I said, "You weren't sure she was the woman in the Earl's room."

He looked up. "Hmmm? No, not until she admitted it. I took a bit of a chance there."

"You were right."

He smiled. "It does happen."

"She didn't seem to know about the passageway. Or about the Earl being able to walk."

"No. If in fact he was." He slipped his hand into his pocket, pulled out his watch, frowned at it. He looked at me. "Enough of the serving class for now, I think. Back to the gentry."

A SERVANT TOLD us that most of the guests were in the drawing room. Sir David was there, and Cecily and Dr. Auerbach and Lady Purleigh. Everyone was gathered in the far corner of the enormous room.

They all looked up at us when we approached, but only Lady Purleigh spoke. "Inspector Marsh. And Mr. Beaumont. Did you need something?"

"I apologize for disturbing you once again, Lady Purleigh," said Marsh.

"Not at all. Please, do sit down. Mr. Beaumont, please."

The two of us sat on the same small sofa. "As I told you earlier," Marsh said, "it's rather important that I ascertain where everyone was located when these unpleasant events took place yesterday. All of you were here in the drawing room, I understand, when the Earl died. It remains for me to determine where everyone was when the rifle shot was fired."

"Yes," she said. "I understand. Did you wish to speak to any one of us in private?"

"Thank you, but that shouldn't be necessary. I have only a few questions." He looked at Cecily. "Miss Fitzwilliam?"

Cecily looked at him, her face composed and empty. "Yes?"

"Could you tell me where you were yesterday, at approximately one o'clock in the afternoon?"

"I was visiting with Mrs. Coburn in the village. She is an old friend of the family's." Cecily had found her drawl and she sounded like someone who planned to be more careful with it from now on.

"At what time, Miss Fitzwilliam," said Marsh, "did you arrive there, and at what time did you leave?"

"I arrived at about eleven, I believe. I left at about two. Shortly after two o'clock. Yes. When Ripley came to fetch me, Mrs. Coburn told me it had just gone two."

"Who is Ripley?" asked Marsh.

"One of the servants. Mrs. Coburn sent her nephew to the chemist's to ring my mother. To tell her I was ready to return."

Marsh turned to the mother. "And you dispatched Ripley, Lady Purleigh?"

"Yes," she said. "The time was a little before two. It takes perhaps fifteen minutes to reach Mrs. Coburn's by auto, perhaps a bit more."

Marsh nodded, turned back to Cecily. "And you were with Mrs. Coburn the entire time?"

"Yes."

"Was anyone else present?"

"No."

Marsh nodded. "Thank you. Dr. Auerbach. Where were you at that time, Doctor?"

Dr. Auerbach nodded. Light sparkled off the lenses of his pince-nez. "Aha, yah. As I explained to Mr. Beaumont, I was in the cemetery of the small church. I enjoy making the rubbings of the tombstones, you see. I have a collection of these."

"And what time did you leave, Doctor?"

"One o'clock?" He ran his hand back over his shining skull. "Yah. One. I returned to Maplewhite on the foot, and this walk required of me an hour and a half, almost exactly. Six miles, it would be. I walk one mile in exactly fifteen minutes. Mrs. Corneille has explained to me that it was two-thirty when I went to examine Miss Turner."

"And why did you examine Miss Turner?"

"Aha, yah. She had fallen off her horse. She was bruised, but otherwise unharmed. A strong, healthy young girl, in the physical sense."

Marsh nodded. "And while you were in the cemetery, Doctor, did you see anyone? Did anyone see you?"

"Yah, Mr. Beaumont, the same thing he asked me. I spoke with the vicar. A very charming man."

"Thank you, Doctor. And you, Sir David?"

"Yes?" said Sir David. He hadn't looked at me since Marsh and I arrived. There was a small mouse beneath his right eye and a gray bruise on his left jaw.

"Where were you, Sir David, between twelve o'clock and one o'clock yesterday?"

"In the village."

"Where in the village?"

"The Cock and Bull."

"That's a pub, is it?"

"It is *the* pub." He smiled. Blandly. "Not by virtue of its cachet, I hasten to add, but by virtue of its uniqueness. It is the only pub in the village."

"And you were in one of the bars?"

"You overestimate its splendors. It has but one. And, no, I was not in it. I had taken a room."

"A room, Sir David?"

"Yes. I was feeling ill. A recurrent ailment—something I picked up in the Bosphorus, years ago. I took a room so that I might rest for a bit."

"Why didn't you simply return to Maplewhite?"

Sir David shrugged. "I should've needed to locate the means to do so, and then suffer through an unpleasant automobile journey back here. I was there, in the pub. A room was available. It was bearable, just. I took it."

"And at what time did you leave the pub, Sir David?"

"Three-ish, I'd say."

"And how did you return here?"

"The landlord laid on transport. A car and driver."

"And what was the landlord's name?"

"I can't imagine." He smiled. "But he oughtn't be difficult to find."

"Do you know the name of the driver, Sir David?"

"Of course not."

Marsh nodded. He stood up. So did I. "Thank you all," he said.

Chapter Thirty-five

OUTSIDE THE DRAWING room, Marsh turned to me. "Charming fellow, Sir David. Tell me. I saw only the finale to your boxing match with him, the last few minutes. For how long did it last?"

"You saw most of it."

"Ah," he said. "Lovely." He smiled. "Well, then. Do you feel up to visit to the metropolis?"

"Purleigh?" I said. "Why not."

"I—"

"Phil?" It was the Great Man, scurrying toward us down the hallway.

"Yeah, Harry?"

He reached us. His hair was wilder than usual, bristling from his temples like the stuffing from an old couch. He adjusted his tie and nodded curtly to Inspector Marsh. "Phil," he said, "I need your assistance for a few moments."

I looked at Marsh.

"You run along," he said, "I'll use the auto and dash into the village on my own." He turned to the Great Man. "Making progress, are we, Mr. Houdini?"

"Certainly. And you, Inspector?"

"One small step at a time." He smiled. "I'll see you at tea, shall I?"

"Naturally."

Marsh nodded, turned, and walked away.

When he was out of earshot, I looked at the Great Man. "What's up, Harry?"

He glanced at the departing back of Inspector Marsh, then turned to me. "Phil," he said, his voice low, "we must proceed to the old mill."

"What old mill?"

"Out there." He waved his hand—vaguely, impatiently—toward the lawn. "Come."

"Why an old mill?" I asked him as we set off down the hall.

"To investigate."

"Uh-huh. And why do you need me?"

He looked at me earnestly. "But Phil. Suppose Chin Soo is out there, waiting? It was your idea that we should be careful, was it not?"

"Come on, Harry. You don't think Chin Soo is out there. What is it? You need someone to fetch and carry?"

We were trotting down a broad stairway now, old pictures of dead people on the walls, the glances from their dead eyes following us.

"It is possible, yes, perhaps," he said. "But still, one is always wise to take precautions." He cleared his throat. Casually—more casually than he was walking—he said, "So. Phil. Have you had a pleasant time with Inspector Marsh?"

"A swell time."

"And has he learned anything of interest?"

We were bustling down a corridor, toward the conservatory. "You think that'd be fair, Harry? Me telling you?"

He raised his head. "Never mind, Phil. Forget that I asked."

I smiled. "It's okay. First we talked to Carson, the Earl's—"

"Beaumont! Houdini!"

Lord Bob, coming up behind us. He was looking rumpled again, and frantic. He strode toward us, his feet thumping against the floor. "They've found the bloody thing," he said to me. He tugged at his big white mustache. "The police. You knew about it, didn't you? That damn bloody tunnel?"

I nodded. "It was Harry who found it."

Lord Bob looked from me to the Great Man and back. His shoulders rose and sank in a heavy sigh. The mustache fluttered as he blew out a long streamer of air. "That big chap, the sergeant. He blundered into Marjorie's room. Mrs. Allardyce. She was resting. Went into fits. Marjorie did, I mean. Clubbed him with a vase. Huge uproar. A servant heard, called Higgens, he called me."

He shook his head sadly. "French. Eighteenth century, I think. A thousand pieces now."

I said, "Why didn't you tell us about the tunnel, Lord Purleigh?"

"I—" He looked around him, then back at us. He nodded. "Come along. We'll talk."

"I'VE TOLD YOU that my father was mad," said Lord Bob.

He and the Great Man and I were in the same small parlor that Doyle and I had used yesterday, not far from the conservatory. Lord Bob sat across the room.

"He was a perfect lunatic," he said. "And not only because he wanted to flog everyone—although that was bad enough, of course. But he did worse. He loved to dress up, you see, as Lord Reginald—the family ghost—and terrify young women. Guests. Wore a nightgown, a false beard, a wig. Attached them with spirit gum, looked quite convincing. Waited till they fell asleep. Used the tunnel to sneak into their rooms. Woke them up with a howl and bellowed that he wanted to ravish 'em. This was before his accident, of course."

"How'd he get away with it?" I asked him. "None of the women reported it? None of them complained?"

"Well, there weren't *that* many, you know. Five or six over the years. And all of 'em actually believed he *was* Lord Reginald. Swooned dead away, or went screaming out into the halls. One of 'em—strange woman, a writer—actually *insisted* he ravish her. And the old swine did, I'm sorry to say. Shocking, I know, but there it is. The Earl boasted of it for weeks."

"He never raped these women?"

Lord Bob's eyebrows sailed upward. "Good Lord, no. Rape? The man was deranged, Beaumont, but he was a *Fitzwilliam.*"

"Miss Turner felt she was in danger of—"

"Yes." Wincing, he held up his hand like a traffic cop. "Miss Turner. I feel dreadful about Miss Turner. All that, the other women, that all happened before his accident, as I said. When we learned he was paralyzed, I breathed a sigh of relief, I don't mind telling you. No more hysterical women running through the hallways. No more silly stories of hauntings."

He took a deep breath. "What must've happened, over the years, he changed. Lying there, he festered. Like a wound, eh? Been mental before, got even worse. Forgot even who he was. *Forgot* he was a Fitzwilliam. By the time he could walk again, he'd gone completely round the bend. He never told us, you know. That he *could* walk. Kept it a secret."

"How'd you find out?"

"A weekend party. Few months ago. Group of people up from London. Friends of Alice—artists, writers, that sort. She meets them there, in town, takes them under her wing. One of the women, young thing named Cora—Dora? Harrington or something. Doesn't matter. Middle of the night, she woke up the entire east wing with her screaming. She'd seen him, she said. Reginald. He'd grabbed at her, she said. He'd never done that before. Actually touched them, I mean. Except for that writer woman, of course. I learned about all this in the morning."

"Did you talk to him? Your father?"

"Of course. Within the hour. Stormed up there, read him the riot act. He denied everything. How could he do it, he asked me. He was paralyzed, wasn't he? All innocence. Nearly persuaded me, I confess. Told myself, this Harrington girl was a nervous sort, mebbe. Had woman troubles, eh? She'd heard the stories, she hallucinated. Talked myself into believing it."

The Great Man asked, "Did you take any precautions, Lord Purleigh, to prevent a repetition of the incident?"

"Locked the entrance to the tunnel. Just in case. His entrance, from the tunnel side. Loops of metal in there, made for that purpose. Centuries ago. Ran a crowbar through 'em. Impossible for him to get through."

"But there was no bar present," said the Great Man, "when I discovered the entrance."

"I know that," said Lord Bob. "Looked for it myself, yesterday." He turned to me. "After I brought you to Carson's room. Used another entrance, down the hall, to get into the tunnel and then back up. Bloody thing had gone missing."

I said, "Your father could've used the same entrance earlier, and taken the bar."

He nodded. "What must've happened. It was still there, though, on Friday morning. I looked."

I asked him, "Who else knew about the tunnel?"

"No one. Family tradition. Only the firstborn son is told. Sworn to secrecy, lots of feudal mumbo-jumbo. Absurd, of course. But so long as he was alive—the Earl—I kept to the oath."

"But Lady Purleigh had to know your father was impersonating the ghost."

"Of course she did. Kinder about the whole thing than I was, Alice. More forgiving. Said it was a sickness, nothing we could do. Except attempt to prevent it happening again. But she never knew about the tunnel. Thought he simply wandered through the halls."

"When were the tunnel and the entrances built?" the Great Man asked.

"The Civil War, so the stories say. Cromwell, the Roundheads, that lot. Think it's older, myself. Late Norman, mebbe. Some of the stonework—"

"Lord Purleigh," I said. "Yesterday, when we were trying to get into the Earl's room, Sir Arthur asked you if there was another way in. You said there wasn't."

He took in another deep breath, slowly sighed it out. He nodded. "Yes," he said. "I know. Wrong of me. Completely. But there was the oath, you see. The tradition. Hundreds of years." He frowned, shook his head, sighed again. "But that wasn't the real reason."

"You didn't want anyone to know about your father."

"No. I didn't. Everyone knew he was a reactionary swine. Most of 'em approved, of course. Preferred him that way. But no one knew about the other."

He looked uncomfortable. "Look, Beaumont, there are things I want to do. Important things. Helping the workers. The farmers. Poor buggers have had a thin time of it for centuries. Exploited by everyone. The aristocracy, the Church, the bourgeoisie, the government. I could *do* something, you see. Oh, they think I'm a fool.

Society. All of 'em. I realize that. Lived with it for years, doesn't bother me. But what would they think of me, think of the earldom, if they learned about *this?* However could I get anything *done?*"

"Do you think your father committed suicide, Lord Purleigh?"

For a moment he only looked at me. Then, slowly, he nodded. "I do, yes. I spoke with him, you know. Yesterday morning, after the others had left for town. Before I saw you at breakfast. I accused him of accosting Miss Turner. He denied it, of course. I told him I intended to have him put away. An asylum. He believed me, I think." He looked away. "I suspect that this is why he took his own life." He looked back at us. "So, in a way, of course, I'm responsible. I expect that's why I drank so much yesterday. Made such an idiot of myself."

"Sooner or later," I said, "you've got to talk to the police."

Lord Bob sighed sadly. "Yes. Yes, I realize that." He shook his head, looked off again. "May mean the end of everything."

"Excuse me, Phil," said the Great Man. "But do you think it is absolutely necessary that Lord Purleigh tell Inspector Marsh about the late Earl? Immediately, at any rate? Perhaps he should wait until—"

"After tea time? Too late, Harry. Marsh already knows." I turned to Lord Bob. "He's talked to Miss Turner. She figured everything out. She went exploring in your father's room last night. She found the phony beard and the wig."

"Ah," he said, and he sighed once more. "She did strike me as an intelligent woman, Miss Turner."

"I'll talk to them," I said. "The police. See if I can get them to keep things quiet."

Lord Bob smiled sadly. "Thank you, Beaumont. I appreciate the thought. Well." He raised his head. "We'll see what happens, won't we?"

"Things'll work out," I told him.

"Yes. Yes, of course." He looked around the room and blinked, like someone who'd just awakened from a daydream. He turned back to me. "I wonder. Do you know where my wife is? I really ought to let her know what's happened."

"She's in the drawing room," I said.

"Thank you." He stood up. He still look rumpled but now he looked worn and defeated and about ten years older. We stood up and he stepped forward, holding out his hand. "Houdini. Beaumont. Thank you for listening."

"TELL ME, PHIL," said the Great Man as we walked across the patio outside the conservatory. "You say that Inspector Marsh has talked with Miss Turner."

"Yeah."

"She told him—"

A voice interrupted him. " 'Scuse me, gents."

It was a policeman, stepping away from the trunk of the tree. I'd forgotten that Superintendent Honniwell had assigned two cops to guard Maplewhite. This one was tall and bulky in his dark uniform, and he needed a shave.

"Sorry, gents," he said, "but I'm s'pose to watch all the comin's and goin's hereabouts. And who—"

"I am Harry Houdini," announced the Great Man. "And this is Phil Beaumont, a Pinkerton man. And, as you see, we are going. You have no orders that prevent anyone from going, do you?"

"No sir," said the policeman, backing away toward the tree. "Sorry, sir. Just doing me job, sir."

"Thank you," said the Great Man. "Idiot," he said, when we'd walked another ten or twelve yards, out onto the sunny lawn.

"Like he said, Harry. He's just doing his job."

"He does not even have a gun, Phil."

"English cops don't carry them."

He looked at me. "But how do they shoot people?"

"They don't."

His forehead furrowed. "They never carry guns? None of them? Not even detective officers, like Marsh and Sergeant Meadows?"

"Marsh could probably get issued a weapon. If he were going up against a band of anarchists. Bombmakers, maybe. But generally, no."

"Amazing." He cocked his head and stared down at the passing ground. "Amazing."

"You wanted to know something about Miss Turner?"

He turned to me. "Yes. Miss Turner told Marsh about the knife in her bed this morning?"

"I told him."

"And what was his response?"

"He didn't give one, Harry. Not to me."

"Do you believe that he thinks it significant?"

"I don't know what he thinks."

He nodded. "To whom has he spoken?

I told him about my morning with Marsh as we walked down the slope of bright green grass and then along the gravel walkway. It was another beautiful day, the second in a row. The squirrels couldn't get over it. They ran up and down the trees like this would be their last chance.

"The Darleen woman," said the Great Man. "The kitchen maid. She had been visiting with the Earl on a regular basis?"

"Yeah."

"But why, then, would the Earl feel obliged to accost these other women, including Miss Turner?"

"I don't know. Maybe the visits from Darleen were what started him wandering the halls again. Maybe Darleen wasn't enough for him."

He made a face. He didn't like that idea. "And why would he steal trinkets from everyone's room?"

"No idea. He was crazy, Harry. Maybe we should ask Dr. Auerbach."

He shook his head, looked off, looked back at me. "And to whom else did you speak?"

I told him.

When I finished, we were at the rear of Maplewhite, the huge gray house rising above the faraway trees. "And what did you find out, Harry?" I asked him.

"Well, Phil," he said. "I believe I have solved the mystery."

"Which one?"

"All of them. Ah, here is the path Miss Turner mentioned. Come along, Phil."

There was a narrow opening in the wall of trees and brambles. The Great Man plunged into it. I followed him.

"So what's the solution?" I asked his back.

"All in good time, Phil," he said over his shoulder.

It wasn't much of a path. As it twisted down into the forest, branches grew across it, and vines and spiderwebs. After a while it came to a wide passageway that looked like it had been a roadway once. This led left and right, off through the towering trees. The Great Man turned left.

I caught up with him. "Where are we going, Harry?"

"I told you, Phil. The old mill. I suspect that there is another path that leads there, closer to the house, but this is the path Miss Turner took."

"When?"

"Yesterday. On horseback."

"When she saw the snake?"

The Great Man smiled. "She saw much more than a snake, Phil. She saw the murderers of the Earl."

I looked at him. "What are you talking about, Harry?"

"All in good time."

I remembered the Colt in my pocket and I thought about using it. I decided not to. We marched along the old road for two or three hundred yards.

"Ah," he said. "The mill."

It was an old mill, made of stone but in ruins now. Its big wooden wheel had tumbled into the narrow rusty-looking stream. The stream flowed from a pool surrounded by drooping cattails. The water was dark and still and the branches of a big willow tree were reflected as they dipped down into it.

"And there is the willow," said the Great Man. He turned to me. "Shall we take a look inside the mill?"

"It's your party, Harry."

He padded through the grasses and jumped over the stream. I followed. The wooden door to the mill was hanging inward on its hinges. We stepped inside. The place smelled of mold and burnt wood.

"Someone has built a fire," said the Great Man.

The building was cylindrical, about fifteen feet across. Against the far wall, on the uneven stone floor, was a huddle of ash and charred lumber, bits of planking, chunks of two-by-four and four-by-four.

"Hobos," I said.

"Are there hobos in England?" He crossed the floor and stood over the small pile.

"Two million unemployed, Lord Bob said. Probably a few of them on the road."

"Lord Purleigh," he corrected me. He looked up. "Do you notice anything interesting about the floor, Phil?"

"No one's swept it for a while." Dust and ashes were scattered over the slabs of stone.

He nodded. "Come."

Outside, he stared across the pond to the willow tree. "They were standing there," he said. "Under the willow."

"Who was?"

"The ghosts that Miss Turner saw."

"Harry."

He turned to me. "You must help me find it," he said.

"Find what?"

"The tunnel."

Chapter Thirty-six

WHAT TUNNEL?"

"The tunnel that runs from here to the manor. It *must* exist." He looked around, narrowed his eyes. "You saw how the pathway curved back to the south? I estimate that we are perhaps sixty yards from the house itself. The west side of it." He nodded toward another wall of trees and brambles. "Beyond the forest there."

"Why a tunnel, Harry?"

He looked at me. "But Phil. How else could the ghosts get from here to the house without being seen?"

I remembered the gun again. "Harry—"

"Please, Phil. We do not have much time. We must find it. It cannot be far."

It wasn't. It was built into the side of a hill about twenty yards from the mill, hidden behind the overhanging leafy branches of a big oak. At its entrance was a pair of broad wooden doors, like the doors to the freight tunnel beneath the formal garden. Lying beside the doors, in the weeds, was a small wicker picnic basket.

"Harry?" I called out.

He was maybe forty feet away, thrashing through some bushes. He stopped and came running toward me. There were scratches on his cheeks that looked like African tribal marks.

"Aha!" he cried. He reached for the door. "You see, Phil!"

It swung open before he could reach it. He danced back.

"Miss Turner!" he said.

She stood there in the opening, a lantern in her hand. Her cheek was smudged and strands of pale brown hair were trailing across her face. She was smiling anyway.

"I heard you coming, Mr. Houdini! Look! I found it!" She said this as if she were talking about El Dorado.

"But Miss Turner—"

"Wait a minute," I said. I turned to her. "Miss Turner, you told me you wouldn't wander off on your own. We agreed. Last night, in Mrs. Corneille's room."

"I know, I know," she said in a rush. "But everyone else had gone to church and I was sitting out on the patio, where it was perfectly safe—there was a policeman on patrol every ten minutes, nearly—and then Mr. Houdini appeared and spoke with me, and I understood what he was thinking from the questions he asked, what he *must* be thinking, about the ghosts—"

"Okay," I said. "Hold on. What's the story on these ghosts?"

". . . AND SO YOU see, Phil," the Great Man said, "logically, this was the only possibility. The tunnel. It was the only way the two of them could have gotten into the house so quickly. And without being seen."

I said, "Seen again, you mean."

"Correct. Miss Turner had already seen them. Unfortunately for her. But, in any event, I determined to locate it. And I *would* have," he said. He looked at Miss Turner. "I suppose," he said stiffly, "that I should offer you my congratulations, Miss Turner."

"But Mr. Houdini," she said. "I should never have considered the possibility of a tunnel if you hadn't spoken with me. It was you, after all, who first realized the significance of the ghosts. Once I understood what you suspected, I realized how important they must be. And how they *must* have returned to the house. I brought a lantern from the stables and I concealed it in the basket and I came out here. I found the tunnel, yes, but all the credit, really, is yours."

He looked at her thoughtfully. "Well. Yes. You are correct, of course. And where does the tunnel lead?"

"It ends at a sort of pantry next to the kitchen," she said. "They must have used it to transport milled grain, years ago. There's an entrance to the kitchen from the pantry. And there's another tunnel there, one that goes off at right angles to this one. I didn't explore it."

"The freight tunnel," I said. "Under the garden."

The Great Man nodded. "It is as I suspected." He turned to me, smiling. "The entire house, Phil, all of Maplewhite, is one enormous gimmicked prop."

"Okay, Harry," I said. "You've figured things out. But you're going to have a hard time proving it."

He raised himself up to his full height. "I have a plan," he announced.

"Uh-huh."

"And Phil," he announced, "there is one additional matter I have discovered."

"What's that?"

He told me. Miss Turner made a small gasp.

"Yeah," I said. "I know that."

"But . . . *how?*" he said. I had never seen him look surprised before. "How could you know?"

I told him.

"But what shall we do, Phil?" he asked when I finished.

I smiled. "I have a plan."

"May I help?" asked Miss Turner

I looked at her. "Maybe you can."

THE GREAT MAN and Miss Turner took the path back to the house. Using Miss Turner's lantern, I took the tunnel.

It led straight into Maplewhite, into the pantry Miss Turner had found, and from end to end it was only about sixty yards long. The floor of the thing was covered with the same gravel that covered the walkway around the grounds. The walls were made of dark stone, damp and slimy.

So were the walls of the other tunnel, leading out under the formal garden. I took a look down that, then came back and left the lantern in the pantry before I slipped into the kitchen. It was empty. The trip from the kitchen to the Great Hall took less than a minute. Lord Bob wasn't there. I found him and Lady Purleigh in the library, sitting together on one of the sofas. Both of them were looking a bit depressed, maybe even a bit lost. I asked Lord

Bob if the Great Man and I could use his telephone. I told him we'd pay for the calls.

"Money," he said sadly, "is the least of my worries just now." Lady Purleigh smiled bravely and took his hand.

"Everything will work out," I told them, but I knew that it wasn't exactly the truth.

The Great Man and I were busy in Lord Bob's office for an hour or so, on the telephone. Miss Turner helped out for a while. She did a good job, and we had some luck we didn't deserve. By one o'clock, Miss Turner and I had done everything we could. She left and the Great Man stayed there, waiting for some calls. I went to find Higgens, the butler, and I asked him to ask Inspector Marsh to come to my room as soon as he got back from Purleigh. Then I went upstairs and lay down. There was nothing useful I could do at that point, and I was tired. It had been already been a long day, and it wasn't over yet. There was still the tea party.

I WAS ASLEEP when someone knocked at the door. My watch was on the night table. Two-thirty. I sat up, swung my feet off the bed, and said, "Come in."

It was Marsh, smiling happily. "Ah, Beaumont. Knitting up the raveled sleeve of care, were we?"

"Yeah. Grab a seat. How was Purleigh?"

"Lovely." He pulled the chair out from under the desk, twirled it around, sat down on it. "A typical Devon hamlet, white walls and thatched roofs and cheerful inbred villagers. Very picturesque. I quite enjoyed myself."

"Good. You find out anything?"

"I did, yes." He smiled. "Would you care to hear?"

"I'm all ears."

"Well," he said, "for starters, Dr. Auerbach was telling the truth. He *was* in the graveyard, making rubbings of the tombstones. The vicar spoke with him, and he tells me that the doctor left on foot, for Maplewhite, sometime before one. But not much before one, and certainly after twelve-thirty. He's a bit cloudy as to time. A bit cloudy in general, really. But I measured the distance between the church and Maplewhite. Six miles. Dr. Auerbach could *not* have returned here before one o'clock, and probably not much before two."

I nodded.

"Sir David Merridale was also telling the truth," he said. "As he said, he took a room at the Cock and Bull yesterday. He neglected to mention, however, that this was not the first time he'd done so. He's stayed there several times over the past few months."

"Must've slipped his mind."

"Let us not burden our remembrance with a heaviness that's gone. The Tempest."

"Right."

"He also neglected to mention that he didn't remain in his room. The room is on the first floor, at the back of the building. I went round to take a look and I discovered, in the ground beneath the room's window, a clear set of footprints. The earth was still quite damp. Up until yesterday, you know, we've experienced heavy rains."

"I noticed."

He smiled. "The footprints were quite distinctive. A small notch was visible in the print of the left foot, where a piece of the leather had been somehow cut away. And, clearly, the prints had been made by someone leaving the room by means of the window, and then returning to it in the same manner."

"Someone else could've left the footprints."

"According to the landlord, no one but Sir David has used the room in a week."

I nodded.

"By a curious coincidence," he said, "the residence of Mrs. Constance Coburn, where Cecily Fitzwilliam was visiting, is only two houses away. The footprints led there, to a bedroom on the first floor, at the rear of the house. From the prints, it is obvious that Sir David climbed into this window as well. I spoke with Mrs. Coburn, and she was good enough to tell me that Cecily was feeling unwell during her visit, and lay down for an hour in the back bedroom. For a rest."

I nodded.

"Mrs. Coburn is nearly deaf," he said, "but I was able, finally, to obtain from her a record of Miss Fitzwilliam's earlier visits to her house. These correspond, exactly, to the times at which Sir David was staying at the Cock and Bull. And, in every case, she lay down for an hour, sometimes longer, in the back bedroom." He smiled. "It appears that Miss Fitzwilliam is rather a faster young thing than she appears."

"Incredible," I said.

"But you do see what this means. If Sir David and Miss Fitzwilliam were occupied with each other, neither one of them could have fired that rifle yesterday."

"Yeah. So who did?"

He smiled. "But surely, Beaumont, you've determined who that was?"

"I've got an idea or two. But who do *you* think it was?"

Another smile. "You shall learn that in"—he took out his watch——"twenty minutes. Now. Did anything of note transpire during my absence?"

"Yeah." I told him about Lord Bob and his father.

"Lovely. So things begin to fall into place at last. And you say Houdini was there at the time?"

"Yeah."

"Has he in fact solved the mystery?"

"He thinks so."

"Lovely. I look forward to meeting with him." He glanced at his watch again. "I must go hunt up Sergeant Meadows." A final smile. "I'll see you in the drawing room, then."

"Right."

After he left, I washed up, checked the Colt, slipped it back into my pocket.

DOWNSTAIRS, SIR ARTHUR CONAN DOYLE was waiting for me outside the drawing room, tall and bulky in another tweed suit. "A moment, Beaumont?"

"Sure."

He led me down the hall a short distance. Frowning, he said,

"I've been attempting to talk to this Marsh fellow, but he refuses to listen to me. This is ridiculous. I possess information that is absolutely critical to his case."

"What information?"

"Madame Sosostris was good enough to hold a small séance this afternoon, with only myself present, and Mr. Dempsey, of course."

"You talked to Running Bear."

"Yes. It is as I thought, Beaumont. Lord Reginald effected the Earl's death."

"The ghost."

"Yes. He drove the Earl insane, you see. Drove him to madness and finally to suicide."

"Uh-huh. And how did the pistol get into the Earl's room?"

"Evidently Lord Reginald dematerialized it from the Great Hall, then caused it to reappear in the Earl's chambers. As you know, perhaps better than anyone, dematerialization *is* a reality."

"Uh-huh."

He frowned impatiently. "I know you pretend to be something of a skeptic, Beaumont. But, look, man, do you happen to know the guiding principle of my detective work? It is this—that when you have eliminated from consideration all the impossibilities, then whatever remains, no matter how improbable, must be the truth. And that is patently the case here. I ask only that Inspector Marsh listen to me."

"I'll tell you what, Sir Arthur. You hold on to your idea for a while. Let's see what happens in the drawing room. If you don't get an explanation that you're happy with, then I promise I'll get Marsh to listen to yours."

"Well . . . I expect that's better than nothing."

"But," I said, "I'd like one small favor in return."

"And what might that be?"

I told him.

Chapter Thirty-seven

LADIES," SAID INSPECTOR Marsh, "and gentlemen. I do thank you all for being present."

Smiling delicately, he looked around the drawing room.

Once again, everyone had plates of food on the tables in front of them, and pots of tea and coffee. Lord Bob and Lady Purleigh and Cecily sat together on one of the sofas. Mr. Dempsey sat beside the wheelchair of Madame Sosostris. Mrs. Allardyce and Miss Turner were together, and so were Sir David and Mrs. Corneille and Dr. Auerbach. Sergeant Meadows was looming against one wall, and Doyle stood a few feet away, looming even larger. I was sitting about a yard from where Marsh was standing. The Great Man sat by himself across the room. He had faintly nodded to me when I entered, and I knew that everything was set up.

"Lord Purleigh," said Marsh, "has graciously permitted me this opportunity to speak with you all, to discuss the recent curious events at Maplewhite. How very bizarre these have been, have they not? A gun suddenly fired across a sunny lawn. An elderly man abruptly dead in his own locked bedroom. *It is a reeling world indeed, my lord, and I believe will never stand upright.* Richard the Third, of course."

He smiled and glanced around the room. "Now. All of you know of the late Earl's death. But what do you know, really, of his life? Did you know that, on the testimony of his own son, the man was mad? Mad, yes, and *no longer paralyzed.*"

There was a small, well-mannered flutter of response. Heads turned, eyebrows arched. Cecily Fitzwilliam leaned toward her mother. Lady Purleigh pressed her lips together and she took her daughter's hand. Mrs. Corneille frowned and glanced over at Lady Purleigh.

"At night," said Marsh, "when the houseguests were asleep, the late Earl prowled through a network of secret passageways that connect the room and chambers of Maplewhite. Dressed as his own ancestor, Lord Reginald, he stalked into the rooms of certain female guests and attempted to assault them."

More turning heads. More arched eyebrows. Lord Bob and Lady Purleigh sat still and stared forward, like a pair of officials witnessing an execution.

"He did this two months ago," said Marsh, "and he did this again on Friday night, when he entered the room of Miss Turner."

Heads swiveled toward Miss Turner.

"Earlier on that same evening," said Marsh, "Lord and Lady Purleigh had spoken with the late Earl in his room." Heads swiveled toward Lord Bob and his wife. "No one else was present, but I believe it likely that in view of the Earl's attempted assault of two months earlier, Lord Purleigh warned his father not to make another attempt that night."

Marsh shrugged. "But as we all now know, the Earl did make an attempt."

He lifted a glass of water from a nearby table, sipped at it, set it back down. "According to his own statement, voluntarily given to Mr. Beaumont, Lord Purleigh spoke with his father on the following morning. He informed the Earl that he planned to place him in a madhouse. Several hours later, when a party of the guests, and Lord Purleigh, were gathered out on the lawn, someone fired a rifle toward the group."

Marsh smiled. "Is it not patently obvious, ladies and gentlemen, who fired that rifle? And is it not patently obvious at whom the rifle was being fired? It was aimed at Lord Purleigh, of course. And it was fired by his father."

"Rubbish!" said Lord Bob. "See here, Marsh—"

Marsh smiled. "All the weapons in the collection were the Earl's. The Earl knew how to use them. He knew, too, that his son intended to remove him, ignominiously, from his own home. And he took the one course that, to his damaged brain, seemed appropriate. He attempted to murder his own son. He made his way down to the Great Hall, loaded the Winchester rifle—"

"What perfect rubbish!" Lord Bob was half out of his seat. Lady

Purleigh reached for him and he turned to her, his face red. She murmured something and he sat back, shaking his head. "But it's *rubbish,* Alice. *Codswollop!*"

"And he proceeded outside," continued Marsh, "and concealed himself in the woods by the formal garden. And when he saw his son return to Maplewhite on his motor bicycle, the Earl fired at him. Fortunately for Lord Purleigh, the Earl missed."

Lord Purleigh's brows were raised. "The old swine would *never* miss a shot like that!"

Marsh paid no attention. "Lord Purleigh understood, of course, what his father had done. He *knew* who had fired that rifle. And he now knew that his father was even more unbalanced than he had believed. Perhaps—and here I speculate—perhaps he realized how nakedly this unbalance might be revealed in any enquiry, any attempt to institutionalize the Earl. And perhaps, too, he was angered by the attempt on his life. Whatever the truth, later that day, while everyone was in the drawing room, Lord Purleigh removed a Smith and Wesson revolver from the Great Hall, used the secret passageway to enter his father's room, and he killed him."

"What?" said Lord Bob. He looked more confused than angry.

"Only Lord Purleigh was absent from the drawing room at the time of the murder," said Marsh. "Only Lord Purleigh had an opportunity to kill the Earl. And only Lord Purleigh had a motive. His father's death would remove not only an embarrassment, but also an actual threat to his own life. And it would, of course, bring him his father's entire inheritance."

"This is sheer nonsense." It was the Great Man, up on his feet, his head raised high. "I will listen to no more of this."

Across the room, Sergeant Meadows leaned away from the wall. Marsh glanced at him, shook his head slightly. Meadows leaned back and Marsh turned to the Great Man. "Do you have some other explanation, Mr. Houdini?"

"I have *the* explanation."

Marsh smiled. "Then I shall gladly, if temporarily, surrender the floor." He sat down and looked up at the Great Man with the same theatrical interest he'd shown in the Earl's bedroom.

The Great Man put his hands behind his back and he glanced slowly around the room. "We have been presented here at Maplewhite," he finally announced, "with a series of totally baffling events."

Then the Great Man said, and pretty much word for word, the same things he'd said when he was explaining how he figured out the secret passageway. That the baffling events had baffled even *him*. That he'd finally realized they were a lot like mediocre magic tricks. "Now," he said, "in order to understand the mechanics of a successful magic trick, we must begin with no preconceptions whatever."

Marsh rolled his eyes. Delicately.

The Great Man looked around the room again, as though to make sure that everyone was still following. "Yesterday afternoon, while Miss Turner was horseback riding, she saw what she believed to be a pair of ghosts under a willow tree, near the old mill. Why did she believe them to be ghosts? Her preconceptions. She had been told that a pair of ghosts often *had* been seen under that tree, a woman and a young boy. And, when she saw two individuals standing there, her preconceptions led her to believe that these were they. She is an intelligent and resourceful woman, but she is not a trained observer. And, perhaps most important, she was *not* wearing her spectacles at the time. Without them, she is extremely nearsighted. Is that not true, Miss Turner?"

Heads swiveled. "Yes," she said. Her voice was strong and clear. Beside her, Mrs. Allardyce frowned.

Inspector Marsh yawned, pretending to hide it behind his hand.

The Great Man nodded. He turned back to the audience. "But these were not ghosts that Miss Turner saw. What she saw were the two people who were conspiring to murder Lord Purleigh."

A rustling sound rippled through the audience.

"And, of course," said the Great Man, "they saw her. So far as they knew, she had recognized them. And for these two to be recognized together would have meant disaster for them both."

He glanced around again. "They acted swiftly. Together they returned to Maplewhite, using a tunnel that runs from the mill to a concealed pantry beside the kitchen. From there, one of them ran to the Great Hall and snatched the Winchester rifle. Perhaps this individual loaded the weapon at that time. Perhaps the two of them had planned ahead, for emergencies, and the weapon was already loaded. No matter. It would have been a matter of seconds only to ready the rifle. Taking the weapon, this individual ran back into the hidden pantry and used the other tunnel, the freight tunnel, to emerge outside the formal garden. From nearby, a clear shot was available at Miss Turner, when she appeared."

The Great Man frowned. "This individual was fortunate. Had Miss Turner known how, she could have returned to the house by a more direct route. But she was unaware of this. And then her horse, bolting, led her past the path she had originally followed. And then she struck her head on the limb of a tree and she was ejected from the animal. She remained unconscious for a time. All of this assisted the would-be assassin. When Miss Turner finally did appear, under the tree by the walkway, the assassin was more than ready. He fired. One shot, and one shot only. Why should he fire another? *He saw Miss Turner fall from her horse, and he assumed he had hit her.*"

"Fascinating," said Inspector Marsh. He smiled, "But just who was this so-called assassin? And who was his conspirator?"

"A more interesting question," said the Great Man, "at the moment, is *what were they doing out by the old mill?* Why meet *there?* And to this, I am pleased to say, I have discovered the answer."

He narrowed his eyes again. "I believe that it was there, at the old mill, that these two, over a period of time, planned their conspiracy. It is there that they *practiced* the technique by which they very nearly succeeded in deceiving us all."

"Oh really?" said Marsh.

The Great Man ignored him. "I examined the old mill with my associate, Mr. Beaumont. On the floor inside it we found the remains of a fire. Not a fire of weeds and brush, such as might have been built by some passing tramp"—he glanced at me, underlining the point—"but a fire that had been constructed of pieces of *lumber.* And why lumber?"

He cocked his head. "Suppose you take a piece of lumber and you saw it neatly in half. Suppose you create a small hollow in one of these halves, and that, within the hollow, you place a live cartridge. You have, previously, removed the slug from the cartridge and crimped shut the opening. Suppose you then carefully glue the halves of lumber back together. Now suppose you place this piece of lumber into a fire. What will happen? At some point, when the heat of the fire at last reaches the cartridge, it will explode. As a consequence of its explosion, some ash may be expelled from the fire itself. Much like the ash that Mr. Beaumont and I found on the floor of the old mill. And much like the ash that was found on the floor of the Earl's bedroom. It is obvious to me that our two conspirators experimented with lumber and cartridge there at the mill, until they discovered exactly the proper combination of both to suit their nefarious purposes."

He turned to Doyle. "It was not our entrance into the room, Sir Arthur, that blew ashes from the fireplace. It was the eruption of a cartridge, hidden within a piece of firewood."

Doyle was frowning. "But no one found a spent cartridge in the fireplace."

"Ah," said the Great Man. "But no one ever looked for it. We did not, because the fire was still burning when we arrived. Superintendent Honniwell and his men did not, because the Superintendent was more interested in currying favor with Lord Purleigh. Afterward, of course, the cartridge was removed."

"By whom, exactly?" asked Marsh.

At the moment, Doyle was more interested in *how* than *whom*. He said, "You're telling us that when Carson heard the shot fired, the Earl was already—"

"Dead, yes!" said the Great Man. "Several minutes before that shot, perhaps as much as half an hour, using the hidden stairway, the murderer had entered the room with the revolver. A single shot was fired, muffled by a cushion, perhaps, and the Earl was dead."

"But according to Superintendent Honniwell," said Doyle, "there were powder burns near the wound. Would these have been present if the pistol had been fired through a cushion?"

"Mr. Beaumont assures me that this is possible, so long as the muzzle of the weapon is brought close to the point of impact of the bullet. It is possible, too, that the autopsy will detect threads of fabric in the wound, thus substantiating my statement."

"And the murderer," said Doyle, "then wiped his fingerprints from the weapon, and placed on it the fingerprints of the Earl."

"The murderer did so," said the Great Man. "Correct. And then, after carefully putting the piece of lumber in the fire, probably off to the side, so as to postpone the explosion, the murderer left. And came down to the drawing room, to join us all in tea."

"And who *is* this murderer of yours?" asked Marsh. "Who *are* these conspirators?"

"Who?" said the Great Man. "Is that not *patently obvious,* Inspector Marsh? They must be two people who knew that if they were seen together, and intimate, their plan would be foiled. One of them, at least, must know Maplewhite, must know its hidden tunnels and passageways. And one of them must be of a stature small enough, slight enough, to be mistaken at a distance, by a woman suffering from nearsightedness, for a young boy. There *are* no young boys at Maplewhite, ghostly or otherwise." He turned to face the audience. "Therefore, the two conspirators *must* be Lady Purleigh and Dr. Auerbach."

The audience made a ragged hissing sound, like a large beast drawing breath. Lady Purleigh looked puzzled. Dr. Auerbach looked alarmed. Lord Bob looked poleaxed, and he stared at the Great Man with his mouth open. Inspector Marsh stood up from his chair. "This is preposterous," he said. "Dr. Auerbach was seen in Purleigh. He walked back from there to Maplewhite. He couldn't possibly have got here by the time that shot was fired."

I took a look at Sergeant Meadows. He was still leaning against the wall.

The Great Man smiled. "Had you investigated thoroughly, *Inspector,* you would have learned that a bicycle was stolen in Purleigh yesterday. Mr. Beaumont learned this from the local constable, Dubbins. Riding a bicycle, using pathways through the woods, pathways detailed for him by Lady Purleigh, Dr. Auerbach easily reached the old mill before one o'clock. The bicycle is no doubt resting at the bottom of the millpond. And had you investigated further, you would have telephoned the University of Leeds, as I did today, and learned that Dr. Auerbach was not in Devon, but in Edinburgh. Where I telephoned and spoke with him." He pointed his finger. *"That* man is not Dr. Auerbach."

The little bald-headed man sprang from his chair and darted for the drawing room doors, running in front of Miss Turner and Mrs. Allardyce. Miss Turner put out her leg. He snagged his foot on it, swung his arms forward as though he were reaching for a trapeze, and went sailing over the coffee table. By the time he landed, I was on top of him with the Colt. I yanked him to his feet. He squirmed like a polliwog until I stuck the pistol in his ear.

Other people were up, too—Sir David, Mrs. Allardyce. Mrs. Corneille was rising.

But the Great Man wasn't finished. He turned back to Marsh. "And the reason, *Inspector Marsh,* that you did not investigate thoroughly, as you should have done, is that you are a most thoroughly incompetent Inspector Marsh." He turned to the audience and smiled. "Ladies and gentlemen, permit me to introduce a man who is almost as inept a policeman as he is a magician." He held out his arm. "I give you Chin Soo!"

This was the signal. The drawing room doors burst open and what seemed like a hundred cops tumbled in, some in uniform, some not. One of them was Superintendent Honniwell. One of them was an angry-looking man who turned out later to be the real Inspector Marsh. Over against the wall, "Sergeant Meadows" reached into his coat pocket, but Doyle was ready and he grabbed the man's hand with his own left and he popped him a very good right on the point of his chin and the man went crashing to the floor.

Epilogue

IT TOOK A few days to get everything straightened out. The key, as the Great Man liked to put it, was Moseley.

Carl Moseley was the man who had been impersonating Dr. Auerbach. Questioned by Honniwell and Marsh, he broke.

A journalist and an unsuccessful playwright, he had met Lady Purleigh in London a year ago, among a group of people who lived in Bloomsbury. It was there, he said, a month or so later, that their affair had begun. One member of the group, a poet named Sybil Prescott-Vane, knew about the affair and let Lady Purleigh and Moseley use her home for their London rendezvous. Her testimony, at the trial, was damaging to both of them.

Lady Purleigh and Moseley had seen each other whenever she went to London, and twice he had visited Maplewhite, both times traveling out there with other members of the Bloomsbury group. They met in his room, or out by the old mill. In both cases, Lady Purleigh used the secret passageways and tunnels. Moseley said that Lady Purleigh had known about the tunnels for some time.

According to Moseley, the original plan had been to kill Lord Bob. Lady Purleigh, he said, didn't want any part of Lord Bob's proletarian golfing club, and didn't really want any part of Lord Bob either. She did want Moseley, said Moseley. The plan was changed during his most recent visit to Maplewhite, when the late Earl wandered into Moseley's bedroom while he was "amorously engaged" with Lady Purleigh. This was the same night the Earl made a grab for a woman named Dora Carrington. The Earl, who was pretty much a loony by then, agreed not to reveal what he'd seen, so long as Lady Purleigh didn't interfere with his "sport".

That cooked the Earl, as far as Lady Purleigh was concerned. She wasn't, she'd told Moseley (according to Moseley), going to gain control of Maplewhite "only to have it ripped from my hands by a drooling sex fiend." This didn't sit too well with the jury, either.

She and Moseley worked out another plan—kill the Earl, and let Lord Bob take the blame. Even if he were never tried for the murder, she was sure she could get him locked up as a nut case.

Moseley had met Dr. Auerbach in Vienna, while he was doing an article about psychoanalysis, and he knew that Auerbach was in Edinburgh now. It was his idea to shave his head and wear a false beard, which made him nearly Auerbach's double. At the trial, the prosecutor asked him what would have happened if the Edinburgh police had talked to the real doctor. Moseley said he'd mentioned exactly that to Lady Purleigh, and she'd said that in that case "we should take care of Dr. Auerbach."

Moseley admitted to firing the shot that missed Miss Turner. As the Great Man said, he thought he'd killed her. He also admitted to a rough time an hour later, when he "examined" her, as Dr. Auerbach. It was then he realized that she was nearsighted, and that she hadn't recognized him and Lady Purleigh. She didn't volunteer anything about ghosts, and he didn't ask.

Lady Purleigh, he said, refused to believe that Miss Turner was no threat. It was Lady Purleigh who had stabbed the dagger into Miss Turner's bed. Moseley, so he claimed, came running after her, using the secret passageway, and dragged her back to her room. In the excitement, both of them had forgotten to retrieve the knife.

The autopsy on the Earl's body had proved that he hadn't committed suicide. As the Great Man had predicted, traces of fabric were found in the fatal wound. Moseley and Lady Purleigh hadn't counted on that. No one ever found the cushion that had been used to muffle the sound of the shot. Moseley said that Lady Purleigh burned it.

And it was Lady Purleigh, said Moseley, who had actually fired the pistol. While her husband was off talking to MacGregor, organizing his posse of tenant farmers, she used the secret passage to go up the Earl's room. She brought along the cushion and the chunk of lumber with the prepared cartridge inside it. According to

Moseley, she killed the old man, put the chunk of lumber into fireplace, and then come downstairs to join the others at tea. She knew when Lord Bob would be coming back—he was always punctual, as Cecily had told me—and she knew he would have no real alibi for the time the shot was fired.

Lady Purleigh's lawyer tried to shift the blame to Moseley. But Moseley had been in plain sight all afternoon. Lady Purleigh hadn't. She was the only one who could've gone up to that room.

From the time she was arrested, Lady Purleigh calmly denied everything. During the trial, Lord Bob told the newspapers that she'd never do such things, had never known about the secret passageways. He was convincing, but I think he realized that she had known, and that she had done all the rest.

They were both convicted. Moseley was hanged. Lady Purleigh is still in prison, serving a life sentence. Lord Bob has given up the idea of a golfing club, and he doesn't give weekend parties anymore.

As for Chin Soo, his real name was Archibald Crubbs and he was English. He'd been an acrobat, a contortionist, and, for a while, a Shakespearean actor before he sailed to America and made his name as a magician. "Sergeant Meadows" was actually a man named Peter Collinson, an old friend of Crubbs's and a former cop who still had connections to Scotland Yard. As Doyle had suggested, Chin Soo had learned on Wednesday, from the newspaper article, that Doyle would be going to Maplewhite for the weekend. Chin Soo assumed, and correctly, that Houdini would also be there. He and Collinson had been staying in Cumbermoorleigh, a village not far from Purleigh, since Thursday.

When the two of them learned that Inspector Marsh would be arriving at Maplewhite on Sunday morning, they brought down a couple of thugs from London, and they all waylaid him. Marsh and his real sergeant, Maynard Vine, spent most of Sunday trussed up in a barn about ten miles south of Maplewhite, guarded by the thugs. They were only discovered because Miss Turner, doing a pretty good imitation of Lady Purleigh's voice, telephoned the Amberly police and demanded that they start looking for them.

The police wanted to move in on the phony Marsh right away, but Lady Purleigh's voice carried a lot of weight with Superintendent Honniwell, even when it wasn't really hers. Miss Turner persuaded them to listen to the Great Man.

Crubbs and Collinson were tried and convicted for kidnapping and for impersonating a police officer, which in England is almost as serious. Both of them were sent to Dartmoor, but while their train was on its way to the prison, they disappeared in what the English newspapers called "the most audacious escape of the century." Neither one of them was ever seen again.

It's a good word, audacious. Sir Arthur Conan Doyle used it that Sunday afternoon, after all the excitement had died down, to describe Chin Soo. "It was audacious of him, really, wasn't it? Pretending to be a policeman while an actual police investigation was going on. Wasn't he the least bit bothered by the notion that Scotland Yard would be expecting reports from the real Inspector Marsh? Didn't he realize that Honniwell might return here at any moment from Amberly? The Amberly police are still examining the rifle and the pistol. The autopsy on the Earl has yet to be performed. How could he possibly put himself in such a position?"

I shrugged. "Like you said. He was audacious."

We were in the library, where Doyle had towed me.

He puffed at his pipe. "Yes, but why put himself in such jeopardy?"

"He wanted to show Harry up. Like I said before, I don't think he ever really wanted to kill him. He was counting coup, in a way, like a Sioux Indian. Getting close enough to kill him, and taking pride in that. Later, probably, if he'd pulled it off, he would've told Harry what he'd done, somehow. And I don't think he planned to hang around long enough to get caught. He wouldn't have stayed as long as he did, probably, if he hadn't gotten involved in that bet with Harry. The idea of beating Harry to a solution was too good for him to pass up."

Chin Soo admitted as much at his trial.

"Yes," said Doyle, "but it was extraordinarily dangerous."

"This is a guy who catches bullets in his teeth."

"But that's merely a trick, you said."

"Harry tells me that two magicians died trying to perform it."

Doyle frowned around the stem of his pipe. "Hmmm. And Lady Purleigh. She was audacious, as well."

"Yeah."

"I should never have suspected her. I've always believed she was a charming woman, and devoted to her husband. I very much admired her."

"I liked her, too," I said. "But if murderers always looked like murderers, and always acted like murderers, we wouldn't need cops." I smiled. "Or mystery writers."

"Hmmm. Yes. Quite so." He looked at me. "Do you suppose that Lord Reginald somehow influenced Lady Purleigh? Somehow warped her perceptions, twisted her nature?"

"You'd have to ask Running Bear," I said. "But he's already been wrong once."

He frowned. "Not as to Mrs. Corneille's daughter. Nor to the Earl's imposing himself upon Miss Turner."

I still thought that Madame Sosostris had gotten her information from Briggs, and that the innocent woman she'd been talking about had been Darleen. But I knew that Madame Sosostris would never admit it.

"You'd think he'd be right about everything," I said.

"Passing over into the next life doesn't make one infallible, you know. One is improved, but one is still subject to human error."

"Then what's the point of dying?"

He smiled. "Still pretending to be a skeptic, eh, Beaumont? Ah well." He stood up. "Nonetheless, it's been a pleasure to meet you. Most instructive. I hope we see each other again at some time. I do mean that. Perhaps we can get together in London."

I stood up. "You're taking off?" I asked him.

"Taking off? Oh yes, yes, I'm returning to London with Madame Sosostris and Mr. Dempsey. We've work to do. Much work."

"Have you talked to Harry yet? About the séance?"

He puffed at the pipe. "Briefly, yes. He isn't as impressed as I'd hoped. He claims that all the miracles she performed at the séance could have been performed, just as well, by a fraud."

"He's right."

"Well, of course he is. I don't dispute that for a moment. But as Madame Sosostris is *not* a fraud, the point is irrelevant. The woman is a marvel, Beaumont. She's brought comfort and peace to literally hundreds of people. How many of us can say that?"

"Not many." Not me, for one.

"I began as a doctor, you know. Medicine. I was helping people. And then I became a writer, and for years all I did was amuse them, really. Entertain them. Now, once again, I can be a part of something that helps them."

I nodded. It seemed to me that being amusing and entertaining was maybe more helpful than confusing them with ghosts, but I didn't think there was much point in bringing it up.

"Well," he said. "I wish you the best of luck."

"I wish you the same, Sir Arthur." We shook hands and he doubled the number of creases in my palm.

He smiled at me again and then he walked off, trailing the smell of burning burlap.

I SAID GOODBYE to Mrs. Corneille, too, late that Sunday afternoon. She was on her way out, ready to drive back to the city with Sir David. I caught her in the Great Hall, asked her if I could talk to her for a minute.

"I don't see," she said, "that we have anything to say to each other."

"One minute. That's all I ask."

She hesitated a moment, narrowing her dark eyes, then she turned to Sir David. "Wait in the car, would you, David? I'll be there in a moment."

Sir David glanced at me and frowned but he said nothing. The bruise on his jaw had become the color of stewed prunes.

"What is it?" she said when Sir David left.

"I just wanted to say that I'm sorry about Lady Purleigh. I know she was your friend."

"She is innocent."

"She'll get a chance to prove that."

"And she will do so. But you've ruined her name. You helped that awful little man. Houdini. You *helped* him build a case against her."

I nodded.

"And you pretended to help that Chin Soo person. That false Inspector Marsh. You deliberately misled him."

I nodded.

"You and Houdini both knew that he was no police officer."

"Yeah," I said.

The Great Man had figured it out when I told him that English cops don't carry guns. He'd felt a gun in Sergeant Meadows's pocket when he tried to move him, up in the Earl's room. That was what he'd told me at the old mill, and that was what had made Miss Turner gasp.

I figured it out while I watched Chin Soo work. No cop, not even a delicate cop, makes a bet about a case with a magician.

"And last night," she said, "you made me promise not to talk to Alice," she said. "Not to inform her of what Miss Turner had found in the Earl's room. You were trying to entrap her even then."

"No," I said. "But she was a suspect, like everyone else."

"Everyone was a suspect?"

"Yeah."

She nodded. "Of course. That's why you came to my room last night, isn't it?"

"I came because you asked me."

She shook her head. "What a fool I was. Things like honor, friendship, loyalty—they don't mean anything at all to you, do they?"

"They mean a lot to me. But so does the job."

She looked at me. "I suppose I ought to respect you for that," she said. "But I'm not required to like you, am I?"

"Nope."

She nodded. "Goodbye, Mr. Beaumont."

"Goodbye, Mrs. Corneille."

And she turned and walked away, her heels clicking on the marble floor, the muscles of her calves clenching and unclenching like fists below the snapping hem of her skirt. The scent of her perfume hung in the air.

I could've reminded her that I hadn't said anything to anyone about her daughter. In the formal garden, she'd said that she hadn't seen her husband for ten years when he died in the war. Later, in her room, she'd let slip that her daughter was born two years after she'd last seen him. Unless she was lying, her husband wasn't the father of her child.

But it was something else that I didn't think there was much point in bringing up.

I SAID GOODBYE to the Great Man a few minutes later. I was in the Great Hall, staring up at the wall of weapons. Everything from cudgels to semiautomatic pistols. People had been using killing tools for a long time, and the tools kept getting better. And they would keep getting better, too, so long as killing was one of the hundreds of thousands of ways we could deny, or escape, our own insignificance.

"Phil. Are you ready to leave? Are you packed?" It was him, carrying his valise.

"Hello, Harry. No, not yet. I talked to Mrs. Allardyce and Miss Turner. I'll be going back to London on the train with them. It doesn't leave till seven." I reached into my pocket, found the key to the Lancia, handed it over.

He looked down at it, looked back up at me. "But Phil. I thought we would be traveling together."

"Chin Soo's in jail. The job's finished. You don't need me anymore."

Frowning, he cocked his head. "What is it, Phil? Are you upset about something?"

"No, Harry. I'm fine. I hope you have a good trip. Maybe I'll see you in London."

"You *are* upset, Phil. Why? I have solved the mystery. That is a cause for celebration, is it not?"

"For who?"

"For you and me. We can leave now. We can meet Bess at the station, and then we can share a huge breakfast, all of us. At the Savoy, I was thinking. It will be wonderful, Phil!"

"Harry," I said, "there were people involved in all this."

"Excuse me?"

"This wasn't just a puzzle, Harry, set up so you could solve it. There were human beings involved. Lady Purleigh and this Moseley character—"

"But they killed the Earl!"

"I know. And they deserve to be punished. But they've got friends, Harry. They've got family. Lord Bob. Cecily. Mrs. Corneille. Even the servants. Something like this happens, it affects everyone close to it. And it keeps affecting them. Forever, maybe. You and I, we can walk away."

"But Phil, *someone* had to solve the crime."

"Yeah. And you did a good job. You were terrific."

"What is it, then?"

I was being foolish. He was who he was.

I put my hand on his shoulder and I said, "Forget it. You go on ahead. Give my regards to Bess. I'll see you in London."

"Phil—"

"Really. It's okay. You go ahead."

"All right, Phil. If you insist." He was beginning to work on a pout.

And then, like the others, he turned and walked away. His back straight, his head high, he stalked across the floor.

I called out, "Drive carefully!"

But he didn't hear me, or he didn't want to, and so for once I had the last word.

The Evening Post

Maplewhite, Devon

August 19

Dear Evangeline,

I hope you receive this. Things here are so entirely topsy-turvy that the evening post may never be posted. Perhaps it will go out tomorrow morning; but by then I shall have left myself. The Allardyce and I, and Mrs Stopes, are taking the eight o'clock train to London tonight.

I really can't tell you what's happened, Evy, not now. It's too complicated and, in a way, really too sad to explain in a letter.

And I'm feeling rather guilty at the moment. Despite all the tragedies that have occurred here, and the losses, I am still valiant in my preoccupation with self. A small part of me (which I should like to but cannot ignore) is fluttering with a wild mixture of confusion and excitement.

It's so ridiculous—

How would you feel, Evy, if you possessed a spinster friend who was not a respectable paid companion but rather a Pinkerton operative? (Operative: that's the word they use for their agents. I think it's awfully silly, don't you?)

Yes. An enquiry agent. Mr Beaumont believes that I'd be 'good at it'. It was he who broached the idea, only an hour ago. He says that the Pinkerton Agency hires women and that in fact one of the best operatives 'in the States' is a woman.

It's preposterous, of course; and so I said to him. He told me that I needn't come to a decision immediately. He'll be in London for a time, he said, at least until the trial (I'll tell you of the trial when I see you), and perhaps longer; and that we can talk of it further, at my discretion. I should 'think about it,' he says.

Evy, it would mean freedom from the Allardyce!

I honestly don't know what to do.

Can you imagine *me* solving crimes and rooting out evil-doers? Well, actually, I suppose that in a way I've already done so, here at Maplewhite, haven't I?

Well. I shall 'think about it,' then. If nothing else, I shall be able to look forward to an occasional visit from Mr Beaumont; and, with any luck at all, these may prove interesting.

All my love,
Jane